Lowcountry
BONEYARD

**The Liz Talbot Mystery Series
by Susan M. Boyer**

LOWCOUNTRY BOIL (#1)
LOWCOUNTRY BOMBSHELL (#2)
LOWCOUNTRY BONEYARD (#3)
LOWCOUNTRY BORDELLO (#4)
(November 2015)

Praise for the Liz Talbot Mystery Series

LOWCOUNTRY BONEYARD (#3)

"Has everything you could want in a traditional mystery: a credible and savvy protagonist, a meaty mystery, and setting that will make you want to spend time in South Carolina. I enjoyed every minute of it."

– Charlaine Harris,
New York Times Bestselling Author of *Day Shift*

"This brilliantly executed and well-defined mystery left me mesmerized... Boasting a superb cast of characters, engaging conversations, a feel good atmosphere and all-around entertaining whodunit, this is the best book yet in this wonderfully charming series."

– *Dru's Book Musings*

"This third in the series continues to smoothly combine elements of the paranormal and romance with a strong investigative plot that delves into the deeply hidden secrets of families...The charming setting, strong writing, and extremely engaging characters that have become hallmarks of this series never cease to entertain."

– *Kings River Life Magazine*

"Lovely writing with well-developed characters, a believable plot and plenty of interesting detail...Boyer may be unstoppable in conjuring mystery as she travels the social circles and back roads of the fascinating southern landscape."

– *Speakers International*

LOWCOUNTRY BOMBSHELL (#2)

"Is there anything more enticing than curling up with a thrilling whodunit that keeps you guessing until the very end? Susan Boyer delivers big time with a witty mystery that is fun, radiant, and impossible to put down. I LOVE THIS BOOK!"

– Darynda Jones,
New York Times Bestselling Author

Lowcountry
BONEYARD

A Liz Talbot Mystery

Susan M. Boyer

HENERY PRESS

LOWCOUNTRY BONEYARD
A Liz Talbot Mystery
Part of the Henery Press Mystery Collection

First Edition
Trade paperback edition | April 2015

Henery Press
www.henerypress.com

This is a work of fiction. Any references to historical events, real people, or real locales are used fictitiously. Other names, characters, places, and incidents are the product of the author's imagination, and any resemblance to actual events or locales or persons, living or dead, is entirely coincidental.

ISBN-13: 978-1-941962-47-3

Printed in the United States of America

This one is for my brother and sister,
Darryl Wayne Jones and Sabrina Jones Niggel.
If they'd let me pick out my siblings,
we'd have come home with y'all.
Blue Whale love to the Sibbles.

ACKNOWLEDGMENTS

THANK YOU—yes, I mean you, Delightful Person Who Bought This Book. You make it possible for me to keep my dream job, making things up and writing them down. It's a delicious thing I do, and I am forever grateful.

Thank you beyond measure, Jim Boyer, my wonderful husband and fiercest advocate.

Massive thanks to everyone at Henery Press—Kendel Lynn, my dream editor, Art Molinares, who always has my back, Erin George, Rachel Jackson, Anna Davis, and Stephanie Chontos—this book is better because of all of you. And of course, here's a shout out to Charlie and Cali, the mascots.

As always, thank you Stephany Evans, my wonderful agent, Kristen Weber, my fabulous first reader who always asks the right questions, and Marcia Migacz and Jan Rubens, for their sharp eyes.

Heartfelt, exuberant thanks to Charlaine Harris. I remain your biggest fan.

Huge thanks to my cousin Linda Ketner. I'm grateful she chose to live in Charleston and even more grateful that she's willing to read galleys. More huge thanks to my dear friends Martha and Mary Rudisill, eleventh and twelfth-generation Charlestonians, respectively, who answered endless questions, helped me find the right cemetery, and pored over galleys.

Thank you...

...Samantha Blundell, whose grandmother gifted her with the character she'd won at a charity auction. Your participation inspired a nice twist in the story.

...Jessica Slaughter at FIG Restaurant, for answering endless questions about chefs, sous chefs, and all things culinary.

...Marcia Beczynski with Magnolia Cemetery.

...Jim O'Neill and everyone at John Rutledge House Inn.

...Phil Sabatino with Queen & King Street Garage.

...and Mike Bowers, who is a real-life private investigator in Charleston, SC.

This book is richer because of all of these folks. Any mistakes are mine alone.

Immense thanks to Rowe Copeland, Kathie Bennett, Susan Zurenda, Liz Bemis, and Erin Mitchell. I have no idea what I'd do without y'all. Thank you Jill Hendrix, owner of Fiction Addiction bookstore, for your continued advice and support.

As always, I have a paralyzing fear I've forgotten someone. Should that prove true, please know it was unintentional and I am truly grateful for everyone who helped me with this book.

ONE

The dead are not generally fretful of mortal affairs. My friend Colleen passed from this world to the next seventeen years ago last June. She can't be bothered with global warming, the national debt, or those Duck Dynasty folks from Louisiana. She's careful to stay focused on her mission, namely, protecting Stella Maris, our South Carolina island home, from the evils of high-rise resorts, timeshares, and all such as that. But occasionally, she fixates on what appear to be random concerns, mostly cases I'm working. Colleen minds my business, is what I'm saying.

To be fair, I make my living minding other people's business. I'm a private investigator, licensed by the state. Roughly half of my casework is pre-trial investigation for criminal defense attorneys. Another quarter involves domestic misunderstandings. The remainder is a mixed bag of human comedy and suffering—everything from conspiracy to kidnap a prize hound for stud services to conspiracy to commit murder. Sometimes it's difficult to know which I'm dealing with at first, but I pray for the wildly farcical.

That Tuesday in mid-October, I was sitting in an Adirondack chair on my deck savoring my second cup of coffee and the music of waves breaking and racing to shore. The sun was warm on my skin. I'd just finished a read-through of my final report on a case when a ringtone named pinball announced a caller not in my contacts list. I glanced at my iPhone. It was precisely nine o'clock. The number was local. I set my coffee down and picked up the phone.

"Talbot and Andrews Investigations."

"Miss Talbot?" The man's tone brought to mind a professor who'd caught me daydreaming in class.

I pulled the phone away from my face and scrutinized the number again. What the hell? "This is Liz Talbot. How can I help you?"

"Colton Heyward here. I'd like to arrange a meeting at your earliest convenience."

Something heavy and dark settled in my chest. The Heyward family and their missing early-twenties daughter had been all over the news. Kent Heyward had vanished from the streets of Charleston one late summer evening. I closed my eyes and forced air into my lungs. "Of course. I'll come whenever you like."

He gave me his home address on lower Legare Street in Charleston and asked me to be there at ten o'clock the next morning. Had I not been familiar with the family, the address—which was south of Broad Street near where the Ashley River converges with the Cooper to sculpt the end of the Charleston peninsula—would've told me I was likely dealing with old money and a family tree including names from history books.

Wednesday morning Colleen woke me at 4:45. She pestered the fire out of me to get an early start, proceeding to inform me of the time every five minutes during my run, shower, and the berry-yogurt-granola parfait that failed to summon my appetite. Kent Heyward's disappearance weighed heavy on my heart. It haunted the entire lowcountry. I was both eager to help and apprehensive. What could *I* do that hadn't been done?

"Are you about ready?" Colleen was working my last nerve.

"What is with you?"

"We can't be late. I'll be in the car."

She rode shotgun on the trip to Charleston. As her sole human Point of Contact, I was the only one who could see her. Across Stella Maris, during the ferry ride to Isle of Palms, and through Mount Pleasant she barely spoke. I knew she was tense. Most days I would've quizzed her about it, but I was preoccupied myself. Colleen relaxed considerably once we crossed the Cooper River Bridge and I drove my green hybrid Escape into the Holy City.

Charleston was christened the Holy City forever ago, owing to the number of churches generously scattered across her cityscape and her history of religious tolerance. Her streets buzzed in the soft October air. Deliverymen unloaded their wares with a brisker step now that the oppressive summer heat and humidity had relented. The Carolina blue sky forecasted a pleasant day for all. October is my favorite month in the Lowcountry. The quality of light renders Charleston and her realm through a filtered lens, obscuring flaws and highlighting our best features. That particular morning, my joy in simply driving through the city was muted.

At nine-fifty—ten minutes early—we rolled through the lacy wrought iron gate and down the tree-sheltered brick drive to the Heyward home. Shades of green surrounded us—magnolias, tea olives, gardenias, camellias, ferns, palms—all manner of tree and shrub. We'd been swallowed whole by the Garden of Eden. I turned off the engine. Everything was still except the gurgling fountain in a bed of massive hostas. We stared at the three-story, clay-colored masonry mansion with triple-tiered piazzas.

"It's magnificent," I said.

"It was built in eighteen thirty-eight. Can you imagine everything that house has seen?" Colleen's voice was reverent, her green eyes round, their color intensified by the similarly hued cardigan she wore over today's dress.

"Do you think there are other ghosts in there?"

She cut me with a look. "You know I'm not a ghost."

"Mmm-kay. Do you think there are other guardian spirits in the house?"

"No. I know all the locals." She shrugged. "The place is crawling with ghosts. We may or may not see them this morning."

The distinction, according to Colleen, was that guardian spirits had passed to the next world and been sent back with work to do. Ghosts were the lingering spirits of the dead who had yet to cross over to the next life.

"This should be interesting," I said. "If you run across any specters, find out where the family skeletons are hidden. That information could come in handy." I climbed out of the car, took a step towards the house, and stopped, startled.

Colleen waited on the lower porch by the front door.

"Would you please stop doing that?" I asked.

"What?" She twirled a finger through her long red curls.

"You know very well what. All that popping in and out disturbs my biorhythms."

She laughed the distinctive bray-snort laugh she'd had since we were children and both mortal.

"Careful. The whole family is probably watching you from a window. You don't want them to think you talk to yourself. I doubt these folks hire eccentrics."

"I'd bet my mamma's pearls these folks *are* eccentric."

"That doesn't mean they aren't discriminating."

"If you would stop chattering at me this wouldn't be a problem." I rang the bell.

Colleen flashed me a mischievous look and faded away.

I fluffed my hair and smoothed my skirt.

The heavy door swung open. A fit salt-and-pepper-haired gentleman studied me. His suit looked to me like a custom-tailored job. I recognized him from all the media coverage. "Miss Talbot?"

"Please, call me Liz."

He extended his hand. "Colton Heyward. Thank you for coming on such short notice."

Why couldn't our culture adopt bowing instead of all this handshaking? It's just unsanitary. His handshake was firm, his perfect posture a testament to his pedigree. He stepped back and opened the door wider. "Please come in, won't you? Can I get you anything? A drink, perhaps?"

"I'm fine, thank you." What I really wanted was my hand sanitizer. I resisted the urge to dig into my tote.

"Very well. Let's talk in my office." He turned and strode down the wide front hall.

I followed him, taking in the heart-of-pine floors, the detailed woodwork, and the smell of furniture polish. This old house was well-preserved and filled with what appeared to be heirloom-quality antiques. If there were ghosts floating around, they were courteous.

Mr. Heyward stopped just beyond a room on the right and gestured for me to enter. "Please, have a seat wherever you're comfortable."

Dark woods and leather greeted me, vouching for his good taste and deep pockets. I chose a club chair by the fireplace, and he settled across from me in its twin. Between us sat a heavy coffee table flanked by a sofa facing the fireplace. Colleen curled her feet under her on the end closest to me. I was long past being rattled by her presence during meetings—provided she kept quiet.

I focused on Mr. Heyward. "May I record our conversation? It will help me remember details."

He looked like maybe he'd caught a whiff of manure but was too well-bred to mention it. "Very well."

I opened the Voice Memos app on my iPhone and pressed the red button to record. "Initial meeting with Colton Heyward, Thursday, October ninth, two thousand fourteen, ten a.m., at his home." I laid the phone on the table between us. "How can I help you?"

He nodded, grimaced, and hesitated. "Ansley Johnson speaks very highly of you. She claims you're the finest private investigator our state has to offer."

"How sweet of her. I've known the Johnson family all my life. Ansley's a good bit younger than me, but her parents and mine are dear friends."

"My daughter, Kent, is quite close to Ansley. They were college roommates. William and Mary. Mrs. Heyward is distantly related to Ansley's mother's family." The creases in his careworn face deepened. He seemed to force the words out of his mouth.

Colleen stared at the ceiling. "I'm going to have a look around." She faded out.

"Forgive me, my dear, but I'm a bit of a traditionalist. You have a solid reputation, but I must say, you're not what one expects of a private investigator. Your appearance suggests you're perhaps on your way to a Junior League luncheon."

I tilted my head and offered him my brightest smile. "Which is precisely why I'm such an effective investigator. Tell me, Mr. Heyward. If you saw me several times any given day, why, it would never occur to you I might be in*vestigating* you, now would it?"

He pulled back his chin and regarded me from atop his nose for a long moment. "I suppose you make a fair point. How much experience do you have?"

Certain he already knew the answer, I humored him. He was taking the measure of me. "I apprenticed with a Greenville private investigator for three years, then worked for him another two. My partner and I opened Talbot and Andrews Investigations eight years ago last May. Altogether, I have thirteen years of experience."

His eyes narrowed. "You don't look old enough to have thirteen years of experience at anything."

Mustering my manners, I stayed sweet. "I turned thirty-four in February, Mr. Heyward. If you require gray hair of an investigator, I can refer you to someone else."

"That won't be necessary." He cleared his throat. "My apologies. My wife and I are beside ourselves with worry about Kent. She's been missing, you see, for a month."

"I'm familiar with the case, of course. At least, what's been reported by the media. I can't even imagine what your family is going through."

"We're devastated. After a brief—you couldn't call it an investigation, really—the police concluded Kent left home of her own volition. Technically her case is still open, but they've as much as told me they aren't looking for her any longer."

I waited to see if he would embellish his story. I'd seen the press conferences. It was hard to believe Charleston PD had stopped looking for Kent Heyward. Something was off. What had been omitted from the news coverage? After a few moments I asked, "Why do they believe she left of her own accord?"

He waved his hand impatiently. "The neighbors."

I tilted my head, signaling my inquiring mind.

He huffed. "They haven't lived here long. We don't know them well. The woman—Mrs. Walsh—is inappropriately inquisitive. She overheard several emotional exchanges. Private, family matters. Called the police. It was nothing, of course, but I'm afraid she's given them the idea that Kent was mistreated here. I assure you, nothing could be further from the truth. If anything, we've spoiled her rotten. Kent is our only child."

"I see."

Emotional exchanges prompting neighbors to call the police must have been doozies. These folks were likely high strung.

"What were these disagreements about? Please forgive me for prying, but I need to know everything about Kent's state of mind if I'm to help. It could be important."

"Kent has been dating a *cook*," he said, like one might sooner date a llama. "Matthew Thomas. He works at FIG. Her mother and I wanted better for her. Kent told us a few weeks before she disappeared that she was moving in with him. Naturally, we were upset."

"Naturally." I was thinking how this didn't seem one bit natural to me, and how Mr. and Mrs. Heyward took snooty to a whole nother level. FIG was one of the top-rated restaurants in Charleston. Everybody from

Oprah to *Gourmet Magazine* had nice things to say about FIG. "Kent is...twenty-three, twenty-four?"

"She's twenty-three."

"Mr. Heyward, I apologize in advance. I know this is painful. I'm going to ask questions you've no doubt answered before. Much has been reported about Kent's disappearance. Unfortunately, I have no way of knowing what hasn't been reported, or if I've missed something."

He nodded for me to proceed.

"When was the last time you saw her?"

He fixed his gaze on a spot above my right shoulder. "September twelfth. It was a Friday evening. She left to go to dinner with friends and never came home."

"What time did she leave?"

"Approximately seven forty-five."

"Was she driving?"

He stiffened. "Yes. A red Mini Cooper convertible. She loves that car as much as I despise it. It's not safe. I would have put her in a Hummer given my choice. As is her custom, she had her way and I bought her the damned Mini Cooper. In any case, her car hasn't been located."

"I'm assuming it has a navigation system with GPS, anti-theft."

"Yes. However, the manufacturer believes it may have been tampered with. They cannot locate the car."

Another possibility was that the car hadn't been turned on since Kent had been reported missing. Surely they'd explained that to him. "Do you know who she planned to meet that night?"

"She didn't say. It was a group Ansley isn't familiar with, either." His eyes burned with a quiet rage. "The police informed me that Matthew Thomas was at work that evening. It appears it wasn't him."

Clearly, Mr. Heyward suspected Matthew Thomas of a great deal. "What do you believe has happened to Kent, Mr. Heyward?"

He closed his eyes and pressed his lips together. After a moment he looked at me. Pain coated his words. "I'm a realist, Miss Talbot. I love my daughter. I pray the police are proven right, and she's run off just to prove she can. But my instincts tell me she's fallen victim to foul play. Either someone is holding her against her will for purposes I'd rather not speculate on, or...something much worse has happened to her."

The ache in my chest made it difficult to breathe. This poor man.

On the one hand, I was terrified he was right and something unspeakable had happened to his daughter. On the other, I found hope in the notion that the police thought she'd run off. I needed to talk to Sonny Ravenel, my friend inside the department.

"Did she take anything with her?" I asked. "Are any of her clothes missing?"

"She typically carried a handbag. We assume she had one with her, but neither her mother nor I saw her leave. I heard her go out and saw her car pulling away. We haven't identified anything that's missing."

I nodded.

"Miss Talbot—Liz—I need you to find my daughter."

"I'll do everything in my power. I give you my word on that. I have a high regard for Charleston's police detectives. If they think Kent simply decided to move out, there's a strong possibility they're right." Just then I was holding on tight to that possibility.

"If you can prove that to my satisfaction, you will have earned your fee. We'll know she's safe." His terse voice made it clear he very much doubted I could do any such of a thing. Colton Heyward was convinced the police had it wrong.

I was convinced that scenario was his best hope. "I understand you don't agree with that theory, but if that's what happened, ultimately that's good news."

His face contorted in a mixture of frustration, rage, and grief. He opened his mouth to speak, then pressed his lips together.

Colleen popped back in. She stood in front of the fireplace. "Great. Could you antagonize him after we get the check? You have property taxes to pay. We have to keep you on the town council."

I patted the air in front of me with my palms in a soothing motion. "Hopefully I can locate her quickly and verify that she's safe." Until I spoke with Sonny, I would not discourage this idea.

"That is my fervent prayer." His gaze locked onto mine, his eyes lit with a desperate hope. His voice had a ragged edge. "Mrs. Heyward and I are worried sick."

"I can't even imagine. Your poor wife must be heartbroken." I was wondering, just then, why Kent's worried-sick mamma wasn't in the room. Her absence was sorely at odds with my experience of worried mammas.

"We both are."

I shook my head in sympathy. "Is she out this morning?"

"Mrs. Heyward is not well." The words came out like a pronouncement that we would discuss Mrs. Heyward no further.

"I see." I pulled my iPad out of my purse and opened a blank client contract. "Do you have a wireless printer?"

"There's one in the console behind my desk." He nodded towards the dark, stately piece of furniture across the room in front of a row of floor-to-ceiling Palladian windows.

Colleen shot me a baleful look. "Really? One of the oldest families South of Broad and you're going to ask him to fill out your questionnaire?"

"It's the law," I snapped.

My heart seized. I'd spoken aloud. To Colleen. And not in a professional tone. I coughed, wheezed, and whooped, demonstrating how the sudden onset of respiratory distress had distorted my voice. I patted my chest.

Finally, I took a deep breath. "Excuse me. My allergies are acting up. Ragweed. As I was saying, private investigators are required by South Carolina law to provide each client with a contract for services spelling out what work will be done and what the fees are."

"Of course." He looked at me from under full eyebrows like he suspected me of something but couldn't decide what.

"Let's get the paperwork done, and I'll get to work right away." I typed case-specific notes into the document and sent it to the email address he gave me, the one associated with the printer. "The contract should print any moment."

He rose and moved to his desk, motioning for me to follow.

I picked up my iPhone, crossed the room, and stood in front of his desk.

He sat in a leather executive chair befitting the head of a major corporation. Opening a drawer with one hand, he reached towards the printer for the contract with the other. "What is your standard retainer?"

"Five thousand dollars. I bill a hundred and twenty-five dollars an hour plus expenses."

He dashed out a check, signed the contract without reading it, then handed me both along with a five by seven photo of Kent.

"I'll expect daily updates."

"Mr. Heyward, sir. That's not my protocol." I took my time studying Kent's studio headshot. Smooth, shoulder-length, chestnut hair, blue eyes, glowing skin—class personified. The same photo had been televised, printed in newspapers, and was no doubt all over the Internet. It was also on posters in the windows of businesses all over the lowcountry. I made eye contact with my client.

He looked at me like I'd spoken in Swahili. Red crept up his neck to his face.

I was not intimidated by his show of temper. I felt an enormous amount of empathy for Colton Heyward. At the same time, to help him, I needed him to let me do my job. "I will call the moment I have anything to tell you. And I will provide a weekly status report, even if the status is I have nothing new to report."

"You indicated that you have a partner, is that correct?"

Nate flashed before my eyes. He'd been my best friend since college, my business partner for eight years, and my partner in a great many other ways for the last two. "I do. Nate Andrews is the Andrews in Talbot and Andrews."

"And will he be assisting you?"

"If necessary. He's currently in Greenville. We have an office there as well. If needed, he's only a few hours away. His time is billed at the same rate."

"I expect every available resource brought to bear to find my daughter."

"Understood." What I understood was that he was accustomed to being in control, and his daughter's disappearance had left him completely helpless. He was coping as best he could by demanding action. "If we need to bring in more help, we have relationships with other agencies."

I glanced through the contract. He'd left several boxes unchecked. I hesitated. "Mr. Heyward, purely as a formality, I need your answers to these questions."

He frowned and reached for the document, glared at me while he put on his reading glasses. He read the first question on page three. "Illegal drugs," he muttered and marked a large, bold x in the "no" box.

For my own protection, legally and physically, I needed to know if my clients were under the influence of anything more than stress. "We ask these questions of every client. It's nothing personal."

I also needed to know if they were armed.

He glowered at me, his tone ripe with sarcasm. "Would you like a complete list of my firearms? I have an extensive collection. Shotguns, rifles, sidearms. I have a handsome pair of dueling pistols."

"Please just mark the box indicating that you own firearms."

He complied, then read the final question. His head jerked up. He squinted at me from under dark eyebrows. "Young lady, my family has served this state—this country—in various capacities for generations. I assure you, not one of us has ever been treated for mental illness."

"Good to know." I gave him a smile that said, "Why of course I knew *that*. Damn all this bothersome paperwork," and made a mental note to figure a polite way to ask about *un*treated mental illness and general bad temper.

He made his final x and passed the contract back to me with a flick of his wrist. "Just find Kent."

Generally at this point I asked for a photo ID and made a copy. I decided to skip that step this once. "I will do everything I possibly can."

"Do whatever it takes."

"Mr. Heyward." I kept my tone neutral. "In the interest of clarity, I need to make sure you understand the terms of the contract you declined to read. I promise to do my very best to find your daughter. Unfortunately, as much as I wish I could, I cannot promise I will be successful."

"Understood." His voice rumbled like thunder. While his word signaled his comprehension, his tone indicated he didn't care for the situation worth a damn.

"I need a bit more information to get started."

He stared at me the way I imagine a bear would before he devoured me for dinner.

"Was anything bothering Kent in the days leading up to her disappearance?"

"Not that I recall. The police asked us that. Her mother had no recollection of it either."

"Can you think of anyone who might have a motive to harm Kent? Did she have difficulties with anyone?"

"Don't you think that would have been the first thing I told you?"

"Of course," I said, thinking he'd been too busy scrutinizing my wardrobe, age, and highlights to tell me anything of value first thing. "Is Kent employed?"

"She works for The Martech Agency. Advertising. They're on Broad. She's in consumer research and social media."

I nodded. "Have you spoken with anyone from the company?"

"The police interviewed them all. No one there knew a single relevant thing."

"How about Kent's other friends, aside from Ansley and Matthew?"

"She isn't close to her friends from high school any longer. The only one of her college friends her mother and I know well is Ansley. She contacted everyone in their circle. The police have interviewed everyone Kent ever met. Several of them started a Facebook page—whatever the bloody hell that is."

"Did the police pull her cellphone records?"

"Of course. There were no calls to or from strangers. She spoke with Ansley and the Thomas boy around lunchtime the day she disappeared. Unfortunately, Kent prefers texting to having an actual conversation these days. I understand there's no way to know who she was in contact with via text. I—" He shook his head.

"Mr. Heyward? Even the smallest thing could be important."

"I want to be clear that incorrect assumptions are being made regarding this piece of information."

"Understood."

"A call home—to this house—was made from her phone at eight-fifteen the Monday evening after she disappeared. According to police, it pinged off a cell tower in Atlanta."

"Who took the call?"

"I did. At the time we were expecting a ransom demand. No one was there, on the line. It was open—no indication the call had ended—for a minute or so. The police confirmed the call duration. I don't believe for a single moment Kent made that call. I implored her to just let us know she was all right. She would've said something. I'm certain of it."

"Was that the last time the phone was used?"

"Yes."

"And, given the neighbors' allegations, the police see this as further evidence she left town? Perhaps called and was too distraught to speak?"

"That's their theory. They also found two separate credit card charges to service stations along Interstate Forty. One near Memphis and one near Amarillo. Neither have outdoor cameras. Neither is the kind of establishment Kent would visit by herself. We taught her to stop for gas during the day, and if she had to fill up at night to go to well-lit facilities in high-traffic areas."

"Were there any other credit card charges after she disappeared?"

"None. Someone wanted to give us the idea she'd headed out west, which is absurd. She would've needed far more than two tanks of gas—not to mention food and shelter."

"Indeed." I was inclined to agree with him that the call and transactions were most likely an attempt at misdirection. "I'll no doubt have more questions later. For now, could I see Kent's room?"

"The police didn't find anything helpful there, but very well. This way."

I followed him up the wide, curved staircase. Generations of Heywards watched from their framed perches on the wall. Except for our muffled steps on the carpet, the house was still. I had the eerie feeling all those ancestors were holding their breath in anticipation. I glanced around. Where had Colleen gotten to?

We went left across a wide landing and down the hall. Mr. Heyward stopped in front of the last door on the right. He straightened, seemed to steel himself, then opened the door. "Take your time. I'll be in my office." He avoided glancing inside and strode back down the hall.

Kent's room most resembled a high-dollar hotel suite. It was tastefully decorated in shades of gold, cream, and beige. Heavy drapes stood open at the floor-to-ceiling windows to reveal sheers. The artwork caught my eye. Impressionist-style paintings hung on every wall. The furniture was dark, substantial, and probably possessed an unimpeachable pedigree. It contrasted nicely with the feminine touches—accent pillows, a stack of hatboxes, and jasmine-scented candles.

I snapped a series of photographs of the room, then checked out her desk. There was a wireless mouse but no computer. Likely the police had taken that when Kent was first reported missing. Unless she'd taken it with her. If she used a laptop, she probably carried it in and out on a regular basis.

But why would she take it to dinner?

A universal charging station occupied a corner of her desk. I checked the drawers for a tablet and came up empty. If her father didn't know the specifics of her electronics inventory, Ansley likely would.

I sat in the chair at her dressing table. Gold cut-glass bottles and jars occupied one corner. The top right drawer held a makeup organizer. Sadness threatened to overwhelm me. The odds that Kent would ever enjoy the comforts of her own space again were long. She was so young. And she was just gone. I spoke sternly to myself. I was no help to anyone in an emotional state. Sometimes the missing do come home. I sent up a prayer that this was one of those times, then focused.

She liked Bobbi Brown cosmetics. Nothing obvious was missing, but she might own duplicates. A travel bag was in the second drawer, but that didn't necessarily mean anything. I had four of various sizes myself.

I took my time on the dresser, sliding my hands between neat stacks of clothes and checking under drawers. Then I went through the most organized closet I'd ever seen in thirteen years of going through other people's belongings. Did Kent love order the way I did, or did the household staff keep it this way?

A complete set of luggage was shelved neatly in a back corner. She could easily own more than one set, but there were no empty shelves. And the closet didn't have that thin feel mine had after I'd packed for a trip. Then again, Kent likely owned so many clothes it would be hard to tell.

The color scheme from the bedroom continued into the bath. The drawers yielded nothing remarkable, and if Kent was taking any medications, she'd left with them. Aspirin and an over-the-counter decongestant were the lone occupants of the medicine cabinet.

I stepped back into the bedroom and let my eyes drift around the room. The paintings were stunning. I wandered over to a nighttime Charleston streetscape reminiscent of Van Gogh's *Café Terrace at Night*. Like Van Gogh's masterpiece, the painting was unsigned. The image of the row of houses along the Battery in moonlight was equally beautiful. I wandered from painting to painting. None of them were signed.

I studied the piece closest to the door. It was an exquisite interpretation of Boneyard Beach at Bulls Bay. Casualties in the never-ending battle with the surf, hundreds of fallen oaks, cedars, and pines line the beach. Some are still standing, their bare arms reaching for the sky. All are sun and saltwater bleached. The painting depicted the boneyard at night, the trees bathed in moon and starlight. It called to mind Van Gogh's *Starry Night*. The paintings were compelling. It seemed odd that they were all unsigned. Curious about the unknown artist, I snapped photos of each painting with my iPhone.

I took a last look around the room as I backed out, then made my way downstairs. Colton Heyward sat behind his desk, his chair at an angle. He examined the air in front of him intently.

"Mr. Heyward?"

He swiveled his head towards me. "Did you find anything helpful?"

"It's too early to know what will be helpful. Did the police take Kent's laptop?"

"No. As I told the police, she must have taken it with her."

"Is it typical for her to carry it along with her to dinner?"

He stared at his hands. "I don't know. She owns a variety of handbags, many large enough to accommodate a laptop. Sometimes she leaves with a backpack."

"Do you know what type of cellphone she has?"

"An iPhone."

"Are you aware of any other electronic devices she owns?"

"She has an iPad—the new one. I'm not aware of anything else."

"Was she taking any prescription medication—something she wouldn't have left behind?"

"Not so far as I know, but unless she'd been ill—and she hasn't been in a very long time—I probably wouldn't know. Mrs. Heyward may be able to assist you with that when she's feeling better."

"Kent has some beautiful artwork in her room. Could you tell me who the artist is?"

He was silent for a moment. "Kent." He looked away, his tone dismissive.

I absorbed that. "She's extraordinarily talented." Why on God's green earth was she working for an advertising agency? This woman should have a gallery on King Street.

"Yes. She is. But my daughter wasn't meant for the world of artists. That world eats its young. She studied marketing in college so as to develop a vocation which would be helpful in charitable work once she marries. She paints for her own pleasure. She's done that since she was a small child. It's a hobby. My father-in-law has a similar interest."

Astounded that he could dismiss such beautiful work as a hobby, I gaped at him. "I'll show myself out."

Colleen waited for me in the car. I climbed in, closed my door, and started the engine. She stared at the house thoughtfully.

"What's wrong?" I asked. "Did you find anything in the rest of the house?"

"Kent's mamma was upstairs in her peignoir set sipping coffee."

"That's odd. Did she seem distraught?"

"Only over her nails. She called to make a manicure appointment."

"You have *got* to be kidding me." My mamma would've been downstairs giving marching orders. "Downright strange that she didn't meet with me along with her husband. Maybe she agrees with the police and thinks Kent simply moved out. Anyone else?"

"A cook, a maid, and a butler—calls himself a 'household manager'—who are still breathing. And a debutante named Sue Ellen in a hoop skirt carrying on about carpetbaggers. She invited me to tea."

"Does she know anything about Kent?"

Colleen winced.

"She's worried about her. Seems anxious that she hasn't been home. But Sue Ellen suffers from time confusion."

"Care to explain that?"

"She hasn't left the house since eighteen sixty-seven. That's when she died. Some kind of fever. She's waiting for her beau to come home from sea. Him and the carpetbaggers are pretty much all she wants to talk about."

"Are you going to tell her she'll need to pass on over to the Other Side to find her true love?"

"Not until I'm sure she can't help us find Kent. If anything was going on in that house that's connected to her disappearance, Sue Ellen might have seen or overheard something that can help."

"Are you going to tell *me* why you were in such an all-fired hurry to get here this morning?"

"I needed to make sure you got across the Cooper River Bridge before nine-thirty-five. That's earlier than you strictly needed to be on the peninsula in order to be on time."

"Why?"

"Turn on the radio. Or check the news alerts on that phone of yours."

I picked up my iPhone and scrolled through the notifications. All inbound lanes on the Cooper River Bridge were closed due to debris in the road. I tapped in my password and pulled up the article. A flatbed truck hauling lumber had lost its load that morning at nine-thirty-five. Miraculously, no one was injured, though a few vehicles suffered damage.

Something thickened in my throat. "I could have been stuck on that bridge for hours."

"You could have been." Colleen's tone was gentle. Her eyes told me the truth.

I could have been killed.

TWO

Colleen went to wherever Colleen goes when she's not saving my hide or working my nerves. As I rolled through the gate and turned left on Legare, I voice-dialed Mamma and scored Nell Johnson's cell number. Nell required way more by way of explanation than I cared to give as to why I needed to reach her daughter. I pulled to the curb on Meeting near the Calhoun Mansion. Twenty minutes later I had Ansley's number. I called and arranged to talk with her when I got back to the island.

My next call was to Sonny Ravenel, a family friend and Charleston homicide detective. Happily, he was free for lunch and agreed to meet me at the Blind Tiger Pub at noon. It was early, but I figured I could take my laptop out to the courtyard and type up my notes from my meeting with Colton Heyward while I waited.

I lucked out and scored a parking place on Broad a few blocks down from the Blind Tiger. My mouth was already watering in anticipation of white corn fritters with secret sauce and crab cakes. I slipped in my earbuds. I'd taken to wearing them most of the time in public. That way, when Colleen popped in, folks assumed I was on the phone instead of Not Quite Right.

I pulled out my black Kate Spade computer bag and headed back up the street. I was the first person through the door for lunch. The hostess escorted me to my favorite spot, tucked into the back corner of the brick-walled courtyard. I ordered iced tea and pulled out my laptop. I transcribed my conversation with Colton Heyward, typing the salient facts into an interview form. Nate and I had cloned an FBI FD 302 a few years ago due to its popularity with attorneys and judges, who become familiar with the format in law school. If we ever had to give testimony regarding a case, this gave our work product an instant pedigree.

I pulled a notebook and pen from my computer bag. I start every case with a list of questions. I began my list for the disappearance of Kent Heyward with, "What happened to her laptop? Did she take it with her to dinner? If so, why?" If I were leaving and not planning on coming back, I would take my laptop, no doubt. If Kent hadn't taken it with her, someone else had removed it from her room. I added the question, "Was she taking any prescription medications?" If prescription meds were missing, it would also point to her leaving with no plans to return.

Sonny took a seat across from me. The redhead at my ten o'clock went on high alert. She stared at his back, no doubt appreciating his broad shoulders and the way his jeans fit. I smiled into his kind, hazel eyes and admired the neat cut of his dark brown hair. I would enjoy telling Nate I had lunch with Sonny. Served Nate right if it got his back up a little. He'd dilly-dallied in Greenville far too long. He might know in his head Sonny was like a brother to me—he was my brother Blake's best friend. But other parts of Nate liked Sonny best at a distance.

"Your timing is impeccable." I stowed my laptop in its case.

"You order yet?"

"No, I was waiting for you."

Sonny flagged down our waitress. We both knew what we wanted, so ordering was quick business. With lunch on the way, he leaned back in his chair and raised his chin. "What are you into now?"

"Kent Heyward. That's a Special Victims Unit case, right?"

"Yep. Technically, she's a missing person. A high-profile missing person. Daddy hire you?"

"Yep. Do you know anything about the case—anything that hasn't been on the news?" I was counting on departmental gossip.

"I've heard a few things. No evidence of foul play whatsoever. No ransom demand. No witnesses to an abduction have come forward. Special Victims handled the case like a crate of C-4. But..." Sonny winced, tilted his head. "You know how these cases play out. After a month there are no more leads to follow."

"She's just gone and not likely coming back. That's got to be a singular kind of hell for the family—not knowing."

"I would imagine it is precisely that."

"Colton Heyward told me the investigators think Kent left home due to family discord?"

Sonny raised both eyebrows, blew out a long breath. "That's one theory. I'm not surprised he latched on to it."

I felt my whole face squint. "See, here's the thing. The way he tells it is exactly the opposite. Like he's mad as all get out at Charleston PD because he *doesn't* believe she ran off. Says he believes something terrible has happened, and he wants me to find out what."

"Hypothetically, in this type situation, we'd be looking at one of two scenarios. Either she decided it was time to get out from under Daddy's thumb, he disagreed, so she left surreptitiously—this being both the best-case scenario and the least likely. Or, she was taken by a person or persons unknown. You ask me, Mr. Heyward can't tolerate the notion that nothing more can be done. He's in denial, wants to hear us say that maybe she's run off, but doesn't believe it for a minute. He hires you because he can." He held his hand out and seesawed it back and forth, indicating things could go either way. His grim expression told me what he really thought.

"Handled?"

"Say what?"

Our waitress dropped off Sonny's iced tea, refilled mine, and moved on to the next table.

"You said they 'handled' the case with care. Past tense. That mean they've stopped working it?"

Sonny lifted a shoulder. "It's still an open case."

"But there wouldn't be any harm in me poking around."

He turned down the corners of his mouth in a facial shrug. "Nobody's going to make any noise about you looking into it. Anything that keeps Colton Heyward—and Abigail Bounetheau, the grandmother—off the chief's phone line is good for all of us. It's not like Kent isn't a priority. We've just exhausted our leads on this one. And every day brings a new batch of victims."

The Bounetheaus had been in Charleston as long as pluff mud. Philanthropic and civic-minded, family members were frequent subjects of newspaper and magazine spreads. Any case involving them would bring an added layer of complexity.

"You think I should mention that I'm looking into Kent's disappearance to the case detectives?" I asked.

"Maybe let me fill them in."

"Thanks." I kept my disappointment out of my voice. While I was grateful for Sonny's help, I would rather have spoken to the detectives myself, maybe find out what leads they'd already worked and discarded.

"Don't mention it."

"Will you ask them if they'll meet with me?"

"I can ask. Not all detectives are as open-minded as me as regards private investigators. Could be, due to the sensitive nature of the parties involved the lieutenant won't allow it. Department told the family there are no more leads to pursue. Lieutenant likely wouldn't want to send a mixed message."

Lunch was served, and for a few minutes, corn fritters and crab cakes got my undivided attention. Sonny dug into a cheeseburger.

We caught up on family and friends while we ate. After all the usual suspects were accounted for, Sonny said, "Hey, you might want to take five-twenty-six back to Mount Pleasant."

I stilled. I wasn't ready to think too much on the bridge accident.

Sonny cocked his thumb over his shoulder in the general direction of East Cooper. "The Cooper River Bridge is closed heading into town. Flatbed lost a load of lumber. It's a bona fide miracle no one was killed. Northbound lanes are open, but folks have been sitting there for a couple hours. Rubberneckers got themselves into a chain reaction of fender-benders. It's a god-awful mess."

"I'll do that—thanks." It was a miracle all right. Hearing Sonny tell it, it finally sank in. If not for Colleen, I would be dead right now. I'd seen it in her eyes. I couldn't catch my breath. I focused. In...out. In...out. How many times in the past seventeen years had Colleen intervened to save me that I wasn't even aware of?

"You okay?" Sonny scrutinized me.

I smiled and shook it off. "I'm fine." I forked another bite of crab cake and dabbed it in lemon aioli. "What do you make of the phone call her daddy got from her cell?"

"Could support either theory. Proves nothing. Detectives flew to Memphis and Amarillo to canvas the areas around the gas stations. No cameras. No one saw her. No evidence she was ever there. But nothing to prove she wasn't, either. Hard to prove a negative."

"It looks bad, her not using her credit cards—except for the two tanks of gas—or bank account. She walked away from her job. Her boyfriend is still in town, right? How is she supporting herself?" I set down my fork and added the question to my list.

"Yeah, the boyfriend's still here. Theoretically, she could be staying with any one of fifty college friends who scattered all over the country after graduation."

"But Ansley—her best friend—called everyone they hung out with."

"And the case detectives called every name on the list she gave them. Local departments followed up. Doesn't mean one of the friends wasn't hiding something."

I weighed that. "This is probably about as much use as a snipe hunt, but I promised Colton Heyward I'd try my best to find her."

"Then do just that. Who knows? Maybe something new will pop."

"Maybe."

He gave me what I guessed was his best try at a stern look. His eyes grew large, his tone emphatic. "Goes without sayin', you find *anything*, you call me first off."

I tried looking earnest and nodded. "Will you keep an ear to the ground for me in case Special Victims gets new information?"

"Not a chance."

"Can't blame a girl for trying."

He gave me his signature tilted single-nod-with-a-grin, signifying I'd gotten all I was going to get from him that day. "The first person they'll tell will be Colton Heyward. I feel sure he'll share."

On the way back to Stella Maris, I called Nate to check in. Typically, when he was in Greenville, we talked on the phone at the end of the day over a glass of wine. But I was struggling to remain objective about the case, and shaken by my own brush with disaster. I needed to hear Nate's voice. Thoughts of taunting him about having lunch with Sonny had flown clear out of my head.

"Well, hey there, Slugger." His voice was sweet and warm, like hot syrup.

"Hey," I said, reaching for casual.

"I sure do miss you. Why don't you leave now and head on up here? You could be home in time for dinner. It's nice outside. We could get a table at The Lazy Goat."

It wasn't lost on me that he still referred to Greenville as home. This was our ongoing tug-of-war—where were we going to live? I couldn't leave Stella Maris, and I didn't want to anyway. For Nate, Greenville was where we'd started our business—our base. It was also his hometown. "Nate..."

"What's wrong?"

"Nothing. I just...had a rough morning. I took a new case. I can't leave right now."

He was quiet for a moment. I knew he was disappointed. The last several times he'd asked me to come to Greenville I hadn't been able to get away. "What'd we catch?"

"Kent Heyward."

"Twenty-something woman missing from South of Broad?"

"Her father hired us." I filled him in on the basics.

"Well, I just wrapped up the work for the Fayssoux divorce. It's all over but the testimony, and that won't come for months. I could head down, give you a hand if you like."

"That sounds real good." I smiled, but felt tears in my eyes. I had frayed nerves and raw emotions on simmer. The complexities of our relationship got folded into the pot. How long could we maintain this not-so-long-distance relationship? Greenville was only three and a half hours away, but it may as well be a thousand miles if he was there and I was here most of the time.

"All right then. I'll see you for dinner. In or out?"

"I'm fine either way."

"Is that a fact?" His voice dropped an octave. He'd read my pensive mood and taken it as a challenge. "Well now, I have to tell you Slugger, I have a preference myself. Why don't I pick something up on the way? Something flexible."

"Flexible food?"

"The kind we can eat whenever it suits us."

"I like the sound of that." My pulse and my spirits picked up. This was part of the problem. I was always so happy to see him it was too easy to sweep the big things under the rug when he was standing in front of me.

"I'll see you around seven." How in this world did that man make the most mundane sentences sound like foreplay?

"I'm looking forward to it." I pressed the end call button on the steering wheel.

Ten minutes later, as I parked on the ferry from Isle of Palms to Stella Maris, I realized I'd forgotten to call Ansley to let her know what time I'd be back. I voice-dialed her. When she picked up, I asked her to meet me at The Cracked Pot at two. Hopefully she had some sliver of information that would give me a solid grip on optimism for finding Kent Heyward.

THREE

"Hey, sweetie." Moon Unit Glendawn called out a welcome as I came through the door of The Cracked Pot, the island's diner. Moon Unit owned the place, had bought it a few years after we graduated from college—her from Carolina, me from Clemson. She'd remodeled it, putting a tropical café spin on the traditional diner. She was there every day to greet customers and gather, embellish, and disseminate town gossip. The Cracked Pot was a touchstone for everyone who'd ever lived in Stella Maris.

I spotted Ansley in the back booth. Silky, pale blonde hair brushed her shoulders. Everything about her shouted "cheerleader." She'd been one at Stella Maris High School.

"Hey, Moon. I'm going to join Ansley Johnson. Could you bring me a glass of tea?"

"Sure thing. Unsweet with Splenda?"

"Please." Drinking sweet tea added a thousand calories to my daily intake.

I slid into the booth across from Ansley. "Thanks for meeting me. How are your mamma and daddy?"

Worry clouded her typically sparkling blue eyes. Her bubbly nature had been supplanted. "They're fine, thanks. And I'm happy to talk to you. I'm just so, so thankful Mr. Heyward hired you. I wanted to call you myself. But he is such a freak about family privacy. I thought if I wanted him to work with you I should do things his way."

"Good call." I reached in my bag for the Purell.

Moon Unit set my iced tea in front of me. "You sure you don't want something to eat?"

"I had lunch in Charleston. Ansley?"

"This is fine." She had a glass of ice water with lemon in front of her.

Moon Unit placed a hand on her chest and leaned back. "So *tell* me."

I blinked. "What?"

She blew out a breath strong enough to fluff her bangs. "About Merry's new *boyfriend*."

I was at a loss. Merry had a new boyfriend? When had I last spoken with my sister? It had been a few days, not long enough for a major development on the romantic front.

"Moon, your sources are better than mine. I don't have a clue."

She pressed both hands to her chest. "Oh, sweetie. I am so sorrrryy. I bet I ruined a surprise. Oh. I am just...*so* sorry." She backed away with a sorrowful look.

Ansley looked at me wide-eyed.

"I guess I better call my sister." I waved it away with one hand and pulled a notepad and pen out of my purse with the other. "May I record our conversation?"

"Sure."

I opened a voice memo and dictated the particulars. "Tell me about Kent."

"She's my best friend. I love her like a sister." Her blue eyes glistened. "We were college roommates sophomore year. We shared an apartment off-campus junior and senior year."

"You've both been out of school about eighteen months, right?" Ansley still had the look of a coed about her, though she was dressed for the office in her silky blue shell and gray skirt.

"That's right."

"You've kept in touch?"

"We talk every day. We see each other at least once a week. We know *everything* about each other."

I was thinking how everyone had secrets. "Have you met her boyfriend?"

"Matt? Of course. I hang out with them all the time." She blushed, smiled. Her teeth were impossibly white against the suntan she'd maintained into fall. "Well, not *all* the time. He is the sweetest thing. If Mr. Heyward thinks Matt had anything to do with Kent's disappearance...well, that's just crazy. Matthew treats Kent like a queen. They were going to move in together. Did Mr. Heyward tell you that?"

"He mentioned it." Clearly, Ansley did not share Colton Heyward's views on the merits of dating chefs. "Okay, so when was the last time you saw Kent?"

"The Wednesday before she disappeared. We had drinks and dinner at Poe's."

Poe's Tavern on Sullivan's Island was named for Edgar Allen Poe, who'd been stationed at Fort Moultrie while in the army. I had a sudden craving for one of their cheeseburgers. "Any particular reason?"

Ansley shook her head.

"We were just hanging out."

"Was anything bothering Kent?"

"Yes. Her parents were making her crazy."

"Tell me about that."

"Her dad is such a snob. Her mamma's not really like that, but she goes along with everything her dad says. He hated that Kent was dating—his words—a cook. Matt is a *trained chef*." Ansley punctuated her words by pointing at the table. "He has a degree in culinary arts from the Art Institute. The Heywards act like he's a dishwasher at a Waffle House."

From the cradle, Southern women in certain circles were molded to adorn, to charm, their position in society preordained. True love with lesser mortals wasn't part of the plan.

"How long had Kent been dating Matt?"

"Her parents don't know this, but they started seeing each other three years ago. Kent and I met him at The Belmont, on Upper King Street? We were hanging out with friends. He was hanging out with friends. We started talking. It was casual—at first. I actually went out with him a time or two before he started dating Kent."

"They were getting serious?"

"Very. Matt adores her. It's mutual. But her parents have to make everything so hard. They keep trying to get her to date—their words— someone more appropriate. They're just always on her about it. *They're* the biggest reason she wants to move out and live with Matt."

"Are Kent and Matt talking marriage?"

Ansley looked away. She brushed her hair back from her shoulder.

"I don't think so. Matt's focused on his future. He wants to own his own restaurant in Charleston."

Something about the marriage question had flustered Ansley. "Does that bother Kent? That he's so focused on his career?"

"Not that she ever said. She's so proud of him."

"I'll need to talk to Matt. Can you give me his phone number?"

"Sure." Ansley tapped her phone a few times and mine vibrated slightly. "I shared all of his contact info."

"Thanks. Was Kent active on social media? Facebook, Twitter?"

"She has a Facebook profile, but she was never one to post much. She talked about deleting the account, said she wanted to interact with people in person."

Was that a trend? Backing away from social media? Seems like I'd heard something about that. I'd've thought twenty-somethings spent a lot of time on Facebook.

"Share Kent's contact info with me, would you? That way I'll have her email, Facebook, cell number, and everything else all in one place."

Ansley tapped her phone a few more times. "Done."

"Are you on Facebook?"

"Yes. But I don't use it much either."

"Mind if I use your profile to check out Kent's friends? Unless you happen to know her password."

"Hers is probably either Van Gogh, Monet, or Renoir, with her birthday. If you can't get in, you can use my account." She took the pen I offered her and wrote her login info on my pad.

"Thanks. Back to that Wednesday night at Poe's, did Kent vent about her parents more than usual? Say anything that made you believe she would leave town to get away from them?"

"No." The word was solid. "There is no way she would leave Matt. Even if her parents pushed her over the edge and she did something that desperate, she would *not* worry everyone to death. Kent is way too thoughtful to treat folks who love her like that, no matter what they did. She would tell us—she'd tell *me*—that she was leaving."

"And you've spoken to all her other friends just to be sure?"

"Everyone I can think of. At least twice. No one has seen or heard from her."

"And you think you could tell if they weren't being truthful."

"Absolutely."

"Could you email me a list of names and phone numbers of all her friends from college? And anyone she was still close with from high school that you know of—anyone you've heard her mention. I need to double check every possibility."

"Sure." Her tone let me know she thought this was a waste of time. "I gave all that to the police. They've checked and rechecked, too."

"Did Kent mention anything aside from her parents that was troubling her?"

"Not a thing."

"Did she like her job?"

Ansley shrugged. "Well enough. She didn't have her dream job, if that's what you mean. She liked the people she worked with. She's very artistic."

I thought about the paintings in her room. "She's quite talented."

Ansley's eyes threw flames. Her mouth drew up into something very near a sneer, which was so far out of character for her I drew back. "Kent could have been a great painter—famous, even. Except her parents didn't think it was a suitable career for her. They imagined her hanging out with drugged-up hippie types. Which is some crazy stereotype they picked up in a sixties movie or something anyway. Kent is not like that."

"She never did drugs?"

"Well, okay, she may have smoked a little pot in school. Once or twice, if everyone else was, and someone offered it to her. It was more not to offend anyone than anything else."

She smoked pot to be polite? That was taking gracious to a whole nother level. "Was she having trouble with anyone—an ex-boyfriend, or a wannabe boyfriend maybe?"

Ansley shook her head. "No."

"No enemies?"

"None. Not for as long as I have known her."

"You said y'all talk every day. Did you speak to her the day she disappeared?"

"Yes. She called me during her lunch break—my lunch break, too. I'm working at Robert Pearson's law office as a paralegal. I'm thinking about law school." She shook her head, aggravated. "You don't need to hear about me. Anyway, it was just a 'hey whatcha doin?' kind of call."

"Did she mention her plans for the evening?"

"Yes—I told the police this. She was going out with a few artists she knew, locals. Painting was Kent's thing. I don't know that crowd. She was super excited because one of them has his own gallery, and he'd been real encouraging to her. *His* name I do know—Evan Ingle. He has a gallery here in town."

That name rang a bell. "In Stella Maris, you mean?" Hadn't Colton Heyward said that Ansley didn't know who Kent was meeting?

"Yes. He opened a gallery on Palmetto Boulevard a few years ago. He lives and paints upstairs and showcases and sells his work in the street-level storefront. You've never been in there?"

"Actually, I have. I've browsed it a few times. I'd be happy to have a few of his pieces hanging on my walls, and I don't usually like abstract paintings."

Ansley tilted her head at me. "That's not all he does. I think that's just the collection he's showing now. Kent loved his work. She raved in painter-speak about him. I didn't understand much of it, but apparently he's a genius with light."

"Did the police question him?"

"Yes, and I did, too. I mean, I went to talk to him. He said they were supposed to meet at Bin 152 on King Street at eight. Only Kent never showed up. He figured something had come up and she'd changed her plans."

Ansley must've been desperate if she'd gone to question this artist herself. Very Nancy Drew of her. "Did he give the police the names of the other folks in the group?"

"He said he did, when I went to talk to him. He seemed like a really nice guy to me. You could tell he cared about Kent. I didn't ask him for the other names. Somehow that seemed rude. Like I was implying he needed an alibi or something."

I resisted the urge to share with her the Ted Bundy lecture my mother had drilled into me regarding how serial killers often seemed like nice guys. Apparently Nell Johnson hadn't been as vigilant as my mamma in her serial-killer training. "So, what do you think happened to Kent?"

"If I had to bet, I'd say someone in her screwed-up family decided they'd get more of the family fortune if she disappeared."

I sat all the way back in my seat. "Her parents are very protective. She's an only child."

"I don't mean Heyward money, though I'm sure there's plenty of that. Her grandparents on her mother's side have the real money. The Bounetheaus. Kent is close to her grandparents. But she has an aunt, two creepy uncles, and a bunch of cousins I wouldn't turn my back on for a minute. There's a pile of money to be divvied up one day. The fewer the piles, the bigger the piles get."

I pondered that for a moment. I purely did not want this to be about Bounetheau family drama. "Any family on her father's side?"

"Not that I know of."

"Do you honestly believe someone in her family would kill her for a bigger inheritance?"

Ansley studied the table for a long moment, her smooth blonde hair framing her worried expression. "This is between us, right?"

"Unless you're involved in a crime or have evidence of one."

Ansley shook her head. "I have *not* committed a crime. And I don't have evidence of anything. But Kent's uncles...I wouldn't put a thing past them."

"What are their names?"

"Peyton and Peter Bounetheau. They're twins. Neither of them has ever married, and they still live with their parents."

"Okay, that's not typical. On the other hand, it isn't criminal. What makes them so creepy?"

Ansley shook her head slowly, like she was searching it and finding nothing. "Honestly, I can't tell you. I just think something is off about them."

I felt my face squinch up. I could hear Mamma now saying I was courting wrinkles. "There's something off about a lot of folks. That doesn't make them killers."

"A lot of folks don't have a missing niece and boatloads of family money."

"Fair enough. Is that your only theory?"

Tears filled her eyes. "I wish I could think of something—anything— that would help. She just vanished somewhere between her house and the restaurant."

"Bin 152, that's just up from the corner of King and Queen. Less than half a mile from home for Kent. Would she normally drive that, or walk?" One of the many benefits of living in downtown Charleston was being able to walk to so many restaurants, art galleries, shops, and the like. It seemed odd she'd drive.

Ansley shrugged. "If she wasn't going anywhere else, and the weather was nice, she'd walk. Except I know she took her car. At least that's what her parents said."

Kent hadn't planned on going anywhere before she met her friends unless she'd planned on being late. Mr. Heyward had said she'd left at seven forty-five. She might've had plans for afterward. Maybe she would've met Matt after he got off work. I needed to establish a timeline for the evening. It would be helpful to know exactly where Kent had planned to be and when.

I jotted down, "What was the weather like on September twelfth?" and "Why did she take her car?" along with, "Where did she park?" I'd love to know what the case detectives had done by way of looking for her car.

As gently as possible, I asked, "Ansley, do you have any reason to believe her parents were abusive?"

"You mean did they hit her? Never. Her daddy has a temper. But he never laid a hand on Kent or her mother. Kent would have told me. Emotional abuse...I guess that's a matter of opinion. I would say so. They would say they just want what's best for her."

"Do you think her daddy has a bad enough temper he could have hurt her in a fit of rage, maybe not meaning to?"

Ansley weighed that. "It's possible, I guess."

A companion to my list of questions was my list of possibilities for each case. I try to imagine all the scenarios, no matter how improbable. If he'd hurt his daughter, Colton Heyward wouldn't be the first person to hire an investigator to make himself look innocent.

FOUR

Mamma sometimes referred to Merry and me as her twins born two years apart. Merry's hair was the same multi-toned blonde as mine, highlights courtesy of Phoebe over at Phoebe's Day Spa, just like mine. Her eyes were the identical shade of cobalt blue she, Blake, and I all got from Mamma. Strangers immediately made us for sisters. I was taller by four inches and didn't care to reflect on the difference in weight. Merry was more petite, is what I'm saying.

We had a complicated relationship. In most respects, our ideas and perspectives were so aligned we often finished each other's sentences. Sometimes I picked up the phone to call her and the phone rang before I had a chance to dial. The things we agreed on, we agreed on with zeal. We both did our dead level best to avoid topics on which we disagreed because the fallout was not pretty. My sister was a mule. No doubt she'd call me worse.

On the way home from The Cracked Pot, I called Merry. When she answered, I said, "According to Moon Unit, you have a new boyfriend."

"Are you coming to dinner at Mamma and Daddy's Saturday night?"

"Yes, but I still don't understand why we're having dinner on a Saturday night. What disrupted the Sunday and occasional Wednesday night schedule?"

"My new boyfriend. He has to fly out of Charlotte Sunday afternoon."

"He's coming to dinner Saturday night?"

"Yeah. You'll really like him." I could hear her smiling.

"And you were going to tell me about him...when?" Hurt and confusion battled for the upper hand in my head.

"I'd planned on telling you Saturday night when I introduced you."

I pondered that for a moment. My sister and I didn't have many secrets from each other. "Why didn't you tell me when you met him? How long have you been seeing this guy? It must be serious if you're introducing him to Mamma and Daddy. And Blake." Our older brother was the Stella Maris chief of police. He took his brotherly duties just as seriously as his professional ones.

"I met him a few months ago on a plane to DC. I was going to a conference. He was going to a different conference. He's an investment banker—municipalities—based in Charlotte. I didn't mention him because at first I didn't see this going anywhere. I can't do the long distance thing."

"I can't believe you. I'm cut to the bone."

"What, because of the comment on long distance relationships? I'm happy it works for you. I just can't do it."

It wasn't working out all that great for me, either. "No—don't play innocent with me. Because you're seeing someone who clearly means a lot to you and you haven't mentioned him to me *at all*. What the hell, Merry?" I was unaccustomed to being an outsider in my sister's life and I didn't care for the feeling the teensiest bit.

"That is odd, isn't it?"

"*Merry*..."

"What's the first thing you would've done?"

I had a clear vision of exactly what this occasion should have looked like. I felt robbed of a memory I should've had. "Well, I would've liked to've shared a bottle of wine with you on the deck under the stars while you told me all the juicy details. I cannot be*lieve* you wouldn't tell me first."

"What's the second thing you would have done?"

"What?" What kind of fool question was that?

"What. Is. The. Second. Thing. You. Would. Have. Done?"

"I don't know..." I squinched up my face.

"Okay. If I'd told Blake, what do you think he would have done straight off?"

"He would've run a detailed background check."

"Ding, ding, ding!"

"I would never—oh, hell's bells. Of course I would have done exactly the same thing." I huffed out a sigh. "But I would've had your best interests at heart."

"I know. And I love that about you. I really, really wanted to tell you. Only I didn't want either of you picking through his life until you knew more about him than I did."

Okay, I was slightly mollified because she'd *wanted* to tell me but couldn't because of my protective tendencies and occupational resources. But what the hell was she thinking? "He could've been a serial killer. Most of them look like perfectly normal people. He could still turn out to be a serial killer. Many of them are highly functional. What did you say his name is?"

"I didn't."

"Well, Merry, before he sits down at Mamma's dinner table, don't you think it would be a good idea for me to just verify he's who he says he is?"

"Liz, seriously. Normal families don't do background checks on dates."

"In *normal* families, you don't have newspaper clippings about how your sister's previous boyfriend tried to kill her." I still had nightmares about the evening two and a half years ago when I nearly lost my sister to a sleazy psycho with a nine mil. "And since when, precisely, did we start aspiring to normalcy anyway? What is his name? You're just delaying the inevitable. You'll have to tell me his name in two days anyway."

Merry heaved a long-suffering sigh. "Joe Eaddy." It came out sounding like, "Joe Eddie."

I was thinking he had two first names, like Billy Bob, or Tommy Lee, which was a common thing in our world. "Last name?"

"Eaddy."

"What kind of last name is Eddie?"

"His name is Joseph Andrew Eaddy. E-A-D-D-Y. Would you like his date of birth?"

"Yes, and place of birth, please. Do you have his social?"

The call dropped.

Shortly after three, I drove down the long oyster shell drive and pulled into the far right garage bay under the beach house I inherited from my grandmother two and a half years ago. It was ridiculously large for one person, but I loved every square foot. It started out as a modest craftsman-style beach bungalow Gram and Granddad built in the sixties. Several additions and remodels later, Gram left me a sprawling yellow house of debatable architectural pedigree, with teak trim. I loved the porches best, from the deep front porch, to the sleeping porch off the side, to the large deck out back, to the veranda off the master bedroom. The house sat atop a four-car garage, which elevated it to protect it from storm surge.

Rhett, my golden retriever, came running into the garage through his doggie door to greet me.

"There's my boy." I ruffled his fur and scratched behind his ear.

He gave me a sloppy grin and wagged his tail to let me know how much he liked the attention. Then he did a little prance that was my cue to come play. This would be good for both of us. I went out to the front yard to throw the ball for him. Rhett was the most uncomplicated male I'd ever had in my life. He helped balance the others. I gave him a beef jerky treat and a big hug before heading in.

I climbed the stairs from the garage into the mudroom, stopping to freshen Rhett's water. On my way through the kitchen, I poured a Diet Cheerwine over some ice for myself and settled behind my desk in the front room. I'd taken to calling my office the front room as it was massive and had multiple functions. After Gram's final remodel, the oversized space had been her living room. She'd been the unofficial social maven of the island and had entertained on a large scale.

My entertaining needs were virtually nonexistent. Aside from date nights with Nate and an occasional night of dancing and karaoke at The Pirates' Den, my social life was family-centric. Everything happened at Mamma's house. These days, in addition to my office, the front room served as my living room and library. The tall windows provided lots of natural light, making it a pleasant space to work or relax.

Joe Eaddy would have to wait. I created an electronic file for the Heyward case, transcribed my notes from my interview with Ansley, and filed them with the ones from the Colton Heyward interview. For me, each case was a puzzle. I needed to find all the pieces, orient them the right way, and fit them together until the picture became clear and complete.

The first piece of the puzzle was Kent. I started an electronic profile for her, pulling together information from several public and private subscription databases, and adding that to what I'd learned. Amelia Kent Rivers Heyward was born March 27, 1991 at Medical University of South Carolina, parents Virginia Bounetheau and Colton Heyward. Kent was a family name that climbed farther back in her maternal family tree than I had time to trace, as was Rivers.

She attended Porter-Gaud private school and The College of William and Mary. I found nothing to contradict the information I'd accumulated from her father and Ansley. Kent had no criminal record, and no civil actions had been filed against her. Though I was reasonably certain that's what I would find, experience had taught me to verify my instincts. Kent was only twenty-three. She had a smaller electronic footprint than most of the folks I profiled.

Next, I created profiles for everyone closest to Kent, beginning with her parents and working my way out. No doubt I would find new people to profile as the case progressed and I learned more about Kent. The software I used made easy work of tracking family connections. It automatically populated information on close relatives. You never knew what would turn out to be important, so I liked knowing everything about my clients and their families.

Colton Heyward was an only child, and it appeared Kent was the last—so far—in a long line of Heywards who'd lived in Charleston for generations. Based on the real estate he owned, the lack of mortgages on any property, the sizable charitable contributions he made, and the lifestyle he and Mrs. Heyward enjoyed, I pegged him as a millionaire many times over.

No software or database I had access to would give me banking information, or the details of his investment accounts or tax returns. There were limits to the information I could gather electronically. But everything I could find indicated that Colton Heyward was a very wealthy man. Another question for my list was what would happen to the Heyward estate should Kent be removed from the equation.

I did a preliminary search for distant Heyward relatives. The closest connection I found was a fifth cousin twice removed. That branch of the family had settled in Minnesota decades ago. It was unlikely they even knew Kent existed. Less likely was that this cousin was a beneficiary of

Colton Heyward's will in any circumstance. Still, I made a note.

I spent the better part of the next two hours documenting Kent's mother's family—the Bounetheaus, another South of Broad family. Virginia Bounetheau married Colton Heyward in 1982 when she was twenty-one. I found no record of her attending college. Her parents—Ansley had been right, they had *big*, old money, the kind that had been growing for many generations—were Charles Drew Calhoun Bounetheau, commonly known as C.C., and Abigail Kent Rivers.

Interesting. Ansley was hardly the "distant relation" to Virginia Bounetheau Heyward that my client had claimed. An early marriage by ancestors two generations back had made first cousins out of Ansley's mother, Shannelle Victoria Rivers Johnson, and Abigail Bounetheau. In the South, that's not a "distant relation" unless said cousins entertained ideas of marriage. If I calculated correctly, Ansley and Kent were second cousins once removed.

Shannelle was an unexpected choice of a first name for a girl from a family with old money in these parts. No wonder she'd shortened it to Nell. Were her bona fides strictly in order? And how had Ansley failed to mention this family connection—especially after casting aspersions on several of Kent's first cousins? I made myself a note to follow up.

Virginia Bounetheau had an older sister, Charlotte, who married Bennett Pinckney. They had four sons, ranging in age from twenty-three to twenty-seven. Virginia and Charlotte also had twin younger brothers—the "creepy uncles" Ansley mentioned—Peyton and Peter. The twins were fifty years old and still lived at home. For men with such apparent resources, this was odd. I'd give Ansley that much. Still, oddity had no bearing on motive, means, or opportunity.

I needed to find out the particulars of C.C. and Abigail Bounetheau's estate planning. I'd found enough to convince me they were worth hundreds of millions of dollars at a minimum. And that was a powerful lot of motive. How that estate was divided could indeed be a factor in Kent's disappearance.

By five-thirty, the Bounetheaus and their money were making the spot behind my left eye throb—the spot where migraines originated. I dug all ten fingers through my hair and massaged my temples with my thumbs. Mr. Heyward's sense of urgency wasn't lost on me. I shared it. However, realistically, Kent had been missing for a month. If it were possible to find her in a day, Charleston PD would've already found her.

I mulled various possible scenarios and fervently prayed we were dealing with voluntary relocation. My plan was to get Nate to work this angle, find out what he could about the phone call from Atlanta and the credit card charges. And follow-up yet again with everyone Ansley and Mr. and Mrs. Heyward could think of who Kent could possibly be staying with—friends from school now living a safe distance away, et cetera. This would leave me free to pursue other possible narratives. If Kent had been the victim of foul play, odds were it was someone she knew. In any case, the first thing I needed to do was interview a gaggle of local relatives and close friends. Hopefully Virginia Heyward had dealt with her manicure crisis today and could speak with me tomorrow. I called the Heyward home and asked the gentleman who answered the phone—the butler?— for an appointment the next day. I waited on hold for ten minutes.

"Mrs. Heyward will receive you at two p.m." Perhaps it was his British accent, but the words came out with triumphant flair. Trumpets. There should've been trumpets.

I wondered if Mrs. Heyward was displeased. She clearly hadn't wanted to see me that morning. She might not appreciate being put on the spot. "Thank you so much. I'm so sorry, I didn't catch your name?"

"It's William, miss. William Palmer. I am the Heyward family household manager."

"Mr. Palmer, would you be available to speak with me after Mrs. Heyward and I finish?"

"If necessary. I can't imagine I'll have anything to add. I was out the evening Miss Heyward disappeared."

"Thank you, Mr. Palmer." I made myself a note to profile Mr. Palmer and the rest of the household staff.

"My pleasure to be of service. Good evening, Miss Talbot."

Matt Thomas answered on the second ring. He was eager to talk to me, and we made an appointment for ten a.m. the next morning at Kudu's on Vanderhorst.

Maybe I could talk to Evan Ingle before I left Stella Maris so I could check that off my list. I wanted to get the names of the other artist friends Kent hung out with. One of them could've been stalking her for all I knew.

This group may not have been the last to see Kent, but they'd been expecting her. They represented the point never reached on her timeline. They were a piece of the puzzle and had to be examined before I would know if they were the main focus or part of the background. A quick call later, I had an appointment to meet Evan at his studio at eight a.m.

Satisfied I'd done all I could for the day, I went upstairs and ran a bath, fully loaded—fizz balls, scented oil, and bubble bath. I docked my iPhone and shuffled my Bathtub Music play list. Kenny Chesney started singing "Always Gonna be You." Then I slipped out of my clothes and into the water and thought of nothing but the feel of silky water on my skin, the scent of lavender, and Nate.

I dressed carefully, but simply. My sleeveless Michael Kors navy and white maxi dress felt like the right choice. I slipped into a pair of neutral, T-strap sandals with pearly-petaled daisies on top. A simple silver chain necklace and a pair of oversized hoops completed my outfit. I kept the makeup simple—a little mascara, a little lip gloss. I could hear Mamma now telling me I needed some color and should put on some lipstick under that gloss.

I wandered downstairs to the kitchen and opened a bottle of pinot noir. Nate texted me as the ferry docked at ten to seven. I texted back to let him know I'd be out back. I set the bourbon and a rocks glass for him on the counter and went out onto the deck. The breeze had cooled, but was still warm enough I didn't need a sweater. I sat in one of the Adirondack chairs and watched moonlit waves chase the sand. Ocean therapy. I needed this. Usually it helped me put the day away. That night, it brought everything I'd stuffed into a corner of my mind front and center.

Fifteen minutes later I heard the door behind me open.

Nate sat in the chair beside me. "I put dinner in the refrigerator."

"Thanks." I smiled, but the surf held my gaze.

"Slugger, are you all right?"

"I am now."

"You seem...subdued. I confess I'm accustomed to a more enthusiastic welcome after three weeks. A man could develop a complex."

I turned to look at him. My mouth went dry. He was wearing a white button-down collared shirt, with the sleeves rolled up, jeans, and boat shoes, no socks. His blond hair was a bit longer than when I'd seen him last. I liked it this way. A curl danced across his forehead in the breeze. His electric blue eyes insisted on a response.

I sipped my wine. "I'm just feeling a bit introspective. This case—the reality that sometimes on a perfectly ordinary day, people you love are gone in the blink of an eye. Then there was a bad accident on the Cooper River Bridge this morning. If I'd been a few minutes later..."

He set down his glass and wrapped his long arms around me. "Thank heavens you weren't."

I snuggled into him. Oh dear heaven, he smelled so good. It would be so easy just to forget everything else.

"Have you eaten anything?" he asked.

"Not since lunch."

"I've got a roasted chicken, some French bread, a few cheeses...picnic stuff. Why don't I bring it out here along with the rest of the wine?"

"Sounds good—thank you. Did you see Rhett on the way in?"

"As a matter of fact, I did. He assured me he'd been keeping a close eye on you. Gave him a great big bone—not a real one. One of those all-natural, fake things. Gluten free. Pet store recommended it."

Nate made several trips back inside. I kept watching the waves. When the food was spread on the table between our chairs, he sat back down. I could feel him watching me. After a few minutes, he said, "Liz, talk to me."

"I just can't stop thinking about it." I turned to look at him. Something grabbed a hold of my heart.

"The accident on the bridge?"

I nodded. "That. Kent. And how none of us are guaranteed tomorrow."

He gave me a quizzical look. "It's not like you to dwell on what-ifs. It scares me crazy how fearless you are, chargin' in when you ought to wait for backup, leaping off Jet Skis to tackle folks in boats...you're not known for your timid nature."

"I know, but..." I chewed on my bottom lip. It was so hard not being able to tell him everything—about Colleen's intervention and all the questions that left me with.

He reached out and brushed my hair back from my face. "We all have close calls every now and then. Some of them we know about, others we don't. You're here, safe and whole. The thing to do is be grateful."

"I am. Very grateful." My eyes sought his out and held them.

"Then I don't understand. What else am I seeing in those gorgeous blue eyes of yours?"

"It just brings everything into focus. How every moment is a gift. I have this instinct to pull everyone I love closer."

"Understandable."

"Today made me want to pull you closer."

His voice was gentle. He set down his glass, reached out and cradled my face in his hands. "Slugger, I'm right here."

"For now."

He sighed and touched his forehead to mine.

The baggage from our shared and separate past set up shop between us.

"Nate, we've been living this long-distance, see-you-when-work-allows kind of life for more than *two years*. How long do you think we can maintain a relationship this way?"

He pulled away, sat back in his chair. "Are you unhappy?"

"Most days I'm too busy to give it much thought. But I think maybe I should. Are you happy?"

"I'm not *un*happy. I've accepted that this is the way things are. I love you. Is this my first choice of how we should live? No. No, it is not."

"It isn't mine, either. People who love each other—they should live together. Or at least live close by and visit often."

"I couldn't agree with you more." His eyes were warm and bright.

The stark white of his crisp shirt against his golden skin made me ache to touch him. Why did he have to be so damned handsome? And why did it hurt so much that I had to ask him this yet again? "But you won't live here?"

"Liz, that's just not reasonable. We have established business relationships with attorneys in Greenville that give us a steady stream of work." His voice was gentle, but firm.

"We have that here now, too." Damnation. It sounded like I was begging him and that galled me to no end.

He grimaced, shook his head. "To walk away from all we've built there—that's a hard thing."

"So is living here without you."

"I could say the same thing about living there without you."

"You know why I can't leave."

"No, I don't." Stubborn crept into his voice. "I know you don't want to leave. I also know you lived in Greenville for a long time and were very happy there."

"I was." I sighed. "We've been over and over this. How many times are we going to have this same conversation? I love Greenville. But it isn't home. This is where I belong."

His eyes hardened. He picked up his glass and took a long drink of bourbon. "Well, Slugger, I guess we're right back where we always land—at an impasse, because Greenville is where I belong."

"I can't wrap my brain around why living there is more important to you than being with me."

"Right back at you."

His voice was ripe with sarcasm.

"My roots are here. My family is here—and family's important to me. And I have a responsibility to this town." I couldn't explain to him that Colleen insisted I had to stay. I couldn't explain Colleen period. She'd been adamant about that. There were rules governing her Point of Contact—me.

"And I have responsibilities in Greenville."

"Greenville will still be Greenville without you. If I leave, my council seat goes up for election, and it's anyone's guess what the outcome would be." According to Colleen and her "alternate scenarios," my leaving would mean big changes for the island and everyone living here. Developers would gain a toehold, and life here would change radically, and not for the better.

Nate stood and walked to the deck rail, put some distance between us. "You know what I don't understand? I can't figure how when *Scott* needed you in Greenville, you were free to be there."

Scott was my ex-husband. He was also Nate's brother. The situation was not nearly as sordid as it sounded. Scott and I had been divorced for years before Nate and I were more than best friends and business partners. "That is *so* not fair. I'd just graduated from Clemson. We were interning, you and I, getting in our qualifying hours to get licensed. I stayed in Greenville for a lot of reasons."

"Exactly. And the primary reason was Michael Devlin. When *you* needed to be where Michael Devlin was *not*, Greenville suited you just fine."

"Really? Are we going to talk about Michael again? I haven't even said so much as hello to him in months." Michael was my college sweetheart. He married my cousin, Marci The Schemer, and I might have been a teensy bit obsessed with him for a while. But that's a whole nother story and ancient history.

"That's not the point. You were content to live in Greenville and let the fate of this island rest on someone else's shoulders for thirteen years. But when *I* need you there, well now, I'm just not as compelling as my brother and your college sweetheart, I guess."

I felt like I'd been punched. It hurt me that he would think I loved him less—that was lightyears from the truth. Things were just wildly damned complicated. "It's not that."

"Well then, by all means, tell me how I've got it wrong."

"I was twenty-two and stupid. Just because I did stupid things when I was fresh out of college doesn't mean I am required, for the rest of my life, to continue to make decisions on how and where I live for the wrong reasons."

I realized how that had come out in the instant I saw Nate's eyes shutter.

I stood and walked towards him. "I did not mean that the way it sounded. You have to know that."

"On the contrary. I think you said precisely what you meant. We all have our priorities, Liz. It's painfully obvious I'm not one of yours." His face looked like it might've been carved from stone, hard and emotionless. He'd retreated, erected a wall between us.

"Nate—"

"I don't believe I'll be staying for dinner after all." He crossed the deck in a few long strides.

"Nate, wait." I dashed after him into the house.

He continued with purposeful strides through the kitchen.

I caught up with him in the hall, reached out and touched his arm. "Nate, please."

He brushed me away and strode out the front door without a word.

He got into his dark grey Explorer and left and didn't look back.

I sank into an Adirondack chair and let the tears come. My heart was breaking, and I was mad as hell at myself and at him. Rhett ambled up the porch and lay down at my feet.

FIVE

I parked in front of Phoebe's Day Spa on Palmetto at 7:30 the next morning. Evan Ingle's gallery was across the street and up a few doors. I hadn't slept well, and my morning run and swim had done little to relieve my stress level. The picture-perfect day only served to make me crankier. I sipped my second cup of coffee from a travel mug and fought back the urge to call Nate. The image of me chasing him burned in my mind. Had he gone straight back to Greenville?

I needed to focus. The gallery was in an old three-story brick building that had once been a furniture store. Brightly colored abstract paintings lined the front windows. Based on the few browsing trips I'd made, none of the artwork fit my budget. I wondered why Evan Ingle had chosen Stella Maris for his gallery. It was a nice addition to downtown, and likely plenty of folks on the island were proud to have his work on their walls. But he offered only his own paintings, none by other artists. Surely he would have sold more of them in Charleston.

I hadn't had a chance to profile Evan Ingle yet, but he was on my list. I needed to know everything about everyone whose life had touched Kent's. There was just no way to know the critical from the irrelevant until I arrived at the truth.

My phone dinged, announcing a text message. I looked at the screen: Send file passcode. What do you need me to start on?

Nate was all business this morning, but at least he was communicating with me. And if he was working the Heyward case, he was probably still in the Lowcountry. Where had he slept last night?

I texted back the passcode to the electronic case file: Please focus on voluntary relocation scenario. Phone call from Atlanta. CC charges. Forwarding email with list of friends. No means of support w/o help.

My fingers hovered over the keypad. Words that would make things right between us wouldn't come.

By the time I'd forwarded Ansley's email, the sign on the gallery door had been flipped to "open." It was eight o'clock. I climbed out of the car and walked across the street. Soothing tones announced my arrival as I walked through the door—very Zen. I took in the man sauntering gracefully towards me. He reminded me a bit of Nate: six foot two, give or take, blond curling hair, very blue eyes, tanned and toned, early to mid-thirties. But this looker had softer features, an angelic vibe. His jeans were worn and the tail of his yellow button-down shirt hung loose. A puka shell necklace peeked out at the open collar.

"You must be Liz Talbot." His voice called to mind the door chimes—soothing.

I smiled. "And you must be Evan Ingle."

He nodded with a slight bow.

Oh, thank heaven, there would be no hand shaking. I returned his nod with gratitude.

"Would you like some tea?" he asked. "I have a pot of Roastaroma brewing. It has a bit of gluten, I'm afraid."

With considerable effort, I kept my left eyebrow in place. I was unaccustomed to hearing men discuss gluten, not that there was anything wrong with it. "Thank you so much, but I just finished my second cup of coffee."

He gestured to a conversation area in the back left corner of the showroom. "Please, make yourself comfortable. I'll grab a cup and be right with you."

I chose one of a pair of gold chenille wingbacks. Two paisley Duncan Phyfe sofas and another pair of wingbacks completed the seating area. An oversized leather ottoman sat in the middle of the group. Mismatched end tables and mosaic tea stands provided a place to set drinks. A bit traditional, a bit whimsical, it was a homey space.

Evan reappeared. He stepped lightly across the gallery, placed his teacup on a table, and settled at the end of the Duncan Phyfe across from me. He stretched out his long legs and crossed them at the ankles. "Have you been through the gallery before?"

"I have. I'm a fan." This was a bit of a stretch, but I did admire the colors in the pieces on display.

His smile was genuinely appreciative, a bit humble. "You flatter me. I enjoy my work. However, my technique has a way to go. You wanted to speak with me about Kent. Is there any news?"

It crossed my mind that the price tags on his paintings didn't reflect his opinion that his technique needed work. "I'm afraid not." I handed him my card. "As I mentioned on the phone, I've been retained by the family to attempt to locate her. I wondered if you might tell me about the evening she disappeared."

He glanced at my card, then laid it on the table by his tea. "Of course. Anything I can do to help."

I pulled out my iPhone. "May I record our conversation? It helps me remember everything."

He sipped his tea, set the cup in the saucer. "Certainly."

I tapped record, and pulled out my pad and pen. "Let's start with how you met Kent."

"She came into the gallery a while back—in the spring. Said she'd seen one of my paintings in a friend's house. She browsed. We struck up a conversation. She mentioned she was a painter as well. I invited her to bring me a sample of her work. I had in mind to offer her pointers—give back, as it were." His eyes widened and he shook his head.

"That didn't work out?"

"Oh, she brought in several paintings. They were magnificent. Frankly, I didn't anticipate she would have that sort of natural talent. I was amazed. There was little I could do but encourage her to focus on her gift."

"I've seen some of her work. It's quite impressive." Her father's dismissal of her "hobby" irked me to no end.

"Such a waste. Her gift is too rare to be discarded for a career in advertising."

"Agreed. So, you became friends?"

"Yes, well, I suppose we were moving in that direction. I invited her to a party here at the gallery. I was showing my new series for the first time. She met a few other local artists. We've been out as a group a time or two—drinks, dinner. I can't say that I know her well."

"The night she disappeared, she was to meet you and others at Bin 152 in Charleston?"

"That's right. At eight o'clock. When she didn't show, we assumed something more pressing had come up. It wasn't unusual for one of us to bail. We're a casual group."

"You were meeting for dinner there?" While I could make a meal out of the menu at Bin 152 any time, it wasn't a typical choice for dinner, more for a glass of wine and an appetizer. Their food menu consisted of meats, cheeses, and bread. The wine selection was divine.

"The menu is a bit limited for some tastes. It's one of my personal favorites." He smiled like he was remembering a good meal. It was a nice warm smile that filled his eyes.

"Who else was with you that night?"

"Sage Farrow, Clint MacLean, Julia Brock, and Greg Weir."

These were names I hadn't heard before, but that was as I expected. Kent kept her artist friends neatly segregated from the rest of her life. "Did all of them arrive around eight?"

"More or less." He shrugged. "I was a few minutes late. Julia came in shortly after me. The others were there when I arrived."

"Clint and Greg...any possibility either of them had a thing for Kent?"

Evan laughed softly. "Probably not. They're quite intrigued by each other."

"Ah. Any chance you had romantic designs on her?" I smiled to soften the question, like I was making a joke.

An emotion I couldn't catch fluttered across his face. He reached for his teacup. "No," he said. "My tastes tend more towards women closer to my own age. I find I have less to explain."

This seemed an unusual sentiment for a guy in his early thirties. Didn't guys always want twenty-three-year-olds? Something made me believe him. When he talked about Kent, I didn't get the sense he harbored impure thoughts about her. "Makes things simpler, doesn't it? Just to cover all my bases, the other two women..." I checked my notes. "Sage and Julia. Where do their romantic interests lie?"

"Sage is happily married. Julia is engaged and expressively passionate about her fiancée."

I nodded. Of course I would verify everything he said with the others, but I expected he would anticipate that. "What time did you all leave the restaurant?"

"About twelve-thirty."

"Where did you park?"

"In the garage on the corner of King and Queen." Wrinkles appeared in his forehead, his expression inquiring what that had to do with anything.

"I'm trying to figure out why Kent would've driven that night. The restaurant was less than half a mile from her home. She would only have saved herself from walking a few blocks unless she lucked out and got a street spot."

"I knew she lived downtown, but I wasn't aware of where. Perhaps she had plans before or afterwards?" His voice was congenial, helpful.

"Perhaps. Do you know if any of the others also parked in the same garage?"

"We all did. We left the restaurant at the same time and walked together."

"Did any of you see Kent's car?"

He spread his hands. "If I did, I wouldn't have known. I've never seen her car. The subject never came up. What does she drive? I doubt the others would know."

"She drives a red Mini Cooper convertible."

"It could have been there, or not. I wasn't paying attention to cars. I doubt I would remember a month later in any case."

I pointed at him with the top of my pen. "Do you happen to recall what the weather was like that evening?"

He searched the ceiling. "Hot, very humid. Typical September weather for Charleston. I do remember the forecast earlier in the day called for rain and possible flooding downtown, though I think they revised that. I took an umbrella with me, but it didn't rain while we were outside."

It was possible the forecast prompted Kent to drive just in case. I made a few notes, gathered my thoughts, then looked up at Evan. "You missed the last ferry back to Stella Maris." The ferry between Stella Maris and Isle of Palms makes its last trip over each day at eleven-thirty.

"I did. I'd had too much to drink to be driving in any event. I stayed at the John Rutledge House Inn on Broad. It's only a block away."

My face squinched. "I thought you walked back to the parking garage with the others."

He lifted his chin and inhaled deeply, then nodded. "Yes, I mean, I walked as far as the corner with them. They went into the garage. I continued on to Broad Street."

"I see. Can you think of any reason Kent would bring her laptop to dinner?" I didn't know that she had, of course. I was fishing.

He shrugged. "Maybe she wanted to show us a photo of a new piece?"

"She has an iPad." I gave him my confused blonde smile. "If it were me, I'd have brought that to show a photo and left the laptop at home."

"Maybe she takes her laptop with her everywhere out of habit? I don't really know her well enough to say." He sipped his tea.

"When was the last time you spoke to Kent?"

"The Wednesday before she disappeared. I called to invite her to go out with us that Friday night."

I studied a vibrant abstract over his shoulder. Shades of blues and greens swirled across the canvas in bold strokes. "Did she ever discuss anything with you, or in your presence—maybe a phone call you overheard—that would lead you to believe she was in any kind of trouble?"

"The only conflict I'm aware of was with her parents. They wanted her to work a few years in a 'suitable' environment. To learn the value of money, I understand. Their plan then called for her to marry well and be a pillar of the community, as it were. Kent had other plans. This is the sum total of what I know about that situation. It came up when I asked why she wasn't devoting herself to her painting."

I was thinking how that was a valid question. "Would you give me the contact information for the others at dinner that night? I'd like to see if any of them know anything helpful. Also anyone else in your circle who wasn't there, but who Kent might have spent time with on other occasions."

"Sure."

He pulled a phone out of his pocket and began tapping and scrolling. He read out the phone numbers for Sage, Clint, Julia, and Greg. "Honestly, I can't think of anyone else."

I stood. "Thank you for your time. If someone or something comes to mind, please call me."

"Of course." He rose to escort me out. "And please, come back when you have more time to browse."

I smiled. "I'll do that. We're lucky to have you in Stella Maris. I'm curious, though, what made you decide to locate your gallery here? The tourist traffic in Charleston would surely make you a wealthy man."

"I would go insane." He laughed. "I prefer the quieter island vibe. I enjoy staying over in Charleston occasionally. But I couldn't work there. Here, my studio is upstairs, along with a small apartment. Not to mention, can you imagine how much this real estate would cost me in Charleston?"

"I see your point."

Back in the car, I texted Nate: Nothing significant from the artist. Need to verify his story. Headed to Charleston to talk to the boyfriend.

We didn't normally share non-urgent details during the day when working the same case. But I was feeling less angry and more anxious by the minute. I needed to reach out to him. I'd hurt him last night with my careless comment. I needed to navigate back to where we were when he'd arrived so we could figure out a way forwards.

He responded: Roger that.

The knot in my stomach tightened. I started the car, turned down a side street, and drove behind the gallery. A late-model turquoise Prius sat in one of the three spaces that belonged to the building. It was the only car in sight. I made note of the plate number. Likely it belonged to Evan and would serve as a starter for my profile. I drove towards the ferry dock.

Once aboard the ferry, I got out of the car and climbed to the top deck to enjoy the morning breeze. There's nothing like the fragrance of salt air. A few deep breaths took the edge off my anxiety. I smiled and waved at friends and neighbors, then studied my pad carefully to send the message I was working. I pushed Nate and our problems firmly to the side. He was working and so was I. There would be time to set things right later.

After a few moments, I raised my head to feel the morning sun on my face. The ferry slid behind the northern end of Isle of Palms, heading for the marina at Morgan's Creek. This early in the morning, most of the passengers were Stella Maris residents. Grace Sullivan chatted with three couples sporting cameras, no doubt tourists enjoying her hospitality at the bed and breakfast. I knew every other person I laid eyes on except for two men in the far corner tapping smartphones. Gelled hair, expensive suits, shoes not made for exploring the local attractions. They radiated impatience. My antennae went up. Were these developers? Where the hell was Colleen?

I pulled out my iPhone and discreetly snapped a photo of the pair. Then I texted it to my brother: Any rumors of developers in town?

He replied: Haven't caught wind of anything. Look like land grabbers to me. Will ask around.

Most Stella Maris residents viewed anyone with designs on our pristine beaches for resorts and the like as land grabbers. I looked at the pair again. Blake was probably right. If so, I could've saved them a lot of time by explaining our zoning laws. For some reason, certain types of businessmen always thought they could get around them.

I put them out of my head and proceeded to Google the phone number for the parking garage on King and Queen Street.

A man answered and identified himself as the operations manager. I explained who I was and offered that he could look me up and call back to verify I was a licensed investigator.

"Nah, that's all right."

"I wonder if you could help me. Does the garage have security cameras?"

"Yeah. In all the potentially vulnerable places. Not every square inch is covered, but it's covered."

"Do you capture cars and plates going in and out?"

"Sure."

"I've been retained by the Heyward family to investigate the disappearance of their daughter, Kent. Has anyone contacted you regarding the case?"

"They contacted the hell outta me. Red Mini Cooper convertible, right?"

"That's right."

"Police called the day after she went missing. I went over the recordings with them several times. They have the footage. Still and all, not a single red Mini Cooper entered that garage that night."

"I see. Thank you so much for your time."

I tried the city garage at 93 Queen and got the same response. Those were the two closest possible places Kent could have parked—unless she'd scored street parking nearby, which wasn't impossible, but unlikely on a Friday night.

I pondered that for a moment, then called Sonny.

He answered on the second ring. "What's up, Liz?"

"Have you had a chance to speak with your buds about briefing me on the Heyward case?" It would save me so much time if they would share. There was a country mile between allowing me to poke around without making a fuss and showing me the file.

"I did. They won't. Too high profile. Plus, they don't know you."

"They have to get to know me sometime." A flock of seagulls flew by.

"I get the impression they don't see it that way."

"Did you vouch for me?" Clearly his enthusiasm had been lacking if he hadn't convinced them.

"Of course."

"Did you tell them my brother is the chief of police in Stella Maris?" I almost never traded on Blake's official status.

"I did. That jogged their memories. They feel bad for Blake. One of them remembered the Jet Ski incident. Another recalled the hog story. Generally, they don't like being in the paper associated with shenanigans. It's just not a good career move."

"Hell's bells, Sonny. I'm trying to help them out. But I need information here. I'm not going to do anything to embarrass them."

"I know you mean well. I told them that. They're skittish."

I sighed. "Mr. Heyward is not going to like this."

"I would not recommend you play that card. Not if you ever want to develop a working relationship with these guys." He used his big-brother voice. As Blake's best friend, Sonny believed he had proxy rights.

He was testing my sunny disposition. "Well, Sonny? Exactly what would you recommend?"

There was a long pause in which I envisioned him studying the heavens for guidance. Finally, he said, "What do you need to know?"

"Was Kent's car caught on camera any time after she left home the night she disappeared?"

"No. And they scoured every piece of footage available from every known camera on the peninsula—ATMs, bars, college feeds, traffic cams, parking garages, home security systems."

"But there are plenty of blind spots, right?"

"Well, yeah. We don't have city-wide video surveillance. Just the chronic problem spots. We have microphones that detect gunfire so we can respond quickly to trouble." He sounded a bit defensive.

"So, there's zero evidence she ever left Charleston?"

"Say again?"

I watched the horizon, where the ocean met the sky. "If there's no trace of her after she pulled out of the Heyward driveway, and no credit card activity with her on camera or anything else tying her—not just her plastic—to another location, as far as we know, she's still in Charleston."

"That's not the narrative they're going with."

"Well, it's the first one I'm working."

"I'll let 'em know." Sonny's voice was calm as always. But I knew him well enough to read between the lines. He wasn't happy and his buddies wouldn't be, either.

My tone was so sweet, hearts and flowers floated out of my mouth. "You do that. Bye-bye now."

I ended the call and growled at my phone in frustration. Nate was right about one thing. Some aspects of our job were easier in Greenville.

SIX

Kudu was doing a brisk business that Friday morning. Classes were in session, and a great many College of Charleston students needed caffeine. I splurged on a cream cheese croissant with my mocha latte. I was stress eating.

Well, hello. A Hollywood-handsome guy walked through the front door just as I was picking up my latte from the barista. Our ongoing challenges notwithstanding, I loved Nate with all my heart, but I wasn't blind. Hollywood looked to be right at six feet tall, and I'd bet he worked hard for the muscles. He had medium brown hair tousled in that I-just-got-out-of-bed look and a day's worth of facial stubble—just enough to be sexy. Worn jeans, low around his hips, and a faded blue t-shirt did nothing to detract from the overall package. I pegged him at late twenties. He was headed my way. I realized I'd been staring, glanced away, and turned towards the courtyard.

"Excuse me," he said.

I cringed, knowing what was coming next and suddenly feeling less-than-professional. He'd caught me ogling him.

"Are you Liz Talbot?"

I'm an idiot. I turned back towards him and flashed a smile. "I am. You must be Matthew Thomas."

Intense green eyes sized me up. "Nice to meet you. My friends call me Matt." He had a firm handshake.

"Is the courtyard all right?"

"Sure, just let me grab some coffee. I'll catch up to you."

"Sounds great." I gathered my latte, the pastry I was no longer in the mood for, and my dignity and went outside. A table in the back corner was open. I chose the chair facing into the courtyard, laid my phone on the table, and pulled out the Purell, thankful for a moment alone. My fondness for good hygiene was often at odds with my sincere desire to avoid a disgraceful breach of manners.

I sipped my coffee. Ansley was right about one thing. It was highly unlikely Kent walked away from Matt Thomas without so much as a goodbye. Unless of course he was a sociopath and she was afraid of him. Or a jackass. No amount of handsome made up for being a jackass.

Colleen appeared to my left. "Boy howdy, he's a looker."

I jumped a little, spilling coffee on my white Michael Kors hammered satin shirt. "Shit." I blotted the stain with my napkin.

"You don't suspect him, do you?" Her tone allowed as to how she thought this was a foolish notion.

"I haven't even interviewed him yet. On the face of it, no. He has an alibi, so I'm told." I gave silent thanks I had my earbuds in.

"I haven't been read in. But he looks innocent to me."

"Read in? What are you, CIA now?"

"Ha. They wish they had my sources."

I rolled my eyes, then turned my attention back to the subject at hand. "Matt Thomas looks a lot of things to me. I'm not sure about innocent."

Colleen blushed, got all fidgety. "I mean I don't think he hurt Kent."

I raised my left eyebrow. "It would be ever so helpful if you could tell me that for certain."

"For some reason, I can't read his mind."

"That's unsettling. The last person you couldn't read at all turned out to be a stone-cold killer."

"I don't get that kind of vibe from him."

"Do you need to be rebooted? If you could just spend the day with me and read everyone's mind, that would make my job so much easier." I may have been just the teensiest bit cranky. But she made me spill coffee on my new shirt.

"It's not my mission to make your job easy." She raised her chin.

I heaved a deep sigh. "I know. When you throw me the occasional bone, I can't help but think how I could close cases a lot faster if it was."

"I help when I can. You know I can't read minds reliably. Some minds are open to me, others aren't. I get information on a need-to-know basis."

"So you tell me. Here he comes."

Matt set down a cup of coffee and took the chair across from me. "Sorry I made you wait."

I waved my hand, shooing the thought away. "I've just been enjoying my coffee."

He leaned across the table, arms circling his round mug. "Do you have any leads on Kent?"

Right to the point. "Not yet. But it's early. I just caught the case yesterday."

He ran a hand through his hair and sat back. "I never thought I'd agree with her daddy on a damn thing. But I wish she'd never gotten involved with this gang of artists."

I squinted at him. "You don't mean gang in the sense that they are involved in anything illegal, do you?"

"No, no. It's just that they are the only new thing in her life. It's hard for me not to suspect them of...*something*."

"Hang on. Do you mind if I tape our conversation?"

"No." He looked me straight in the eyes. His face was open. I couldn't read a flicker of objection.

I tapped the record button and read in the interview particulars. "You were saying you have reservations about Kent's new artist friends. Have you ever met them?"

Frustration flashed across his face. "No."

"Why is that? I get the impression this part of her life is important to her."

He shrugged. "It's mostly a scheduling thing. I work nights. She works days. We don't have much time together as it is. We tend to spend what little we have alone or with close friends."

"Okay. Let's start at the beginning. Tell me about you and Kent. When did you meet?"

His story matched what Ansley had already told me. When he talked about Kent, his voice went softer, his eyes bright. He looked and sounded like a man in love.

"When was the last time you saw her?" I asked.

"The night before she disappeared. I was off that Thursday. I made dinner for us at my place. She didn't leave until after two a.m. Friday morning. I wanted her to stay. I didn't want her out that late by herself.

She wanted to be home for breakfast so her daddy wouldn't lose it."

Colleen piped up. "He'd've had a conniption fit."

I bit back the urge to tell her to hush up. "Where do you live, Matt?"

"I have a bungalow over on St. Margaret. Wagener Terrace area. My house is about the size of Kent's closet. Honestly, I'm amazed she agreed to move in with me. It'll be a huge lifestyle adjustment for her. She doesn't care." He blinked and looked away.

While it wasn't South of Broad, Wagener Terrace wasn't exactly a low rent district. The area near the Ashley River, north of The Citadel was hip. Young professionals were snapping up houses built from the nineteen-twenties through the nineteen-fifties and renovating them.

"When are y'all planning on her moving in?"

"We talked about next month. Kent wanted to give her parents time to adjust. She was hoping they'd warm up to me. It breaks her heart, the way they act. I tried telling her it doesn't matter to me. But it matters to her."

Colleen said, "He's just the sweetest thing."

I ignored her. "I get that they have other plans for Kent, but is there any reason you can think of aside from that why they wouldn't like you? I mean—and, not to put too fine a point on it, but I will verify what you tell me—have you ever been arrested? Do you abuse drugs? That kind of thing."

"God, no." He looked like he wanted to spit something out.

Colleen said, "What is wrong with you?"

"I have to ask. Nothing personal."

He canted his head and blew out a long breath. "I work hard. I have plans. One day I'm going to have my own restaurant in this town. Everything Kent's parents suspect I am, I'm the opposite of *that*."

"Noted. So, she left your place around two that morning. Did you talk to her after that?"

"She texted me when she got home. I texted her back. We said goodnight, that kind of thing."

"And you didn't speak to her on Friday at all?"

"Yes, I did. We spoke briefly around lunchtime. She was excited about seeing her artist friends that night." He closed his eyes, then opened them. "Look, I shouldn't have said what I did about them. They've been very encouraging to Kent, and she needs this. The guy from

Stella Maris—Evan Ingle—he was going to help her set up a virtual gallery website. Kent has plans, too. That restaurant I'm going to open? We're going to showcase her work on the walls."

"Wait. He was going to help her set up a website Friday night at dinner?"

His forehead creased. "No, not during dinner. I had the impression they were going to do that after dinner."

"She told you that?"

He thought for a minute. "Yeah. I mean, she wasn't specific about where they were going to do that. She just said she didn't know how late they'd be when I asked her about coming over after I got off. I should've asked more questions. Damn. Do you think that's important?"

Only because Evan hadn't mentioned it. And I'd asked him specifically if he knew why she would've brought her laptop. "Probably not. It's too soon to tell what's important. I'm just figuring out a timeline right now. What she planned to do, and exactly where things went off track."

"Seems pretty clear. She never showed up at Bin 152. That's why I never gave much thought to what she had planned after, I guess."

I pondered that, unconvinced that whatever had happened to Kent had occurred in the fifteen-minute window between seven forty-five and eight p.m. "What time did you get off?"

"Around one."

"Is that typical for a Friday night?"

"Yeah. Restaurant hours...they're hard on relationships. But I love it. I could never do anything else."

"How long have you been at FIG?"

"Three and a half years."

"What do you do there?"

"I'm a sous chef." There was pride in his voice, and just a touch of prickly.

"You didn't just walk into that job, I'm guessing." I needed to fill in details I wouldn't be able to get online about Matt. I needed a better sense of him, needed him to keep talking.

"No. I started in restaurants right out of high school, washing dishes at High Cotton. That fall, I started culinary arts classes at the Art Institute. By the time I finished, I had worked my way up to sous chef at High Cotton. I left in May twenty eleven. I really wanted to work with the team at FIG. I gave up a sous chef position for a job as a line cook at FIG. Don't get me wrong. The folks at High Cotton were good to me. It was just time for me to move on."

High Cotton was another popular fine dining restaurant, part of a small chain specializing in Southern cuisine. "The night Kent disappeared, what did you do after work?"

An expression I couldn't put a name to slipped across his face and then evaporated. "I went home. I was exhausted."

"Did you see anyone else that night?"

"What do you mean?"

"Oh, for goodness sake!" Colleen said.

I swiveled my head so fast it felt like it might spin all the way around. "Hush up." Ever so slowly, I eased my face back in Matt's direction.

He was staring at me wide-eyed, his expression chiseled in shock.

I beamed at him. In a real sweet, soothing voice, I said, "I mean, after you left the restaurant, did you see anyone else you know—a neighbor, a friend..."

"Why?" Irritation raked through the question.

At least I'd distracted him from my lapse. I dropped Little Miss Sunshine. "Because right now, I don't have a timeline to work with. All I know for sure is that Kent left home at seven forty-five and didn't show up where she said she was going. But she could have changed her plans. Women do it all the time—trust me. For all I know, she went shopping, browsed for hours, bought nothing, and met you at your place when you got off work."

He looked at me with unvarnished horror. Clearly he understood the implications of Kent meeting him after work on that particular evening.

"Or," I continued, "she could have driven straight to your house, let herself in, and watched TV until you got off from work."

His enunciation was precise. "That did not happen." His voice rose, and the words came out in a rush. "You've gotta believe me. I never saw Kent after she left at two that morning."

"Does she have a key to your house?"

"Yes." Clear green eyes met mine.

"You see my problem? Right now, all we know is the impossible. It's impossible that she disappeared into thin air. She went *somewhere*. I have to examine everywhere that's possible until I figure out what happened. Give me a reason why it's impossible that she came to your house that night."

He dropped his gaze. "I don't have one. All I know is that she didn't."

He was hiding something. I could smell it. "Did the Charleston Police detectives interview you?"

"Are you freaking kidding me? I spent six hours in a little room at the police station. Kent's daddy put the idea in their head I'd done something to her. I guess he gave you a load of that horseshit, too. I was at work. They talked to everyone else working at the restaurant that night to be certain I couldn't have snuck out and come back. Clueless. None of them ever worked in a restaurant."

I pondered this for a moment. "So their theory was that whatever happened to Kent happened before one a.m.?"

"How do I know what they thought?" Wounded, confused green eyes stared back at me. "I guess. When they accepted that I had an alibi, I never heard from them again."

"What are you not telling me?"

He pursed his lips and glared at me like maybe he thought I was evil.

"There's something. And maybe you don't think it's important. But let me tell you something, buddy. You don't know what's important. I need to know *e-ver-y-thing*. You love her. I can see that. Tell me."

He looked at the patio to his left and shook his head. "I'm not hiding anything. That's the truth."

"For your sake, I hope it's the whole truth." I wasn't convinced by any means, and he would stay on my radar until I was. "Was Kent taking any medications she wouldn't have left home without?"

"No. Kent doesn't take pills."

"What about birth control?"

He scowled. "We use other methods."

"So what are you not telling me?"

He stood. "If you figure out what happened to her, call me. Please. But if you want to pursue the crazy-assed idea I had something to do with this—that *I* hurt Kent?—then you call my attorney. Maybe you've heard of him. His name is Charlie Condon. He's in Mount Pleasant."

He strode across the courtyard without looking back.

I wondered what the salary range for sous chefs was. This one owned real estate in an up-and-coming area and could afford arguably the top attorney east of the Cooper—an attorney who'd served eight years as the South Carolina Attorney General, and ten as a district attorney. Why did Matt have any attorney's name to whip out? Why did he hire an East Cooper attorney when he lived in Charleston?

Colleen said, "He looks just as good going as coming."

"Lookit," I said. "You and I are going to have to come to an understanding where *you don't talk* when I'm talking to other people. Do you want folks to think I have Tourette's syndrome?"

"You were antagonizing him for no good reason."

"You just think he's cute. You and I both know that doesn't make him innocent. How do you know what my reasons were?"

"Because I can read *your* mind." Colleen shimmered and then grew transparent. "See you at the Heywards' house. Prepare yourself." She disappeared altogether.

"I need some liquor in this coffee," I said to no one in particular.

The gentleman at the next table turned around. I pegged him at roughly eighty. He wore a pink seersucker suit and a bowtie. "They don't sell that here, darlin', but I could spare a dash." He opened his jacket to show me his flask.

"How nice of you to offer. Thank you so much." I hopped up. "I've got to be running along. You have yourself a good day, now."

SEVEN

William Palmer opened the door to the Heyward home. I recognized his voice immediately, his British accent quite elegant. Tall, lean, and wearing a nice suit, he was a distinguished-looking gentleman of African descent. "Good afternoon, Miss Talbot."

"Good afternoon, Mr. Palmer." I stepped into the wide hall.

He closed the door. "Please, address me as William. This way." He led me to the first door on the left and stepped inside. "Miss Talbot has arrived."

From inside the room a woman said, "Thank you, William. That will be all."

He stepped back and nodded, indicating I should enter.

I stepped through the door. Elaborately carved moldings, gilt-framed art and mirrors, antiques, and cream-colored upholstered furniture set the traditional Charleston living room stage. Five actors were on the set. Hell's bells. The two identical men seated on one of the cream sofas stood. These had to be the twin uncles—Mrs. Heyward's brothers.

From a wingback near the fireplace, the oldest of the three women stood. Her shoulder-length bob was a lighter shade of chestnut than Kent's, and it had a teased look to it. There was only so much even the best colorist could do to maintain a youthful look past a certain point. Her skin was stretched tight, but well cared for. I'd bet she'd had work done. Her beige St. John skirt suit and pearls testified to her good taste. "Hello, Miss Talbot. I'm Abigail Bounetheau, Kent's grandmother. After speaking with my daughter, we felt this would be the most expeditious way to move forward, don't you agree?"

I'd been ambushed. Hell no, I didn't agree. I offered her my brightest smile, crossed the room, and extended a hand. I would never get away with bowing and nodding in this crowd. "It's so lovely to meet you, Mrs. Bounetheau."

She took my hand and gave it a firm shake. "And you as well." She looked to her right and nodded. The two women seated on a second, matching cream sofa stood. "These are my daughters. Virginia is Kent's mother, of course. I'm sure you understand how much she needs her family beside her at this difficult time."

"Of course. Mrs. Heyward." I extended a hand to the middle-aged, well-maintained version of Kent.

She slipped hers in, then out of mine. "Pleased to meet you." Her voice was cultured, but wispy. The elsewhere vibe she gave off screamed heavily medicated. Bless her heart, she likely needed a little something to help her get by. She had a missing child, after all. Mrs. Heyward's St. John skirt suit was a darker shade than her mother's, more of a taupe.

Abigail Bounetheau continued. "And this is her older sister, Charlotte."

Charlotte made eye contact as she extended a hand. "Thank you for coming." She neatly flipped the dynamics. This was their meeting, not mine. Charlotte's hair was a shorter bob than Virginia's and Abigail's. But the family resemblance was unmistakable. No St. John suit for her— Charlotte wore a classic navy sheath. I didn't recognize the designer, but the fabric and fit signified high-end.

Abigail gestured to her left. "My sons, Peter and Peyton."

Peter and Peyton looked nothing like the women in the room. The gentlemen had blond hair, cut very short, with a touch of wave. The only common denominator seemed to be blue eyes. The twins were trim and slightly built. They wore identical navy suits. We said hello, shook hands, and the family sat back down. Two occasional chairs with cameo backs sat at the end of the conversation area nearest the door, across from the fireplace. "Please," the matriarch gestured, "make yourself comfortable."

What would make me comfortable was to get out my hand sanitizer. I didn't dare. "Thank you for seeing me this afternoon." I took the seat closest to the sisters and pulled my pad and pen out of my bag. If I read Abigail Bounetheau right, she would resist me recording the conversation, and might use it as an excuse to cancel the meeting. "I need a bit more background information. I'm sure Mrs. Heyward can help me." I smiled at Virginia. "I hope you're feeling better today."

She looked at something over my left shoulder. "I am, thank you."

"Tell us, Miss Talbot." Abigail Bounetheau's regal tone commanded everyone's attention. She was not about to let me take control of the conversation. "How do you believe you can help us find our Kent?"

"I'm a private investigator, Mrs. Bounetheau. I have a great many tools at my disposal to assist in missing persons cases."

"Tools which the police do not have access to?" Frost formed on her voice.

"Ma'am, as I explained to Mr. Heyward, I have great faith in the Charleston Police Department. Likely, things are precisely as they suspect. Kent chose to leave and chose not to tell anyone where she is. I hope to contact her and verify her safety."

"I see." Mrs. Bounetheau looked down her patrician nose at me. Clearly, she did not approve of me nor any of my ancestors.

I took the opening. "Mrs. Heyward, are you aware of any prescription medications Kent was taking?"

Mrs. Heyward looked at her mother.

Mrs. Bounetheau arched an elegant eyebrow as if to say, *go ahead and answer, but this is a complete and utter waste of time.*

Virginia Heyward looked directly at me for the first time, her expression demure, deferential. "She wasn't taking anything as far as I know. Kent doesn't like to take pills. She suffers from allergies, but on the rare occasion she takes something, it's natural."

Clearly, her mother did not share Kent's aversion to pharmaceuticals. "Can you think of anything she wouldn't dream of leaving behind that's still here?"

Virginia's hands lay crossed in her lap. She stared at them a long moment. Something was definitely wrong with this woman. I couldn't decide if she was indeed heavily drugged, indifferent to her daughter, suffering from PTSD, or simply accustomed to deferring to others. Finally, she raised her chin. Desperate blue eyes met mine. "I can't imagine she'd leave her diamond studs. We gave her those for graduation. Or her pearls. She has several nice pieces that I wouldn't think she'd leave." Virginia's voice got softer as she spoke and her eyes glistened with tears. "Then again, if she were very angry with her father and me...well, we gave her all of her nice jewelry, so it's hard to say. And of course, *things* don't mean as much to Kent. She isn't materialistic in the least." Where was the woman who coldly made herself a manicure appointment yesterday while I met with her husband?

"We've been over this with the police." Charlotte's tone was clipped, not as imperious as her mother's, but she was training hard at it. "There's nothing missing from Kent's belongings that one can draw a conclusion from one way or another."

"What about clothes, luggage?" I asked.

"None of her luggage is missing," said Abigail. "If she took any of her clothes, she took them out a piece or two at a time and she only took a few things. None of us has her closet inventory committed to memory." That last bit was sprinkled with sarcasm.

If Abigail wanted to tangle, we'd just get to it. "Mrs. Bounetheau, one of the things I do in a case like this is eliminate all the possibilities, one at a time, until only one is left. One of the possibilities is that someone stood to gain financially if Kent were removed from the equation. Since so much of the family is here, let's put our heads together, why don't we? Can any of you think of anyone, on either side of the family, who stood to gain from Kent's...disappearance?"

Abigail Bounetheau turned an interesting shade of fuchsia. "I beg your pardon," she said, in that indignant tone that suggested unseemly things for both me and the horse I rode in on.

Simultaneously, Charlotte inquired, "Exactly who do you think you are?"

Virginia gasped softly.

The twins commenced whispering to each other.

I looked at Charlotte and Abigail in turn. "I'm the investigator, hired by Kent's father, to find out what has happened to her. I aim to do just that. I mean no offense. But I need to know if anyone stands to gain financially if Kent doesn't come home."

"That's insulting," one of the twins spoke up.

"Revolting," said the other.

Those two were a piece of work. "Mrs. Bounetheau," I said, "forgive me for asking such a personal question, but what is the impact, hypothetically speaking, on your and Mr. Bounetheau's estate should one of your heirs be...unaccounted for?"

Abigail Bounetheau stared at me like she was trying to melt me where I sat. "Our financial affairs are private family business."

And most of the time when folks went missing their family was behind it. "Of course," I said. "I'd just hoped that since we all want the same thing—to find Kent—that perhaps you would give me the big picture."

"The only people who would have anything whatsoever to gain are family members who adore Kent and would never dream of harming her." Abigail straightened her back, which I would have thought impossible, as it appeared to have a rod in it to begin with.

The twins went to whispering again. Charlotte spoke softly to Virginia. I couldn't make out what she was saying.

"Naturally," I replied to Abigail. I buttered my question and slid it in with a smile. "So, you have trust funds set up for each of the grandchildren, and the children as well, I expect?"

The four siblings stilled and looked at their mother. Mrs. Bounetheau pressed her lips together.

Before she could order me out, I said, "If you prefer, I could speak to Mr. Bounetheau. I suppose it's better to ask him about financial matters, anyway." My statement hung suspended in the air. It seemed everyone in the room had stopped breathing.

In a regal tone, Mrs. Bounetheau said, "Do not bother Mr. Bounetheau with your outlandish ideas. He has no time for this nonsense. If nothing else will satisfy you—and I assure you, it has no relevance whatsoever—Mr. Bounetheau and I have established a family trust, which owns all of our holdings. Professionals manage it all, of course. There are separate trusts for each child and grandchild, but should tragedy befall any of them, their assets would revert to the family trust. When Mr. Bounetheau and I have both passed on, after charitable bequests, the family trust will be split equally between our children. Are you quite satisfied?" Mrs. Bounetheau was the only person I'd ever met who shot more lethal death rays with her eyes than my sister, Merry.

"Quite," I said, reflecting on just how far from satisfied I was. "Mrs. Heyward, what becomes of your and your husband's estate should Kent be unavailable to inherit?"

She took a moment to draw herself together. "Everything is divided between several charities."

I kept my voice low and gentle.

"I asked your husband this, but if you don't mind, I wonder if anything has occurred to you that may have been bothering Kent before she disappeared?"

Mrs. Heyward looked over my right shoulder for a moment, then squared her eyes to mine, seeming to rally. "She and Matt were having problems."

I felt my face scrunch up. "I thought they were getting ready to move in together?"

"What?" Abigail Bounetheau cast an accusing glare at Virginia.

Virginia Heyward kept her eyes on mine, as if I were her lifeline. "That was their plan. I don't think that had changed. Kent would have married him, I think. Except he wasn't ready to make that commitment. That was the source of the friction between them."

"*Virginia.*" Abigail spoke sharply, as she would to a disobedient child, which I suppose is how she saw her, but Virginia Heyward was fifty-three years old. "Why on earth did you not tell me about this?"

Slowly, Virginia turned her head towards her mother. She was looking away from me, so I couldn't read the message she was sending. For a split second, I would have sworn I saw fear in Abigail's eyes. Then her face went completely expressionless. Damnation. Where was Colleen? I seriously needed a peek into a few of these gentrified heads.

Virginia looked back at me. She took several deep breaths, swallowed hard. "Forgive me for not meeting with you yesterday. I should have been there. For Kent. I'm holding on as tight as I can to the idea that she has run away. She'll call any day, I tell myself. But I know that isn't right. Colton is right. We need your help, Miss Talbot. Thank you."

Abigail brought a hand to her temple and remained quiet.

Maybe Virginia wasn't on drugs. Seemed like that would be harder to rally through than emotional distress. You can't turn drugged on and off that fast.

"Of course," I said. "You have my word. I'll do everything I possibly can. Did you mention this to the police? That Kent and Matt were having problems?"

"No," Virginia said. "At first it seemed so...prejudicial. Colton was giving them all sorts of ideas, pointing the finger at Matt. I didn't want to make more trouble for him. I really don't think he'd hurt Kent."

"Did your husband know Matt and Kent had been quarreling?" I asked.

"No, that's not the kind of thing she would confide in him. I didn't dare tell him. He's convinced as it is that Matt is guilty of something, even if it's just exposing her to the wrong element, putting her at risk."

"Just to clarify, by the 'wrong element,' do you mean her artist friends?" Matt hadn't introduced Kent to those folks. He'd never even met them.

Her forehead wrinkled. "Colton doesn't approve of what he refers to as the service crowd. Restaurant workers. We weren't aware that Kent *had* artist friends until Ansley mentioned that's who Kent was meeting."

"Mr. Heyward indicated that Ansley didn't know who Kent planned to meet." I didn't mention how Ansley had a different story.

"Well, she didn't, actually," said Virginia. "I think she gave the police officers one name. Ansley doesn't know that group." Her words were dismissive.

Under the circumstances, I could understand why Kent wouldn't bring her artist friends home for dinner. Still, there was something odd about the way Mr. and Mrs. Heyward were eager to dismiss the fact that Kent planned to meet a group of artists the very night she vanished given their distrust of the entire vocation. Naturally, this piqued my curious nature. "Is there anything else that has come to you—anything you've remembered that might be helpful?"

"I've wracked my brain. Kent and I are close. If there's anything else, I don't know the significance of it. I keep going over and over everything in my head. There's something I should have done differently. I just don't know what it is." The helpless look in her eyes touched me. But there was something else swimming around in there. Guilt.

Charlotte put her arm around her sister. "Virginia, that's nonsense. You've done nothing wrong. Kent's just blowing off steam. She'll be home soon."

Virginia collapsed into her sister's embrace and sobbed softly.

I looked over at the twins, who were staring at Abigail. I followed their gaze. She seemed to be calculating a difficult equation. They seemed to be waiting for her to come up with an answer.

I took that as an opening. "Gentlemen, what do you all do? For a living, I mean?"

They both jumped a little. The one on the left said, "We manage our personal portfolios."

"That must be very time consuming," I said.

Two sets of identical eyes widened. The other twin said, "You cannot possibly imagine." He looked down his aristocratic nose at me. Good grief, how did they tell themselves apart?

"Peyton?" I inquired.

"Yes?" said the one on the right.

They should be required to wear nametags. "Are you close to your niece?"

"Kent?"

"Do you have another niece?"

"No. That is, I do not have another niece. I suppose we're as close to Kent as any uncles would be, wouldn't you say, Peter?"

Peter was already nodding. "Absolutely."

"Are you aware of anything that was troubling her?"

They looked at each other, then me. Simultaneously they said, "No."

I couldn't decide if I agreed with Ansley that they were creepy, or if I simply found them comical.

I turned to Charlotte. "Mrs. Pinckney, how about you?"

"Kent and I are very close. I have four boys. She's like the daughter I never had." She stroked her sister's arm.

Virginia quieted, seemed to pull herself together.

"Have you met Matt?" I asked.

"Yes," said Charlotte. "Virginia, Kent, and I had dinner at FIG once. We went on a Monday night, so it was slow. He made a special appetizer for us, and he came out to say hello. He seems like a nice young man. I don't disapprove of their relationship, if that's what you're asking."

I kept my tone soothing. "Mrs. Heyward...what do you think of Matt?"

"He loves Kent. That's good enough for me. My only fear is that he doesn't want the same things she does. I worry he'll hurt her."

"What kinds of things?" I asked.

"Kent wants a home, children. I think his priority is his career," said Virginia.

"They're so young," said Charlotte. "They have plenty of time for children."

I looked at Abigail, who was still curiously quiet. I kept waiting for her to interject. I turned back to Virginia.

"So it's your husband who strongly objects to the relationship?"

Virginia's gaze returned to her hands.

"We both object, but for different reasons. Colton wants a more appropriate match for her—someone with a similar background. And he's not wrong that certain things would be easier. I worry Matt will hurt her in the end."

"You said they'd been having problems," I said. "Do you think Kent was upset enough that she would leave?"

Virginia and Charlotte both shook their heads vehemently. Charlotte said, "She would never put us through this. Family is important to Kent. She could just break things off with Matt. Why would she leave town?"

"I can't come up with a single reason...yet," I said. "Mrs. Heyward, I apologize in advance. This will seem an insensitive question. But I have to ask it, or I wouldn't be doing my job. You want me to do my job, right?"

"Yes, of course."

"Is there any trace of a possibility in your mind that when Mr. Heyward was beside himself—not himself at all—perhaps during a heated argument with Kent, that he could have unintentionally hurt her?"

Virginia Heyward looked at me levelly.

"That's the one thing that is simply not possible. Colton never raised a hand to anyone to my knowledge, least of all Kent. He positively dotes on her. In time, he will make his peace with Matt. Please, don't waste precious time pursing that scenario. I gave birth to her. If I thought for a second...no." She shook her head.

"Thank you. I had to ask." I trusted a mother's instincts. She had me convinced.

"Is that all, Miss Talbot?" Abigail Bounetheau had found her voice, but she'd dialed down the imperious tone.

"Yes," I stood. "I think that's all I have for today." I handed each of them a card. "If you think of anything at all that might be helpful, please call me. I'll see myself out."

"Please find her."

Virginia's voice was thick with tears shed and more pent up.

"I will do my best." I walked out of the room and down the hall with my bag in one hand and my pad and pen in the other. William Palmer waited by the front door. I was certain he'd overheard every word. "Do you have a moment, Mr. Palmer?"

"It's William, miss. Of course. At your service." He gave me a precise half nod. I half expected him to click his heels together.

"If I recall correctly, you mentioned you were out the evening Kent went missing?"

"Correct."

I moved over to a chest and set down my bag and pad. "What time did you leave?"

"Just after five. I had dinner with my family, read for a while, and turned in early." He seemed well-prepared.

"You don't live here?" Why had I thought that?

"No, miss. None of the staff lives in. Cook—Alice George—arrives at six, the maid, Loretta King, and I at seven each morning, Monday through Friday. Loretta and I leave at five. Cook stays until after dinner is served. She has a break in the afternoons."

"So they're both here right now?" I looked up at him from my pad.

"Yes, miss."

"Would it be possible to speak with them as well?"

He hesitated, no doubt wondering how Mrs. Bounetheau would react. Loyalty to his employer won out. Finally, he nodded. "Of course. Please, come with me." He headed down the hall and made a left.

I followed. A few turns later, we were in a large, sunny, modern kitchen. It looked like what I envisioned a Southern Living test kitchen would look like—high ceilings, industrial appliances, and all the modern conveniences folded into a warm décor, complete with a large stone fireplace. Two women were seated by the fireplace, one on a yellow and white checked sofa, the other in a slipcovered chair to the left. They stopped talking as we entered the room.

William did the introductions.

"Miss Talbot, please meet Alice George, the cook..." The woman on the sofa stood. I pegged her at mid-forties. She was plump, with short brown hair and a warm smile.

"...and Loretta King, the maid." The other woman stood. She seemed of a similar age, though she was trim, perhaps from cleaning this huge house. She wore her blonde hair short as well. Both women wore black pants and black blouses.

William continued, "Ladies, this is Miss Talbot. She's been retained by Mr. Heyward to find Miss Kent."

We all said hello, shook hands, and all that. The women wore somber expressions. William remained inscrutable.

"Let's sit, shall we?" William settled into one of the wingbacks and motioned that I should take the other.

I sat and jotted names on my pad. "Thank you all for taking time to speak with me. This shouldn't take long. First, how long have each of you worked for the Heyward family?"

"I came from the Bounetheau home with Mrs. Heyward when she married Mr. Heyward. That was in nineteen-eighty-two." William's posture was as good as Abigail Bounetheau's.

Alice said, "I came five years later. I've worked here twenty-seven years."

"I'm the newbie," Loretta said. "I've only been with the Heyward family for fifteen years."

"So all of you have known Kent for a very long time," I said.

They nodded and murmured agreement.

"Do any of you have any reason to believe that Kent left home and moved elsewhere, possibly due to tensions or disagreements with her parents?"

The women looked at William, as if asking permission to speak freely.

William nodded.

"Not in a million years," said Alice.

"No way," said Loretta. "That is the sweetest, most compassionate young woman I've ever known. She would never worry her mamma and daddy like that. Sure, they had ideas she didn't go along with. But these folks care about each other."

"Exactly," said Alice. "Now they did argue, and I won't say different. It's like I told the police. Sometimes the arguments got hot. But nobody ever hit anybody—nothing like that."

I looked at William. He seemed content to let the women talk. I continued to look at him expectantly.

"No, I do not believe Miss Kent would leave and not tell anyone where she could be reached," he said.

"Loretta, how often did you clean Kent's room?" I asked.

"Every day. Well, except Sunday. I'm off on Sunday. Wednesdays and Saturdays I work half days."

"You're familiar with what she keeps in her room and her closet?" I asked.

"Of course."

"Are any of her clothes missing?" I waited with my pen poised.

"No," she said. "Maybe a piece or two I wouldn't miss. If she took anything—and I'm not saying she did—it was only enough for overnight."

"Did she generally keep her laptop on her desk?" I asked.

"I dusted it three times a week," Loretta said. "She rarely took it anywhere. Kept her iPad and her phone in her purse. If she took her laptop, she put it in a backpack she kept under her desk."

Why did I not just talk to the help to begin with? Surely the police had questioned everyone in the household. But I'd gotten information through the filter of what Colton Heyward deemed important enough to retain in his frazzled state. "Do you remember if it was there that Friday when you cleaned?"

"It was," said Loretta. "I remember noticing it was gone the next day, when she didn't come home."

I turned to Alice. "You were the only member of the staff here when she left that Friday?"

Alice said, "Yes. I made dinner for Mr. and Mrs. Heyward, then left after I cleaned up the kitchen."

"Did you see Kent leave?" I asked.

"Yes." Alice nodded. "She came through the kitchen on her way out. The garage is down that hall." She pointed across the room at a short glassed-in breezeway. "She stopped. Asked me about my kids, my new grandbaby." Alice's eyes moistened.

"What did she have with her?" I asked.

"Her backpack—the one she carried the computer in. She could've had an extra change of clothes in there, too, I guess. And her purse."

"Did anything seem amiss?" I asked. "Did she seem upset about anything? Give you any indication that she wouldn't be coming home that night?"

"No," Alice said. "She seemed happy."

I looked at William.

He gave me a look that said, *honestly, don't you think I would have mentioned it?* Then he cleared his throat and said, "Although I did not see her that Friday, I did not observe anything unusual about Miss Kent's behavior in the days leading up to her disappearance."

"Did Kent confide in any of you? Talk to you about her friends, her boyfriend, that kind of thing?"

William didn't dignify that with an answer.

Alice said, "When she was younger she did. Not since she turned thirteen."

"Loretta?" I looked at the maid.

"Not me," she said.

"Okay," I said. "I think I have what I need. Thank you all so much. Here is my card." I handed one to each of them. "Please call me if you think of anything that might be helpful."

Alice said, "We're just praying you find her, and that she's safe."

William showed me out. I noticed that Virginia and her family had cleared out of the living room. Did they notice I'd gone to the kitchen? If they did, apparently they were okay with it. William opened the front door for me. "Good afternoon, Miss Talbot. Godspeed."

I climbed into the Escape. Colleen waited in the passenger seat.

"Where have you been?" I asked. "I needed you in there."

"I was having tea with Sue Ellen. You remember, the debutante ghost."

"How nice," I said.

"It was, actually. Her two sisters were here today, and several of the servants. We actually did have tea. With little sandwiches and cakes."

I tried to parse that.

Colleen continued, "Sue Ellen doesn't understand part of what she knows. She said Kent cried a lot at night lately, and that she talked to herself a lot about Matt. Sue Ellen mentioned strings Kent put in her ears. I think she's talking about earbuds. I think Matt and Kent were fighting on the phone."

"About what?"

"Kent is expecting."

"What?" *Oh dear heaven, no.* I needed to rethink everything. "Are you sure? Wait...*is*? Does that mean she's alive?"

"I don't know. I'm trying to find out." Colleen faded away.

EIGHT

The first person I needed to speak to was Matt Thomas. We hadn't parted on the best of terms, and he wasn't taking my calls, so I decided to pay him a visit. I pulled out my laptop and activated the Wi-Fi hotspot on my phone. A quick search of the Charleston County real property database yielded Matt's house number on St. Margaret Street. I like to know if potential suspects are in debt, and if so, just how far in debt—money being the root of so much evil and all. I checked public records. Not only did I not find civil judgments and the like for unpaid bills, I couldn't find a mortgage recorded against the house. Interesting.

I headed down Legare and made a right on South Battery. A few blocks later, I turned right on Ashley Avenue and drove two miles northwest, to the other side of Highway 17. Ashley more or less parallels Meeting Street, but this way I'd miss the tourist traffic. A few quick turns later, and I was on St. Margaret Street.

A mix of frame and brick homes lined the street, some clearly renovated, others not. Matt's house was on the right, a few houses past Tenth Street. I pulled to the curb. Well, he couldn't pretend he wasn't home. Matt was on the front porch, shirtless, touching up the trim paint on what appeared to be a nicely renovated, well-maintained frame bungalow. He'd added some craftsman touches—shingle accents, stained shutters, and square porch pillars which were stone at the bottom with tapered wood columns at the top.

He set down the paint cup and put the brush inside it. Then he crossed his arms and stared at me. Hostility radiated off him.

I got out of the car and walked around the front end towards the sidewalk.

"Unless you have news for me, you can get right back in your car."

I glanced up and down the street. A woman with a stroller was a block away on the other side of the street. Two houses up, an older couple sat on their front porch. I kept quiet and continued towards Matt. I hadn't expected him to be happy to see me.

"Okay, you're trespassing now," he said as I passed through the vine-covered pergola that framed the walkway to his house.

I kept walking. When I was close enough to speak in a conversational tone, I said, "If you'd like to make a scene for the neighbors, I'm game."

He screwed up his face and shot missiles at me from his eyes.

It wasn't the first hateful look I'd received that day. "We can talk inside or out. Your call."

Without a word, he turned, opened the wood-and-stained-glass front door, and walked through it. I followed, but he stopped in the cozy den just inside.

He said, "You've got five seconds to tell me why I shouldn't call my attorney and get some sort of restraining order against you. I asked you to speak to him."

"We'll get to that in a minute," I said. "First maybe you could tell me why I shouldn't call the Charleston Police Department and tell them about all the fighting going on between you and Kent, and how *she's* pregnant and *you* don't want children."

He drew back like I'd taken a swing at him. "Who told you that?"

"It doesn't matter. Is this what you were hiding from me this morning, or is there more?"

"I don't have to talk to you."

"You're mighty right. You don't. I can call up my friend Sonny—he's a Charleston PD detective—and have him come on over and you can talk to him instead."

Matt dug a hand through his hair.

"So what's it going to be?" I tilted my head. "I guess technically it wouldn't be Sonny who showed up. He'd no doubt call those nice detectives you spent so much quality time with before and send them over to pick your ass up."

He rubbed his face with his hands, covered his eyes. Then he drew a deep breath and let it out. "Fine." He walked over to the leather sofa and plopped down. "Sit wherever you want."

I sat at a right angle to him on the loveseat that matched the sofa. I pulled out my pad, pen, and phone, and tapped record. I dictated the date, time and parties present. "Is it true that Kent Heyward is pregnant?"

"Yes. At least she was the last time I spoke to her."

I slid back in the loveseat, stared at him for a moment. "Do you have reason to believe she's gone off somewhere to get an abortion?"

"It occurred to me maybe that's what she did. But she never told me she was going to do that. Last I heard, she was dead set against an abortion." His tone softened. "Kent wants this child."

"You don't?" I kept my voice neutral.

"No. I'm not sure I ever want kids." He worked his jaw. "I had a perfect childhood. I know exactly how lucky I am, because way too many of my friends didn't have what I had. Two parents who loved me, who were *involved*. Every. Single. Day. Two brothers who've always had my back. Dinner with the family every night. Church on Sunday. Grandparents— the nineteen-fifties textbook ideal childhood. I know what raising kids takes. And I know I don't have that to give."

"That's the life Kent wants?"

"It's not that simple. Kent thinks we can make it work—it'll be all right. She's willing to take what I can give her and the baby and be happy with it. She deserves more. So much more. I thought we could make it work, too—just the two of us. But kids...that's a whole nother thing."

"You want her to have an abortion?"

He jabbed his finger at me. "I *never* said that."

"Then what, exactly, do you want?"

He tilted his head back, looked at the ceiling. "I don't know, all right?" It was almost a howl from an animal in pain. "Right now, all I want is Kent. Safe. Here with me."

I processed that for a moment. "How much do you make a year?"

"Why?"

"Because I like to know everything. I'm nosy like that."

"Forty-five thousand."

Single guy. Probably ate in the restaurant a lot. "This house is completely paid for?"

"Yes," he ground out.

"How—on forty-five thousand dollars a year—can you afford this house? Why do you have an attorney? And how can you afford Charlie Condon?"

"How is any of that related to Kent?"

"I don't know. Maybe she's been giving you money?"

"I never took a dime from her."

I shrugged. "Then answer the questions."

He rolled his entire head. "I have an attorney because my girl-friend's family sicced the police on me. I have no idea where Kent is, but innocent people like me have been railroaded into prison plenty of times by people like them. I can afford Charlie Condon *only* because my father knows him. Dad's a contractor. He's done work for him. They aren't friends, exactly. But Dad asked, and Charlie said he'd help."

I had to admit that was a smart move, getting a high profile attorney any way you could. If I were in Matt's shoes, that's what I would've done. "And the house?"

"My grandmother left us each a CD—me and my brothers. She pinched pennies like you couldn't believe. My grandparents lived below their means. She left us each a hundred thousand dollars. Not a fortune, but a lot of money to us. I lived at home for years and worked my ass off. I saved my money, added to what she left me. A couple years ago I bought this place for a hundred and fifty thousand. It was falling down—probably should have been torn down. But, like I told you, Dad's a contractor. I worked summers for him since I was fourteen. He helped. My brothers helped. We fixed the place up."

I was starting to feel bad. The more I knew about Matt Thomas, the more he seemed like a good guy. Sonavabitch. I hated when Colleen was right. "It looks great."

"Thank you." He sighed, brushed a hand through his hair. He rolled his shoulders like he was working tension out of them.

"Are you absolutely certain Kent's child is yours?"

"Oh my—*arrrgh*." He held both hands in front of him, close to-gether, like maybe he wanted to wring my neck. I fully expected him to breathe fire.

"Last question," I said.

"And then you'll leave?"

"You have my word."

"Yes. I am absolutely certain. Kent and I are committed to each other. Have been since the day we met. Ask anyone who knows us. Ask Ansley Johnson. She's Kent's best friend."

"I already have." I stood and walked towards the door. Did Ansley know Kent was pregnant? If so, she was holding out on me. Something else tickled the back of my brain, but I couldn't quite grab it.

"Wait," he said.

I turned.

"You're not going to tell the police about the baby, are you?"

I sighed. "It's a moot point. I'm obligated to tell my client. *He* will tell them, and likely demand your head on a platter."

"Look...God, this is the last thing I even want to think about. I just want you to find Kent, okay? But I need my job. This is my life. If they arrest me, even if they never convict me of anything, it will destroy my reputation—my future—in this city."

He could be right. Then again, if he was innocent, the scandal might make him a tourist attraction. It could go either way. A bikini wax was more appealing to me than telling Colton Heyward his daughter was carrying the "cook's" love child. But Mr. Heyward was my client, and I would tell him. I just needed more than Matt's word and that of a guardian spirit before I had that conversation. "I'll wait a day or so, see what else I come up with. If I can locate Kent, that's all her daddy's gonna care about."

He closed his eyes and let go the breath he'd been holding. "Thank you."

He followed me out and waved goodbye as I pulled away from the curb. Though I believed Matt, it seemed prudent to be able to find him in a hurry if I needed to. I parked one block over and sneaked into his backyard through the adjoining property. Then I slipped through the gate to the driveway out front. No one in sight. I attached a GPS tracker under the back driver's side wheel well of his ten-year-old Ford pickup truck.

NINE

By the time I drove off the ferry onto Stella Maris, it felt like that day had lasted five years. But I knew I couldn't rest until I'd cleared up a few things. I called Ansley and asked her to meet me at the Pirates' Den for a drink. It was just after five and I needed one.

The Pirates' Den was a favorite local hangout. The restaurant and bar had a tropical décor and served great local seafood, lowcountry dishes, and burgers. A stage provided a venue for local bands like my brother's, The Back Porch Prophets—Blake played pedal steel guitar and keyboards and wrote some of their music—and the dance floor was well worn from use.

John Glendawn stood behind the bar. He had the look of a salty old sailor right out of central casting—tanned and wrinkled, curling gray hair underneath an old captain's hat, twinkling blue eyes. "There's Lizzie," he said. As always, his warm smile let me know he was happy to see me. Very few people got away with calling me Lizzie. The owner of the Pirates' Den and his wife, Alma, had been close friends of my grandmother.

"Hey, John. I need a margarita." I slid a hip onto one of the barstools.

"Coming right up. Bad day?" His calloused hands went to work mixing my drink.

"Long day. And it isn't over yet. I'm meeting Ansley Johnson."

"How did the judge's daughter get mixed up in your business?"

"She's not really. Just a friend of someone who is."

"Eh law. That's a blessing."

I knew what he was thinking. If Ansley were directly involved in a case, I'd have to deal with Nell Johnson, a notoriously protective mother and bona fide nutcase.

"That it is," I said. "I'm treading closer than I'd like to Nell's family."

John sat my drink on a napkin in front of me. "You'll likely need another."

Ansley walked through the door and approached the bar. Her heels clicked on the floor. She looked very professional in tailored black slacks, a blouse that brought out the blue in her eyes, and a striped scarf. "Hey y'all."

"Afternoon, Ansley. What can I get you?" John asked.

"A glass of Chardonnay, please."

"Let's grab a table," I said.

We paid for our drinks and carried them to a quiet corner by the wall of windows overlooking the Atlantic. Ansley's eyes were bright with anticipation. "Have you found something already?"

"Unfortunately not. I just have a couple follow-up questions. I spoke with Matt—twice today, actually."

"Okay." Ansley looked surprised, curious.

"Before we get to Matt, I'm trying to figure why you would leave out that you and Kent are second cousins."

Ansley blinked. "Once removed. And I wasn't trying to hide it, if that's what you mean. It's just something I don't think about. We don't associate with the Bounetheaus at all. I've never considered them family. Hell, Liz, everyone on this island is related if you go back far enough."

I sipped my margarita. "The other thing that's niggling me..." There was no good way to ask this. "Ansley, did you know Kent was expecting?"

A sip of her wine must have gone down the wrong way. She sputtered and coughed. "*What?*"

"I'll take that as a 'no.'"

"I can't believe she wouldn't tell me. Are you sure?"

I studied her for a long moment. "Very."

Ansley propped her elbow on the table and her head in her hand. "We're like sisters. Why wouldn't she tell me?"

"She and Matt were having problems. Maybe she wasn't sure she was going to keep the baby."

"But still. And *he* never mentioned it."

"Is that something you and Matt would discuss?" I remembered what had eluded me that afternoon at Matt's house. Ansley.

"Well...probably not, I guess. But still." Confusion and disbelief swirled into an odd expression. She took a long sip of wine.

"Matt does seem to be in love with Kent," I said.

"I told you. He adores her."

"He said they were totally committed to each other." I glanced out the window.

"Exactly."

"Have been, since the moment they met."

"They have."

"He said I should ask anyone who knew them, mentioned you specifically."

"Stands to reason...." She nodded.

"Except you told me just yesterday that you and Matt went out before he dated Kent."

Ansley jerked slightly. She moistened her lips. "Well, okay. We did go out, that's true. I mean, we met for drinks a couple of times. And at first, I thought maybe...I mean, Matt's ridiculously hot. You saw him. Who wouldn't be interested in *that*?"

I tilted my head left, then right, weighing that statement. I saw her point.

Ansley continued. "He made it clear from the start he only had eyes for Kent. I guess I like to think of it as dating. It's good for my ego. Except he was chatting me up trying to see if I thought she'd go out with him. They didn't exactly run in the same circles."

"But you and Kent did. What made you more approachable?"

Ansley shrugged. "I guess I tried to be approachable. Things like that don't occur to Kent. She isn't class conscious at all. She doesn't understand that she can be intimidating."

"So there was never anything between you and Matt?"

"No. He wanted to be with Kent from the night we first met him. I was a little jealous, I admit." She had the grace to blush, look sheepish. "I wished it'd been me he wanted. But Kent is my best friend. I was happy for her, too."

I pondered that a bit. "Okay. So think about this for a minute. Kent is pregnant. She decides she's either going to give the baby up for adoption, or she's going to have an abortion. Either way, she doesn't want anyone else to know about the baby. Given that scenario, doesn't it seem more likely to you that she simply left town to deal with this?"

Ansley was quiet for a long moment. She shook her head. "I still don't see it. She'd tell us something, even if it wasn't true, to account for her being gone. I mean, Kent is not typically a liar. But in that situation, she'd lie before she'd just leave without a word."

"I know y'all are close. Think about it. She didn't tell you she was expecting."

"That's different. She's very private. But you'll never convince me she left without a word to anyone."

"I'm not trying to convince you, Ansley. I'm just ruling it out."

I considered calling Evan Ingle, but often I learned more from watching how people react to a question than their words. I drove down Palmetto Boulevard. The gallery was closed. I circled around back and saw the Prius parked behind the building. I pulled back onto Palmetto, parked on the street, and called him. He answered the phone and agreed to speak with me. He didn't inquire, and I didn't offer a reason, why I couldn't just ask him what I wanted to ask on the phone.

A few moments later, he unlocked the front door of the gallery and held it open for me.

I stepped inside. "Thanks so much for seeing me. I purely hate to bother you again so soon."

He smiled and his blue eyes twinkled a bit. "Not a bother at all. Can I get you anything?"

I was thinking he looked happy to see me, and about catching flies with honey and all. I returned the smile. "No, thank you. I won't take but a moment of your time."

"Well, have a seat at least." He led me back to the conversation area. This evening his well-worn jeans were accompanied by a faded blue t-shirt. His feet were bare.

I followed and sat in the same gold chenille wingback I'd occupied a year ago that morning.

He sat at a right angle to me and slid back into the sofa, getting comfortable. "Do you have new information?"

"I'm afraid not. It's just that often, when I start asking questions one person at a time, something comes up that prompts another question for someone I've already spoken with."

"I can see that." He smiled again, slow and warm.

I wondered what he was thinking about, and had an idea I knew what sort of thoughts he entertained. "Remember how I couldn't think why Kent would take her laptop to dinner?"

"Yes."

"Her boyfriend told me that you were helping her with a website for her paintings."

Evan raised both eyebrows. "Yes, of course. I did offer to help her with that now that you mention it. We hadn't planned on working on it that night. I don't recall settling on a specific plan for when we'd get started." He appeared relaxed, his arms open, one on the arm of the sofa, the other by his side. His body language said he was being forthcoming with me.

"I see." I conjured my best confused look and waited to see if he'd offer more.

"Perhaps she misunderstood something I said? Or maybe she was hopeful that we would get to that project? Certainly if she'd asked after dinner, I would have done whatever I could given the setting."

"A wine bar slash restaurant wouldn't be the best place to work on a website, would it?"

"No. Not at all."

"Well, I feel silly. I should have just asked you that on the phone and saved you the trip downstairs."

"Nonsense. It's a pleasure to see you again. In fact, if you don't have dinner plans, I'm making chicken piccata. I could use some company."

"Thank you so much. I really appreciate the offer. It's been a long day. Another time, perhaps?" I smiled like I was hoping he'd ask again. He seemed to like me. I needed to keep it that way. While I didn't plan on ever having dinner with him, I didn't need to tell him that just then.

"I'll look forward to it."

TEN

Driving home I had three things on my mind. I needed to talk to my partner. I also needed to talk to my guy, but he didn't want to talk to me, which made matters messy. And I had half a bottle of pinot noir left from the night before. As soon as I parked the car in the garage, with Rhett in tow, I climbed the stairs to the mudroom, went straight to the kitchen, and poured a glass of wine. Rhett sat on the heart-of-pine floor, tongue hanging out, and cocked his head at me like he was inquiring about my day.

"It's complicated," I told him. "Let's check your kibble supply." I went back into the mudroom, or, more aptly, Rhett's lounge. A huge bed with his name embroidered on it took up most of the far end. I'd taken no small amount of abuse from Nate and Blake, who thought it hilarious to point out Rhett can't read. A mat in one corner held his personal water cooler—the upside down jug replenishes the bowl—his elevated kibble dish, and the airtight container where the kibble is stored. I opened it and added a few scoops of Blue Wilderness Salmon Recipe to his dish.

Rhett chowed down, and I wandered back into the kitchen. With a sigh I pulled out my iPhone. I looked at it for a minute and took another sip of wine.

Then I texted Nate: I need to talk to my partner, please.

While he might not want to talk about us, he would talk to me about the case. We could start there.

It took him an inordinate amount of time to reply: Be there in 30.

I was weak-kneed with relief. He was coming. Oh my stars, I had thirty minutes to freshen up. I dashed up the stairs, took a quick shower, dressed and reapplied makeup faster than I have since I was a teenager. What to wear? Casual. Keep it casual. Just going over the case. What would I have worn before—when he was my partner and my friend, but not my lover?

Oh hell no. No yoga pants and comfy tee tonight. I slid into a pair of ankle-length jeans that fit me real good. Next I pulled out my cute Anthropologie blouse with the cartography print. Perfect—casual, but elegant. I rolled up the sleeves to my elbow, and added a group of delicate silver chains that dripped towards my cleavage. Silver hoop earrings...ballet flats or sandals? I checked my toenail polish. No chips in the Cha-Ching Cherry. I slipped on my favorite blue Kate Spade sandals and buckled the straps.

I fluffed my hair, applied mascara and reached for the lip gloss. My hand hovered over it a moment, then I grabbed the tube of Chanel Passion lipstick—I love it when pretty colors have evocative names. Mamma popped into my head with an approving smile. After a generous coat, I applied the gloss. I glanced in the mirror. Not bad for thirty minutes, if I ditched the needy look. I squared my shoulders.

Nate was pulling into the drive as I walked downstairs. I waited for him at the door. As he climbed out of the car, something clutched at my stomach and my eyes glistened. Sweet reason, how much I missed him. I'd barely had half an hour with him yesterday before things blew up. I inhaled slowly, savoring the view—broad shoulders, narrow hips, long legs. Nate did wonderful things for a chambray shirt, faded jeans, and boat shoes.

As he got closer, I could read the look in his eyes. The blue in them looked more like steel this evening. I opened the door as he walked up the steps. "Hey." I reached for casual and missed by a mile.

"Hey." His voice was curt. His gaze dropped to the porch by the door. "You have a package." He picked up a large cardboard box and handed it to me.

"I came in through the garage. I didn't see it." I glanced at the label. It was from Omaha Steaks. "Who would be sending me beef?"

He stepped inside and walked straight to my office. "I spoke with all of Kent's friends—the ones Ansley gave you, anyway."

I followed him into the room and placed the box on the corner of my desk. Since we were keeping things all businesslike, I sat in my desk chair. I steeled myself not to show how much I was hurting. "Any of them give you anything?"

Nate settled into one of the club chairs in front of my desk, extended his legs, and crossed his ankles. "No. Of course, every last one of them had already been contacted by Charleston PD, local law enforcement, and Ansley. I spent the most time on three college friends who've moved west of Amarillo. Nothing. Could be someone's had plenty of time to get their story straight."

"Maybe."

"I also told every one of Kent's friends that they could be in legal trouble if they were hiding her. That's a stretch of the truth, but I guess if Colton Heyward wanted to sue them for pain, suffering, and what-all, he could. We live in a litigious society."

"Any of them sound worried?"

"Not a one. My instincts say they were telling the truth. They all sounded scared for Kent. Got a lot of 'Please find her,' and the like. Sounded sincere."

"Still…"

"It's covered. I subcontracted investigators in Memphis, Amarillo, and the three cities where the west-bound college friends landed—Denver, LA, and Seattle. Too much ground for us to cover in a timely manner. They're going to run surveillance on those three friends, look for any sign of Kent. And the Memphis and Amarillo PIs are re-interviewing the service station staff, talking to local law enforcement. I know Sonny said Charleston PD covered that, but it seemed prudent to double check."

"Agreed." I rubbed the spot above my left eyebrow. "Things got more complicated today."

"Did they now?"

I gave him the highlights: Kent's secret pregnancy, the tension that created between her and Matt, the Heyward-Bounetheau family dynamic, et cetera. "I've got a glass of wine in the kitchen." I stood. "Bourbon?"

He looked away from me and then back, his gaze stopping at the package on my desk. "Who puts holes in a box with perishable food?"

I studied the box. There were three round holes on the side facing me. I stood and examined the box more closely. All four sides had holes. "Could be fruit or something. Is Omaha Steaks like Harry and David? Do they sell other kinds of food gifts?"

"I have no idea. Are you expecting a gift?"

"No, but I have gotten thank-you gifts from clients on occasion."

"Really? No one sends me gifts. Come to think of it, I do recall the occasional fruit basket when we both worked in Greenville. I'm not sure what to think about that. Hurts my feelings." He stared at the box.

I shrugged. "You can have half of whatever it is." I reached in my desk drawer for a letter opener to slit the packing tape. I opened the cardboard and lifted the Styrofoam container inside. "Hold on to the cardboard."

Nate did as I asked. "There are holes in the Styrofoam, too."

"Well it wouldn't make any sense to put holes in the cardboard and not the Styrofoam, would it?" I set the thick-walled container on my desk.

"I'm just wondering what kind of food you pack in something designed to keep it cold or hot, and then poke holes in it."

I gripped the lid, ready to lift. "Let's find out."

"Wait," Nate said.

I gave him my *oh puh-leeze* look. "What, you think there's a bomb in here?"

"No. Bombs don't need air. Let's take this outside." He picked up the box and headed towards the hall. "Get the door."

"This is ridiculous." I humored him and opened the front door.

He walked down the steps and set the container in the driveway. He studied it for a few moments. "Do you own a shotgun?"

"Granddad had one. It's in the hall closet. What on earth do you think is in there?"

"Something that needs to breathe. Pets are not a typical thank-you gift."

"Good point." A bomb seemed like such an outlandish idea I hadn't taken it seriously. The prospect of something alive that would be quiet inside a box was a whole nother thing. That seemed credible. Dread crept up from the pit of my stomach and lodged in my throat.

"Turns out it's not a pet you want to keep, I may need to dispatch it. Depending on what's in there, a shotgun is likely a better choice than my Glock."

"I'll be right back." I dashed inside, verified Rhett was in the mudroom, and slipped in the panel that would prevent him from going out through the doggie door.

Naturally, this aroused his curiosity. He followed me through the kitchen and down the hall. I grabbed Granddad's twenty-gauge Remington and headed towards the front door. Rhett followed.

"Stay," I said.

He cocked his head at me, but sat on the hall floor.

"Good boy." I slipped out the front door and closed it behind me.

Nate waited at the bottom of the porch steps.

I handed him the gun.

"Now bring me something with a long handle—a hoe or a shovel."

I sprinted to the garage and brought back a gardening hoe.

"Stay on the porch," Nate said.

He didn't have to tell me twice.

With the gun cradled in his right hand, he overturned the box with the hoe in his left. The lid didn't come off. "Shit."

He used the edge of the hoe to pry the lid open on one side. Once loosed, the lid fell over.

The biggest rattlesnake I have ever seen slithered out. It looked to be six feet long. And it was highly pissed off.

Someone screamed. I realized it was me. Dear Lord, I purely hate snakes.

Inside the house, Rhett went to barking.

Nate dropped the hoe, chambered a round and raised the gun to his shoulder. "I got this."

The snake coiled and rattled its tail.

Boom. My ears rang. Too late, I covered them.

Nate chambered another round.

We stared at the snake. It lay in several pieces near the Styrofoam container, which had also sustained damage.

My hands still covered my ears for no good reason. I was shaking.

"I'll take that bourbon now," Nate said. "Go on inside. I'll clean up out here."

Rhett jumped up and down inside the front door, barking like crazy. "It's okay, boy." Carefully, I opened the door and slid in. He scampered around me. I knelt and hugged him, patted him a few times. Still in a daze, I went inside, wandered down the hall, passed through the dining room, and stepped into the kitchen. Rhett trotted after me, as if looking for an explanation.

I picked up my wine glass, held it with both hands, and drank deeply. Then I refilled it. Nate typically drank his bourbon on the rocks. I fixed his drink and dropped onto a counter stool.

Rhett paced the room.

No doubt someone would report a gunshot. I made a preemptory call to my brother and told him simply that I'd had to kill a snake, which was the truth, if not the whole truth. He could pass the word along to whoever was working at the station that night. I ended the conversation before Blake could interrogate me to his satisfaction.

I heard Nate come in and go back out, then come back in and close the door. "All clear," he called as he walked down the hall. He came into the kitchen, walked over to the island, and picked up his drink. He sipped the bourbon. "I got rid of the cardboard box on your desk. Knowing how you feel about both germs and snakes, I figured that was best."

"Thank you." Shudders crawled up and down my spine. The thought of that snake right there on my desk the whole time we'd been talking...Deep breaths.

"Nothing else inside the box. I did save the shipping label. Nothing helpful on it. Someone took a used Omaha Steaks carton and put a new delivery label on it. Looks like a UPS delivery, except the barcode is missing. I think it was personally delivered."

"I'll check the security system footage directly. My outdoor cameras should've caught whoever brought it." I pondered that for a moment. "I didn't get an alert, which is odd."

He took another sip, rolled his lips in and out, then stared at his glass. "Are you working any cases aside from the Heyward case?"

"No."

"Any dissatisfied customers, angry subjects of investigations—anything like that you haven't told me about?"

"None that aren't locked up somewhere."

"Then, Slugger, I would say that someone just served notice of their displeasure that you're looking for Kent Heyward. What say we go back over all the things that got more complicated today?" He rubbed my arms, then pulled me up and into a hug. "Come on, let's go relax a bit. You're still looking a little pale."

I snuggled into him. Oh dear heaven, it felt so good to be close to him, to have him touch me. He reached around and picked up my wine glass, and then gentled me down the hall. Rhett passed us. He seemed to know where we were headed.

We went back into my office and settled on the green velvet sofa facing the wall of windows that looked out on the front porch. I curled my feet under me on the end. Nate propped his on the tufted ottoman. We sipped our drinks for a few minutes. Rhett checked out the room, then lay down at my feet.

"Why did it have to be a snake?" I said. A shudder made its way up my spine. "I hate snakes."

"Can't say I know many folks who have a fondness for them. I'm sure that was the point—to rattle you. No pun intended."

I flashed him a look that said *very funny.* "You'd think in the interest of clarity they would've at least enclosed a note. What if I did have an angry client or some such thing?"

"They went to a lot of trouble. I'd say they counted on the timing making the message clear. You aren't second-guessing who was behind it, are you?"

"Nah. I just would've expected specific instructions: 'Stay away from the Heyward case'—*something.*"

"Seems to me they delivered the message they intended."

"Well, all they succeeded in doing is making me bound and determined to repay the gesture with something equally unpleasant."

"There's my girl." Nate grinned. "To revenge." He raised his glass. We clinked and sipped. Nate's gaze touched mine. My eyes held his as long as he allowed. He was still angry and hurt. But something else stirred in the unhappy cocktail of emotions in his eyes. Hunger.

An electric current flowed between us. I almost dropped my glass. Nate looked away.

That cut deep. I swallowed hard, then tried to navigate back to safer ground. "I'm going to check the security cameras." I stood and crossed the room, settling in the chair behind my desk.

Nate stayed on the sofa. Was he thinking we needed distance?

I brought up the security system log for the day. "No incidents were recorded. The cameras indoors and out are motion activated. Something prevented the system from making a record or notifying me."

Just as I was thinking it, Nate said, "That points to professionals. Someone who would suspect you might have a security system tied into the Wi-Fi. If we're dealing with individuals who anticipate that sort of security and know how to jam a Wi-Fi system, that's even more worrisome."

"Clearly, I need to explore countermeasures for jammers. Or replace my security system with a hard-wired version. We've never run across a case where criminals with this level of technical sophistication came after us at home."

Nate grew pensive.

I moved back to the sofa. "All the more reason to solve this case as quickly as possible. Do you think we should set aside the voluntary relocation scenario?"

He shook his head, looked baffled. "See, I'd've thought it *more* likely, considering the pregnancy. Clearly someone does not want you looking for her. But that wouldn't necessarily rule out that she left home of her own free will. Right up until you said the security system didn't function, I'd've said, could be she has friends trying to discourage you from looking for her because she doesn't want to be found. Now..."

"I don't see her hiring professionals."

"Exactly."

"At first I thought the pregnancy pointed to her leaving on her own, too. Except the one thing everyone agrees on is that Kent would never put the people who loved her through this kind of pain. People don't change their core values overnight."

Nate studied his bourbon. "No, but if they're pushed farther than they can stand, sometimes they act out of character."

What did he mean by that? Were we talking about Kent, me, or him? "That's true to a point. But I don't see Kent punishing everyone she knows because she was upset at Matt and her parents. She'd at least tell Ansley where she was going and why."

Nate shrugged. "No way to know for sure. We're seeing Kent through the lens of how others perceived her. Some people are predictable. Others are reliably unpredictable. Maybe we put that theory on the back burner for now."

"Makes sense to me. Let's figure out which two of the other possible narratives are the most likely. I'll take one, you take the other, go from there."

"All right. I like money for a motive. You said Kent's share of the big pot would revert to the family trust, and that gets divided between the Bounetheau progeny, is that right?"

"Right. We can definitely rule out Virginia, Kent's mother, in that scenario. Kent is her only child. Virginia is desperate to find her. And besides, she has her husband's fortune in addition to her own money. That leaves Charlotte, the aunt, and Peyton and Peter, the twin uncles."

"You pulled background on the whacko uncles yet?"

"Preliminary. We need to dig deeper. They stated their occupation as 'managing their portfolios.'"

"Don't folks with giraffe money have people to do that for them?"

"That's what I would've thought."

"They have to pass their days doing something. I'll start with them, work my way on to the aunt if nothing pops. Maybe she wants more of the family fortune for her own babies."

My ribs tightened their grip on my lungs. "Sweet Lord, I hope this doesn't turn out to be family. Why is it always family?"

Nate just shook his head.

"I'll keep working the Matt angle," I said. "His alibi only holds up if you're positive of when things went pear-shaped for Kent. Maybe Charleston PD is somehow sure of that, but so far they haven't shared."

"Can't you get our client to induce them to be more cooperative? Seems like he'd have a lot of influence, could make a call."

I bit the corner of my lip. "I asked Sonny about that. He said best not to go there if we want to develop a relationship with members of Charleston PD aside from him. Seemed like a bad career move."

Nate sipped his drink. I knew exactly what he was thinking, but he didn't say a word. He was thinking that we already had strong relationships with detectives in Greenville. This wouldn't be a problem if we stayed in Greenville. My eyes started to water. I blinked quickly. I. Would. Not. Cry.

I cleared my throat. "Maybe Matt's neighbors saw Kent or her car that night. Or, maybe they were outside and *didn't* see her car."

"All right. I've got family for the money, and you've got boyfriend because of the baby."

Something didn't sit right about the notion of Matt harming Kent. More to myself than to Nate, I said, "He could have hurt her accidentally, panicked, and covered it up. I don't make him for a stone-cold killer.

Then again...sociopaths are adept at appearing normal. I'm also going to keep the mother and grandmother as a side project. Something odd was going on between them this afternoon. Might be unrelated family drama. I'll be happier when I know that for sure."

"Out of everyone you've spoken to since you left Colton Heyward's house yesterday morning, who do you peg as the most likely to pull the stunt with the snake?"

I pondered that for a minute. "None of them would get their own hands dirty, of course. But any of the Heyward/Bounetheau clan, aside from Kent's parents, could have hired someone to discourage me."

"They've hired help to scare off the hired help. This takes messed up family to a whole nother level."

"It likely was professionals, but it was an amateur move when you think about it. Someone was kind enough to confirm for us that at least one person *who knows we've been hired* knows what happened to Kent. That eliminates the two hardest to solve scenarios altogether."

"You make a fair point, Slugger. Human traffickers would have no way of knowing we'd been hired, nor would a serial psycho. It had to be someone connected to Kent's family and friends."

I glanced at the round, wooden wall clock. "It's after eight. Have you eaten?" I wasn't the slightest bit hungry. But we'd just finished conducting our business, and I didn't want him to leave.

Nate stared at the corner of the ceiling to my left. Just before the silence became more than I could bear he said, "No. I haven't eaten."

"Want me to pull out the food from last night? It's in the fridge."

"Why not? Partners eat together all the time." His voice sounded strained, but he was staying, at least for the moment. Every moment he stayed was another chance to find our way back to each other.

He stood and followed me to the kitchen. I set out the chicken. Nate sliced some breast and made short work of cutting apart the other pieces. I put a wedge of brie, a block of Vermont cheddar, and some smoked Gouda on a cheese board and added some grapes. We worked quietly. Celery sticks, pepper wedges, and baby carrots along with some hummus I had on hand became a veggie plate. Nate sliced the day old baguette. I freshened his drink. Somehow, the routine tasks eased the tension between us. We climbed onto stools at a right angle to each other at the end of the bar.

For a few minutes we sipped and nibbled. Finally I asked, "Where did you sleep last night?"

He watched the piece of baguette he smeared with brie. "Hampton Inn in Mount Pleasant. Figured if I went to the Bed and Breakfast, Grace would have questions. My disposition being what it was, a hotel seemed a better choice."

Grace Sullivan was my godmother and a bona fide psychic. Nate had been wise to avoid her. I set my wine glass on the granite and looked at him, willing him to look back.

After a moment of silence, he raised his gaze to mine.

I said, "I am *so* sorry about what I said last night. The words came out all wrong. I love you. You have to know that."

"You know what they say." He took a long swallow of bourbon, but didn't look away. "Actions speak louder than words."

My insides felt like wrung out laundry. I was in an impossible situation. This wasn't just about what I wanted, but I couldn't tell him all the reasons I had to stay in Stella Maris. But dammit, I did *want* to stay. "That goes both ways."

"I think we've established we're at an impasse in our personal relationship. I told you a long time ago if we went down this road there was no going back. But I guess we're going to have to find a way back." His voice was quiet, his eyes hurt but resolute.

"Nate, no—"

"Best we focus on being partners for now. It's in both of our best interests. We have a lot invested in our business. We're a good team."

Dammit to hell. I was going to cry and that pissed me off. Tears slid down my cheeks. "You're my best friend."

"And you're mine. But if we're going to clean up the mess we made, we need to back away from each other every way except professionally. At least for now."

"This is not what I want. Dammit, Nate. I finally feel like I know what love is. How it's supposed to feel."

"It's not what I want, either." He stared out the window into the night.

I reached out and touched his arm, willing him to look at me. "Then fight for me—for us. Let's figure this thing out."

"You said it yourself." He dropped his gaze to the granite. "We've been trying to figure it out for more than two years. If we haven't resolved it by now, we're not going to."

Every cell in my body rebelled at his words. "I don't believe that. I refuse to believe that."

Finally, he looked at me. His handsome face was a study in contrasts, his jaw firm, his eyes searching mine. "Tell me what you want."

"I want you."

"For your what...your long distance boyfriend? Because I think we both agree that portion of the program has gone on way too long." His voice wasn't unkind, but resolved.

"What do *you* want? You said yesterday that you'd accepted this was the way things are." Oh dear Lord how I wanted yesterday back.

"Well, maybe I shouldn't have settled for that."

"Answer my question. What do you want?"

He set down his glass. "I want a life with you in it every day. I'm fine with dividing our time between here and Greenville. Only I want us in the same place at the same time most of the time. And, someday..." He looked away.

"Someday?" That word punched me in the gut. "You want children." Instinctively, I wrapped my arms around my stomach. I'd had a bad case of endometriosis, which had required a hysterectomy a year ago. I wouldn't be having children, a heartbreak I'd finally come to terms with.

"Liz, listen to me." He slid off the barstool and folded me into his arms. "That is not what this is about. We don't exactly have a child-friendly profession." He kissed the top of my head. "I love you, too, Slugger. We just want different things. And I can't live with knowing you had stronger feelings for—for other men before—than you do for me."

"But that's not true. It's so far from the truth it's beyond ridiculous."

"That's how I feel. And I can't get around it." He stepped back, hooked a finger under my chin and lifted it until I knew he could see the mascara that must be running off my face in rivers. "Make sure you get this part right. This has nothing to do with whether or not we might someday want children. Do you understand that?"

I nodded.

He sighed. "This isn't going to be easy on either of us. But we'll get through it. We just need to focus on the job right now."

"No, dammit." I wasn't ready to give up.

He closed his eyes for a long moment, then opened them. "Liz. We just can't chew on this all night, going over and over the same things. It tears me up to see you cry. I'd like to stay here, but that's just not a good idea right now. I'm going to move to a hotel downtown. It'll be more convenient to track the uncles from there. You said the Heywards live on Legare. Where do the Bounetheaus live?"

I sniffled. "East Bay. Not far from South Battery."

He was quiet for a minute. "The inns in that area are pricey. I'll move to the Hampton Inn downtown. It's not as close as some of the other choices, but it'll do."

I stood and walked around the island to the far end of the kitchen. There was a box of tissues on the end of the counter nearest the door. I grabbed a handful and dabbed at my face, keeping my back to Nate.

"I'll touch base tomorrow," he said.

I listened as he walked down the hall and out the front door.

In my peripheral vison, I watched Colleen fade in. She sat quietly on the counter near the sink. After a while, she said, "You really love him, don't you?"

"Yes. I do." I gave in to the blubbering. I almost never blubbered. I hated myself afterwards.

"Do you want to live in Greenville?"

"Not all the time. My family is here. I love my family. I love this island. This is my place in the world. I also love Nate, and I love Greenville. I could be happy dividing our time between here and there."

"But you can't be happy without Nate," Colleen said.

"It will be the hardest thing I've ever had to do. Only it doesn't look like I have a choice, does it? I can't take my happiness at the expense of everyone else who lives here. You said if I left, things would change—your alternate scenarios."

"That's true," she said. "Let me work on it. That's the thing about alternate scenarios. Choices people make every day create new possibilities, some good, some bad. Things change."

"I always thought you meant I'd have to live here for the rest of my life."

"I'd like that," she said. "But I want you to be happy. I just have to figure another way to protect the island. Give me some time."

Colleen hopped off the counter and glided over to where I stood. She wrapped her arms around me, enfolding me in warmth. Like she'd flipped a switch, my despair became utter peace. I knew in that moment that no matter what happened, everything would be okay.

"Colleen?"

"Yeah?"

"Why didn't you tell me there was a snake in that box?"

She bray-snorted exuberantly. "I didn't get here until Nate had it outside. If you'd been in any danger, I would've known it, and would've been here sooner."

"Good to know."

ELEVEN

Saturday morning I ran hard. I did my usual five-mile route around the north point of Stella Maris, past the marina, to Heron Creek, then retraced my steps past my house all the way to the end of Main Street and back. I pounded the clay-colored sand as if I were trying to outrun something with large teeth. Rhett raced beside me, occasionally detouring to chase a shore bird, then galloping to catch up.

By the time I stripped out of my running clothes and ran into the surf, he sprawled panting by my chair. I'd blown off my steam on the run. I swam at a more leisurely pace, then bobbed around a bit just for the feel of water on my skin. Finally, I rode a wave back to the shore. I slid into the robe I'd left on my chair. I was lost in the rhythm of the surf when I heard footsteps on the walkway.

"Got your clothes on yet?" I recognized Blake's voice. My older brother knew and thoroughly disapproved of my habit of swimming in the altogether after my run.

"Yes, you're safe from being scarred. Come on out."

He took the canvas-and-wood beach chair beside mine. My brother is a good-looking man—five-ten, well-built, fit, blue eyes, medium-brown hair, nice cheekbones. But he has a tendency towards bossy and ornery, which likely explained why he was still a bachelor at thirty-five. "Isn't the water getting too chilly for this nonsense?"

"Feels good to me. Usually I can swim through late October. I'm hot natured."

He blew out a long breath. "I'll be glad when November gets here."

"Why does it bother you so much that I skinny dip in the mornings? I do it before the walkers are out. No one's ever seen me."

"I'm your brother. I prefer that you keep your clothes on in all situations."

"Is that what you came out here before breakfast to tell me?"

"No. I came to find out exactly what happened here last night that required you to discharge a firearm. Experience has taught me that I didn't get the whole story. Plus, I wanted to save you some time. I checked out Joe Eaddy. No sense in you duplicating the effort."

"So Merry broke down and told you?"

"Moon Unit told me first."

"Me too. What'd you find?"

Blake shrugged. "Nothing bad. Guy's clean. Seems to be a responsible, upstanding citizen. 'Course that could just mean he's a smart criminal. No red flags, anyway."

"Good to know. Thanks." Merry's love life looked a lot more promising than mine at the moment.

"Sonny tells me you're working the Heyward case."

"Yeah...oh dear Lord. That's a mess of heartbreak. I can't figure why Nancy Grace isn't all over it."

"Because the girl moved out of her parents' house. She's twenty-three. No crime in that."

"Her parents don't see it that way." I sighed. "I guess they're not the type to call in Nancy. They likely prefer to keep things discreet. Probably wouldn't care for camera crews South of Broad."

Blake lifted his Boston Red Sox cap and settled it back on top of his close-cropped hair. "Yeah. They called you instead. Not sure how I feel about this case."

"What do you mean?"

"On the one hand, I'm glad you're not working on my island. I like it when the police blotter in *The Citizen* reports nothing but animal control and teenage mischief. On the other hand, I like it best when I can keep an eye on you."

"Oh, *puh-leeze*. I have been working as a PI for more than thirteen years, most of it without your attempt at oversight."

"Only when you worked in Greenville, I could imagine you taking pictures from a safe distance of men sneaking out of bedroom windows and such."

I tilted my head left and right.

"I've done my share of fidelity cases over the years."

"Is Nate in town?"

"Yes and no."

"The hell does that mean?" He looked like he'd taken a bite of something nasty.

"He's staying in Charleston."

"Issue with the case?"

I sighed long and hard. "Lots of issues. But tonight at Mamma and Daddy's house? This is Merry's night to introduce Joe. Let's just leave it at Nate is working the case, okay?"

"Anything you want to talk about?"

I reached out and laid a hand on his arm. "Thanks. But not right now."

"I like Nate. Seems like a good guy. Nothing whatsoever like his scumbag brother. That said, if he needs his ass kicked, you let me know and I'll help him out."

"I don't think it will come to that. Let's just focus on making Merry's beau feel welcome, and try to act as normal as possible so as not to scare him off."

"Yeah, past a certain age she's not gonna look any better."

"Frank-lin Blake Tal-bot!"

He barked out a laugh. "You sound exactly like Mom."

Oh good grief. I did. I covered my face with my hands.

"Now about the gunfire..."

The look he leveled at me, which he might've stolen off a bull, told me I'd just as well get it over with. I sighed long and loud, then told him all about it, after which he let fire an elaborate string of curses.

After a shower, coffee, and a Greek yogurt, berry, and granola parfait, I settled in at my desk. My first order of business was security. I'd installed my high-tech Wi-Fi system myself. When it worked, it let me monitor the house while I was away, and gave me an early warning of trouble when I was home. But it was vulnerable to anyone with a jammer. Jammers were designed as countermeasures—to stop folks from spying on you. They also had nefarious uses.

Sometimes Nate and I used them, but we were on the side of the angels, so I never lost a minute's sleep about it. Anyone who had the spe-cial delivery of snakes in their wheelhouse was not working for the good guys. I called Mack Ryan at Security Solutions Incorporated in Charles-ton to get his advice. Our paths had crossed on a previous case. He was an ex-Navy Seal and owned SSI. He listened as I explained my problem.

"Nothing you can install in a residence is going to be one hundred percent unassailable," he said. "Your best defense is a protected wired system. You can still tie it in to your network. As long as you have Inter-net access you can still get alerts. Or keep the wireless system and install a redundant wired system. You want me to send out a team of techs?"

This was beyond my skillset and what I had time to deal with. "Yes. Thank you. Redundancy sounds good. How soon can they come?"

"For you? ETA thirteen hundred hours."

"Thanks, Mack. I really appreciate it."

"Don't mention it. You want us to monitor it?"

"Thanks, but no. Just make the cameras motion activated when the system is on, and have the feed go to a DVR." His monitoring and the response team that went along with that were pricey. And I was squeam-ish about someone else having access to cameras inside my home.

"Let me know if you change your mind."

"Will do. Tell the techs the golden retriever doesn't bite."

"Roger that."

With that settled, I turned my attention to the profiles I'd started Thursday afternoon. Based on the way Nate and I divvied things up, Matt was my priority, even though my gut said he wouldn't hurt Kent on purpose. I needed to know everything there was to know about Matthew Thomas. But in an hour of digging, I added little to what I already knew. He'd grown up in Mount Pleasant, attended Wando High School, and had two brothers. His father was a well-respected contractor, his mother a homemaker. Matt had been a baseball standout, and could likely have gone to college on a scholarship had he not chosen a culinary degree at the Art Institute. No one in the family had a criminal or civil complaint history. On paper, they were the poster family for the American dream.

Every detail of what Matt told me, from his grandmother leaving him and his brothers each a hundred thousand dollars to how he'd worked his way up at High Cotton, then left to go to FIG was verifiable. I'd talk to the neighbors next.

After trying several combinations Ansley had suggested, I logged on to Kent's Facebook profile. Her last update was two months before she disappeared, and it was a check in from dinner at Poe's with Ansley. I scrolled through Kent's two hundred eighty-six friends. How well did she know them? All of them seemed to be in the same age group as Kent. But online predators would disguise themselves as just that. Who's to say one of these "friends" wasn't actually a stalker?

A few were family—her cousins, Charlotte's boys, Lyndon, Fraiser, Wyeth, and Charles Bennett. Some of the names I recognized from the list Ansley had given me. I clicked through to each of their pages. Many had shared a post Ansley put up the day after Kent went missing with her photo, asking everyone to help look for her and pray for her safe return. The posts had accumulated thousands of likes, comments, and shares.

All two hundred eighty-six of Kent's so-called friends had to be vetted. An online predator was a real possibility. This was going to be a time consuming process. I needed someone to delegate this to. Ansley. She could do it faster than I could. She'd be able to spot someone who didn't belong. I called, gave her the password that worked, and told her what I needed.

"Absolutely," she said. "I'm on it right now. It's a relief to be able to do *something*."

"Thanks. If you find anything remotely suspicious, call me right away."

"Will do."

I turned my attention to Evan Ingle. His birth certificate was interesting. He was born at home in West Ashley with a midwife attending. Did people do that anymore? The women I knew birthed their babies in a hospital, with the comfort of all the painkillers modern medicine allowed. Evan's mother was Talitha Ingle, but in the box for the father's name on his birth certificate, the word "unknown" was typed.

He'd attended Porter Gaud and then, hell's bells, Evan Ingle had a BFA from Clemson. He was only a year younger than me, which meant we were there at the same time. That was an odd coincidence, but I couldn't see any relevance. I moved on.

Evan's timeline got sketchy between college and April 2007, when he opened his gallery in Stella Maris. I did a quick real property check. He owned the gallery outright, and had apparently paid cash for it because there was no record of a mortgage. He would've been twenty-six at the time. Where did the money come from? Was his mother wealthy? The West Ashley neighborhood where he'd grown up was nice, but not affluent.

A few clicks later I learned that Talitha Ingle had died August 10, 2014 in a two-car accident on Highway 17 in West Ashley. I pulled up the *Post & Courier* article. There was a photo of a Camry and a minivan, both crumpled, surrounded by emergency personnel and vehicles. I scanned the article. The driver of the minivan had run a red light and broadsided the Camry. Talitha Ingle was killed at the scene. The driver of the minivan died later at the hospital. There were no passengers in either vehicle.

I clicked over to the obituary section. Talitha was buried at Magnolia Cemetery the following Saturday. She was predeceased by her parents, who had tragically also been killed in an automobile accident. What were the odds of that happening? She was survived only by her son, Evan Ingle of Stella Maris.

I turned all of that over and over in my head. Evan's mother had died two months ago. He hadn't mentioned it, but why would he? He didn't appear to be in mourning—he was going out socially—but people grieve differently. And as riveting as his story was, there was no connection I could see to my client or his missing daughter.

Because the timeline was still uncertain, and by way of dotting my i's, I called the John Rutledge House Inn and spoke to the innkeeper. I asked her to go to the Talbot & Andrews website and call me back on the number listed there to verify my identity. Then I asked nicely if she would verify that Evan Ingle had checked in on Friday night—technically Saturday morning—between twelve-thirty and one. She was happy to confirm, though she made a point to tell me she wouldn't have given me information I didn't already have.

I profiled the remaining artists who'd been at Bin 152 the night Kent disappeared. There were no red flags, so I moved them all with Evan to my "most likely not connected" list.

Time to go talk to Matt Thomas's neighbors.

The GPS I'd attached to Matt's pickup truck emitted a clear signal from a few blocks off Coleman Boulevard in Mount Pleasant. He was at his parents' house. Hopefully he would be there a while. I circled through the two-block area around Matt's bungalow a few times to see who was out and about. The weather was near perfect. Several mothers with children in tow headed in the direction of Hampton Park. I pulled to the curb a few houses down from Matt's on St. Margaret Street.

I'd mulled pretexts on my way from Stella Maris. Sometimes, the truth is the best strategy. I approached the modest red brick house on the immediate left of Matt's house. No one answered the door, though I rang twice and waited patiently. I left my card in the crack between the storm door and its frame.

The neighbors on the right didn't come to the door, though there were two cars in the drive. Maybe they'd gone to the park. Or maybe they thought I was selling something. I walked across the street and tried a smallish but neat white frame house. The lovely front porch, with its swing and wicker furniture, beckoned me to come sit a spell. Hanging baskets and pots on the steps overflowed with flowers.

A fresh-faced, thirty-something woman with short, dark hair answered the door promptly. Dressed in yoga pants and a tee, she waited behind the storm door for me to state my business.

"Hey," I said with a warm smile. "I'm Liz Talbot, a private investigator." I offered her my card.

She gave me an appraising look, then opened the door a crack and took my card. She studied it, then looked at me squarely. "What can I do for you?"

I slipped my hand inside my thin sweater and tapped the record button on the app I'd already opened. "I'm looking into the disappearance of Kent Heyward. You may recall reading about it?"

"Yes."

"That was a Friday night, September 12. Four weeks ago last night. Are you generally home on Friday nights?"

"Yes. My husband and I both work high-pressure jobs. Friday nights are our crash night."

"You have a lovely front porch." I glanced towards the swing with its brightly colored pillows.

"Thank you." She flashed me a look that telegraphed how she had no patience for small talk with strangers.

I smiled. "I love porches. I practically live on mine. Do you relax out here on Friday nights this time of year?"

"Sometimes." She crossed her arms.

"Do you know your neighbor across the street, Matt Thomas?" I nodded in the direction of Matt's house.

"I know who he is. We wave, say hey."

"Do you happen to notice if he has a lot of company?"

"If he does, they aren't loud." She shifted from one foot to the other.

"I'm so sorry. I know I'm asking a lot of questions. It's just...well, that poor girl..."

She lowered her arms, nodded. "Of course."

"Do you know what he drives?"

"A white pickup. Older."

"Do you notice other cars there regularly?"

"A red Mini Cooper is there a lot, though not recently. A pretty brunette drives it. Oh no. That's the girl who's missing, isn't it? I remember reading that she drove a red Mini Cooper."

"That's right. Can you remember the last time you saw it?

She studied the floor in front of her intently, thinking. Then she looked up at me. "I'm sorry. I wish I could help. I just know it's been a few weeks at least."

"Do you recall any other cars you may have seen over there?"

She thought for a minute. "A couple of other trucks. There for a while, they were working on the house. The only other car I can remember is a dark grey BMW. The sporty one. I remember it because I told my husband I wanted one just like it." She smiled. "As if."

Ansley drove a late model grey BMW Z4. "Do you remember when you saw it last?"

"One night this week. Tuesday, maybe? I saw it when I came home around seven-thirty."

"Did you see the driver?"

"Not this week, but I've seen her before. Long blonde hair, early twenties. Really cute girl."

Ansley. What the hell? "Is she a frequent visitor?"

"Not that I've noticed." She squinted like she was concentrating hard. "One time I remember seeing the car *was* on a Friday night. I remember because we were sitting out here sipping wine and daydreaming about what we were going to do with the bonus check I was expecting at the end of September. I saw that car and was teasing my husband that I wanted to make a down payment on one of those."

"Think back on that conversation. Does it feel like you were getting the check the next week, or was it earlier in the month?"

"It was earlier. Hang on a minute. Let me get my phone."

She left me on the front porch, closed the door, and returned a few minutes later. When she came back, she joined me on the porch. "Please, have a seat." She sat on the swing.

I took a wicker chair to her right. "I'm so sorry. I didn't catch your name." Of course, I could look it up several different ways, but it was easier to ask.

"Wendy. Wendy Ryan. My husband's name is Steve." She tapped her phone a few times. "We had takeout Chinese that night. And looking at my bank statement, the debit to Red Orchid's was on the twelfth. My husband picked it up on his way home from work."

"Do you remember what time you saw the BMW?"

"Oh wow. We'd both worked late. I can't say if it was here when we got home or not. That would've been nearly nine. We ate in the kitchen. Then we came out here. The weather was nice. We didn't go inside until right around midnight."

I leaned in towards her. "This could be very important. Are you sure you saw the grey BMW parked across the street sometime after nine on the night of September twelfth?"

She blinked rapidly. "Yes. I'm sure."

"It was still there at midnight?"

"Yes. And..." She hesitated.

"And?"

"And it was still there the next morning."

I sat back in my chair, mulling that. "You're positive?"

She nodded.

"And the red Mini Cooper was definitely not here that night up until you went inside?"

"No, it wasn't. Does this have anything to do with the Heyward girl's disappearance?"

"Honestly, I don't know yet. Maybe." My head was spinning. What the hell had Ansley been doing at Matt's house while he was at work—

and overnight? What did it mean that Kent's car wasn't there while Ansley's was?

"Should I call the police?"

I rubbed my left temple. "Have they been around to talk to you about any of this?"

"No. You're the first person to ask."

I pondered that. If Ansley was involved in Kent's disappearance in any way, I couldn't—wouldn't—protect her. But if she wasn't, and there was an innocent explanation, this could still create a world of hurt for her.

"Don't call the police just yet. Let me see if I can determine if it's relevant before we get you involved in this."

Now Wendy looked worried. "I'd appreciate that."

"Please call me if you remember anything else regarding that particular evening, or either of the two young women or their cars. You have my number. May I have yours?"

She recited the number and I wrote it down.

I stood. "Thank you for your time."

Wendy looked a bit shell-shocked. "Of course."

I headed down the steps and back to my car at a fast clip. I was so mad at Ansley I could've spit nails. Either she was wasting my time by feeding me bites of half-truths to avoid making herself and Matt look bad on account of their bad behavior, or much worse, she was involved.

TWELVE

On the ferry ride back to Stella Maris, I mulled all the possibilities regarding Ansley, Kent, and Matt. It crossed my mind that Ansley could be playing me, and the thought made me sick. If she were involved in Kent's disappearance and knew Colton Heyward planned to hire a PI, she might've lobbied for him to hire me so she could steer me where she wanted to and find out what I was thinking. It would never have occurred to me that she was capable of such things. Ansley had always struck me as softhearted, gentle—made from the traditional Southern lady mold. She seemed genuinely concerned about Kent. Then again, anyone who'd taken high school drama could fake that.

I decided not to confront her until I'd had more time to think things over and talk it through with Nate. If she was involved, I didn't want her to know I suspected her. One possibility was that she'd helped Kent leave and then helped cover it up. Her potential involvement generated several new possible narratives.

It was just after three o'clock when I drove my car off the ferry. I went home to get ready for dinner at Mamma and Daddy's. At Mamma's request, we were gathering earlier than usual, at four. Apparently, we were going to spend quality family time with one another.

Mack's team was hard at work. I petted and reassured Rhett, then spoke briefly to the team leader, who told me they'd leave the codes and instructions on my desk. I logged into my network, and he walked me through setting up the interface. After getting the techs a pitcher of iced tea, I headed upstairs.

It was three-forty already. I moved into high gear. I changed into my Ann Taylor dark blue and white polka dot shirt and a pair of white jeans. Mamma did not sanction wearing white after Labor Day, but it was in style according to a recent article I'd read in the newspaper. Besides, the jeans went with the shirt and were my most comfortable pair.

I arrived right at four as instructed. Apparently, an updated memo had gone out and I'd missed it, because everyone else was already there. Blake's Tahoe sat in our parents' driveway along with a late model green Subaru Forrester which I assumed belonged to Joe Eaddy. I took a quick photo of the tag. It's a habit. As soon I had time, I'd expand on Blake's research.

I climbed the front porch steps. Mamma and Daddy's house was built in the style of a Lowcountry Cottage, but the size—five thousand square feet, give or take—made use of the word "cottage" absurd. When I opened the front door, the hall and adjacent rooms showed no signs of life. "Hey, y'all?" I called as I walked down the wide hall. "Where is everybody?"

"In here," Merry answered from the kitchen.

I followed her voice. Mamma and Merry stood in front of the door leading to the screened porch, their backs to me. They had their heads together, Mamma's auburn bob a contrast to Merry's multi-toned blonde, shoulder-length style which was virtually identical to mine. Chumley, Daddy's basset hound, sat at their feet, an extra yard of skin hanging off him in folds. All three were glued to something going down in the backyard. I slid into the group beside Mamma. Daddy, Blake, and a tall sandy-haired man were in the backyard. Daddy was gesturing.

"Is that Joe?" I asked.

"Yeah," Merry said.

"My, my. He's a looker," I said.

"He gets even better up close," Merry said.

"And this one has a legitimate occupation," said Mamma.

Merry rolled her eyes dramatically.

Mamma turned and gave me a quick hug. "Hey, sugar. Where's Nate?"

"He's working."

"On a Saturday?" Her look held me accountable for this outrage. Then she took in my wardrobe choice. "Maybe if you took a little more care with your appearance he wouldn't be working on Saturday afternoons."

"Really, Mamma? You think Nate isn't here because I'm wearing white after Labor Day? Do you think men even know there's a rule against that? I have on lipstick." I might have sounded the teensiest bit cranky.

Mamma tilted her head, scrutinized me. I felt like I was being scanned by a superior race who could read my thoughts and take my blood pressure simultaneously. "What's wrong?" she asked, concern in her voice.

"Nothing. Everything's fine." I gave her my sunniest smile and rubbed her arm.

She raised her left eyebrow and shot me a look that put me on notice we'd discuss this later.

I nodded towards the backyard. "What's going on?"

"Rats are burrowing tunnels in Chumley's front yard," said Mamma.

Chumley spent most of his time indoors near Daddy's chair. For times when Mamma and Daddy were away for a few hours, or the weather was nice and the hound needed fresh air, Chumley had his own quarters out back. Because he paid no mind whatsoever to electronic collars, Daddy and Blake had built a large fenced-in area—no one ever referred to this as a pen or kennel—around Chumley's house, which had its own covered front porch.

"Rats?" I scrunched my face.

"Big ones," said Merry. "They've been eating Chumley's food."

"What's Daddy up to?" Dread blossomed deep within my chest.

"He said he was going to take care of business." Amusement bubbled up in Mamma's voice. "He took a shotgun out there."

"And you didn't try to stop him?" I asked.

Mamma and Merry both looked at me like I was a simpleton. My daddy did whatever he damn well pleased. Any attempt to control him was a fool's errand.

And yet, knowing this full well, I reached for the doorknob. "I'll be right back."

"You'd better stay in here with us," Mamma said.

"I don't even know what manner of crazy is on his program, but I have an idea somebody needs to put a stop to it."

Merry snorted. "And you think you can do that? Blake made a similar pronouncement before he went out there fifteen minutes ago."

"I'm just going to get a closer look."

Mamma and Merry stepped back to let me out. Chumley woofed a warning.

I crossed the screened porch, went out the side door, and walked across the backyard to join the menfolk by the dog compound. They didn't notice my approach. Blake and Joe Eaddy were listening to whatever Daddy was saying that went along with all the dramatic gesturing.

"Daddy, what's going on?" I asked.

He turned and looked at me, his face all twisted up with indignation. "These damn rats are eating the hunting dog's food."

I parsed that, unsure if Chumley had ever actually been hunting. Daddy had a pack of hunting dogs when I was little. But as far as I knew, he hadn't hunted anything aside from his reading glasses in years.

Daddy continued. "Chumley likes it outside this time of year. He's been having his lunch out here. But he doesn't eat all of it. Been leaving a little taste. Damn rats figure they've got a good deal. Dug themselves all these holes and tunnels. Just look at this." He gestured at a group of eight holes in Chumley's front yard.

"So...isn't there something you can buy over at Steven's Hardware to take care of the problem?" I asked.

"No need to do that. I'm gonna take care of it," Daddy said, like I'd recommended extreme measures, and he had a more sensible plan.

Blake said, "Dad—"

"Go on in the house if you want to. I can handle this. Then we'll get us a drink."

I noted the five-gallon gas can at Daddy's feet. One of his shotguns was propped against a nearby live oak. This was going nowhere good.

The tall, sandy-haired man extended a hand. "Joe Eaddy."

"It's so nice to meet you," I said, wishing I'd brought my purse out with me so I could discreetly reach for the hand sanitizer. "I'm Liz, Merry's sister. Merry's told us all about you."

He grinned wide. "Nice to meet you, too." I wasn't sure if he was grinning because of something Merry had told him about me, because of what maybe she'd told us about him, or because he was just a friendly sort.

For Merry's sake, I had a conviction we needed to get Joe Eaddy inside. I was shocked she'd let him stay out here this long. "Blake, let's you and me and Joe go inside and fix a round of drinks. Daddy can finish up out here and join us in a few minutes."

Blake gave me a worried look.

Joe Eaddy said, "I want to watch."

"Really?" I smiled. "Oh, there's not much to see out here." I took his arm. "What would you like to drink?"

"Anything's fine. Y'all go ahead. I'll be in with FT," said Joe Eaddy.

FT? Daddy's initials—Franklin Talbot. Apparently Daddy and Joe were fast friends and Daddy had a nickname already. Usually he was on the giving end of nicknames.

Blake and I looked at each other. We couldn't leave Joe out here alone with Daddy, five gallons of gas, and a shotgun.

"Y'all do whatever you want to." Daddy picked up the can of gas and strode purposefully into the dog fence. Blake, Joe, and I watched as Daddy crouched and poured gas into each hole, muttering all the while.

"Hand me my gun," Daddy said.

Blake said, "Dad, there's an ordinance against discharging a firearm inside the city limits. I have to cite Zeke Lyerly once a month for shooting squirrels."

"So cite me," Daddy said.

Joe Eaddy reached for the gun, walked inside the fence, and handed it to Daddy.

I schooled myself to stop thinking of him as "Joe Eddie." I said, "Joe, come on back here and tell me all about yourself. We've just met, my goodness."

"We'll talk later." He smiled over his shoulder. "I've never seen a rat kill." He looked real excited, like maybe he was on safari in Africa, about to see big game.

"A rat kill?" I'd never seen one either, and was happy for it.

Daddy pulled out a box of matches. He propped his gun against a post, struck a match and dropped it in the closest hole.

Flames shot out of the hole.

"Daddy!" I yelled.

Daddy grabbed his gun and Joe's arm and jumped backwards. "Get ready!"

Clack-snap. Daddy chambered a shell and pulled the gun to his shoulder.

"Oh my God," I said.

An ominous *pouf* came from the battleground.

"Dad, get back," Blake hollered.

Countless rats flew out of the remaining seven holes. Several were on fire.

I covered my ears just in time.

Boom! Dad started taking out the enemy.

Blake and I retreated another few yards.

Clack-snap boom! More of the rats went down.

After another round, all seemed quiet.

"FT, over there," Joe pointed at an escaping rodent.

Daddy chambered, aimed, and fired. "Got 'em!" He chambered another round, swept the corner of the yard once more with his eyes, shotgun at his shoulder. "I think we got 'em all." He lowered the gun. He stepped back and surveyed the area once more, then discharged the gun overhead.

Joe said, "That was awesome, FT."

"Tutie, bring me a trash bag," Daddy said. Tutie was the latest in a long line of odd nicknames he'd given me. Its origin eluded me, though once or twice he'd called me Fruity Tutie, which made me think he was making fun of my fondness for good sanitary habits.

"I'll get it." Blake jerked his head at me to follow him.

Together we headed back to the house.

"So much for acting normal," Blake said.

"Well, if that didn't scare him off, nothing will," I said.

My mamma's fried chicken is legendary. She stands over an enormous cast iron skillet and painstakingly turns each piece until it's golden on all sides and tender in the middle, just like her mamma did, and her mamma before her, et cetera. And just like all the Southern cooks before her, she serves it with mashed potatoes and pan gravy, and at least a half dozen other side dishes that vary depending on what's in season and her mood.

The spread she put out that afternoon included fried okra, squash casserole, collard greens, butter peas, tomato pie, and green beans. And biscuits. Because all that food would not fit on her antique mahogany dining room table and still allow room for plates, cutlery, and glasses, she served dinner buffet style.

When we were all seated in the dining room, she held out her hands to Blake on her left, and Merry on her right. When we'd all joined hands and bowed our heads, Mamma returned thanks. "Father, thank you for this glorious day and the gift of family and friends. Thank you for delivering Franklin and our precious children from harm's way as he was shooting up the backyard a short while ago. Bless this food to our use and us to thy service. Amen."

Daddy looked at Mamma indignantly. "I did not shoot up the backyard."

"That's what it looked like from where I was standing," she said.

"I got rid of the rats, didn't I?" he asked.

Mamma smiled a warning at Daddy. "Frank, let's enjoy our dinner. Our guest must be starving from all this commotion."

Joe's grin spread across his handsome face. His blue eyes lit with excitement. "I've never seen anything like that."

"Neither have I," I said.

We all dug into our plates. After a few minutes, Joe said, "This is the best fried chicken I have ever tasted."

Mamma beamed. "I'm so glad you like it. There's plenty more in the kitchen."

"Oh, I'll be going back for more," said Joe. And he did—several times.

He wasn't the only one. We all went back for more of something. The second time Joe went back to the kitchen, I looked at Merry. "I think Mamma's chicken canceled out Daddy's crazy."

Merry said, "I think he enjoyed the crazy as much as the chicken."

I squinted at her. "Does that concern you at all?"

"Not really. His family isn't all that close. I think he thinks we're normal."

"God help him," Blake said.

"Didn't you say he was a banker?" I asked.

Merry said, "An investment banker. He puts together bond deals for municipalities."

"I picture him wearing a suit and tie to work," I said.

"Yeah." Merry smiled. "He cleans up real good."

I forked a bite of okra. "See, I'm thinking folks like that are more often entertained by something a little more highbrow than a rat kill."

Merry shrugged. "Daddy wore a suit and tie to work for years."

She had me there. "Hey." I looked at Blake. "You ever have any trouble out of Ansley Johnson?"

"Ansley? Nah. Her mother's nuttier than a box of Goobers. Poor Hank. Ansley's a good kid. Why?"

I shook my head. "Just tying up loose ends."

"Nobody here has anything to do with your Charleston case," Blake said. "You and Sonny and Nate keep your business on the other side of the Arthur Ravenel Junior Bridge." The latest version of the Cooper River Bridge was named in honor of a former congressman. I had a flash back to Thursday morning's near miss.

Merry looked at Blake. "I've been meaning to ask you. I know you and Sonny Ravenel go way back."

"Yeah?" Blake said.

Joe and Daddy returned to the table with full plates.

Merry said, "Is he related to those Ravenels on that reality TV show?"

Joe's eyes lit up. "Southern Charm?"

Blake gave Merry a Big Brother stare down. "Don't ever mention that show around Sonny."

"What's wrong with Southern Charm?" Joe asked. "Everybody knows it's not real."

My gaze collided with my sister's. She smothered a laugh.

Daddy said, "Got 'em a sweet young girlfriend, don't he? She looks real enough to me. And a poor little baby to prove it." Daddy pressed his lips together and shook his head.

Daddy had a peculiar fascination with reality TV. *Swamp People* was his favorite. Apparently he'd been watching South Carolina's contribution to the genre. Our former state treasurer, Thomas Ravenel, had resigned a few years back after being arrested and later incarcerated on cocaine charges. He now had a so-called reality TV show, which I had never seen, and a love child with a young woman reportedly thirty years his junior who was a descendant of John Calhoun. Oh, and Thomas was running for the U.S. senate.

Blake rubbed his forehead.

"Is that a 'yes' or a 'no?'" asked Merry.

Blake closed his eyes. "Distantly."

"Do I need to remind everyone that we do not discuss politics at the dinner table in this house?" asked Mamma.

"Politics?" I scrunched up my face at her.

"Wrinkles, darlin'," she said.

I consciously smoothed my face. "No one mentioned politics."

"Political families and their...unfortunate situations crosses that line in my book." Mamma smiled firmly, putting us all on notice that her book was the one we went by. "Merry, bring the biscuits and gravy from the kitchen. There's room on the table. Y'all save room for chocolate cake, now."

Joe said, "Oh, man. You made chocolate cake, too? I haven't eaten like this in...I don't think I ever have." He bit into a chicken leg.

Moments later, Merry returned with the biscuits and more gravy. She set both directly in front of Joe, smiled at me, and sat back down. I knew exactly what she was thinking. My sister doesn't cook. But if she brought Joe over for Mamma's fried chicken often enough, he might not care.

THIRTEEN

Sunday morning, Nate and I met for breakfast at The Cracked Pot. We snagged the back booth, and Moon Unit swooped in with coffee, juice, and menus.

"Good *mornin'*, y'all!" Moon's perky nature bubbled out all over us. "Nate, it's so good to *see* you. When are you gonna stop hopping back and forth and settle down here where you belong?" She put her hand on his shoulder and gave him an inquiring look.

I felt like I'd been punched in the gut. Moon Unit had no idea her words would hurt me. She was just being friendly.

"Good to see you too, Moon Unit," Nate said. "I declare, I have dreams about your grits and red eye gravy."

Moon blushed. Nate had that effect on women, especially when he poured on the Southern drawl and flashed his baby blues. "*Awww*, aren't you the sweetest thing?"

I'd run an extra mile so I could enjoy my breakfast without guilt, then remembered the fried chicken et cetera from the night before. I would be having the fruit plate for breakfast.

Nate handed Moon his menu. "I'd like three eggs, over easy, country ham, grits with red eye gravy, and biscuits."

Moon looked at me, pen poised. "What about chu, sweetie?"

Colleen popped in beside me, next to the window.

I jumped a little.

"What's wrong?" Nate asked.

"Oh, nothing. Just a nerve in my leg. I'm fine."

Colleen said, "Life's short. Eat what you want and enjoy every bite. And order extra ham biscuits to go. I've been working on solidifying. I think I can eat."

I smiled brightly at Moon and played with my earring. "I'm starved. I'd like two scrambled eggs with lots of cheese, country ham, biscuits and gravy."

"All righty." Moon scribbled my order.

"And Moon, will you wrap me up two ham biscuits to go?" My smile didn't waver.

"Who's that for?" Nate asked.

"Oh, you know. I might be hungry later on," I said.

"I'll put those in after I bring out your breakfast." Moon Unit put one hand on her hip. "Did you meet him? I heard y'all had dinner at your mamma's yesterday. What's he like?"

Nate looked confused. "Who?"

"Merry's new boyfriend. Joe Eaddy," I said.

"Joe Eddie who?"

"His last name is Eaddy. E-A-D-D-Y."

"Is he good lookin'?" Moon grinned slyly.

"He is quite handsome," I said.

"You think they're serious?" Moon asked.

"Glory, Moon, I don't know. You know Merry." I purely did not want to discuss my sister's love life just then. I had my own to worry about, and a guardian spirit to deal with. "Yum. I just can't wait for your grits and gravy. I was thinking about them the whole time I was running this morning." This was the unvarnished truth.

"Oh." She clutched her chest. "I am *so* sorry. Coming right up." She spun away.

"So, I think I've worked something out," Colleen said.

I set down my coffee cup very carefully. I looked at her, or out the window, depending on your perspective. I knew she could reliably read my mind. *Can I agree to part-time in Greenville?*

"Yes," she said. "I've got a backup plan. But there's a catch. I can only officially protect the person who holds your Gram's seat—your seat—on the Town Council. If you give that up, well, there may be times you need me when I can't come."

I pondered what that might mean. Colleen had likely saved my life more times than I even knew. Then again, most people walked through this world without guardian spirits to look out for them. At least I was assuming they did. Except most people didn't court disaster quite as enthusiastically as I did. Oh, for the love of Pete. I needed to live my life with the man I loved, even if it turned out to be shorter than it might otherwise have been.

Nate said, "What are you thinking about?"

"Think about this before you mention it to him," Colleen said. "You've had a few close calls. I'm trying to look after you."

My eyes grabbed onto his and held on tight.

"I was thinking about maybe...maybe we should revisit living in Greenville part-time. That's reasonable. I'm truly sorry I've been so stubborn-headed."

Colleen said, "Why do you never listen to a word I say?"

A series of expressions flickered across Nate's face.

"At the risk of being redundant, Slugger, you are a confusing woman. I'm happy you're feeling that way right now. But I think you should sleep on it and let's see how it settles with you tomorrow."

"He's right," Colleen said. "Sleep on it. And remember how no one died in that accident Thursday morning. And the ferry boat incident, and—"

"All right," I said to both of them. My voice may have been sharper than the situation called for, so I reached across the table for Nate's hand. "I'll sleep on it."

Confusion clouded his face. He looked out the window for a minute, then back at me.

"I've come up with something on Peyton and Peter Bounetheau."

"Really? What?"

"They own a warehouse up Shipyard Creek a ways."

"Mmm-kay."

"They own it through several layers of holding companies—like they're trying to keep it at arm's distance."

"What's in the warehouse?"

"Funny you should ask. I paid a call last night. Sign says it's Trade Winds Import and Export."

"Any idea what they're importing and exporting?"

"Not as of yet. The place has sophisticated electronic security—cameras with motion detectors and the like. Roll of barbed wire on top of the fence. And a few onsite individuals who patrol more regularly than one would expect for your garden-variety home décor inventory. These security officers are not the sort who wear uniforms with nametags. They're the kind with prison tats."

"Exactly how close did you get to these thugs?"

"Relax. I used the night vision binoculars."

"Interesting. Could be drugs. Maybe guns, human trafficking. Nothing good."

"My thoughts exactly. I followed two of the security staff at shift change. Guess where they went?"

"Where?"

"Bridgeview Village Apartments."

I went cold, like someone had shoved me in a walk-in freezer and slammed the door. "Please tell me you didn't follow them to Bayside at night." The place was named Bridgeview Village now, but it had been Bayside Manor for many years, and most folks still referred to it as Bayside. If it was in the news, most likely someone had been shot, or the SWAT team had been called out, or a drug deal had gone south—or all three. A YouTube video had been posted of the Bayside brawl, a free-for-all with a crowd of angry women engaging in a violent disagreement in the parking lot last year.

He lowered his eyebrows, gave me a look that said, *what's wrong with you?* "Bridgeview. I didn't even get out of the car. I just followed to see where they went."

Colleen shimmered. "Make him understand. His life depends on it."

"Nate. Promise me. *Promise me* you will not go back there for any reason. Stay off North Romney Street altogether."

"Slugger, calm down. All I did was a drive-by."

I was on the verge of hyperventilating. "You don't get it. SWAT doesn't like to go in there—but they do. The police keep the street blocked off so there's only one way in or out. Management hires off-duty police officers to patrol it in addition to the surveillance cameras and additional regular patrols."

"Sounds like it would be hard for anybody to commit a crime with all those cops and cameras around."

"There's a reason all of that is necessary. To be fair, a lot of folks arrested there are from North Charleston. But the trouble still goes down in Bayside. There's tension between the police, both on duty and off, and the residents. It's just not a good situation for anyone. Some of Merry's kids live there, and she's told me heartbreaking stories." Merry was the executive director of a non-profit organization in Charleston that worked with at-risk youth. "Heaven knows, my heart hurts for the good people who live there, folks without any other recourse—especially the kids. It's Section Eight housing. But it has a very long, violent history. This is not the kind of place you go asking questions at night. You drove out by the grace of God. Don't go back. Promise. Me." I grabbed his arm and clamped down hard.

"Okay, okay. I promise." He gave me a look that said he thought I was way overreacting.

"If that's where this case takes us, I'll give Colton Heyward his money back. We'll just turn over what we know to Charleston PD and walk away."

"All right. Slugger, I've never seen you this rattled."

"I need you to take me seriously. Your life depends on it," I said, taking Colleen at her word.

"I won't go back." He sat back in the booth and studied me careful-ly, like I was a puzzle he was trying to solve.

I took a few deep breaths and a sip of orange juice. After a few minutes, I said, "What the *hell* are the likes of Peyton and Peter doing mixed up with folks from Bayside?"

"That would be the question of the day," Nate said. "No doubt they know what's going on in that warehouse, or why go to so much effort to hide that they own it? If the warehouse was simply an investment, and they leased the space, there would be no reason for all that paperwork."

"Agreed. Only there's no evidence whatever they're doing is con-nected to Kent." Moon Unit approached with our breakfast. "Shhh."

"I'll put your to-go order in now, hon. Can I get you anything else?" she asked.

"This looks fabulous, Moon." My appetite had gone clean out the window.

"Mmmm-*mmmm*." Nate smiled at Moon. "This looks mighty fine. Thank you. I think we're all set."

"Just wave at me if you need anything." In a whirl she was gone.

Nate dug in. I tried a few bites and found my appetite could be lured back. We ate in silence for a few moments. Colleen stared longingly at our food.

"Could be Kent stumbled onto whatever illegal activities her uncles are involved in, and they found it necessary to deal with the situation," Nate said.

I mulled that. "I say we run down every other possibility. If we come up with nothing else, we put it in the report and let the police and God sort it out."

"What's the downside to giving Colton Heyward what we have on them? He'll take it to the police. Meanwhile, we work the other scenarios."

"All right. But we'll need documentation on the trail that ties them to the warehouse. And your report from last night's surveillance," I said.

"We take that to him now, we're keeping him in the loop. He's happy, right?"

A warning light flashed in my head. "Riiight. Except, you know he'll confront Peyton and Peter. And they'll know exactly where his information came from."

"We'll just have to convince him how it's not in his best interests to get us killed."

"I don't know," I said. "Why not just give it straight to Sonny? That seems safer to me. We can still give it to Mr. Heyward in our final report if we don't come up with anything more likely."

"That'll work." A few bites later, he said, "So tell me what you've got."

"Nothing quite so dramatic," I said. "I did talk to one of Matt's neighbors who puts Ansley's car at Matt's house from around nine the night Kent disappeared until sometime the following morning."

"How did she explain that?"

"She hasn't yet. Up until the Peyton and Peter revelation, I thought she and Matt must be involved with Kent's disappearance. I wanted to sleep on it, talk to you, before I tipped her off."

"They could still be behind it. Just because Peyton and Peter are embroiled in one illegal enterprise doesn't mean they also made their niece disappear. Matt and Ansley—that's still a plausible narrative."

"If one or both of them are involved, they either helped her disappear, covered up an accident, or covered up a crime of passion," I said. "And it almost had to have gone down in his house."

"Want to search it?"

I put together the perfect bite of eggs, grits, and gravy, delivered it to my mouth, and savored the mix of flavors. I studied the ceiling. "Charleston PD looked at Matt hard. He's not stupid. If something happened to Kent in his house, the only evidence remaining by now is the kind we'd need Luminol to find." Often accidents and crimes of passion resulted in bloodstains. It was virtually impossible to clean up all the blood unless you knew what you were doing. Matt and Ansley were not pros at crime scene cleanup.

"And we don't need to be spraying a crime scene with Luminol. We could screw up evidence in the process."

"Precisely." I chewed a bite of biscuit. "And if we don't come up with something else pretty damn quick—preferably Kent—we have no choice but to tell Colton Heyward about the baby. Once we do that, he'll go straight to the police."

"And they'll arrest Matt within ten minutes."

"At which point they'll get a search warrant, and go over his house with a fine-tooth comb. Best we not disturb anything there."

"Agreed."

"I think it's time for me to talk to Ansley." I looked at Colleen. I could use her help with Ansley.

"And we need to make an appointment to speak with Colton Heyward tomorrow morning if possible," said Nate. "That's as long as we can put off telling him about the baby. We've sat on that for nearly two days already."

"All right. I'll make the call."

"Meantime, I'll get the documentation ready for Sonny. That will take most of today."

"I know that's a lot, but do you think you could squeeze in talking to the other artists who were with Evan Ingle that Friday night at Bin 152? I haven't had a chance to verify his story." I flashed him my best pretty-please look.

He gave me a look that said he knew what I was up to. "As I am not immune to your feminine wiles, I will find a way to work it in, provided they are available and willing. Names and contact info in the file?"

"Yeah." I grinned a silly grin. He was not immune to my feminine wiles. That was welcome news, since he hadn't exactly jumped all over my earlier offer to live in Greenville part-time. "Thank you so much."

"My pleasure to assist," he said in a tone that suggested other things he might assist me with.

Moon Unit arrived with a to-go bag and our ticket. "Here you go."

Nate paid at the register, good-naturedly parrying all attempts from Moon Unit to discuss his residency status. He might not want to live full time in Stella Maris, but he could never claim he wasn't welcome.

I waved the bag of biscuits at Colleen. If she wanted what was inside them, she was going to have to help me out with Ansley.

FOURTEEN

My Escape was parked on the street a few doors down from The Cracked Pot. Before I had my seat belt buckled, Colleen faded into the passenger seat. "Okay, watch this."

I cocked my head at her and waited. At first I couldn't tell a difference. Then gradually, she appeared denser, until she looked just like any mortal human.

"Wow," I said. "That's what you mean by solidifying?"

"Yep." She grinned. "It's an advanced skill. Takes tons of practice. What did you do with the biscuits?" She looked around the car.

"I have them in my bag."

She looked past me, to where my purse was wedged between me and the door. "Let me have them."

"In a little while. First we need to talk about what you have up your sleeve relative to where I'm going to reside. Then I need your help with Ansley."

"Really? You're holding my biscuits hostage? After I saved your hide yet again just a few days ago? *Really*?"

I sighed, cut my eyes heavenward, pulled the biscuits out and handed her the bag.

She held it like it was a precious butterfly that might float away if she moved suddenly. "Oh. I'm so hungry."

I was having a hard time processing ghosts—whatever—with an appetite. "Seriously? Do guardian spirits get hungry?"

She gave in and tore open the bag and unwrapped one of the biscuits. She rolled her eyes and moaned when she took the first bite. The look of sheer ecstasy on her face called to mind a whole nother experience—something I liked even better than biscuits.

I said, "I'm guessing that's a yes."

She swallowed. "We crave things that we miss from when we were human, but we don't actually feel hunger, or any kind of pain. The next world is infinitely better than this one. But they don't have biscuits."

"Can other people see you now—when you're solid?"

"They can. Except most people see what they expect to see, and hardly anyone would recognize me anyway." Posthumous Colleen was a perfect version of mortal Colleen. Her skin was clear and luminous, her red curls long and shiny. Her figure was lean, her movements lithe. And she was right in that no one in town would be expecting to see her. She'd been gone quite a spell.

"Enjoy your biscuits. I need to take care of something right quick."

I texted Ansley: Need to talk ASAP. How quick can you meet me at Lighthouse Park?

It was a few minutes after nine on Sunday morning. I'd expected Ansley to be with her parents, in a pew a few rows behind Mamma and Daddy at St. Francis Episcopal. Surprisingly, she texted me back right away: See you in ten.

I started the car and headed towards the city park just south of Devlin's Point. "Help me out here. What is the tactical advantage for a guardian spirit in solidifying? Like you once told me, your most reliable skill is eavesdropping without being seen."

"I can talk to humans this way—aside from you. In my normal state, I can only see and talk to you."

"Who do you need to talk to?"

"No one right now. But you never know when I might need to distract someone while you're someplace you're not supposed to be."

"Hmm...I can use you for diversions now?" I parked near the lighthouse, rolled down the windows, and opened the moonroof.

"Sometimes. Depending on what you decide." She bit into the biscuit.

"About that."

She was inhaling the biscuit, eyes closed. "Can you hear me?"

She nodded, but kept eating.

"It seems to me if the goal is to keep someone in my town council seat who will protect the island, several other candidates could do this as easily as me. Candidates with no desire to live anywhere else."

Colleen swallowed a bite. "The problem is that nearly everyone is persuadable with the right argument. Sometimes people think they're doing the right thing, when they're really being manipulated. You're stubborn."

"I have to say, no one has ever appreciated that quality in me before."

"I have a thought. And really, it's good to have a couple possibilities in reserve. Things happen. Your Gram should have held that seat another ten years at least."

"Who is your other thought?"

"Calista."

"Oooh! She'd be perfect. And trust me, she has stubborn down." Calista McQueen was a former client, now a friend, who lived just down the beach from me. She bore an uncanny resemblance to Marilyn Monroe, which had caused more than her share of grief in the past. But she'd settled into Stella Maris life as if she'd been born there. Lately she'd taken up teaching Mamma's Jazzercise class.

"Still," Colleen said. "I worry about you. Calista doesn't have the same risk factors. I can only protect the council members who I can depend on to serve the best interests of the island."

I tilted my head at her. "You watch out after Daddy, too?"

"Among others."

"I would have thought everyone serving now would be dependable: me, Daddy, John Glendawn, Grace Sullivan, Michael Devlin, and Robert Pearson. Even the mayor, Lincoln Sullivan—and I'm likely not his favorite person, which goes both ways—but I'd still say he'd always put the town first."

"It's complicated," Colleen said. "Some of them are vulnerable to persuasion. It's important to keep a majority who are not."

That made me wonder a great many things. I'd long suspected Robert Pearson had secrets. And were there yet more developers who had the island in their sights? I thought about the two men I'd seen on the ferry Friday morning. I filed all of that under "things to ponder when I get time." "Okay, so, we replace me with Calista, and I can be a part-time resident."

Colleen unwrapped her second biscuit slowly.

"I will only be able to help you very sporadically—when it doesn't interfere with my other duties. Think about it. This impacts both you and Nate."

I couldn't live with myself if Nate were hurt—or worse—and it could have been avoided.

"How about this?" I said. "I mean, it's not like the other council members never leave the island, right? They travel all the time. As long as I own a house here and it's my primary residence, I qualify as a resident of Stella Maris. Isn't the real issue showing up for council meetings? As long as I do that and am here part of the time...who's keeping island attendance?"

Colleen thought and chewed for an eternity. Finally, she said, "You'll get away with that for a while. At some point, your residency will be challenged."

"Well, maybe I'll just cross that bridge when I get there. And who's to say a challenge would be successful? The remaining council members would decide, right?"

"Except that you have to run for office every four years. If folks notice you're not here much, it will be easy for someone else to win over enough votes to beat you."

"I need to mull this over. But I can get away with being in Greenville part-time for a while, right?"

"Yes."

"So, when it looks like I'm getting into trouble, you let me know, and I'll spend more time here. If it becomes impossible to balance, then we recruit Calista. Now. If you're through devouring those biscuits, I could use your help with Ansley."

Ansley parked her Z4 in the space beside me and got out. I could see why Wendy Ryan had noticed the car—and why she wanted one.

To Colleen, I said, "You'll need to get in the back. See if you can read her mind. Get me anything to do with Matt Thomas or Kent Heyward."

"I'll see what I can do," Colleen said, slightly miffed. She liked to call the shots, not take requests. She faded, disappeared, and popped into the backseat.

Ansley climbed into the passenger seat. "Did you find something?" she asked. Her face told me she was excited and eager, hoping I had good news.

She was so...kittenish with her big innocent eyes, shiny blonde hair, and petite build. I sighed and used my stern voice. "Yes, as a matter of fact I did. I found out that your car was parked overnight in front of Matt's house the night Kent disappeared."

She looked like she'd been sucker-punched. "I—oh no." She put one hand over her mouth and furiously fumbled with the other to get the door open. She did, just before she started retching. Then she sobbed and retched alternately for a while. She was all tore up, is what I'm saying.

When she was finished, I handed her the tissue box. She took a few and dabbled at her mouth and eyes. "It's not what it looks like."

Colleen said, "She's genuinely upset."

I threw her a look over my shoulder that telegraphed, *ya think?*

"Ansley."

She sobbed on.

"Ansley. Tell. Me. What. It. *Is*. Now, please."

She nodded, sobbed a few more times for good measure. "I didn't want to say anything because it looks bad."

"That's the understatement of the century."

"Matt and I are friends. I told you that. He was upset—really, really upset. He loves Kent, but with the baby—"

"I thought you didn't know about the baby?"

She started crying again.

"Would you stop that and talk to me?"

She sniffled and then quieted and nodded. "I knew about the baby. I knew that was causing most of their problems. I went there that night because he needed a friend. Kent had other plans. He just wanted someone to talk to who knew them both—knew the situation."

"And you thought Kent would be okay with you spending the night?"

"He didn't get off until one in the morning. There was no way I could go home. The last ferry left at eleven-thirty."

"Why were you there before he got off work?"

"I had to come over while the ferry was still running. I just came early, hung out, watched TV."

I had a sinking suspicion Ansley harbored feelings for Matt she'd had from the get-go. "You like being in his house."

She nodded, looked out the window.

"You have a thing for him still, don't you?"

"Okay, yes. I'm crazy about him. But Kent is my best friend and I have *never* done anything but be a friend to both of them. Never."

"Why didn't you tell me this to begin with? I gotta tell you, Ansley, you're making it hard for me to believe anything you say. This is the second—no, third—time you have either lied to me or left things out. It makes me wonder if you talked Colton Heyward into hiring me so you could feed me the information you wanted me to have and try to keep me from finding out the truth."

"*No, no, no.* That's not it at all. I only wanted to protect Matt. This just looks bad."

"Ansley, do you know what Luminol is?"

"No."

"It's a chemical you spray on things—floors, walls, pretty much everything. Then you turn out the lights. If there's any blood at all, even a speck—people always think they can clean it all up, but they really can't—the Luminol lights up. The police use it to solve crimes. Sometimes Nate and I use it. What do you think we'll find in Matt's house?" I hadn't changed my mind about tampering with a potential crime scene, but I wanted to see her reaction.

"How should I know? No one's ever been bleeding when I was there."

I studied her for a long moment. She seemed not to connect my question to Kent at all. But Ansley had gotten an "A" in lying these past few days. "So that wouldn't trouble you? Us performing a Luminol test?"

"Of course not. But that house is like almost a hundred years old. Matt's only owned it for a couple of years. Who knows what happened there before he bought it?"

She was awfully quick with that. Then again, she did work for an attorney. How much did she know about crime scenes? "That's the beautiful thing about blood types. Kent's is on file." Of course it must be, but Luminol wouldn't give us a blood type. Maybe Ansley didn't know that.

"You will not find Kent's blood in that house unless it's a drop from a nosebleed or something. Matt would never, ever hurt her."

"How about you?"

"*What?*" Her face froze, mouth open, eyes wide with indignation.

I shrugged, kept my voice casual. "She was getting ready to move in with the man you love."

"*Oh*. I can't *believe* you would think such a thing. How could you?" The sobbing commenced again.

"Ansley, I have to look at every possibility. That's what I get paid for. I'm sorry if you thought I would do anything less. But here we are. Tell me why I shouldn't think you got rid of your competition?"

She cowered against the passenger door and stared at me like I'd beaten her down to a pulpy mess. "Because I'm not capable of hurting anyone, much less Kent, who I love like a sister."

"I don't think you have murder in you. I don't. My problem is I believed everything you said the first time we talked about this case. And the second time. Now, you're a habitual liar. And you're good at it. Really good."

"But I'm helping you."

"Really? Aside from feeding me half-truths and outright lies, how are you helping me?"

"I stayed home from church this morning to work on Kent's Facebook friends. I've been going through them nonstop since you called. I think I found something."

"What?"

"There's this girl—well, the profile identifies her as a girl, but it could be anyone, right? Supposedly, she lives in Bakersfield, California and is a high school student. Her name is Samantha Blundell. I don't know who this is, or how Kent knows her. She's never mentioned her to me. I don't know how their paths would've crossed."

"Hunh." Bakersfield, CA was west of Amarillo. I pulled out a pad and pen and wrote down the name. "Everyone else checks out?"

"Yes. All two hundred eighty-five of the others are either family, friends from high school, friends from college, or other friends Kent and I both knew—with the exception of a few local artists who also have professional pages."

I watched Ansley for a few moments, hoping Colleen would have something to offer. She was regarding Ansley intently, like she was trying to read her but couldn't. I said, "Ansley, you have violated my trust. I'm only going to ask this once. Is there anything else you haven't told me?"

"No. I promise. There's nothing."

"I have to report all of this to my client. He will likely report it to the police. He is already predisposed to be suspicious of Matt. This could get very rough before it gets better. Best you talk to Robert—or better yet, your daddy—about everything. You may need an attorney before this is over."

She pressed her eyes closed, clearly trying not to cry again.

I said, "I give you my word I will not stop working this case until Kent is found or I'm satisfied the person responsible for her disappearance is in jail—preferably both."

Ansley nodded. "Thank you. I believe you. And I really am sorry I didn't tell you everything to begin with. I realize how stupid that was."

"Well, when all of this is over, after you've graduated from law school, maybe you can use it as a cautionary tale for your clients when you are trying to impress on them the importance of telling you the whole truth."

Ansley jerked with a humorless half chuckle. "When all of this is over. Right."

"Are you all right to drive?"

"I will be in a few minutes." She opened the door and climbed out, taking the box of tissues with her. "I'll get you a new box."

"Okay." I started the car, rolled up the windows, and closed the moon roof. "Anything?" I asked Colleen.

"I'm sorry. I can't read her—it's like Matt. I don't think that means anything either way. It's simply a case of there's no valid reason for me to know what's going on inside their heads."

"Does that point to innocence?"

"Not necessarily. Remember—my mission doesn't include solving your cases."

"Right." I sighed.

FIFTEEN

I made a run by The Book & Grind for a mocha latte on the way home. My brain needed a caffeine boost. So many scraps of information floated around in my head. I had the feeling someone had mixed the pieces to three different puzzles in the same box, and I didn't know which ones I needed and which ones I didn't.

When I walked out the front door, coffee in hand, I glanced up and down Palmetto Boulevard. It was a storybook downtown with window boxes, awnings, trees with border beds, and brick sidewalks. Most of the businesses were closed—it was Sunday morning. I shared the street with one runner headed back towards Main. Stella Maris was blessed with a wealth of locally owned businesses that occupied historic buildings along the two streets that made up the business district—Main and Palmetto.

Across Palmetto, Evan Ingle's gallery caught my eye. The vivid colors and bold strokes of the paintings lining the windows made me smile. Evan's was the only art gallery on the island, but it gave me hope others would follow. Opening a gallery must be a huge undertaking for a young artist. Evan had paid cash for that building. How *had* he pulled that off? Were his paintings popular with collectors? He'd bought the building several years ago. Surely if he was a phenom there would've been more press about him. Unaccounted-for money bothered me. I took another sip of coffee and climbed in the car. I couldn't call Colton Heyward until after one on a Sunday. Maybe after I checked out Samantha Blundell, I'd have time to satisfy my curiosity regarding Evan Ingle's finances.

I zipped home, settled in at my desk, and turned on my laptop. Rhett, having greeted me and escorted me in, scampered right back down the hall towards the mudroom. He was on his way back outside and I didn't blame him.

From Kent's Facebook account, I brought up Samantha's profile page. Cute girl. She had an open smile, dark blonde wavy hair, and evidently liked big round sunglasses. It was a good look for her. Assuming this was a real person, of course.

I clicked around her profile a bit, browsed her photos—almost seven hundred of them—and checked out her friends. If this account belonged to a predator in disguise, it was the best disguise I'd ever seen. She looked sprightly. This girl liked beaches, Jimi Hendrix on vinyl, and Harry Potter. She'd been to church camp over the summer and was Facebook friends with her mother, her grandparents, and a slew of other family members. She was the personification of the word "wholesome." How did Samantha know Kent Heyward, a girl five years older and a continent away?

A closer look at her family showed some in Texas, where Samantha was born, and, hello, grandparents in Greenville. Progress. A connection to South Carolina.

I scrolled through her timeline. Lots of family stuff. Shared links to funny videos and thoughtful articles. And her college visits: Appalachian State and College of Charleston.

In April, Samantha had visited both campuses. She had an album of photos from the trip. I scanned through them. Tons of shots of the C of C campus. Samantha and her parents in front of Randolph Hall. Pictures from all over Charleston, mostly of historic homes and landmarks.

Then I got to the beach scenes. Of course. A beach lover wouldn't come to the Holy City and not visit the Atlantic. I recognized Sullivan's Island, Breach Inlet, and the beach near the pier on Isle of Palms. I scanned forwards until I saw the photo taken from the ferry looking back at the Isle of Palms marina. Samantha Blundell had been to Stella Maris.

Apparently, they'd spent the better part of a day here. She'd snapped photos from all over the island. There was a cute pic from one of the booths at The Cracked Pot. The three of them had their heads together over the remnants of what looked like lunch. I'd bet Moon Unit had taken the photo. Another photo from The Pirates' Den showed they'd dined on one of John and Alma's specialties—Lowcountry Boil—for dinner. There were streetscapes and beach shots. But there was no sign of Kent. And, however the friendship came to be, it was hard to imagine Samantha knew anything about Kent's disappearance. Unless for some reason Kent was hiding out in Bakersfield, California. No one would think to look there, for sure. Perhaps that was the point.

I flipped back to Samantha's "about" page. Her phone number was listed. I bet telemarketers worried her to death. I couldn't think of a reason not to call. It was a little after nine in California. Maybe I'd catch her before church.

"Hello?" She answered on the third ring.

"Hey, I'm trying to reach Samantha Blundell?"

"I'm Samantha."

"Great. I'm Liz Talbot. I'm calling from Stella Maris, South Carolina. How are you today?"

"I'm fine." Her tone telegraphed, *What is this about?*

"Samantha, I'm a private investigator. Would you like me to speak to your parents?"

"I don't think so...."

She sounded confused, but curious.

"I'm investigating the disappearance of a young woman from Charleston. I think you know her—Kent Heyward?"

"Yes—I mean, we've met. I saw the posts to her Facebook page about her being missing. It's horrible."

"How did you meet her?"

"When I was in Charleston for one of my college visits. I met her at an art gallery on Stella Maris. My parents and I were over there for the day. That evening after dinner, we were walking around town, and the artist was having an exhibition. We went in, and Kent was there. It was funny. She and I had on the same shirt—one that kinda stands out, I guess. Anthropologie. Blue paisley, but the sleeves are yellow striped. We just looked at each other and laughed. And we started talking. She's really nice. I told her I might go to college in Charleston, and she offered to show me around the city. She friended me on Facebook."

"Have you spoken to her since you met her? Aside from connecting online, I mean."

"No. Gosh, I just pray she's all right."

"Samantha. This is really important. A lot of people are very worried about her. The police are looking for her. Are you sure you haven't heard from her?"

"I'm sure. I would tell you."

"If she were in trouble and asked to stay with you, would you let her?"

She hesitated. "Maybe. I mean, I'd have to talk to my parents. If she were in trouble they'd want to help, I guess. Unless she was in trouble with the police. We only met that once. Do you want to talk to my parents?" The tone of her voice told me how odd she thought the question was.

Which told me Kent wasn't there. It had been an incredible long shot. "Okay. Well, if she contacts you, would you please let me know?"

"Sure. But like I said, I barely know her. We talked for maybe fifteen minutes. I don't think I'm the one she'd turn to."

I gave her my contact info just in case.

With the Samantha lead exhausted, I turned my attention to the source of Evan Ingle's financial security. I clicked over to his website. On his home page, there was a brief statement about his education. There was a list of artists he'd studied with after earning his BFA—several abroad. More money unaccounted for. But that filled the gap in his timeline between college and opening his gallery.

On the tab for exhibitions, there were drop-down boxes for "Current," "Upcoming," and "Past." Only the current tab had photos of his work, and it was what I'd seen in the gallery. His website was a bit bare, which called into question why Kent would've turned to him for website advice. There was no indication anywhere of who had purchased his paintings or how many he'd sold. Had he made enough money from selling his work to pay for the gallery? Financial records were the hardest to come by online, even with my variety of databases.

Evan's profile held no more revelations that morning than it had when I'd pulled it together the day before. His mother must've left him money. Maybe she had a life insurance policy. As a single mother, that would've made sense. Except Evan had gone to Porter Gaud, a private school. Where had that money come from? The unaccounted for resources started way before Evan studied abroad and opened his gallery.

I opened a file on Talitha Ingle. First, I pulled her birth records. She'd been born in Charleston, parents Mark Ingle and Melanie Turner Ingle. I documented the single car accident that had taken both of their lives in 1979. Next, I pulled obituaries and discovered that Talitha had a brother, Turner Ingle, four years her junior.

A few clicks later, I was looking at Turner Ingle's death certificate. Unbelievable. He had also died due to internal injuries sustained in a single car accident. What, could this family just not drive worth a damn? Coincidences like this made me itchy. Turner had died in 1981, barely two years after his parents. According to his death certificate, he had lived and died in Greenville. The address listed was on Trails End, a street I recognized from a neighborhood near Cleveland Park. Some of the homes there were large and pricey, others more modest. In recent years anything in the area was high-dollar real estate. But in 1981, it would have been more affordable. It would've had to've been. The occupation listed on Turner Ingle's death certificate was "welder," and his employer was GE Gas Turbines.

Oddly, the box "married" was checked, but no spouse's name was listed. The informant was his sister, Talitha Ingle. There was no indication where Turner was to be buried, but he'd been released to the J. Henry Stuhr funeral home in Charleston. Talitha had brought her brother home. Was he buried beside her at Magnolia Cemetery? What had happened to his unnamed wife? Who were their people? Sometimes you could find answers about a person's life in their final resting place.

I glanced at the clock. It was a few minutes past one. I called Colton Heyward and made an appointment for nine o'clock the next morning. Then I grabbed my keys.

Magnolia Cemetery occupied a former rice plantation on the upper neck of the Charleston peninsula and backed up to the Cooper River, roughly where the Wando River flowed into the Cooper. It opened in 1850, and its residents included a who's who list from historic Charleston. I drove through the white painted brick columns and wrought iron gate. A beautiful, park-like place, the grounds were divided into several sections, with roads and paths that wended through and around marshes, two lagoons, and wooded areas.

I needed a map, but the sign at the white, two-story cemetery office informed me it was open Monday through Friday. According to Talitha's obituary, she'd been buried in the Greenhill section. I proceeded along the road I was on. Massive live oaks draped in Spanish moss dotted the grounds, some performing improbable acts of contortion. I didn't see another soul. Being as well acquainted with the departed as I am, I wondered how many of the folks whose names were carved in the monuments were wandering among us on missions similar to Colleen's.

Before long, the road turned to dirt and gravel. Elaborate monuments—crosses, angels, and spires—many much taller than me, stood inside iron fences and stone borders marking family plots. Presently, I came to a sign pointing right to Greenhill.

I passed between two marshes. The Greenhill section of Magnolia Cemetery was in the back, isolated, and surrounded by a combination of woods and marshes. This was definitely not a place I would care to visit at night.

"Creepy, isn't it?" Colleen said.

I jumped so high my seat belt locked down. "Are you trying to give me a heart attack?"

"What?" Her attempt at an innocent look was ruined by the smirk she couldn't control. "This place make you nervous?"

"What do you think?"

"I admit it looks spooky. Beautiful and peaceful, too. There's no one here but you, me, and a bunch of alligators. And snakes."

I shuddered. I'd seen one more snake than I wanted to already that week.

"And of course birds and small critters. But these folks..." She waved her hand like Vanna White. "...they're either resting a spell, or they're on assignment somewhere, like me. Or they're like Sue Ellen and haven't crossed over. Either way, they're not here. The folks you need to be afraid of are the ones still living and breathing."

"Tell me about it."

"Turn left," she said.

"Why?"

"Do you want to visit Talitha Ingle's grave?"

"Yes."

"Then turn left. It's down there." She pointed.

I turned left as instructed and drove halfway down the grid-like section.

"This is it," Colleen said.

I pulled over as far as I could, cut the engine, and got out.

A border of granite surrounded a plot large enough for eight graves, if I were to guess. Only three markers stood there, roughly in the middle. These were simple but elegant granite markers. The one farthest to the left was Turner Mark Ingle, March 9, 1959 – October 14, 1981. The inscription read: Beloved husband, father, and brother. What had become of his loving wife and children?

Next in line was a smaller stone, with an angel engraved on top: Eva Drew Ingle, October 14, 1981 – October 14, 1981. A stillborn child. How sad. Was she Turner's child, Talitha's, or another family member's I hadn't yet discovered?

The third stone was Talitha's: Talitha Anne Ingle, January 21, 1955 – August 10, 2014. Her inscription read: Beloved mother.

My eyes darted back to the child's stone. I hustled back to the car, pulled out my iPad, and tapped icons until I had Evan Ingle's file open.

His birthdate was October 14, 1981. Eva had been his twin sister.

Who were their father? And who was Turner Ingle's child or children? He was someone's "loving father." And he'd died on the same date the twins were born.

"Can you get any kind of read on this?" I asked Colleen.

She held out her arms, looked to the heavens, and closed her eyes. After a few moments, she said. "Tread carefully. I sense danger for you here."

"Here in this cemetery, or here as in asking questions about Turner, Eva, and Talitha?"

Colleen studied the sky. "Perhaps both."

"Danger from who?"

"I don't know." She shook her head. "That's all I've been given."

I took photos of the headstones for my files. Slowly, I turned and scanned the area. It was deserted. The surrounding marsh and woods were dense and wild. "Colleen?"

"Yeah?"

"How much of the Charleston peninsula do you suppose is like this?"

"Like what? Graveyards, you mean?"

"No, I mean, how much of it has this kind of tree canopy, these thick woods surrounded by marshes?"

"Not much. It's pretty built up."

I opened Google maps on my iPad. "Exactly." The satellite view confirmed what I already knew. Charleston had several beautiful parks near tourist areas and neighborhoods. But the biggest green spot on the map was right where we stood. My gut clenched when I noticed how close we were to Bayside—and to Shipyard Creek, where Nate had located Peyton and Peter's warehouse. Magnolia Cemetery sprawled between the two locations, not immediately adjacent to either, but close by.

"It wouldn't be a bad place to hide a car, if you wanted to make one disappear. Or a person," I said.

Colleen's eyes grew. "You'd need a machete to hack through the thickets between all the big trees. And the marshes are right behind the trees."

"Maybe."

I climbed into the car and started the engine. I drove down the dirt road until I came to the road that looped all the way around the biggest part of the Greenhill section. I turned right and slowly circumnavigated the area. A dirt road forked off to my left. I turned down it. Shortly there appeared a massive pile of dirt. A backhoe, and various other pieces of heavy equipment I couldn't name sat over to one side. The kinds of heavy machinery one needed to dig large holes and move extra dirt around. "This is a working area. Someone comes back here regularly." I put the car in reverse.

"Maybe you should call Nate," Colleen said.

"I will if I find anything."

She bit her bottom lip and looked worried.

I stopped the car and looked at her. "You always know way before I do when trouble is coming. Should I get the heck out of here?"

She looked at me for a long moment, then shook her head.

"No. There's no immediate threat."

I breathed a little easier, turned the car around and went back out to the main loop. The open marsh wouldn't hide a car. I drove past less dense spots where the tree canopy thinned. After a moment, we were back at the fork in the road at the entrance to the Greenhill section. I made a hard right, and continued along the border. No crushed undergrowth or broken limbs betrayed a disturbance. Could you even tell a month later?

Like a hunting dog with a scent, I persisted. This may well have been a wild goose chase, but I had a feeling in my bones that I was close to discovering something important. I rolled forwards. For her part, Colleen was unusually quiet.

At the elbow where the border road made a right turn, another service road forked left. A chain attached to simple posts let visitors know this area was off limits. I pulled over and got out of the car. The entire area was still deserted. I walked to the chain and stepped across. A short ways down the dirt road, a section of woods had clearly been disturbed. Weeds and saplings lay flattened. A few limbs were snapped. I approached the dented forest with dread, for both what I knew I would find—wildlife—and what I was very much afraid I would find—a red Mini Cooper.

I glanced around, thinking maybe Colleen could scout it out. Alligators and snakes wouldn't bother her one bit. Where had she gotten to? "Colleen?"

Damnation, she picked the wrong time to evaporate. On the other hand, the fact that she wasn't there confirmed I didn't need her to survive whatever I found. I took a deep breath, pushed back a hanging limb, and stepped into the woods. The ground became mucky almost immediately. I was busy watching where I put my sandal-clad feet and stepped straight into a gigantic spider web.

Batting, brushing, sputtering, and cursing ensued.

Finally clear of web and spiders, I focused again on where I was headed.

I stilled.

Thirty feet in front of me, a red Mini Cooper appeared to squat in the woods. It had sunk into the marsh about halfway. The canopy of trees was impenetrable. It would never have been seen from the sky. I pulled my iPhone out of my pocket, snapped photos in every direction.

I crept a few steps closer, tried to see inside the car. Oh sweet Lord, how I did not want to find Kent in that muddy, infested with who-knew-what car, but I had to look. I pulled back a pine branch. Just a few more steps. Oh, thank goodness. The front seats were empty. Weak with relief, I backed out as carefully as I'd come in.

I called Nate, then Sonny.

Ten minutes later, the first Charleston PD vehicle arrived. It was an unmarked car. Two gentlemen in street clothes emerged.

"You Liz Talbot?" the short one asked.

"Yes."

"See some ID?" the tall, broad-shouldered one said.

"Sure." I pulled out my PI and driver's licenses and handed them to the tall one.

He scrutinized both, then me, then handed them back. "I'm Detective Jenkins. This is Detective Bissell. I understand you've run across a red Mini Cooper."

"I have. I was retained by Colton Heyward to look into his daughter's disappearance. It's back there a ways." I pointed down the service road.

"How did you come to look for it back there?" asked Detective Bissell, his tone neutral.

"I've given a lot of thought to where one might hide a car, assuming it was still in Charleston. There aren't many places it wouldn't be found in a month's time. This seemed like a good spot."

"So you got lucky." Detective Bissell sounded defensive.

"I guess you could say that." I was more concerned about Kent's luck just then. I heard more cars approaching and glanced to my right. Nate and Sonny arrived at the same time, but under separate cover.

They both got out of their cars and approached our group. Nate walked over and stood by me. Sonny took the spot between us and the other detectives, so that we formed a semi-circle. The Charleston PD guys all did this little chin lift in acknowledgement of each other.

"This is my partner, Nate Andrews," I said.

Everyone said quick hellos.

Detective Jenkins said, "We'll go check it out." He made eye contact and nodded. He didn't say, *Y'all stay here*, but he conveyed the message nevertheless.

"It's not too far down, on the right. You'll see where the woods are disturbed," I said.

Sonny and the other two detectives headed down the service road.

Nate canted his head at me and squinted. "What have I missed since breakfast?"

I gave him the Cliff's Notes version.

"You went walking into a swamp—in those shoes?" He glared at my sandals.

"Well, I didn't go very far."

"Why didn't you call me?" He spread his arms wide and gave me a look that asked *what am I going to do with you?*

"I did."

With his free hand, he gestured in the direction the detectives had disappeared. "If you'd called me earlier, you wouldn't've had to've gone traipsing through a marsh, all's I'm saying."

"It worked out," I said with no enthusiasm whatsoever. I'd tried to keep a realistic view of the prospects for this case. But it weighed heavy on me how this turn of events made the chances of finding Kent safe less likely.

"This narrows our possible narratives quite a bit. Could you tell if anyone was in the car?"

"The front seats were empty. That car has a tiny backseat and a trunk. It's possible she's somewhere I couldn't see her."

We stood around simmering in our own thoughts for what seemed like an hour. Finally, the three detectives reemerged, mucky in varying degrees.

Jenkins said, "It's her car. Good news is she's not in it. We're going to call in crime scene techs, rope this area off." He looked at me. "You mind coming in tomorrow morning, giving us a statement?"

"Not at all."

"Nine o'clock?"

"See you then."

Jenkins got busy on his cellphone.

Nate and I turned and headed towards our cars. He'd parked in front of me. I spoke quietly to Nate. "We need to talk to Colton Heyward today instead of tomorrow."

"Liz." Sonny's voice came from behind me.

I stopped and turned.

He walked in long-legged strides towards us, stopped a few feet away. He raised his chin in acknowledgement. "Good job."

"Think your friends will play with me now?"

He huffed out a half chuckle. "I wouldn't count on that."

SIXTEEN

I called Colton Heyward and asked to change our meeting to immediately. I wanted to tell him about the Mini Cooper. Because I knew someone from Charleston PD would be knocking on his door sooner rather than later, I needed to do it lickety-split.

We left my car at the Hampton Inn, climbed into Nate's Explorer, and headed towards the Heyward home.

He let out a low whistle as we rolled down the driveway. "Would you look at this?"

"I know, right?"

"You seen the Bounetheau place over on East Bay?"

"I've driven past. Haven't been inside. Have you?"

"I've been inside the gardens. Mansion is easily twice the size of this one."

We climbed out of the car and hustled towards the front door. Mr. Palmer let us in and showed us to the living room. Thankfully, today only Colton and Virginia Heyward were waiting for us. They both stood as we came in the door.

"Mr. and Mrs. Heyward," I said, "this is my partner, Nate Andrews."

Nate shook hands with them. Since I'd already done that once, on two separate occasions, I didn't feel compelled to repeat the process.

"Please, have a seat." Mr. Heyward gestured to the sofa facing the one he and his wife stood in front of.

Nate and I sat. Mr. and Mrs. Heyward both perched on the edge of the sofa across from us, dressed in what I supposed passed for casual wear for them. He wore pressed khakis and an open-collared blue oxford shirt. She looked elegant in a fine gauge cream-colored sweater, pearls, tan slacks, and flats.

"You have news." Mr. Heyward said.

"Yes," I said. "We've located Kent's car."

His eyes bored into mine, his face hard, hope and dread battling for the upper hand. "Where?"

Mrs. Heyward raised a hand to her mouth.

"It was hidden in a marshy area, in the woods, at Magnolia Cemetery."

"And Kent?" Mr. Heyward's voice was ragged.

"There is no sign of her," I said.

Mr. and Mrs. Heyward seemed to be holding their breath. Neither of them moved.

"Mr. Heyward, Mrs. Heyward. This is good news—Kent not being in the car. She could easily have hidden it there herself before leaving town." I was trying hard to sell this to myself as much as them.

"Why on earth would she do that?" Mrs. Heyward reached for her husband's hand.

He wrapped her tiny, pale hand in his much larger pair.

"Because she doesn't want to be tracked and the car has a built in GPS," Nate said. "The police can find the car if it's turned on. She couldn't drive away in it and hope not to be found."

"So this supports the police department's theory?" Mr. Heyward lowered his chin and looked at me from under dark eyebrows.

"It could," I said. "We're still looking at several possibilities."

"And they are?" Mr. Heyward asked.

"We're talking to all of Kent's friends. Everyone from college and high school—even her Facebook friends," I said.

"You found her laptop?" Mrs. Heyward was far more functional when her husband was in the room as opposed to her mother.

"No," I said. "Ansley helped us access Kent's account from my computer."

"I see," she said.

Nate said, "So far we haven't had any luck in locating her, but we have eliminated a lot of possibilities. And we are also looking at other scenarios." He looked at Mr. Heyward.

Mr. Heyward nodded.

The three of us silently agreed not to discuss those other scenarios in front of Mrs. Heyward.

"What happens now?" Mrs. Heyward asked. The hope in her voice, combined with how much she looked like Kent, ate at me.

"The police have secured the area," Nate said. "They're bringing in crime scene technicians to go over every inch of the car and the area around the car to see if there's any further evidence. We would appreciate it if you would share that information with us."

Colton Heyward jerked his head up. "Are they not cooperating with you?"

Oh boy. I sighed.

"Well...actually, no. Honestly, we didn't want to mention it. I know you can make a call and fix this—"

"And I shall," he said. "As soon as we conclude our meeting."

This would no doubt be a mixed blessing. "Thank you."

"Our daughter's well-being is all that matters. This is no time for pettiness."

"Agreed," I said. I searched for the right words to break the news of Kent's pregnancy. It made no sense to come back tomorrow. Nate and I had discussed it on the drive across town. I hadn't had enough time to figure out how to make this easier. Likely there would never be enough time to work that out.

Nate must have sensed my hesitation.

"We do have some more information to share with you," Nate said. "This may not be welcome news."

Mr. and Mrs. Heyward looked at him expectantly.

Nate leaned forwards, his face solemn. He spread his hands wide. "In the course of our investigation, we came across a piece of personal information about Kent that we are assuming you are not aware of."

Two creased foreheads looked back at us.

"Kent is expecting a baby," Nate said, his voice soft.

Colton Heyward blinked rapidly.

Mrs. Heyward gasped, flattened both hands at the base of her throat.

"*What?*" Colton Heyward asked.

Very gently I said, "We learned from Matt Thomas that Kent is expecting." While this was not the first place we'd heard the news, I was not about to tell my clients a Civil War-era debutante had told me through my guardian spirit.

"I can't believe it," Mr. Heyward said. "I *don't* believe it. You can't take his word for something like that."

"She didn't tell me," Mrs. Heyward said.

"Virginia, for goodness sake, we can't take this seriously."

I said, "Ansley confirmed it. I suspect Kent was nervous to tell you because of the tension regarding her relationship with Matt."

They both fell silent and stared at us. Finally, Colton Heyward said, "The fact that he withheld this is very suspicious."

"I was afraid you might feel that way," I said.

"That's what they've been arguing about," Virginia said.

"They've been arguing?" Colton Heyward looked at his wife.

"Yes," she said. "I didn't say anything because I knew you'd think it just confirmed what you already thought—that he'd hurt her."

Colton worked his jaw. He looked from me to Nate, his face hot with controlled anger. "Do you have further news?"

I debated with myself for a long moment. "I don't think this is related, but I did learn that Ansley was at Matt Thomas's house the night Kent disappeared. They're all friends, and as Kent had other plans, Ansley was there to visit with Matt."

"But he was working." Mrs. Heyward's brow creased.

"Yes," I said. "Ansley took an early ferry and waited for him to get off work. They spent some time together, and she stayed in the guest room as the ferry service back to Stella Maris stops at midnight."

"I see," said Mrs. Heyward, disappointment in her voice.

"So do I." Mr. Heyward appeared both livid and satisfied that he had proof Matt was not to be trusted.

Nate said, "I think it's important we don't jump to conclusions."

"Have you shared this information with the police?" Mr. Heyward asked.

"No," I said. "As Kent's condition is of a personal nature, and Ansley's visit isn't evidence of anything, we haven't. Unless we come across direct evidence, like the car, we bring everything to you. You are our clients."

Mr. Heyward nodded. "I appreciate your discretion. My wife and I will discuss this. However, I'm inclined to share every shred of information with the police. Just as I want them to share what they have with you."

"Whatever you decide. We're still working on several angles." We had discussed it again, and still both felt we were better off not sharing information on Peyton and Peter and their nefarious pursuits with Colton Heyward. It left us too exposed. I brushed Nate's leg. We both rose.

"We'll be in touch as soon as we have anything else," I said.

Mr. and Mrs. Heyward stood.

"Thank you," said Mrs. Heyward. "You've given us more information in just a few days than we've had in a month. Thank you." Her eyes told her story. She was clinging to every scrap of news as somehow proof her daughter would be coming home.

We headed back to Nate's hotel room. He needed to finish the documentation on Peyton and Peter's suspicious activities and cohorts before we met with Sonny. Since Kent wasn't Sonny's case, he likely wouldn't be tied up long at Magnolia Cemetery. I stepped out to the courtyard to call him while Nate worked.

"We have some information for you," I said when Sonny answered the phone. The courtyard was empty. I settled into a chair in the far left corner, my back to the planting bed that bordered the garden wall.

"For me? This isn't my case. And you've done enough for one day, really."

"You're welcome," I said, perhaps a tad sarcastically.

"I meant what I said. You did real good. It's just...I hate to see the shit storm Jenkins and Bissell are going to have to deal with because you found that car and they didn't."

"I played a hunch, got lucky. Anyway, this other thing may not be related to Kent. It's something we stumbled across along the way."

"All right. Kudu's got live music tonight. Not the best place for talking. Where do you want to meet?"

"How about Bin 152? I'm feeling like some prosciutto, a few creamy cheeses, and a glass of pinot noir. It'll be quiet there on a Sunday night."

"That's fine. What time?"

It was nearly six-thirty. "How about eight?"

"See you there."

It was a nice evening. No use in me rushing back upstairs to look over Nate's shoulder. I relaxed and let my mind drift. Huge crape myrtles and live oaks shaded the courtyard. The pool called to me, but I didn't have time for a swim. It had been a long day. Things were happening faster than I could properly analyze them. While it was possible Kent had dumped her car like I'd suggested to Mr. and Mrs. Heyward, it was more likely she would've simply dropped it at the airport or in a Walmart parking lot if she were ditching it so she couldn't be tracked. I hadn't wanted to give them false hope, but at the same time, there was no sense in having them believe the worst until we knew it for a fact.

The door to the hotel lobby opened and closed. Two hulk-like figures ambled my way. One was Caucasian, the other of African descent. Both wore caps low on their heads, obscuring their faces. They were dressed in jeans and t-shirts with long-sleeved collared shirts over the top, long tails hanging out. My skin tingled and my heart picked up its pace to a trot.

I hadn't brought my purse outside with me. No gun, no Taser, no pepper spray. *Sonavabitch.* All I had was my phone. I reached for it to shoot Nate a quick text.

"Thas jus rude," said the white hulk. They stopped on either side of the table, effectively boxing me into the corner.

"Your mamma din't teach you no better than to text when folks are right in front of you, tryin' to conversate?" said his friend.

I laid the phone down, smiled, and tried to keep my tone light. "I wasn't aware you gentlemen wished to speak with me. What can I do for you?"

They stepped closer.

My claustrophobia kicked into high gear.

"It's not what you can do for us," said black thug.

"We're here to do you a favor," said white thug.

"Do tell?" I said.

"Thas right," said black thug. "See, you're fixin' to get yosef hurt."

White thug pulled a very large automatic weapon from the back of his jeans. He didn't point it at me. He just held it with one hand and stroked it with the other. "We jus wanna help you stay safe."

I licked my lips, steadied my breathing. "How's that?"

"You've been stickin' your nose where it don' belong," said black thug. "Walk away. We done tried sending you a nice, gentle warnin'.""

These thugs had sent the snake? Who did they belong to? "Just so I'm clear, because, you know, my nose has been lots of places lately, where specifically do I need to keep it away from?"

The thugs looked at each other.

"Shee-it," said black thug.

White thug smiled, his face shining with pure evil. "Watch yourself, sweet thang. We don' have to be nice to you. We ain't paid to be nice, you feel me?"

I nodded.

"Just keep your nose outa Bounetheau business, and it might stay above ground a while longer," said black thug.

"Fair enough." I held my hands up in surrender. "So, you want me to stop looking for Kent Heyward?"

White thug scowled at me. "We don' care nothin' about you hunting for that girl. Jus keep out the Bounetheaus' private business. It ain't got nothing to do with her."

"Got it," I said. But I so did not get it. Nate had been poking around the Bounetheaus, not me. And these hoodlums hadn't said word one about Nate or his nose.

"Now, we gone go back inside," said black thug. "And you gone sit your pretty ass right there for at least ten minutes before you get up. Got it?"

"Got it," I said.

"This gone be the last warnin' you get, sweet thang. Third time you dead." White thug caressed my face with his gun. "After we have ourselves a party." He grinned like he was looking forward to that.

They backed away a few steps. White thug put his gun back in his jeans and pulled his shirt down over it. They turned and walked back towards the hotel door.

I gasped for breath but didn't move. As I watched them retreat, I memorized as many details as I could. Their shoes were wrong. Both of them wore loafers too nice for the rest of their look. Their swagger shifted to a smooth stride. Something was off. They disappeared inside the hotel.

I replayed the scene in my head. I couldn't be sure, but I had a strong suspicion these were the men I'd seen on the ferry Friday morning. They'd seemed heftier this evening, and they were dressed very differently. But I'd bet money those were the same shoes.

After I was sure ten minutes had passed, I picked up my phone and went inside. My head swiveled in every direction. The lobby was deserted except for an older couple looking at brochures and the cheerful desk clerk.

She smiled and said, "Have a good evening."

I nodded and walked towards the elevator.

Once I calmed down, I realized I'd never been in any danger. Colleen hadn't showed. Or maybe she was making a point. Nate was not one bit amused by the incident, nor mollified by my protestations that these were wannabe gangsters. He held forth on the matter during our eight-tenths-of-a-mile walk to Bin 152, alternately checking who was around us on the sidewalk. Nate was on high alert, agitated. Sonny waited at the table by the front left window.

"Light staff tonight," he said. "Order at the bar and they'll bring it out."

Nate and I glanced at the menu. He went to the bar and made short work of placing our order. I settled into a chair across from Sonny. Nate took the chair in the middle, facing the street.

"Any news on the car?" Nate asked. He seemed to be settling down a bit.

Sonny looked at him for a long moment.

"Not my case. Only thing I heard is that it's wiped clean inside. No prints anywhere."

"That's not encouraging," said Nate.

"She could have done that to throw us off." I realized immediately how outlandish that sounded. I was clinging to hope we'd find Kent alive.

Nate nodded in my direction but looked at Sonny. "She had a scare a little while ago," he said by way of explaining my irrational statement.

Sonny raised his eyebrows.

We started with Peyton and Peter, pausing when a waiter delivered wine, bread, and an array of meats and cheeses. Then we dug in and took turns talking and eating. Finally, I told Sonny what had happened in the courtyard at the hotel right after I'd spoken to him.

"Can you describe these guys at all aside from their clothes and skin color?" Sonny asked.

"They weren't right," I said.

"Come again?" Sonny said.

"First, they both had really short hair, because not one strand of it was visible under their ball caps."

Sonny shrugged. "It's Charleston. It's hot here. Not all criminals have long scraggly hair."

"I'll give you that, but...Did you ever see that movie with Steve Martin and Queen Latifah? *Bringing Down the House*?"

The menfolk looked at each other and then back at me. "No," they both said.

"Okay, there's this scene in it where Steve Martin tries to go all gangster-homeboy, but he's horrible at it."

"You're saying these were inexperienced criminals?" Nate asked. "Because you were pretty shook up not an hour ago. You don't shake up easy."

"Fine. I'll admit, I was scared out of my mind at the time. They took me by surprise. In hindsight, I think they were trying a little too hard to sound like uneducated thugs. And their shoes were totally wrong. They were businessmen shoes—polished loafers."

"But one of them threatened you with a gun and they told you they'd kill you if you didn't stop nosing around the Bounetheaus. Do I have that right?" Sonny asked.

I sighed. "Yes."

Nate said, "So, you think they are a legitimate threat, just not uneducated."

"Yes. And I think they were trying to disguise their appearance."

"You think maybe you've seen them before?" Nate asked.

"I can't be positive," I said. "But I think they were on the nine o'clock ferry leaving Stella Maris Friday morning. I saw two guys I didn't recognize, and they didn't look like tourists. *Them* I snapped a photo of." I pulled it up on my iPhone and texted it to Nate and Sonny. "See? They're dressed much nicer. No ball caps. They don't seem as large...Shit, the shoes aren't in the photo." I sipped my pinot noir.

"Padding is an easy thing to add," said Nate. "But why would they do that?"

I shrugged. "Maybe they're afraid I'll recognize them in a different context?"

"Well, if you do, give me a shout and I'll come pick 'em up." Sonny said, "So you think Peyton and Peter Bounetheau are importing and exporting things not allowed by state and/or federal laws?"

"That would be my guess," Nate said. "The security they have around that warehouse is too ridiculous to be anything legitimate."

"And you think Kent stumbled across their operations and they did away with her?" Sonny asked.

"It's possible," I said. "But right now we're working with several other narratives. Bottom line, Peyton and Peter Bounetheau are likely doing something illegal, probably drug related. The people they're working with live in an area known for violent drug crime. This is not an investigation for private investigators. If you go after them for whatever else they're up to and happen to run across evidence linking them to Kent's disappearance, well, you've solved both cases."

"And we'll keep working on every other possibility until we know for sure what's happened to Kent," Nate said.

"Only here's where things get fuzzy," I said. "The thugs sent me a rattlesnake Friday afternoon. Nate didn't snoop around the twins' warehouse until Saturday night. And it was me the pretend hoodlums came to warn, not Nate."

"They probably know you're partners—work together," Sonny said.

"But they didn't even mention him. And what about the snake—the timing of the delivery?" I asked.

"You're thinking your visitors this evening were upset about something you did before Friday, and continued to do even after the snake was delivered?" Nate asked.

"I think that has to be the case," I said.

"That makes no sense," Nate said. "We haven't investigated any other Bounetheau family member or their interests."

"I think maybe I did something to make Charlotte and her family, or maybe even Abigail or C.C. Bounetheau, feel threatened," I said. "They're not the ones who hired me."

"So you're going to just keep right on doing whatever you've been doing?" Sonny asked.

"Of course," I said. "I'll just make sure I take Sig with me everywhere I go." My Sig Sauer nine millimeter went by Sig, after an imaginary childhood friend.

"That's not all you're taking with you everywhere you go," Nate said.

"What?"

"You'll be sticking close to me until this is over," Nate said.

"I think that's smart," said Sonny.

"I do not need a babysitter," I said, thinking how messed up it was I had to stand on principle here because I wanted to stick as close to Nate as allowed by the laws of biology, physics, et cetera.

"Liz, for once will you be reasonable?" Nate said.

"You know who you sound like? You sound exactly like Blake Talbot," I said, as if I'd compared him to a sidewalk soapbox preacher.

Nate and Sonny both stared at me.

Sonny said, "I'll look into what the Bounetheau twins are up to." He turned to Nate, patted the folder of documentation. "Thanks for this."

"I hope it helps," said Nate.

"Saves me a lot of time. 'Preciate it. I'll report this as a lead from a confidential informant."

"Thanks for keeping us out of it," Nate said.

Sonny nodded. "I'll start rattling that cage, see who gets riled. If the guys who threatened Liz tonight are connected to the twins, I'll give them something else to worry about."

"I'm telling y'all, those guys were not connected to Peyton and Peter," I said.

"When did you first meet with Mrs. Heyward, her mother, her sister, and the twins?" Nate asked.

"Friday afternoon at two."

Nate said, "I think Peyton and Peter anticipated you might run across their illegal business as soon as they heard Colton Heyward planned to hire you. Likely started having you followed as soon as you left the Heyward house on Thursday—or before. Then, when you asked them what they did for a living Friday, they got agitated."

I pondered that. "You think they ordered that snake up for delivery as soon as I left?"

"I think that makes more sense than anything else," Nate said. "And then Saturday I started poking around their warehouse. Maybe someone saw me. They followed me back to you. Knew the best way to threaten me was through you. Kill two birds with one stone."

"Makes sense to me," Sonny said.

I stared at my wine glass, swirled the wine. "Maybe that's how it went."

"One other thing y'all might not have considered given everything that's happened this evening," Sonny said.

We both looked at him.

"Now that car's been found, Jenkins and Bissell will be under a lot of pressure to find the Heyward girl. Case looks a lot more like a homicide now than it did before. Just be aware your case isn't on our back burner anymore."

SEVENTEEN

Outside the restaurant, the fall night air felt cool but pleasant. The jitters I'd had earlier in the wake of my encounter with the two hoodlums had evaporated. I was still kicking myself for leaving my purse in Nate's room and myself vulnerable, but even that irritation was fading on the breeze. It had been a long and eventful day. Discovering Kent's car was a major break. But it still left open several explanations for what had become of Kent. I was at that point where I needed to let my subconscious work on the problem for a while.

"Let's cut across Queen and go back up Meeting," I said. The Hampton Inn occupied the corner of Meeting and John Street. King and Meeting ran parallel to each other all the way from the upper neck of the peninsula to White Point Gardens at the tip.

"As you wish," said Nate.

"My second three favorite words." So much remained unsettled between us. Screw it. Life was too short for games. I smiled at him and reached for his hand.

He didn't resist, just shook his head with a wry smile.

We turned left onto Queen. I studied the parking garage across the street. "That's where the group Kent was supposed to meet parked. Could've been where she was headed when she left home. Impossible to know, really. She could've looked for street parking, or changed her mind and gone somewhere else altogether." So much for giving it to my subconscious.

"Or," Nate said, "she could've planned another destination all along."

"I struggle with the idea of Kent having this elaborate scheme she didn't tell anyone about—not even her best friend."

"Maybe she knew her best friend had inappropriate thoughts about her guy. That sort of thing typically makes a woman behave unpredictably."

"You know a lot about women, do you?"

"I study up on things I'm interested in and things I'm afraid of. Women are both."

I laughed. One of the things I loved best about Nate was how he made me laugh. We passed the Elliott House Inn. "But seriously, you don't believe Kent ditched her car in a marsh at a cemetery and left town any more than I do."

Nate sighed, "No, I do not. At this point, I believe the most likely scenario is that she was the victim of an unfortunate accident."

"An accident?"

"I'm afraid she may have accidentally stumbled across her uncles' criminal enterprise, and, while I'm sure they regretted such a distasteful thing, they had no choice but to have their associates deal with the problem. That's not to say we shouldn't continue to explore all other alternatives like we planned. I'm just telling you how I see it right now."

"Yeah, that's looking likely to me, too." We passed Husk and Poogan's Porch on our left. "Did you know there's a ghost in Poogan's?" The restaurant occupied a Victorian home built in 1888.

"Is that a fact?" Nate asked.

"Absolutely," I said. "Two sisters, Zoe and Liz St. Amand lived in the house for years. Zoe, they say, went mad from grief after her sister died. She fell down the steps and died in the house—Zoe, I mean. Sometimes she shows up in photographs as a green misty figure. Sometimes she pops into the lady's room upstairs. Occasionally she plays practical jokes on the kitchen staff. Poogan was her dog. His ghost still runs around the porch and yard."

"Well, now, that tale does make for entertaining stories for the tourists, I suppose," said Nate.

"You don't believe in ghosts?"

"I haven't given the matter much thought." He tilted his head, pushed his lips out, then in, as though in careful consideration. "No, I don't guess I do."

"I can tell you for an absolute certainty that ghosts—and all manner of supernatural creatures—are all around us."

"Can you now?"

"I can."

"Have you ever seen a ghost?"

"Maybe." I smiled up at him. "Charleston is a hotbed of supernatural activity. Haven't you heard?" I glanced over his shoulder at the pink masonry building with white carved window trim and wrought iron balconies. The Mills House occupied a large piece of real estate on a corner of Queen and Meeting. "Interesting."

"What?"

"Evan Ingle missed the ferry home the night Kent disappeared. And he'd been drinking. He stayed at the John Rutledge House Inn on Broad Street. But the Elliott House and Mills House were right around the corner."

Nate shrugged. "Maybe he likes Rutledge House."

"He did say he stayed in Charleston often. Maybe that's just his regular place."

"Now about these ghosts..." Nate said. We turned the corner and headed up Meeting Street.

"We could take a stroll through the graveyard up here at the Circular Church. We'll walk right past it. Probably a few ghosts out and about."

"I'd say we've seen all the graveyards we need to for one day."

"You're right about that. It's after ten, anyway. By the time we get back to the hotel, I probably need to head on back to the ferry dock."

"Are you sure you're okay to drive?"

"I only had two glasses of wine, along with plenty of food. And we're walking. I'm fine, really."

"Why don't you stay with me tonight?" he asked, like he was just stating the most logical course of action.

I studied his face for a clue as to whether he wanted me to stay because he thought I'd had too much to drink, he was trying to keep me close because of a perceived threat, or if possibly he just wanted my company.

He gave me his poker face—relaxed, impossible to read.

Finally, I said, "I think that will just complicate things more. You seemed unaccountably lukewarm this morning when I suggested we revisit dividing our time between here and Greenville."

"It's not that."

I waited for him to elaborate, but he fell silent. I was not going to chase this man. I loved him, true and strong. But I was all done with pining after men who didn't want me, or didn't want me enough. It was time one of them fought for me. I had offered to meet him halfway. His response was to tell me to sleep on it. The next move was his, and he was going to have to do better than *why don't you stay with me tonight.* A whole lot better.

A soft voice inside my head whispered, *maybe he wants you to fight for him. He's suffering under the wrong-headed assumption that he means less to me than his brother did. Than Michael did.*

I rubbed my temple. I really did need to sleep on all of that. Perhaps I did have something to prove. For tonight, I moved things back to safer ground. "Did you get a chance to talk to Evan's artist buddies?"

"In fact, I did. The cemetery drama made me forget. I talked to each of them over the phone. His story checks out."

"Well, at least that's one more thing we can check off our list."

We walked in silence for a while, each to our own thoughts. As we approached Hasell Street, I looked across Meeting at FIG. The restaurant was closed on Sunday night.

"Have you ever eaten there?" Nate asked.

"Twice. The food is fabulous."

"I've never been. Want to go tomorrow night? We can check out Matt in his work environment, have a nice meal at the same time."

"You'll never get a reservation on this short a notice, even on a Monday night."

"Well, how about this? Will you have dinner with me tomorrow evening? If I can get a reservation, we'll go to FIG. If I can't, we'll seek nourishment elsewhere."

"I'd like that." I watched the sidewalk in front of me, in part because I suddenly felt shy with him, but mostly because it's best to watch your step on Charleston sidewalks, many of which were constructed of slabs of stone or brick, and you'd trip if you weren't careful.

"All right then." Nate smiled.

It hit me then.

"Oh, no."

"What's wrong?"

"We told Mr. and Mrs. Heyward about Kent's car, but I didn't tell Matt."

"Liz, he's not our client. And he's one of a few likely suspects."

"Truly, I don't think he hurt Kent. And I don't want him hearing this on the news. Or worse, when the police are at his door because Colton Heyward got his way."

"What if you're wrong, and when you tell him he runs?"

"You're right. I can't tell him or Ansley. But it just feels wrong."

"Part of the job, Slugger."

"I know." Damnation.

We walked on in silence. When we reached the hotel entrance, I slid my hand out of his, walked another step and turned to face him. "I'll talk to you tomorrow."

"You sure I can't talk you into stayin'?"

"Thanks, but I need to go see about Rhett." There were other reasons I needed to leave, but that one would do just fine.

"I'll walk you to your car." Both his face and his tone were neutral.

"That's not necessary." All that neutrality was making me cranky.

"All the same."

"Nate. Stop it. I can take care of myself."

"Okay, Slugger." He backed off easier than I expected. "Since we just handed off Peyton and Peter, tomorrow I'll do some digging into Charlotte and Bennett Pinckney and their brood. Just to check them off the list."

"All right," I nodded. "Just be careful. Charlotte is a Bounetheau. Goodnight." I held his eyes with mine for a moment, trying to read what was there, then turned to go.

I arrived just as the ferry began loading for the last trip of the evening to Stella Maris. I pulled the Escape onto the ferry, got out of the car, and slammed the door. Hands on my hips, I watched as Nate parked his Explorer behind me. He took his time getting out. He closed the door behind him and grinned. "You need a jacket?"

"I have one in the car, thank you." I put as much ice in my tone as I could manage. "You weren't even trying to hide the fact that you were following me home."

"Didn't see the point. You're pretty good at spotting a tail. You know my car." He spread his hands wide, shrugged.

"So, when you couldn't talk me into staying with you, you decided you'd just follow me right on home, stay at my house tonight?" This whole situation was maddening. I wanted him to stay with me—for the right reasons. Not because he thought I needed him to keep an eye on me.

"That's about the size of it."

"And what if I decide I'm not receiving overnight guests?"

"You are genetically incapable of that grievous a lapse in manners. To make me sleep on the porch—"

"Precisely what makes you think I'd allow you to sleep on my porch?"

"Well, darlin', you'd pretty much have to stay up all night to stop me. Do you object to the idea of my presence so strenuously you'd do such a thing?"

He had me there. I was plenty mad, but I wasn't going to stand guard to keep him away. Besides that, he had a key and the alarm codes. As soon as I was asleep he could come inside if he wanted to. "Fine. You can sleep in the guest room." I opened the back door of my car, grabbed my jacket, slammed the door, and climbed the stairs to the top deck of the ferry.

The ferry pulled away from the dock. I snuggled into my jacket and stood at the rail, gazing at the stars. The evening air was cold on my cheeks as the boat picked up speed.

A few minutes later, Nate walked up to the rail beside me. "I remember another night we were up here on this deck enjoying one another's company. As I recall, we were rudely interrupted."

"I'm still mad at you," I said.

"Why, because I want to make sure you're safe?"

"Because you're not trusting me to take care of myself. You used to do that—when we were partners and friends, but not lovers."

"Maybe I was just more careful about letting on how much I worried."

"You've never trusted me to take care of myself?"

He sighed.

"Let's just say I'm a big believer in contingency planning and safety in numbers. And, to be fair, most days armed criminals don't threaten you with death outright."

He wasn't wrong. And if the situation were reversed, I'd want to keep him close. We passed the rest of the ferry ride in something approaching companionable silence.

When I opened the garage door, Rhett came bounding out to greet me. I baby-talked him a bit and scratched his belly, then climbed the stairs to the mudroom and scooped out some kibble. I heard Nate in the kitchen.

"I'm going up to change," I said as I passed through.

He poured two fingers of bourbon over ice in a rocks glass. "I'll be out on the deck."

I went through my normal bedtime routine. The warm water in the shower felt like heaven. I tried to scrub the day away. I washed and conditioned my hair, and combed it out to air dry. I slathered myself with lavender lotion. Then I pulled on my favorite orange cotton pajama pants with yellow flowers and a matching yellow tank. Because I tend to take a while getting ready for bed, I figured Nate had come upstairs. I slipped down the hall and checked the guest bedroom. No sign of him. I grabbed a sweatshirt, slipped into my fleece-lined ballet slippers and went to investigate.

As I reached the door leading onto the deck, I could see Nate in one of the Adirondack chairs. The sight made me smile. I paused to enjoy it for a moment. Rhett was curled up at his feet. The bottle of bourbon was on the table between the two chairs. I could hear Nate talking. He was gesturing with his left hand and periodically delivering the glass of bourbon to his lips with his right.

"You know what I mean, don't you?" Nate was apparently addressing Rhett.

Rhett cocked his head, his tongue hanging out in a sloppy grin.

Deciding to join the party, I opened the door and walked out.

"Shhh," Nate said.

"What?" I whispered.

"Nothing." Was his voice slurred just a bit?

"Were you talking to Rhett?"

"Yep. Man to man."

Moonlight bathed us, casting its magic over the water and up onto the deck, framing the moment. I sat in the chair beside him. "I see. How much bourbon have you had?"

"Why? I'm not driving anywhere tonight."

"Fair enough." The sound of the moon-driven surf and the salt air eased the last of the tension out of me. "Are you trying to drink me off your mind?"

"Slugger, there is not enough bourbon in Kentucky."

"I don't understand you," I said. "I offer to do exactly what you have asked me for two years to do—divide our time between here and Greenville so we can be together—and you immediately start pulling away. And yet, here you sit, drinking and talking to the dog like I've kicked you to the curb. Can you explain that to me?"

"Yesss. I can." He nodded his golden head emphatically.

I smothered a grin. "Well then, by all means, please proceed."

He drained his glass and poured in two more fingers. He studied the caramel-colored liquid. "I am an ass."

"Do tell?"

"Yes. Of the highest order." He raised his glass, as if toasting the notion.

Rhett barked.

"See?" Nate gestured at Rhett, then nodded. "He knows."

"Could you elaborate?" I turned in my chair to face him directly.

"Yesss. You see, Slugger, I *know* how much this island means to you. Your family is here. You said it yourself. This is your place in the world."

"And Greenville is yours. I get that." I kept my voice gentle. He was clearly in a vulnerable state.

"Ahh. But there's the rub." He gestured dramatically.

"The rub?"

"See, as long as you wouldn't live there with me, at least part-time, it felt like you didn't love me the way you loved Michael. I know you never loved Scott—not really. Hell, how could you. But you were you, and my brother is smooth, I'll give him that. I digress.

"When you agreed to a split-residency, I realized the truth." He examined the contents of his glass.

"And that is?"

"You must really love me if you're willing to give up the things that are even more precious to you now because you spent so much time away. People who mean the most to you—aside from me and Rhett here—part of the time. And then I just felt like an ass for asking you to do that."

"Nate—"

"Because I like Greenville, don't get me wrong. It's been home my whole life. But when you're not there, it's just a pretty town where things are familiar, nothing more. It's not like I have family keeping me there. Mom and Dad are in Florida most of the time. You know we're not close. It's not like you and your family. You have the kind of family everyone wants."

I was tearing up, so I let him keep talking.

"And I was ready to take that away from you, just to make you prove you loved me. What kind of an ass does that? And then I started worrying, am I really just afraid you'll belong more to your family—to this island—than to me if we live here all the time? And that's even more messed up." He looked at me, all walls down, storms in his beautiful blue eyes.

"Oh, sweetheart, that's just crazy talk."

I reached out and touched his cheek with the backs of my fingers.

"Is it? Are you sure?" His tone begged me to convince him.

"Yeah. There's plenty of me to go around."

I tried putting an arm around him, rubbing his arm with the other, but he was too far away.

"I'm an ass," he confessed to the moon.

I took the glass out of his hand and put it on the table. Then I climbed into his lap. "You are the furthest possible thing from an ass."

Rhett yawned, snorted, stood and left, just like a child who didn't want to watch his parents cuddle.

"Well, that is a hell of a thing." Nate watched him leave. He whipped his head back around. "No." He shook his head emphatically. "See...I'm an—"

I put two fingers over his lips. "Shhh." I brushed a lock of hair off his forehead with my other hand. My eyes captured his and he drank me in like he was dying of thirst. "We can settle the details tomorrow."

He kissed my fingers. "No need. I've already decided. I'm going to sell my condo and—"

"I guess I'm going to have to distract you from this topic of conversation."

His eyes turned a deeper shade of blue. "I do like the sound of that."

I gave him a slow smile full of promises. Then I leaned in and kissed his neck just below his ear and worked my way down from there. I inhaled his scent. "I just want to breathe you in. Sweet reason, how I've missed you."

He wrapped his long arms around me. His mouth found mine and he kissed me soft and slow.

He pulled back, touched his forehead to mine. "Not nearly as much as I've missed you. I've all but screwed this up. But I'm going to make it right. Just give me a chance."

"All I need to know is that you love me, and you're willing to fight for us."

He kissed me again, deeper. "I love you so much it scares me half to death."

"I love you back." Moonstruck and crazy for each other, we floated, lost in each other's eyes. Then, our lips met and we devoured each other. Tasting, holding, touching, rocking.

Nate pulled back. "Slugger?"

"Umm-hmm?"

"I'm hoping you've changed your mind on that whole guest room policy."

I laughed out loud. "Do tell?"

Based on the amount of bourbon he'd had, and given the angle of the chair, it was nothing short of impressive that he could stand while holding me against his chest and carry me inside and up the stairs to my room. But he did, without dropping me once.

EIGHTEEN

The three of us ran together the next morning, Nate, Rhett, and me. I was still drunk from the night before, and I hadn't had a drop to drink. I was positively giddy and had to speak to myself sternly to get my head back into the case. Realistically, we both leaned towards Peyton and Peter as the most likely culprits in Kent's disappearance, and we'd agreed we weren't going to pursue that avenue of investigation. We were at the point of running down the remaining scenarios to eliminate them. It's frustrating when you face accepting you may not be able to solve a case, but it happens.

Miraculously, Nate wasn't hungover. While we ran, I told Nate about what I'd found at Magnolia Cemetery before I'd found Kent's Mini Cooper—Talitha Ingle, her brother, and Talitha's child Eva, who'd been Evan's twin. So much had happened in the last twenty-four hours, I hadn't had a chance to get into any of that.

"That's all very intriguing," he said, "but I don't understand the connection to Kent's disappearance."

"I don't know for certain there is one," I said. "But there's a story there. We run down every lead, right? Lookit, I know we can't bill Colton Heyward unless I can find a connection. What I'm saying is, while you're verifying that Charlotte, her husband, and their offspring are upstanding citizens, maybe I could run with this just a little ways."

Nate shrugged. "I can't see any harm in that."

"You know how when I put a puzzle together, I always want all the edge pieces together first? I feel like we're missing edge pieces. This could be one of them. It's a gut thing."

"Seems to me we have enough 'edge pieces' for two perfectly workable theories of the crime: the Matt and/or Ansley narrative, or the Peyton and Peter narrative. That said, if your gut says there's something there, well, then, by all means, go with your gut. Just don't forget we're having dinner at seven."

"Like I would forget a date with such a handsome Southern gentleman. Hey, if you finish with Charlotte and her family, would you stop by Martech Agency—the place Kent worked? We haven't spoken to those folks yet, and I need a list of employees to profile. Could be there's yet another possibility we haven't considered—a workplace problem."

"Sure. I'll drop by. It's downtown, right?"

"Yeah. On Broad Street."

We'd run up to the chairs at the edge of the ocean. I pulled my shirt over my head.

"You sure the water's not too cold for a swim?"

I shrugged and unhooked my sports bra. "You don't have to come in if you don't want to." I continued undressing.

He took in the view. "That is so not fair." He slipped out of his shorts and pulled off his shoes and socks. By the time he was finished undressing, I was already running towards the water.

He caught up to me fast enough. "Hold on there just a minute." He wrapped his arms around me and pulled me to him.

"I'm going for a swim." I squealed and struggled to splash him with zero success.

"If you're going to lure me into the water, you're going to have to warm me up first. And likely after I get out."

Talitha Ingle's home wasn't listed with a realtor. She'd only passed two months ago, so that wasn't a surprise. As far as I could tell, Evan was her sole surviving relative. He would have to either hire someone to go through her things or do it himself. Perhaps he wasn't ready to face that yet. Whatever the case, it worked in my favor.

Since I planned on breaking and entering in broad daylight, even though I had a very strong pretext as a realtor, I decided to go incognito. I tucked my hair under a chin-length brunette wig, slipped in brown contacts, and went trés dramatic with the eye makeup.

My black Ann Taylor suit, a cute pair of Kate Spade polka-dot pumps, and my black tote completed my eager realtor look. In all likelihood, any neighbors who happened to be at home would be expecting a realtor.

I snapped a selfie and printed out a few business cards with the photo, identifying me as Laura Beth St. Vincent, a realtor with an agency I made up out of whole cloth and named Lowcountry Homes. If I ran across any of the neighbors, I'd show them my card and make a pretense of offering it, but then make sure they didn't leave with one. I had a story ready that involved me getting them a folder full of detailed information which would include a card in the mail that very day.

Gram's silver Cadillac convertible, which I'd held on to for sentimental reasons and occasions such as these, would make the perfect realtor car.

The modest brick bungalow on Colleton Drive was in an established neighborhood off Savannah Highway, not much more than a half mile on the other side of the Ashley River Bridge. I drove through the neighborhood a few times, looking for joggers, walkers, mothers with strollers, et cetera, just so I'd be aware of them. But the streets were quiet. Few cars were parked in the drives. Most of the neighborhood appeared to be at work that Monday morning. I pulled to the curb right in front of Talitha's house. A huge loblolly pine took up most of the front yard.

I took photos of the exterior, as many realtors would. Some, like the one I'd hired in Greenville to sell my loft, would send out a professional photographer later. But she'd take her own shots for reference in the meantime. This gave me a good excuse to walk all the way around the house, looking for signs of a security system. There didn't appear to be one.

Back out front, I strode purposefully up the walkway, clipboard in hand. At the foot of the brick porch steps, I stopped to make notes just in case any of the neighbors were at home and happened to look out the window. Once on the porch, I set my tote, clipboard and phone by the door. Discreetly, I slipped on latex gloves, shielding them from view with my body. I had a standard door key in my pocket just in case someone approached. I would pretend someone had given me the wrong key, or perhaps the lock was sticking. Meanwhile, I pulled out my lock pick set.

Talitha Ingle had not been particularly security conscious. The lock took less than a minute. I gathered my belongings and went inside, closing the door behind me. The front door opened into a small living room.

It was neat and decorated in a traditional but not overly formal style. The stale air made me wrinkle my nose. A layer of dust coated the tabletops.

I toured the house. It was maybe fourteen hundred square feet, no more. Three bedrooms, one bath, the living room, a galley kitchen, and a dining room. One of the bedrooms had clearly been Talitha's. It was decorated in cream and pale greens, a pile of accent pillows on the bed. The second bedroom must have been Evan's up until he'd left home. Here browns and darker greens provided a backdrop for sports trophies and framed paintings with his signature, from childish preschool-era efforts which were far better than anything I would ever create to a marsh landscape I'd guess he'd painted much more recently. The style was different from anything I'd seen in his gallery, much closer to impressionist than abstract.

The third bedroom held a sewing machine and a table I'd guess was used for cutting and the like—I'd never been one for the needle arts—and a desk and file cabinet. The blinds were closed. I tried the light switch. The electricity was on. That would be helpful.

Two files lay on top of the file cabinet, papers spilling out of three sides as though they'd been recently rifled through and dropped there carelessly. One was labeled "Insurance." I flipped through it and found the usual home and auto policies, and one for long-term care for Talitha. I didn't find a life insurance policy, but if Evan had gone through his mother's papers looking for a life insurance policy, perhaps he'd found it and taken it with him.

The second folder was labeled "Banking." The bottom of this folder had flattened out, like it had once held substantially more than it did now. Statements for a savings account at First Federal went all the way back to 1971. Deposits of $57.85 were made weekly for a year, then they increased to $68.47. How old was Talitha then? I pulled out my iPad and opened her profile. She was born in 1955, so these were likely paychecks from jobs she'd held in high school.

I laid my iPad on top of the desk and opened the top file cabinet drawer. Talitha had kept excellent records. There was an "Employment" folder with documentation of jobs going back to 1971 when she got her first job at the Piggly Wiggly.

After high school, she'd worked eight years at Medical University of South Carolina as a data entry clerk before quitting her job in March of

1981 and moving to Greenville, where she'd held a part-time job at Greenville Memorial.

Why had she moved to Greenville? I did some quick math. She would've been pregnant then. It made no sense. Her parents were already deceased, so she wouldn't fear their wrath because she was an unwed mother. Back then, pregnancy would've been a pre-existing condition. Her insurance in Charleston would likely have covered her expenses, but a part-time job she'd gotten after she was pregnant? Not likely.

The last piece of paper in Talitha's employment file was a letter that had apparently been enclosed with her last paycheck from Greenville Memorial. It had been mailed to Talitha in Charleston in November 1981. Had she left that job abruptly as well? And was that the last job she'd ever held? How had she lived?

I turned back to the bank statements, flipping through the pages. When Talitha went to work at Medical University of South Carolina, she'd opened a checking account. There were statements for every month through March 1981, but nothing more recent. The deposits appeared to be biweekly paychecks of $403.82. I pulled out my iPhone and did some quick calculations. Allowing for taxes, she'd been making somewhere in the neighborhood of $14,000 per year. Definitely not enough money to retire at the ripe old age of twenty-six and send her son to private school.

I checked the file cabinet for another folder with more recent banking or investment records, but with no luck. One by one, I checked the other files for anything that would shed light on how Talitha had lived since the twins had been born. Whoever the father was, he must have paid generous child support. Did Evan know who his father was?

I pulled up Evan's birth certificate again. The midwife's name was Aurora Luiz. Maybe she knew something. A quick check of the database I used to access DMV records showed thirty-five women with that name in the state. I'd have to run them down later and see if I could determine if one of them had delivered Evan and his sister.

According to the real property database, only two current nearby neighbors had been living here at the time Evan and Eva were born. The Mitchells, who lived a few doors down and across the street on Colleton Drive, and the Spencers, who lived on Tynte Street, just around the corner. I put the files back the way I'd found them and continued my search with Talitha's desk.

Two hours later, I'd gone through every room in the house and had come up with nothing. If Talitha had left clues to her past, someone— presumably Evan—had removed them from the house. Time to introduce myself to a few neighbors. Hopefully someone was home after all.

I gathered my belongings, turned out all the lights, and did a final walkthrough to make sure I'd left no trace that I'd been there. Then, I walked out, turned the knob lock, and pulled the door closed behind me. I slipped the latex gloves and iPad into my bag and my iPhone into my jacket pocket. Leaving my car parked in front of Talitha's house, I walked towards the Mitchells' house. The yard was neat, the brick house similar in style to Talitha's. I rang the bell and waited. A small dog went to barking—at least it sounded small.

"I'm a comin'," a woman's voice called from inside.

I smiled and waved enthusiastically when she pulled back a curtain near the door to take a look at me. The dog continued to bark.

She must have decided I didn't look dangerous, because she opened the door. "Mabel, be quiet." She looked from the white fluffy dog at her side to me. "Yes?" I pegged her as approaching eighty. Her hair was silver and permed within an inch of its life. The burgundy velour jogging suit and white tennis shoes she had on were perhaps used for walking. She seemed fit, her eyes sharp. Mabel sported a bow on top of her head.

"Good morning, how are you?" I offered her my brightest smile.

"Well, I can't complain. How are you?"

"I'm fine—thank you so much for asking. Ma'am, my name is Laura Beth St. Vincent. I'm a realtor, come to see about poor Mrs. Ingle's house." I pointed to my car, evidence of my story.

"I wondered when Evan would list it. I hope you get a good price for it. Helps everyone's property values."

"Indeed, it does. I was just trying to get a feel for the neighborhood. That helps me know which of my clients are a good fit. Ma'am, do you mind telling me...have you lived here very long?"

"Boyd and I bought this house right after we got married. I'm Sarah Mitchell. I've lived here sixty years come June."

"You must like it here, then, I guess." I widened my smile.

"Well, it's home. Of course I like it. Boyd passed on three years back. My sons would prefer me to move to an *assisted living* home." She made a noise and a face that let me know what she thought of that idea.

"Ungrateful scoundrels. The very idea. I don't need assistance. I'll leave when they carry me out in a box. That's all the *assistance* I'll require."

I chuckled. "You certainly seem capable of taking care of yourself. This looks like it would be a good neighborhood for walking."

"Oh, it is. Mabel and I walk every morning. Well, my goodness gracious, come in the house, why don't you? We don't need to stand here in the doorway flapping our gums." She stepped back and ushered me inside.

"Thank you so much. That's so sweet of you." I walked in and paused while she closed the door.

"Come on in the living room and sit down."

The living room was about the size of Talitha's. The décor was one I could only think of as country-beach. A blue-and-white plaid sofa and matching love seat, pine coffee table, and a recliner made up the seating area. A framed print of a beach scene hung over the sofa. Family photos and containers of seashells were everywhere.

The recliner sat in the far corner of the room, angled to get a good view of both the front window and the television. Mrs. Mitchell settled into the recliner, clearly her spot, and Mabel hopped into her lap. I sat on the end of the sofa nearest them.

"It's such a shame about Mrs. Ingle's accident. Did you know her?" I asked.

"Of course I knew her. Lived across the street from her all her life. That was her parents' house before her."

I kept my eyes on hers and slipped my hand into my jacket pocket to tap record on my voice memos app.

"I never had the pleasure, of course, but Evan is certainly a nice young man."

"Isn't he though? Such a sweet boy. Adored his mamma. *Adored* her. This like to broke his heart. They were all the family they had." She pressed her lips together and shook her head. "I remember the day she brought that baby home. She didn't know the first thing about how to tend to a newborn. I had to teach her everything. There wasn't anyone else to show her. Her parents died—another car accident if you can believe it—two years before that."

Brought him home? The birth certificate had indicated a home birth.

"How awful. I guess his father wasn't much help with changing diapers and all such as that."

"Hmmphf. Some father. I never laid eyes on him. Far as I know, neither did Evan. The daddy paid his child support regular, I'll say that for him. But that's all he ever did."

"What kind of man just ignores his own child?"

"Some man from Greenville. Talitha moved up there that spring and met him right off. Something went bad wrong. Talitha never did talk about it. She came home from up there with Evan when he was no more than a couple days old, and he was premature if I recall." She raised a finger to her brow.

"Mmm, mmm, mmm." I shook my head.

"It was a sad, sad time. Her brother Turner had just died—*another* car accident. Can you believe that? She brought him home to bury him. I kept Evan while she went to the funeral, if you could call it that. She didn't have the means for a proper service. It was just her and the preacher to say a few words at the gravesite."

I brought my hands to my face in a show of horror and waited to see if she had more to say. After a moment I lowered my hands and said, "For some reason, I thought Evan had a sister."

Mrs. Mitchell dipped her chin, tilted her head, and raised an eyebrow at me. "Sounds to me like maybe you and Evan have more than just a business relationship."

"I'm sorry?" Holy shit. I'd stepped in it.

"All those years, I never knew he'd had a twin sister. Poor little child didn't even live a day. I guess Talitha's heart was broken and she just couldn't talk about it. Must have buried the baby girl the same day she buried her brother. Evan never knew he had a sister, either. He and I both found out at the cemetery the day we buried his mamma. He was in shock—just too much to take in at once."

So Eva hadn't been stillborn. Evan appeared to have rebounded quickly from his discombobulation.

"Tell me," Mrs. Mitchell said, "are you and Evan seeing each other socially?"

"Oh, my, no," I said. "I can't think where I heard that about a sister. I may be confusing him with another client. I'm so terribly sorry to have brought back painful memories."

She made a tsk-tsk noise. "It's a pity. He's a looker. You could do a lot worse."

"Well, maybe after we finish our business we'll have to see about that." I gave her a sly grin, like we were plotting romance together, she and I.

"I do like a happy ending." She grinned back at me.

"Me, too. Oh, not to change the subject, but do you know Mr. and Mrs. Spencer over on Tynte?"

"I've known 'em forever, bless their hearts. Say a prayer for them, will you? Poor Margaret is back in the hospital. It's her heart. I don't think she'll be with us much longer. Howard spends every minute by her side. Only comes home to take a shower. I try to keep him fed, but he won't eat much."

"I'm truly sorry to hear that. I will keep them in my prayers. Forgive me for taking up so much of your time." I stood. "Thank you so much for talking with me. You've been a big help."

She put Mabel down and stood to follow me out. "I don't see as how I've been any help at all. But it's a good neighborhood. Find me some nice neighbors, you hear me?"

"I'll do my best."

I smiled and waved, then turned to walk down the steps. I made my way back to Gram's caddy more convinced than ever that I was on to something. Talitha Ingle had a boatload of secrets. Whether or not uncovering them would help us find Kent remained to be seen. But I sensed a connection, a wisp of something glimpsed perhaps by my subconscious. Or was it a thought planted by Colleen? *Hell fire.* It irritated me to no end that I could never be sure if she'd been messing around in my head.

I slammed the car door closed. "Colleen?"

For once she appeared when I called her. "What's up?"

"Are you throwing thoughts into my head?"

"Why would I do that?"

"I don't know the half of why you do anything. But I've watched while you threw thoughts into other people's heads—planted ideas. Do you do that to me?"

She rolled her eyes elaborately. "No. I can *talk* to you. Before I could materialize, the only way for me to communicate with others was by throwing or planting thoughts. Now I can talk to other folks, but only people I'm absolutely sure won't recognize me."

"So my instincts...they're all mine."

"Of course," she said. "What's for lunch?"

"I've got to go by the police department and give a statement. I was supposed to do that first thing this morning, but I could hardly go there in disguise."

"Well hurry it up. I'm hungry." She disappeared.

I drove out of the neighborhood and into a parking lot on Savannah Highway where I slipped the brown wig off, fluffed my hair, and used a cotton round to dial my eye makeup back a bit. Then I headed to the Charleston Police Department.

Colleen insisted on lunch at Poogan's Porch. We both loved the food, and she wanted to play with Poogan, the ghost dog. I had no business taking a long lunch that day—or eating fried chicken—given that I was going out for a nice dinner that evening. But some days Colleen is a bad influence. The corner table in the courtyard was a glorious venue for lunch, I'll give her that. The sky was postcard-blue, the breeze warm. As always, the food was decadent.

"Enjoy your chicken," she said. "And have some of this macaroni and cheese. I ordered it for us to share. Things are unfolding as they should."

"Is this a philosophy lesson, or is there a cryptic message for me there?"

She forked a bite of chicken breast and swirled it in gravy. "Both."

"Could you give me just a teeny bit more information? Where to find Kent would be helpful."

Colleen chewed thoughtfully.

"I can't tell you where to find her, but you will. Two things to re-member. One, rational people often do irrational things. Two, use the angel to smite the enemy."

"Smite? I'm smiting people now?"

"Do you like the word clobber better? I thought smite sounded more mysterious—and classier."

I deliberately ignored her and delivered a bite of macaroni and cheese to my mouth. They made it with country ham and Gouda. I closed my eyes and savored the combination.

"Let's order dessert," she said.

"No. Absolutely not. I've got work to do and a date tonight."

A grin slid all the way up Colleen's face.

"What's that grin for?"

"I notice Nate is warming up to island life."

"*When* did you notice that? Have you been popping into intimate moments? There's a line, Colleen."

She bray-snorted out loud. "No, I have not been spying on your 'intimate moments.' But I did happen to overhear him mention selling his condo. Seems to me he's coming to his senses."

"We have not settled that issue. I have no more desire to take my happiness at the expense of his than he does mine."

"Oh no. Please tell me you are not going to mess this up yet."

"I told you. I will spend plenty of time in Stella Maris. I love that island as much as you do. We're going to spend some time in Greenville, too. But I will do whatever I need to do to protect my council seat."

"I'll be holding you to that," she said. "And don't forget about the angel."

NINETEEN

By the time I'd driven home, seen to Rhett, showered and primped, it was nearly time for Nate to arrive to take me back to Charleston. There was no way he'd gotten us a reservation at FIG, but we'd go someplace equally nice. The cobalt blue dress that matched my eyes with the draped neckline would be perfect. I slipped into it and buckled the thin black belt. The hem hit just above my knees, and the V in the back was suggestive without issuing improper invitations for a public venue.

I hooked Gram's pearls around my neck and tried several pairs of earrings before deciding on the drop pearl beauties Nate had given me for my birthday. My nude peep-toe pumps completed my ensemble. I was checking the results in the mirror when I heard Nate in the driveway.

He was coming in the front door as I started down the stairs. He closed the door behind him and didn't say a word as he watched me descend. But his eyes were telling me how much he appreciated the care I'd taken in dressing that evening, as well as the way I placed each step very precisely on the stairs, moving slowly, so he could enjoy the view. I don't know what message he could see in my eyes, but the one I was sending said, *I am one lucky girl because you are the best looking thing I have ever laid eyes on.* He did wonderful things for that steel grey suit and white shirt with an open collar.

When I was two steps from the bottom, he said, "You're so damn gorgeous."

I smiled real slow, took the last two steps, and crossed the foyer until I stood right in front of him. "You always make me feel that way. You look mighty fine yourself."

"Thank you, darlin'." He planted a soft kiss on my lips. "I think we'd best hurry along before I change my mind about taking you out this evening." He opened the door and I walked through it and waited while he set the alarm and locked up. Then he helped me down the steps and into the car like I was some fragile treasure.

Neither of us spoke much at first. Nate drove towards the ferry dock and I watched him, appreciating the profile. Finally, he said, "How was your day?"

"Confusing," I said. "Do you want to talk business?"

"I figure that's inevitable under the circumstances. Why don't we get it over with now, then I can try to distract you during dinner?"

I smiled. "Sounds good. Where're we headed?"

"FIG."

"How did you manage that?"

"I guess I should make something up to impress you with my ingenuity, but truth be told, I called and asked for a table at seven. It happens they'd had a cancellation."

"Well, our good fortune."

"Indeed. So, I found nothing of any consequence regarding Charlotte and her family. No red flags in any of the usual databases. Bennett Pinckney doesn't appear to have a mistress. Kids have never been in any trouble. All four boys are out of college, all have jobs in the father's investment firm. Aside from being, best I can tell, slightly snooty, they're the embodiment of the American dream. And the Bounetheaus have so much money to spread around, it's hard to imagine Charlotte offing her niece for a bigger share. Any of them for that matter."

"How could you tell they're snooty? I met Charlotte, and yeah, she gave me that vibe. But did you meet any of them face-to-face?"

"Nah, I just arranged to sit at the next table while Bennett had lunch at the Yacht Club over on East Bay with three of his cronies. Shameless name-dropper, that one."

"Exactly how did you get into the Yacht Club for lunch? That's a private club, membership by invitation only."

Nate sighed. "Here again, I'd love to regale you with my cunning, but I simply called Colton Heyward and he arranged a reservation. Then I asked for the table I wanted right by Bennett. I'm a big fan of the asking nicely strategy." He parked the car on the ferry. "Want to ride up top?"

"Sure." We climbed out of the Explorer and made our way to the top deck. The wind made a mess of my hair, but I had a comb in my purse and it felt good.

"By way of wrapping up my day, I stopped by the Martech Agency. Small outfit. I emailed you a list of employees. Only five in this office. Four women and one guy. Company's headquartered in Columbia. Honestly, I don't think there's anything there. They all like Kent, seemed real concerned about her. None of them socialized with her outside of work. I figure we can profile them just in case and put them on the back burner unless we come up with any red flags."

"Thanks. I appreciate you handling that."

"Had to be done." Nate brushed my hair out of my face. "Now tell me what about your day was confusing."

"I played realtor. Visited Talitha Ingle's house over in West Ashley. Apparently, Evan has already removed any paperwork that might've been helpful in determining how she supported herself and him, sent him to private school, college, to study abroad, et cetera."

"That's unfortunate."

"Exactly. There's a whole lot of unaccounted-for money that flowed to Talitha and Evan over the years, presumably in the form of child support from the unknown father."

"Have you tried asking Evan about that nicely?"

"No, because I can't connect it to our case aside for the fact that Evan knew Kent and he was supposed to meet her the night she disappeared."

"There is that. Slugger—"

"There is a connection. I just haven't found it *yet*." Some cases required a bet on instinct to solve. This felt like one of them. My instincts told me there was a connection. I just needed to find it.

"Okay, so what else did you get into today?"

"I had a lovely chat with one of the two neighbors still living there from when Evan was a baby. Sarah Mitchell. Sweet lady. Anyway, according to her, Talitha came home from Greenville with a newborn baby—Evan—and the body of her brother to bury. Turner Ingle. Incredibly, he also died in a car accident, by the way. Sarah never knew Evan had a twin until Talitha's funeral when Sarah and Evan and anyone else who cared to see saw Eva's grave. And Sarah said Evan never knew he had a sister."

"And his birth certificate said he was born in Charleston?"

"Yes. A home birth with a midwife. I had planned to try to find her, but that would be a fool's errand since the twins were actually born in Greenville. There's a reason why Talitha falsified that on the birth certificate."

"Could still've been a home birth. Almost would had to've been if there's no birth certificate filed in Greenville County. The hospital wouldn't've just let her waltz out of there with two babies and no paperwork."

"Hmm. She worked at Greenville Memorial. Maybe she somehow did away with her own records."

"Possible. But why?"

"I think everything she did was to hide the identity of the baby's father. And it must've been someone with deep pockets, because he paid her a fortune over the years to keep his name out of it. I think they had a deal. Both parties kept up their end."

"Sounds solid as far as it goes."

"So there are three things I want to know. Who is Evan's father, why was it so critical for him to be anonymous, and what became of Turner Ingle's family after his death?"

"Why are you so sure he had a family?"

"Because his tombstone said he was a 'beloved husband, father, and brother.'"

"I know this sounds distasteful, to say the least, but have you considered that maybe Turner was the twins' father? Maybe we're looking at incest here, which is why everyone wanted to hush it up."

"See, there's the problem. Evan Ingle is literally the last person alive in that family. There was no one to hush it up aside from Talitha. The money had to come from somewhere. Turner was a welder at GE who died in a car accident—no lawsuit with a big settlement."

"Fair point. Always follow the money."

As buildings go in downtown Charleston, the one that housed FIG—Food is Good—was unremarkable. It sat on the corner of Meeting and Hasell, a one-story brick building painted creamy white, with flat, modern-looking brown awnings and accents. The sign was three simple squares with round cutouts for orange letters that spelled the name.

Inside, the décor was simple—earth-toned walls in brown and gold, with stained concrete floors. The artwork was understated, seascapes in tones that complemented the walls. I had the impression that the interior design had been carefully planned to never compete with what was served. The artisans at FIG framed their work with plates and bowls.

The hostess seated us at a window looking out onto Meeting Street. A waiter appeared and Nate gave him our standard cocktail order: two fingers of Woodford Reserve on the rocks for Nate, and a Grey Goose Pomegranate martini for me.

We studied our menus.

"I love the John's Island Tomato Tarte Tatin," I said. "I'm tempted to order one for my appetizer and another for my entrée."

"What the lady wants, the lady gets," Nate said.

"On the other hand, the poached salmon is calling to me. I'll say this, Matt must be very good at his job. To be a sous chef here? Everything I've ever tasted is fabulous."

"I'm feeling the Alabama Pork Schnitzel. Want to share some of the skillet okra on the side?"

"Sure." I'd never been known to turn down okra. "Are you going to get the tomato tarte?"

"The gnocchi looks good to me as a first course."

"Fine," I said with a lift of my eyebrows.

"What, you were going to have your appetizer and then some of mine?"

"Maybe just a bite."

He chuckled and shook his head. The waiter arrived with our drinks. When he'd slipped away, Nate lifted his glass. "To whoever made that gorgeous blue dress. The color is nearly as amazing as your eyes."

"Thank you. I declare, you Southern boys purely know how to turn a girl's head." I sipped my martini, my eyes locked on his. The connection between us was far more intoxicating than the liquor. I felt the happy wash over me. The rough spot had passed. We were going to be fine.

Another waiter arrived to take our dinner order. Nate spoke to him and I glanced out the window. Sticky Fingers, a chain barbecue restaurant, was directly across the street. Pedestrian traffic was light. A bicycle taxi rode by with two passengers. The traffic light changed and cars stacked up at the intersection. A large truck with ads for Sailor Jerry Spiced Rum stopped in front of the window.

I stared at the truck for a minute and turned back to Nate, who was still speaking to the waiter. "That'd be great, thanks." The waiter retreated.

"Could you put a Mini Cooper in the back of a truck like that one?" I nodded towards the window.

Nate turned to look. "Sure. You'd just need a ramp to drive it up. Could've been what happened. Do any of our suspects distribute rum?"

"Not that I know of."

"Theoretically, any large truck would do the job—some vans even. But I don't see that happening. Why go to that much trouble when you could just drive the car away? Most criminals are basically lazy."

"Because there are a lot of security cameras downtown. The culprit could have been caught on camera driving Kent's car."

"Criminals with that much forethought and imagination are generally the ones you see in movies," Nate said. "Matt is working tonight. I asked the waiter. Told him we knew him. He's going to let him know we're here. I'd like to look him in the eye. See if he impresses me as innocent the way he does you."

"Well, he hasn't been arrested and he hasn't left town."

"Thus far."

The waiter brought bread and wine glasses for the pinot noir Nate had ordered to go with dinner. A few minutes later, I saw Matt headed our way. He looked profoundly anxious.

"Good evening," he said. "I hope everything is all right." He was in professional mode, inquiring about the food, which was off, because we hadn't had any yet.

"Everything's great," I said. "Matt Thomas, this is my partner, Nate Andrews."

They shook hands.

Matt said, "I heard on the news they found Kent's car."

"Yes, well, actually, I found her car." The news accounts had left me completely out of the story, which was as I expected and fine by me.

"Why didn't you call me?" Anger and fear flashed across his face.

"Because that would've been a conflict of interest. I informed my client."

"What else did you tell him?" Matt asked.

I looked at Nate. If I told Matt I'd left out the pregnancy, he'd never believe me. And he'd run or he wouldn't, no matter what I said at this point. A mixture of pain and frustration seemed to radiate off him and he was fidgety. He looked wound pretty tight, is what I'm saying.

I said, "I gave Mr. Heyward a full report, as I'm obligated to do."

Matt nodded. "I understand. Guess I'll update my attorney."

"That's probably a good idea," Nate said. "Always good to keep them in the loop."

"Enjoy your dinner," Matt said. "Please let me know if you need anything at all." His tone was practiced. He turned and headed back to the kitchen.

"Well?" I looked at Nate.

Nate looked at his bourbon, the hint of a smile on his lips. Then he raised his eyes to mine. "I'm just wondering if the fact he looks like a model for men's underwear has any bearing at all on your steadfast belief in his innocence."

"Nate Andrews. You are a rascal of the first order for saying such a thing. First and foremost, I am a professional."

"You're not denying he has a certain appeal to the fairer sex?"

"Oh good grief. So he's good looking. What about it? Most of the sociopaths I've run across were quite attractive. His appearance has nothing to do with it. I just don't see him hurting Kent."

Nate laughed. "I'm just yanking your ponytail, Slugger."

I rolled my eyes with as much flair as I could muster without pulling a muscle. "Well, what's your read on him?"

Nate tilted his head, winced. "It's hard to say. You've had a lot more interaction with him than I have. Nothing about him shouts guilty to me. Your instincts are usually good about these things."

Our appetizers arrived. I was so engrossed in my tomato tarte I forgot all about having my professional objectivity called into question. Our entrees were equally fabulous, as were the chocolate crepes we shared for dessert.

After dinner we walked hand in hand back to the Hampton Inn. We'd both had cocktails and several glasses of wine, so we'd agreed to spend the night there. As the elevator door closed, Nate brushed my hair back and kissed my neck. "Intriguing as it might be to stop this thing between floors and have my way with you," he murmured, "I'm afraid we'd be rescued far too soon."

"Not to mention, there are likely cameras in here."

"At a Hampton Inn? I doubt it."

The doors opened on the third floor, ending the discussion. Nate put his hand on the small of my back. "Well then, let's seek our entertainment in the privacy of my guestroom. I have a king-size bed and a do-not-disturb sign. I promise there are no cameras. And I confess I've been wondering all evening what you have on underneath that dress."

He slid the key card in the door lock, opened the door, and held it for me.

I plugged my iPhone into the alarm clock and shuffled the playlist labeled "A Little Romance." John Legend started singing "All of Me." Nate came up behind me and wrapped me in his arms. He held me there, gently, but firmly, and bent to press his head against my neck. "I'm a lucky man."

I shivered all the way down to my toes, which curled.

And then he proceeded to undress me and show his appreciation for my choice in lingerie.

TWENTY

We slept in until after eight the next morning. More romping under the covers ensued, followed by showers, me first, because according to Nate, I spend forty-five minutes playing in the water, which is a flagrant exaggeration. When I'd dressed and combed the tangles from my wet hair, I unplugged my iPhone from the radio.

Sonovabitch. I had ten missed calls and two voicemails from Ansley. And one from Colton Heyward. What the hell? How had I missed all those calls?

I listened to the first voicemail: "It's Ansley. Matt's been arrested. The police came early this morning. They barely even let him get dressed. Liz, they charged him with murder. They had a warrant to search the house. Some of them are still here. I called Charlie Condon. *Call me.*" She sounded like she was on the verge of hyperventilating. Hell's bells. What on God's green earth was that girl thinking that she'd be over at Matt's again, apparently overnight?

Her second message was shorter, the frantic in her voice dialed to a new high: "Liz, *where are you?* Call me as soon as you get this."

Colton's message was to the point: "Miss Talbot, please come by this morning at ten."

It was nine-thirty.

"*Nate?*"

He came out of the bathroom, a towel wrapped around his waist. "What's wrong?"

"Matt's been arrested. Ansley was apparently at his house when the police arrived this morning. Does that girl not have the first lick of sense? She's already called his attorney. Colton Heyward wants us—well, me at least—at his house at ten."

"I can be ready in five." He pulled a shirt from the closet. "I think we should both go talk to Heyward."

"We need to be rolling by ten 'til." I was already dashing for the hair dryer. "I'll call Ansley on the way and let her know we'll be there as fast as we can."

As Nate navigated the Explorer through tourist traffic, I examined my iPhone.

"How did the Do Not Disturb setting get turned on? I never turn that on when we're working a case."

"You know I didn't do it."

"I didn't think that. It's just very strange. I don't see how that could happen by accident." I made myself a note to chat with Colleen.

William Palmer escorted us to the living room in the Heyward home.

"Good morning," I said as we entered the room.

Nate nodded his greeting.

Mr. Heyward sat in the wingback by the fireplace that Abigail Bounetheau had occupied the first time I'd visited this room. His face looked haggard, like he hadn't slept in a very long time. Mrs. Heyward was on the end of the sofa to his right. Both of them were immaculately groomed. Neither stood.

"Please, have a seat."

Mr. Heyward directed us to the sofa across from his wife.

When we were settled, Mr. Heyward said, "I suppose you've heard the police arrested Matthew Thomas this morning."

"Yes," I said. "Though I am far from convinced he harmed Kent."

Mrs. Heyward looked at me as if I were her lifeline. She still held out hope her daughter was alive and well. My heart hurt for her.

"Be that as it may," said Mr. Heyward, "the police are now actively working the case. I hired you because they had stopped doing that. It seems to me at this juncture the best course is to let them do their job."

"With all due respect," I said, "I don't believe they can establish anything beyond a trumped up motive for the charge they've filed." I avoided saying the word "murder" in front of Mrs. Heyward. "I'm shocked that they jumped straight from finding the car to arresting Matt on so little evidence."

"Have they shared whatever evidence they have?" Mr. Heyward asked.

"No," Nate said. "They have not. And I think it's worth mentioning here that the only break they've had in the case is the one Liz handed them—the car."

"The only break you know about," said Mr. Heyward.

"Have they shared any new information with you?" I asked.

He exhaled slowly, looked away. "No. They have not."

Nate said, "There's a very good reason for that. They don't have anything new. If they had a shred of an idea they could stretch into something resembling a lead, they'd be rushing over here to serve it up on a silver platter."

"Mr. Heyward, you shared with them what we told you about the baby," I said.

"Yes, as we discussed."

"Sir, did you, perhaps inadvertently, give them the idea that you had concluded Matt was guilty?"

"Absolutely not," he said.

"Because I believe they likely feel an immense amount of pressure to solve this case."

"As they damn well should," he said.

"Agreed, of course," I said. "But sometimes operating under a great deal of pressure can lead to a rush to judgment."

"What other leads are you pursuing?" Mr. Heyward asked.

Oh boy. I needed to give him something, but I didn't even have a suspect yet connected to my Talitha Ingle puzzle. I grabbed the only thing I could think of fast. "We've uncovered a possible connection to alleged illegal activities involving other family members."

I could feel Nate tense beside me.

Colleen popped in and perched on the mantle. "Do *not* name names."

Mr. Heyward straightened. "Members of our family?"

Mrs. Heyward's voice was low and filled with dread. "She's talking about Peyton and Peter."

"Is that true?" Mr. Heyward asked.

Colleen hopped off the mantle and went to sit by Mrs. Heyward. She wrapped her arms around her, comforting her.

I'd experienced Colleen's hugs for myself, and they were truly soothing.

Nate and I looked at each other.

He shook his head indicating how bad an idea he thought this was. "There are very good reasons why we don't share every detail of a case until we either solve it or exhaust all of our leads. One of those reasons is that a few days into an investigation, we might have a lead that doesn't pan out. That's where we are right now. We have several leads, some of which will prove either invalid or unrelated, or both."

I picked up on where he was headed.

"The last thing we would ever want to do is cast aspersions on the good character of any family member. We just need more time."

Mrs. Heyward said, "I've always suspected they were up to no good. Daddy has bailed those boys out of more trouble than you can possibly imagine. And kept it quiet, of course."

Nate said, "We have no evidence that your brothers are connected in any way to Kent's disappearance."

"However," I said, "we would like to further pursue several avenues of investigation. Until Kent is found, the case hasn't been resolved."

A silver aura glowed around Colleen. It shimmered, and sparks of gold radiated from her fingertips. She brushed back Mrs. Heyward's hair, and spoke to her soothingly. "Matt didn't hurt Kent. He doesn't have that in him. If Liz and Nate stop investigating, Matt will go to jail— or worse."

I had seen Colleen do this before. She was planting thoughts in Virginia Heyward's head. No one spoke for a few moments. I cocked my head at Colleen and threw her a question, since she could read my mind so well: *Is this a fact, or more of your hopeful intuition?*

Colleen glanced at me, but continued ministering to Mrs. Heyward. "Matt is innocent."

Mrs. Heyward's voice was stronger than it had been moments before.

"Colton, let them continue their work."

"My dear," Mr. Heyward said, "what can they possibly do that the police can't?"

"It's not a matter of can't. It's won't. I'm afraid this poor boy will be sent to jail and we still won't ever know what's become of Kent."

"They will get the truth out of him," Mr. Heyward said.

"Only if he knows the truth," said Mrs. Heyward. "What if he doesn't?"

Mr. Heyward nodded. "Very well. I think the police are on the right track. However, if Mr. Andrews and Miss Talbot are exploring other possibilities, well, there's no harm in that, is there? Until Kent is found, we should leave no stone unturned, as it were."

"Thank you, Colton," Mrs. Heyward said.

"Is there anything else?" Nate asked.

"No." Mr. Heyward stood.

The rest of us followed suit.

"Just please let us know the moment you have news," said Mrs. Heyward.

"Of course," I said. "We'll show ourselves out."

Colleen followed us into the wide front hall.

Mr. Palmer was nowhere to be seen.

I glared at Colleen. *I need to talk to you.*

She gave me a solemn look. "Remember what I told you a long time ago. There's only one battle, and it's good versus evil. I didn't touch your phone. Entities who aren't on the side of the angels may have wanted you out of the way this morning. If you hadn't shown up at ten, you'd be off the case." She faded out.

Nate and I continued to the car. Had Colleen gone to check in with Sue Ellen?

When we were turning left on Legare, from the backseat, Colleen said, "Mr. William Palmer was on an important phone call."

I glanced over my shoulder.

"What's wrong?" Nate asked.

"Nothing. Just admiring the garden."

Nate gave me a look that said *fine, if you don't want to talk about it.*

Colleen said, "He was reporting to Abigail Bounetheau that you and Nate think Peyton and Peter are involved in something illegal, and may be responsible for Kent's disappearance. I have the distinct impression that he is in the habit of reporting all manner of things to her."

"*Damnation,*" I said.

"Yeah, that could've gone better," Nate said.

"What?"

"We should not have mentioned Peyton and Peter," said Nate.

"*We* didn't."

"Apparently, Mrs. Heyward is under no illusions about her brothers. Maybe we'll get lucky and they won't mention that to the rest of the family."

"Abigail Bounetheau already knows." *Sonavabitch.* How was I going to explain this? I needed a drink already and it wasn't even noon.

"How can you know that?" Nate asked.

"I overheard William Palmer, the house manager, talking to her on the phone when we were walking out. Didn't you?"

Nate pulled to a stop at the intersection of Legare and Lamboll.

"There's no stop sign. Why'd you stop?"

"Because I want you to look at me and tell me how you could hear both ends of a phone conversation that I didn't hear at all. Even if you overheard William Palmer telling tales on the phone—and I did not—how could you know who he was talking to?"

"He had the call on speaker. I can't believe you couldn't hear it. I recognized Abigail's voice immediately. Maybe you had your mind on something else?" I reached for an innocent look and prayed I pulled it off.

For her part, Colleen bray-snorted exuberantly in the back seat.

Nate stared at me for an endless moment. "Why would he have a call he presumably wanted to make surreptitiously on speaker?"

"That is a very good question." I pointed at Nate with emphasis to underscore how I was every bit as mystified as he was by this whole episode. "Looks like he'd have gone way in the back—that's a huge house—and been careful to keep that quiet. Maybe he had the maid or the cook on the line making reports, too." Oh my sweet Lord, how I hated lying to Nate.

He shook his head. "Dammit, Liz. There's something you're not telling me."

I made my eyes bigger.

"What could that possibly be? We were right there together the whole time. I simply heard something you didn't. I think we need to focus on our bigger problem. Colton and Virginia would maybe have kept it to themselves. But Abigail Bounetheau will surely tell her sons we suspect them. She just doesn't know we're not investigating them."

Nate cursed under his breath. He drove through the intersection. "How do I get to Matt's house from here?"

TWENTY-ONE

Ansley slumped in the swing on Matt's front porch, leaning on the chain. Her Z4, a patrol car, and a forensics unit were parked by the curb. Nate pulled in behind the forensics unit. A uniformed officer emerged from the front door and headed down the steps in purposeful strides. Ansley was fast on his heels. We met him halfway down the front walk.

"We're executing a search warrant on this residence. What is your business here?" His nametag read Gambrell, but he didn't offer an introduction.

Nate and I pulled out our identification. I gave him a quick glance that said, *let me talk.*

I said, "We've been retained by the Heyward family to investigate the disappearance of their daughter, Kent. I'm Liz Talbot. This is my partner, Nate Andrews."

Gambrell looked at our IDs, then at us. "You the ones who found the car?"

"Yes, as a matter of fact," I said.

"Thanks for the assist. Looks like you all can move on to your next case. We arrested Matthew Thomas this morning for the murder of Miss Heyward. This case is closed."

"So you found her body, then?" Nate asked, a touch of challenge in his voice.

I flashed him a warning look.

Gambrell bristled. "We will soon enough. He'll tell us where to find her to keep a needle out of his arm."

I offered him my sunniest smile. "Officer Gambrell, the last thing we want to do is step on any toes. But I'm sure you are familiar with our client, Colton Heyward? He insists we keep working this case until Kent has been found. If you could tell us anything at all—perhaps new information that's come to light?—to help us convince him, well, then, we'd be out of your hair in a skinny minute."

Gambrell said, "I'm not at liberty to discuss the case, ma'am. You'd need to speak with Detectives Jenkins and Bissell. And they asked me to advise you this case is closed."

"Are they inside?" I asked, knowing full well the answer.

"No, ma'am. They've taken the suspect in for processing."

"I see. Well, we'll just speak with Miss Johnson here, then, and be on our way."

Gambrell worked his jaw and glared at Ansley. "Make sure you're available for further questioning." He stalked back inside.

Ansley flew into my arms, sobbing.

I patted her back. "Ansley? Honey? I need you to pull it together. Let's go sit in Nate's car, okay?"

Nate walked towards the car, irritation written all over his face. He had little patience with folks who did stupid things and then cried about it, especially if the crying was literal and messy. He turned on the ignition and lowered the windows while I climbed in back with Ansley. I pulled out a pack of tissues from my purse and handed them to her.

Gradually, her sobs slowed to hitched breathing. She dabbed at her eyes.

I said, "Ansley, what were you thinking spending the night at Matt's house again? It looks *bad*. You'll be one lucky girl if you are not arrested as an accessory or even an accomplice before this is over. If your daddy wasn't a judge, you'd likely be at the police station with Matt right now in a separate interrogation room while they tried to get y'all to turn on each other."

She sucked in two quick breaths. "We're just trying to help each other through this. We both love Kent. We're hanging on to each other for support—that's *all*."

"Exactly how tight were you hanging on?" I asked.

"Not like *thaaat*." Her words were a cross between a moan and a whine. "We have never, ever, *ever* had any sort of physical relationship. I swear."

"Okay, okay," I said. "What did Charlie Condon say?"

"Just that he was on his way, and he would try to arrange bail, but it might not work out. I just can't bear to think of Matt in jail with…with…criminals." She commenced crying again.

Nate's eyes met mine in the rearview. He was losing all patience.

"Ansley, focus," I said. Since someone in the Bounetheau family had taken to hiring muscle, it stood to reason one of them was hiding something. It was odd that the muscle hadn't objected to me looking for Kent. Something I'd done along the way had crossed the line to "Bounetheau Business." I needed to know what that was. "You mentioned early on you suspected Kent's uncles of being involved in her disappearance. Think. Did Kent ever say anything about them to you? Was she afraid of them? Did she suspect them of anything?"

She dialed back the waterworks to sniffles and appeared to think hard. Finally, she said, "Not that I can recall. I mean, we joked about them sometimes, how odd it was they still lived at home. How weird it is they seem to share a brain—finish each other's sentences and all. But she never seemed afraid of them."

"Tell me about her grandparents," I said. "The Bounetheaus."

"Kent is very close to them, her granddad especially. He's a painter, too. Not professionally, of course. He and Kent are tight. I had the impression she got along well with her cousins, too. I've met her grandparents—been to parties with Kent where they were and all like that. Mr. Bounetheau's a good guy. Mrs. Bounetheau…she's a little cold, kinda uptight. I mean, she loves Kent. Only she's…well, she's just a snob."

That was consistent with my impression of Abigail Bounetheau. "How about Kent's mamma?"

"What about her?"

"Is she more like her mamma or her daddy?" Nate asked.

"Definitely her dad. Mrs. Heyward isn't snooty at all. She's a nice lady. It's sad…Mrs. Bounetheau has controlled Virginia Heyward her entire life. I don't know why she lets her get away with it. She has her own husband and household, but you'd think she was still a teenager the way she just does whatever her mother tells her."

I squinted at her. I had noticed an odd dynamic between Virginia and her mamma the first time I'd met them. "What kinds of things does her mamma tell her to do?"

Ansley had recovered enough to execute an eye roll. "She's always telling her the 'proper' way to do things. What is and isn't done in better households. Nothing big, I guess. But I know I couldn't tolerate it."

"Does she treat Charlotte that way?" I asked.

"No," Ansley said. "I always thought it was because Charlotte was the oldest and she just never put up with it. For some reason, Kent's mom does. Maybe Charlotte did everything the way her mamma wanted because she wanted the same things. She graduated with honors from Wellesley. Married a Pinckney. Birthed four babies. She's on every charitable board in the county."

"Have you ever heard any gossip at all about Charlotte or her family—or the twins—any of the Bounetheaus? Something scandalous they'd want kept quiet? Something you might have thought unimportant?"

Ansley was quiet for a moment. "Nothing. None of Charlotte's boys were ever in trouble. We went to school with the youngest, Charles Bennett. They call him Benny. We'd have heard if any of those boys had gotten into trouble."

I sighed. Ansley was my best resource on all things Bounetheau, and she'd given me nothing new. I patted her on the leg. "We need to get you out of here."

"But that police officer told me to stay."

"Did he place you under arrest?" Nate asked.

"No."

"Listen to me," I said. "You get in your car right this minute and hightail it straight back to Stella Maris. Go to your daddy's office and wait there. Let his secretary know you need to see him and it's urgent. He's likely in court, and his lunch break may be over by the time you get there. You might not be able to see him until his session ends for the day. Wait for him. Tell him everything. Don't leave a single thing out. You hear me?"

The sobbing recommenced. She nodded.

"He'll know who to call. You need an attorney on standby and not Charlie Condon. You need a different attorney from Matt."

"O-okay," she said.

I looked towards the house. No sign of the police officers. "Go on."

Ansley opened the door, climbed out, and closed the door quietly behind her. She jogged to her car, slipped in, and drove away.

Officer Gambrell came to the door just in time to watch her turn right at the stop sign. He glared at us. I smiled and waved as I got out of the backseat and into the front.

TWENTY-TWO

Three blocks away from Matt's house, I said, "Let's go to Greenville."

"You took the words right out of my mouth," Nate said.

I knew he and I had different things in mind, but that didn't matter just then. We made a quick stop at the Hampton Inn to pick up what few things I had there for overnight. Since Nate was still spending most of his time in Greenville, his condo had everything he needed aside from the electronics he carried with him.

While I took his room key and went inside, Nate did a thorough sweep of the Explorer for GPS trackers, listening devices, and all such as that. With Peyton and Peter warned of our suspicions, we were on heightened alert. Assuming the gentlemen I'd met in the Hampton Inn courtyard worked for them, the twins had already sent us two warnings. They would not be kindly disposed to learn we'd mentioned them as possible suspects to Mr. and Mrs. Heyward.

I called Blake from the hotel room phone. "Hey," I said when he answered. "I'm in a fix. I need you to take care of Rhett for a day or two. Can you swing by this morning? Nate and I are heading to Greenville."

"Why are you calling me from a Charleston landline? What kind of fix?"

I heaved a sigh. I didn't want Blake to worry, but I wouldn't lie to him, either. "It's this case we're working. We're just being overly cautious, paranoid, really."

"Being overly cautious is not in your nature. Tell me what's going on."

Maybe it was better if he knew, just in case. Also, he'd be pissed if he heard about the Sunday night goons-with-a-gun incident from Sonny. I probably should've already told him. Quickly, I outlined what had transpired since Saturday and where we stood with the investigation. "Maybe you should take Rhett to stay with you on the houseboat tonight. Maybe tomorrow night. We'll be back tomorrow, Thursday latest. I don't like the idea of him being by himself so long."

"You're worried the muscle is going to show up at your house." My brother's voice held layers of concern and anger.

"It's possible they might come looking for me. If I'm not home…Just please take Rhett to your place at night." I felt horribly guilty having left him by himself the night before.

"I've got Rhett. Take your time in Greenville. The longer you stay the better."

"That is a hell of a thing to say to your sister." I tried to lighten the tone.

"Dammit, Liz. Does someone have to shoot you before you'll take a threat seriously?"

"I've got to go. Thank you so much for seeing about Rhett."

"Be careful."

Nate was waiting in the driver's seat when I returned. I climbed into the car. "Are we ready?"

"All clear. Thankfully. I should have scanned for listening devices before we had that chat with Ansley. That was a bit spontaneous. We caught a break. Let's run counter spyware on our phones and tablets. Since we don't know who all the Bounetheaus subcontract their intimidation and enforcement needs to, we don't know what kinds of tools they have. We should assume they have access to every toy we do plus potentially anything professional law enforcement brings to the party."

"I was thinking the same thing." I pulled out my iPhone and iPad and ran an app that looked for remote spying software. Anyone who knows how can track anyone who owns most modern phones and tablets. "I'm clean. Turning off Wi-Fi and Bluetooth. And turning off both devices for now."

"Roger that. I'm good to go." Nate drove out of the parking garage, made a right on John, and a left on Meeting Street. "I'm heading towards Mount Pleasant, like we're going back to Stella Maris. Maybe take a few detours. Let's keep an eye out for tails. When we're sure we're clean, I'll catch 526 back to I-26." Five twenty-six was two-thirds of a loop, connecting Highway 17 in Mount Pleasant to Highway 17 in West Ashley, passing through North Charleston and intersecting Interstate 26 near the airport along the way.

"Sounds good."

After driving around Mount Pleasant for fifteen minutes and stopping three times, neither of us had seen the same car twice. At a Walgreens on Highway 17, we stopped and I ran inside and paid cash for two prepaid cellphones, some bottled water, and some snacks. Shortly thereafter, Nate turned onto I-526.

"I'm driving towards Greenville for one reason," Nate said. "Because I believe you'll be safer there. We still don't know for sure which Bounetheau paid your snake-handling friends. My theory, as I've mentioned, is that the twins were proactive in dissuading you from investigating their enterprise. If I'm wrong, and that does happen on occasion, we don't know what tripwire you snagged that brought on the goons, since the gentlemen themselves magnanimously allowed that you could continue investigating Kent's disappearance.

"Either way," he continued his soliloquy, "now that we know for sure the twins *think* we're investigating them, we'll both be that much more a target for their merry band of uber hooligans. Now, that could be an additional threat, or an increased threat level on an existing problem, depending on whether I'm right or wrong. But what I am genuinely interested in hearing, Slugger, is why *you* wanted to leave forthwith for the Upstate. I'm certain of one thing—your reasons are not mine."

"I want to find out who Evan's father is. According to Sarah Mitchell, Talitha's neighbor, he's from Greenville, and he has very deep pockets. Greenville is our turf. We should be able to suss this out in short order."

"Follow the money."

"Exactly," I said. "Evan had already taken Talitha's banking statements from the time he was born until she was killed—at least I assume it was Evan who took them. He would have legitimate reason. I'll check his apartment when we get back. But...the statements themselves likely reflect transfers from a company or trust that may be hard to trace. It will be easier if we can find out who his father is another way."

"Like the layers of companies separating the twins from that warehouse."

"Exactly. Except we'd start with the company names instead of the person's name. It's harder that way. If you know who you're looking for to begin with, a trace like that is still tedious, but you hit fewer brick walls."

"Agreed."

"Someone took very good care of Talitha and Evan. If we find out who, that might lead us to what happened to Turner's family. Sarah Mitchell said that Evan and Talitha were all the family each other had. But somewhere, Turner Ingle had a wife and at least one child. They are pieces to this puzzle."

"With a little luck, by the time we've identified everyone in Evan's family tree, someone will've locked up Peyton, Peter, and all their cohorts. That will make for a much safer working environment for you and me." Nate took the exit to I-26 West. "Like I said, I'm just happy to be headed towards the foothills."

"I'm going to check in with Sonny."

"Probably a good idea. Will he answer a number he doesn't recognize?"

"Sure he will. He's a detective. You never know who might be on the other end of a line. It would eat me alive not to answer a call. I would lie awake at night and wonder who that was, what they wanted. I'd end up having to call back just to find out. Might as well answer to begin with."

"I'm just guessing here. I don't know the man well, but I'm going to go out on a limb here and speculate that Sonny is not as neurotic as you are. And I mean that in a lovin' way."

I laughed out loud. "I'm neurotic, but you love me anyway?"

"Of course."

Sonny answered on the third ring. "Ravenel."

I smiled at Nate. "Hey, it's Liz."

"Why are you calling me from what I'm guessing is a burner phone?"

"Recent events have conspired to make me paranoid. Nate and I are in the car. I'm going to put you on speaker so I don't have to repeat all of this, okay?"

"All right."

I pressed the speaker button.

"Okay, so, I had to tell Mr. and Mrs. Heyward that we suspect Peter and Peyton of illegal shenanigans that could be related to Kent's disap-

pearance. We have to assume additional individuals of the criminal persuasion will be unhappy with us. Is there anything new regarding the
twins you can share?"

Sonny was quiet for so long I thought the call had dropped. "Sonny?"

"I'm here. Just needed to step outside. Look, all I know is there's a
task force assigned to whatever the Bounetheau twins have going on over
at Shipyard Creek. All over the alphabet—DEA, FBI, SLED, the Coast
Guard. Task force has been in place for months, but the specifics have
been real hush-hush. Technically, we've got guys on the team, but I'm
not sure how much they even know. But your instincts were good. You
guys need to stay away from that for all kinds of reasons."

"Any way to find out if their investigation uncovered anything related to Kent?" I asked.

"In a surreal act of interagency cooperation—*I've* never seen anything like it—the Special Agent in Charge told Jenkins and Bissell that he
had techs check recordings from a week before Kent disappeared until
three days after. Nothing there that points to her stumbling into her uncles' operation. They're convinced there's no connection."

"Recordings?" I said.

"Yeah, I don't know what all they have going on. Wiretaps at a minimum would be my guess. Could be they're listening to whatever's going
on inside the warehouse, offsite offices—I have no idea. They just mentioned recordings."

Nate asked, "You think they're playing straight, not just brushing
them off?"

"Yeah, I think the non-criminal members of the Bounetheau family
still have plenty of influence. Speaking of which, as soon as that car was
found, the grandmother—Abigail—called God and everybody—the chief,
the solicitor's office, the state attorney general, a couple of senators, a
few judges, et cetera—demanding Matthew Thomas's arrest. Which, between you and me, was premature by any reasonable measure."

I said, "I would've bet Colton Heyward was behind that."

"He did talk to the chief. Except Jenkins told me Heyward just
asked the chief to keep the pregnancy confidential and keep him updated. He was pleased the case was active again. His agenda is he wants his
daughter found. Demanded hourly updates and whatnot. I'm not saying

he was a pleasure to deal with. But he didn't pressure anyone to arrest Matthew Thomas."

"Interesting," I said. "I wonder if these people talk to each other at all. You'd think they'd be singing from the same hymnal."

"I hear tell the grandmother is convinced the boyfriend did it. If she had her way, they'd hang him at dawn at White Point Gardens where Stede Bonnet and all those other pirates were dispatched."

"You're saying she's not pressing y'all to find Kent, just to prosecute Matt?" I asked.

"Yep. And isn't that the damnedest thing? Strikes me that maybe she knows the longer we're investigating anything related to her family, the more likely we are to run across Peyton and Peter's import and export business."

"You think she knows about that?" Nate asked.

"It's a theory."

"Seems awfully cold," I said. "I mean, she's potentially sweeping whatever happened to Kent under the rug to protect two grown men who should've had the least motivation of anyone in Charleston to undertake criminal activities."

"Hell," Nate said, "for all we know she's in charge of the family import export business."

I mulled that for a minute. "I think she's too proud of her pedigree. Which is probably why she's desperate to keep the whole mess quiet."

"Sounds right," Sonny said. "I've got to get back to it. Keep your heads low."

"Will do." I ended the call.

Nate said, "Task force operations can take years. I hope they're being forthcoming. Sonny's right about one thing. It's rare for the alphabet gang to give anything to another investigation before they've wrapped up their case."

"I say we assume the info is good. We aren't working that angle anyway. This gives me peace of mind checking it off our possible narratives list."

"I like it better when we eliminate a narrative ourselves before discarding it, but in this case, I think we're going to have to live with it."

"If we can't prove an alternate theory, and all we're left with is the possibility that Kent somehow bumped into her uncles' criminal enterprise and they felt obliged to make her disappear—then, like we agreed, we explain that to Mr. and Mrs. Heyward and walk away. Unfortunately, that will not get Matt out of jail."

"They don't have anywhere close to enough evidence to convict him."

"That's because he's innocent," I said.

TWENTY-THREE

We stopped by Nate's South Main Street condo just long enough for me to print a picture of Talitha from her online obituary and search the county property database. I scoured records for the neighborhood Turner Ingle had lived in near Cleveland Park looking for neighbors who'd been there in nineteen eighty-one and hadn't moved. I printed names and addresses as I found them. When I had four, I stopped. It was pushing five o'clock. If we didn't get what we needed from any of these folks, we'd start again tomorrow.

The shaded neighborhood perched on a hillside above Cleveland Park consisted of a mix of bungalows and ranch-style homes, with an occasional two-story colonial and a few newer homes best described as craftsman. The landscaping was mature and well-tended. It was a pretty, established neighborhood, the kind where it was easy to imagine families sitting down to dinner together. Nate pulled to the side of the street near the former Ingle home.

Turner Ingle had purchased a small grey cottage near the intersection of Trails End and Dogwood Lane in early 1980. His was the sole name on the deed. I'd searched every database I had access to and found no marriage license. A little more than a year after he'd bought the house, according to Sarah Mitchell, Talitha had moved to Greenville. I knew she'd lived here with her brother, and worked at Greenville Memorial Hospital. I stared at the cottage.

"It's not going to confess," said Nate.

I scanned the street. "The house two doors down is for sale. There's nothing over the windows, no cars. I make it for vacant. Why don't you pull in there? If anyone asks, we can pretend we're waiting for a realtor."

"As you wish."

I smiled and pulled out my property records and Talitha's picture. "I'll look less threatening by myself."

"Holler if you need me."

"I'll start with the closest neighbors and work outwards. John and Marcia Clark live across the street. It's still early, but these folks are all retirement age. Maybe someone will be home." I climbed out of the car and made my way to the white frame ranch.

The Clarks weren't home, nor were the Hannahs or the Stouts. At the fourth house I tried, a painted brick cottage further down Trails End, a gentleman answered the door. "Can I help you?" He was trim, maybe just under six feet tall, with gray hair and a close-cut beard and mustache. His posture suggested ex-military.

"Are you Bob Elmore?"

"Yes." His tone was guarded. He likely suspected I was selling something or running a scam.

I pulled out my PI license and my ID. "My name is Liz Talbot. I'm investigating the disappearance of a young woman in Charleston. Could I trouble you for a moment of your time?"

"Charleston, you say? I don't know anyone in Charleston."

"I understand, Mr. Elmore, but it's possible there's a connection to your former neighbors, the Ingles, from down the street. Did you know them?"

He scrutinized me for a moment. "Yes. I knew Turner. He was a good man. Welder at GE. Come to think of it, he was from Charleston, but he's been dead...Vicki?" He called inside the house. "Darlin', can you come here a minute?"

"Coming." A fair-skinned brunette approached and stood beside Bob.

Bob said, "This is my wife, Vicki. She knew them better than I did. Vicki, this young woman is a private investigator up from Charleston. She's asking about Turner and Kathy."

Kathy? I went on full alert. Was this Turner's bride?

Vicki said, "They were such nice folks. Such a tragedy."

"I was trying to think how long Turner's been gone. He died in a car accident. When was that, hon?"

"Oh, gosh, they hadn't been here but...let's see...it was less than two years. Turner and Kathy moved here in the early eighties. It was a February. I don't recall what year. He died not that October, but the next. He was on his way to the hospital. Kathy gave birth to twins that same night."

"Kathy was his wife?" I said.

They both looked at me like I was a bit slow. "Uh-huh. Yes."

"And Kathy was the twins' mother?"

"Why, yes, of course," Vicki said.

"Did you know Turner's sister, Talitha?"

"Yes," said Vicki. "She came up from Charleston to help out. The doctors put Kathy on bed rest early on. Turner had to work. Talitha worked part-time, but her hours were different, so one of them was always there. Twins are sometimes difficult."

I showed them Talitha's photo. "And this woman is Talitha Ingle?" I wanted to make sure no one was borrowing her name.

Vicki took the photo. They both looked at it and nodded.

"Course, she was a good bit younger," said Bob. "But that's her."

"Can you tell me what Kathy looked like?" I asked.

"She was average height," said Vicki. "Medium brown hair—pretty hair. Blue eyes. I'd say she was very attractive, wouldn't you?" She turned to Bob.

"She was a beautiful woman."

"Was she from around here?" I asked.

"No," Vicki said. "They were all from Charleston."

"Any idea what her maiden name was?" I asked.

They looked at each other and shook their heads. "No," Vicki said. "She never talked about her family."

Vicki said, "It was so sad, but a little strange, I'd say. Wouldn't you, Bob?"

"Yeah," Bob said, like he was telegraphing how that was a doozey of an understatement.

"What was strange?" I asked.

"Kathy went to the hospital and had the twins. When we heard about the accident, we went by the hospital to check on her. She was distraught, of course. Turner was dead, and one of the twins—the girl, I think—was in an incubator. But Kathy didn't say a word to us about going back to Charleston."

Bob said, "She just never came home. Neither did Talitha. A few weeks later movers came. After several months the house went on the market. We never saw either of the girls again."

"That is odd," I said.

"It wasn't one of them that disappeared in Charleston, was it?" Bob asked.

"No," I said. "It was a much younger woman. I'm sorry to give you sad news, but Talitha was killed in a car accident two months ago."

Vicki's hand went to her chest. "That's just awful. Another car accident?"

"That is strange, isn't it?" I said.

"They never did find out what caused Turner's wreck. Just said he lost control of the vehicle. It was a clear night—no rain. He was coming straight from work to the hospital. Talitha had already taken Kathy. Accident happened on Garlington Road, not far from the plant. No witnesses. It's like he swerved for no reason on a straight stretch of road and hit a tree."

"Talitha's accident involved another vehicle," I said. "But it is odd."

"Do you know whatever happened to Kathy?" Vicki asked.

"I'm afraid I don't," I said. "Thank you both so much for your help."

"You're welcome," Vicki said. "I hope you find the girl you're looking for."

"Thank you." I smiled and walked down the steps and back up the street.

"Find out anything?" Nate asked as I climbed in the car.

"As Colleen would say, 'Boy Howdy.'"

"Colleen?" Nate gave me a blank look.

I closed my eyes and took a deep breath, then opened them and gave him a sad smile. "You remember, my friend who died when we were in high school? It's just something she says—said." Life would be so much simpler if I could tell Nate about Colleen. Or he'd think I was crazy.

"Anyway," I said. "Talitha Ingle was not Evan's mother."

"Say what?"

"Turner Ingle was his father, and his wife—Evan's mother—her name was Kathy." I filled him in on everything I'd learned.

"And you've already scoured online records and databases for these folks?"

"Yep. Which means tomorrow morning, we'll be waiting at the door when the county offices open." Occasionally, documents didn't make their way into electronic databases, but could still be found on file in the county of origin.

"If Turner was the father, and he was a tradesman of modest means, then Kathy's family is the one with money."

"That's what I think. Welders don't have life insurance policies big enough to cover the amount of money funneled to Talitha and Evan over the years given that she didn't work from the time he was born."

"And this Kathy…just gave her son to Talitha and walked away?" Nate sounded skeptical.

"Doesn't sound right to me either. I'm wondering if Kathy had an accident as well. The question is, did Talitha kidnap the children, or rescue them?"

"Good question."

"So here's narrative number three: Kent was getting close to Evan. Evan had a past someone—not Evan, but his wealthy, anonymous family—wanted to stay in the past. Kent found out something she shouldn't have. Someone took Kent out of the picture."

"It's sketchy, but we have a lot more than we had this morning." He blew out a long breath. "My turn, I guess. Regrettably, our voluntary relocation scenario just got considerably less plausible."

"What do you mean?"

"While you were chatting with the Elmores, I got updates from the agencies doing our out-of-state legwork."

"And?" My heart rate quickened.

"Kent's college friends living in Denver, Seattle, and LA have been under surveillance since Friday. No sign of Kent. The investigators have also done some poking around. In all three cases, they're reasonably confident she's not there."

I closed my eyes. "I was hoping hard one of them would find her."

"That would've been the best outcome, no doubt. There's more bad news."

I opened my eyes, turned towards Nate.

He stared out the front window. "You remember Wade Montgomery?"

"Yeah, he was one of Blake's fraternity brothers. Why?"

"He left SC Highway patrol a while back. Moved to Dallas. He's the PI I contacted about Amarillo. It's less than six hours away—reachable—and we know him. That last transaction on Kent's credit card at the service station in Amarillo was at ten-thirty p.m. Wade went through the other transactions from around the same time, found a witness who remembered seeing a guy pumping gas. Long story short, eventually he came up with Hart Feldman, age nineteen. Former College of Charleston sophomore, native of Amarillo."

"Did he admit using Kent's credit card?"

"As a matter of fact, he did. And her cellphone. His story is he wanted to get home. Missed his girlfriend. He'd only been on campus a week but he couldn't stand it. True love and whatnot. But his funds were tight. He went in to sell plasma for gas money the Saturday morning after Kent disappeared. Says he found her wallet and cellphone literally on the sidewalk on Ashley Avenue on his way out. The kid swears he thought it was a gift from God, at first, anyway.

"So, he heads for Texas. By the time he got to Atlanta, he's worried something bad happened to Kent, but he hasn't been watching the news, he's been driving. He calls the number labeled "home" in her favorites list, but when Colton Heyward answered, he lost his nerve. Then he got nervous about getting caught, and how bad it would look if Kent had met with foul play. He destroyed the cellphone and put it in a dumpster in Atlanta with her wallet. He just kept the one credit card.

"Because he still needed gas to get home. He figured if he alternated fill ups with what cash he had, and only used her card when he had to, maybe he wasn't digging his Karma hole too deep. Wade emailed the full report."

"Dammit all to hell." My chest and throat tightened. Someone had left Kent's wallet and cellphone precisely where someone desperate would find them in hopes of creating a false trail. And it had worked.

"Slugger, we always knew this wasn't likely to have a happy ending."

"I know. But I wanted like hell to be wrong."

TWENTY-FOUR

Nate parked in his street-level garage, a luxury for downtown Greenville. We took the private elevator to his third floor Customs House condo. He'd bought the unit new a year ago and moved from his smaller place at Poinsett Corners. He said it was a good investment, and no doubt that was true. But I suspected the bigger reason was to make more room for me. I had my own office in his professionally decorated home, which I rarely used. The sweetness of the gesture touched my soft spot again.

I'd gone into the master bath to powder my nose. When I came out, he waited by the bedroom window. He turned and scrutinized me as if I perplexed him. "Slugger, I'm not a hundred percent sure if this will make you happy or piss you off. Maybe a bit of both. But I bought some things for you a while back—to keep here. I went to some of the stores you like and asked the sales clerks for pity. In any case, you have clothes here if you need them."

I felt tears fill my eyes. How much this man must love me. I walked into his arms and hugged him, speechless.

"I'm guessing this means I haven't screwed up." He rested his face against my head.

"No." I pulled back to look at him. "That's the sweetest thing—so thoughtful. Thank you."

His voice was soft, husky. "I hope you like them. Everything's in your closet. I thought, since there's nothing more we can do tonight, we might have dinner at The Lazy Goat if you like?"

"That sounds perfect." The Lazy Goat had long been one of our favorite Greenville restaurants. "I'll grab a shower."

"I'll wait until you're finished. I'm guessing you're getting hungry, and if I join you, you're not going to get fed for a while."

I flashed him a playful look, then dashed into the bathroom and closed the door.

"There's no lock on that door, by the way. Didn't see the need."

"Well then, I'll hold you to your word," I said through the door.

"I think I'll go make myself a drink."

Thirty minutes later, I emerged wrapped in a fluffy towel and went to explore the contents of my closet. It was a huge walk-in affair, better described as a dressing room, custom built just for me. On a hook behind the door was a spa robe. I traded the towel for it, and slid into the matching slippers.

There were shelves for shoes, with black flats, brown ankle-boots, strappy evening sandals, and Keen walking shoes already in place. The drawers held a full assortment of lingerie in my favorite brands. On padded hangers, half a dozen outfits waited for me to choose what to wear to dinner. Nate had taken great care to make sure I had what I needed here.

I pulled out a flouncy pumpkin-colored skirt and a neutral pullover. The ankle boots would look cute with that ensemble. A long tri-metal necklace and earring set I had with me would go well. I selected a lacy bra and matching boy shorts with bows.

A built-in dressing table provided a comfortable spot for me to primp. From beyond the door I'd left ajar, I heard Nate go into the bathroom. I smiled at the lit mirror and pulled my makeup tote from my overnight bag. Light base, smoky eyes, just a touch of lipstick and gloss. I wore my hair loose, just a bit tousled.

When I rose and turned to check the results in the full-length mirror, Nate stood in the doorway. Our eyes collided and a jolt of electric current seared my core. His face was lit with warmth, love, and lust. The power of what I felt for him left me weak-kneed.

He wore jeans, a white oxford shirt, and a black leather jacket. "It's turned chilly," he said. "Better grab something warm."

I looked around the closet. Two cardigans were folded on a shelf, one black, one ivory. Beside them was a multi-colored pashmina that had a swirl of the color of my skirt running through it. "Oh, my goodness. This is lovely." I picked it up to look at it closer. It was as soft as it was beautiful. "Nate..." I shook my head at him. "You shouldn't have done all of this. I mean...thank you, so much. But really, you shouldn't have."

"I can't think of a solitary reason why not. If there's something you don't like, you can take it back. I saved the receipts."

"No, it's not that. Everything is gorgeous."

"And so are you. Ready for dinner?"

"Sure." I smiled and walked towards him.

He didn't budge from the doorway. When I was right in front of him, he bent down to kiss me. It was soft, but stirring. He pulled back and looked at me. "We'd best go." He escorted me through the condo, out the door, and into the elevator.

"The decorators did a wonderful job with the condo," I said.

"I'm happy you like it."

"Nate, please don't sell it."

The perplexed look returned. "I thought we had all that settled."

"No, we don't settle things after you've had more than three bourbons."

"Tell you what, let's leave it be for tonight."

I studied his face. He was happy. I was happy. We'd leave it alone.

Main Street in Greenville looks festive year round—white lights in the trees lining the street, happy people on their way to dinner or a play. A guitar player strummed and sang at the entrance to Falls Park. We made a left onto Camperdown, and a right past the entrance to the Hampton Inn and we were at the restaurant. Nate had once again magically finagled one of the best tables in a corner window overlooking the Reedy River.

I looked at the familiar scene and remembered all the nights we'd spent mulling cases and chatting about everything and nothing while watching wedding receptions at the Wyche Pavilion, the charming two-story brick shell of a building originally intended as a paint shop for coaches and wagons. I felt a tug of homesick for Greenville. My decision to live here part-time settled around me and I wrapped up in it like a quilt.

"Feel like grazing and nibbling?" Nate referred to the small plates section of the menu titled "Graze and Nibble," which was our favorite. Our custom was to order a selection and share. If we wanted more, we ordered more.

"Yes. Order anything you like as long as it includes the Moroccan lamb and the fried goat cheese."

"I'm thinking the roasted Brussel sprouts. The Burrata cheese...."

The waiter appeared and Nate ordered a spread of food which would likely have fed four of us along with a bottle of pinot noir. We chatted about little things—what was coming up this season at the Peace Center, new restaurants in town, friends I hadn't seen in a while.

The food arrived and we grazed until we couldn't nibble another bite. Then we walked back up Main Street hand in hand. It was a perfect evening. Once we were back in the condo, Nate went to the stainless steel refrigerator and pulled out a bottle of Veuve Clicquot.

"What are we celebrating?" I asked.

He set two champagne flutes on the granite counter. For a moment he just looked at them. Then, he said, "I feel like we've turned a corner. Maybe I've gotten past something, I don't know. All I know is that it's clear to me now that it doesn't matter where or how we live, as long as I can spend my days and my nights with you."

I smiled at him, a slow, come-and-get-me smile. "Then let's celebrate, by all means. How do I turn on the music? I can't recall."

"Media closet. I'll get it." He popped the cork, filled our glasses, dimmed the kitchen lights, then brought me my flute. "Hold on to that." He stepped down the hall, opened a closet, and seconds later "Marry Me" by Train filled the room.

I'd always loved that song. It had been in both our music libraries for years.

Nate went back to the bar and picked up his champagne flute, then made his way to where I stood by the window looking down Main Street. "Cheers." He touched his glass to mine.

"Cheers." I raised my glass and drank deeply.

He transferred his glass to his left hand and wrapped my right one with his. Pulling me into an embrace, he moved with the music. We danced by the soft light of the streetlights coming in from the window.

The last few lines of the chorus played.

Nate caressed my face with his empty hand. "Will you?"

My chest felt tight. Terrified I'd somehow misunderstood his intent, I managed to eke out the word, "What?"

"Say you will. Marry me."

And I knew that's exactly what I wanted to do. My heart felt full. Fireworks went off in my brain.

"Liz?"

"Yes. I will." I laughed and spun around. "I will marry you, Nate Andrews."

"Really?" His eyes were bright with hope and disbelief, his jaw slack.

I laughed again. "Of course, really. I sure hope that wasn't like an impulse thing, because I'm all in."

He threw back his head and whooped, drained his glass, and crushed me to him.

"I'm going to spill my champagne."

"Drink it quick."

I tipped the glass and finished it off.

He handed me his glass. "Hang on to this one, too."

"What?" I was still laughing.

He scooped me up and carried me to the kitchen. "Grab the bottle."

I complied and he walked down the hall to the master bedroom. "Hang on now." He laid me down gently on the bed, propped me against a pile of pillows I'm sure the decorator chose, then took the bottle and glasses from me, refilled them, and handed me mine back. He sprawled out beside me and looked at me in wonder. "I love you so much."

"I love you, too. It's...overwhelming. It fills me up inside."

"I'm sorry I don't have a ring. To be honest, I was afraid to jinx it by buying one. We'll pick one out—whatever you want."

"Would it be all right if I wear Gram's ring?" The piece held sentimental value, and I'd always thought it a shame to leave such a pretty ring in a jewelry box.

"Well, sure, if that's what you want. But I want to give you something—something important. Something that means forever."

"We'll need to pick out bands, probably have to have them made to match the ring. Gram has her band."

"Okay, but we still need to shop for engagement jewelry. Your choice."

"All right." I held up my glass. "To spending all my tomorrows with you."

We drank to that and many other things while we undressed each other. Our lovemaking that night was slow and tender, cherishing each other with every touch. I was happier than I'd ever been.

TWENTY-FIVE

Greenville County Square occupied an entire block of University Ridge, with The Governor's School between it and the back side of Falls Park. The building most resembled a shopping mall because that's exactly what it was designed to be. Bell Tower Mall languished in the eighties when downtown department stores relocated to Haywood Mall. Nowadays, Greenville's downtown thrived, anchored by Falls Park and The Peace Center for the Performing Arts.

Nate pulled into a parking spot near the probate court entrance. He'd been building his case.

"No, sweetheart, we can't just pick up a marriage license while we're here," I said. "I'd rather Daddy not kill you before I get you to a church."

"I'm pretty sure they're good anywhere in the state." He turned off the ignition. "Uhh, I've got nothing against church weddings..."

"That's good, because that's the only kind Mamma holds with."

He appeared to have something stuck in his throat. "Slugger, just so I understand your intent here, do you have in mind to fill up St. Francis Episcopal and get married in front of God and everyone who witnessed you marrying my brother a few years back?"

I grinned. "Yes. That's exactly what I have in mind."

"That's likely to cause folks to talk."

"Let them. I don't care. We are native South Carolinians. Eccentricity is our birthright."

"All right then." He blew out a long breath and widened his eyes. "And why again can't we get a marriage license today? I'd rather not give you too much time to overthink this."

"I think they're only good for thirty days. Weddings take months—a year—to plan."

"The hell you say."

I laughed as I climbed out of the car. "It'll go by fast. There's so much to do. We have to pick out flowers, and a cake, and my dress of course."

"I can have all that done by this evening."

"Sweetheart, you'd best leave the details to me. And Mamma, of course."

"Of course."

"But first there'll be an engagement party."

"Naturally," he said, like he was thinking how he should have seen that coming.

"Okay, marriage records are in probate court, suite 5600. We may need a story. I don't think they hand these out like candy."

"Perhaps a delicate family matter?" Nate said.

"Yes. Involving a critical health issue. Genetics and all. We're looking for a bone marrow donor. That's much more compelling than a will."

He held the door for me. We made our way to suite 5600. We'd arrived right at opening time, so there was no line. We walked straight up to the counter. A woman I pegged at mid-fifties approached from the other side. Her hair was likely from Clairol's medium brown family, styled short and teased a bit. "Can I help you?"

"I surely hope so," I said. "Ma'am, we have a family emergency. My sister Laura Beth has been diagnosed with leukemia. I tried donating, but I'm not a match. So far, none of us are."

"I'm so sorry to hear that. How can I help?" She oozed empathy.

For a split second, I felt bad about playing this nice lady. Then I visualized Kent. "We're hoping to locate our half-sister. I'm afraid it was a family scandal. Mamma thinks Daddy was married once before—a long time ago. Daddy was much older than Mamma. He's passed on."

"I see." The clerk blinked several times behind her glasses.

"I was wondering if you could help us find out if Daddy really was married to someone else before Mamma. If he had other children, you see..." I choked up.

Nate put his arms around me. "It's going to be all right, darlin'. This nice lady can help us, I'm sure of it."

"What was your daddy's name?" she asked.

"Turner. Turner Ingle."

She wrote that down. "And about what year do you think he was previously married?"

"Nineteen eighty, perhaps eighty-one."

"I'll see what I can find." She turned and went to a computer station. She tapped and clicked for a few moments, then rose, walked to a printer, and retrieved a piece of paper. "Here you go. I hope this helps." She walked to the counter, arm extended with the document in hand.

"Oh, thank you so much," I said. "Bless you."

"You're welcome," she said.

We walked out of the office and a few steps down the hall. I stopped and studied the piece of paper with Nate looking over my shoulder.

In the box labeled "wife" on the marriage license for Turner Mark Ingle, dated February 9, 1980, was the name Virginia Mary Katherine Bounetheau.

"Sonavabitch," I said.

"I did not see that coming," said Nate.

"Kent is Evan's half-sister."

"Evan Ingle is a Bounetheau."

TWENTY-SIX

Nate pulled the Explorer to a stop at the parking lot exit. "Are you ready to head back to Charleston?"

"Not just yet. We need to talk to someone who knows what happened after the twins were born." How could we get information from Greenville Memorial?

"I'd say your best bet there is Virginia Bounetheau Heyward," said Nate. "Though I predict her mother orchestrated the operation."

"I'd like to talk to someone who is not a member of the family." Talking to any of the Bounetheaus prematurely seemed like an invitation for them to tie up loose ends.

"You're thinking a doctor, a nurse?"

"Exactly."

"The doctor's name would be on the birth certificates. Only Vital Records isn't going to give us those," he said. "The bone marrow thing won't work on them. We'd have to prove we were immediate family."

I stared across the street at the Health Department. "And I'd be willing to bet those birth certificates were never filed. They disappeared at the hospital. Talitha could've seen to that, and if she filed one in Charleston County for a home birth, she'd have had to've known another wouldn't surface in Greenville."

Nate peered into space. "So how else do we find out who delivered those twins? Or...the twins were in the hospital for at least part of a day, because the Elmores visited. Maybe a nurse who tended newborns. Someone who worked that floor of the hospital in nineteen eighty-one."

I shook my head, looked out the window over my shoulder. "Privacy regulations being what they are today, going to the hospital will be a waste of time."

We both mulled that for a few moments. Nate said, "Let's go back to the condo. Search through the databases for births the same night in the same hospital. If we can find a doctor who was there, that's a start."

"Women have their own OB-GYNs. Kathy's—Virginia's—doctor wouldn't necessarily have delivered any of the other babies. She would have seen the same doctor once a month at least. It's a long shot, but maybe the Elmores remember who she was seeing."

Nate pulled over into the shade while I looked up their phone number.

Vicki answered on the second ring. "Hello?"

"Mrs. Elmore, this is Liz Talbot. I spoke to you and your husband yesterday afternoon?"

"Oh, hey. Of course."

"I have one more question, if you don't mind."

"I'm happy to help if I can."

"Do you happen to recall the doctor Kathy was seeing? Her OB-GYN?"

"As a matter of fact, I recommended him. I saw the man myself until he retired. It was Doctor Redrick Lawrence. His office used to be over near the hospital, in Cross Creek."

"Thank you so much. I really appreciate your help."

We said our goodbyes.

"Back to the condo to research the doctor?" Nate asked.

"Sounds good."

I started a profile on Redrick Lawrence. Fortunately, no one had seen a need to obscure his digital footprint. He'd lived in Greenville his entire life except for the time he attended the University of South Carolina at Columbia and its School of Medicine. He resided on McDaniel Avenue, a high-dollar, well-established neighborhood with a solid pedigree. Within an hour, I'd created a timeline of Doctor Lawrence's life. His wife was deceased. He had one daughter, Lynda.

Something was niggling me. I picked up the marriage license and studied it. Talitha had been a witness, as had a woman whose last name was the same as the minister's. Here was proof Evan Ingle was a Bounetheau. Did he know that? Had he known it all along? And had they all kept him at arm's length all these years, funneling money to him anonymously? Or had one or more of them reached out?

I pulled up Kent's Facebook profile again, and looked through her photo albums. Most of the pictures were more than a year old. There were hundreds from high school and college, but few recent, and none with Evan.

I went back to Samantha Blundell's profile and scanned the album from April. She told me on the phone she'd been to Evan's opening for his new collection. But there were no photos posted from the gallery. Did she have other photos she hadn't posted? Who might be in those photos? An opening exhibit was a big deal.

It was eleven o'clock—seven on the West Coast. That was painfully early for a teenager. Then again, she'd be getting ready for school. I scrolled through the contacts on my phone and tapped her name.

"Hello?" She didn't sound like I'd woken her.

"Samantha, this is Liz Talbot, calling from South Carolina."

She laughed.

I didn't pause to ask what amused her. "I have a quick question if you have a moment. I hope I'm not catching you on your way out to school."

"No," she said. "I'm on fall break. I'm actually at my grandma's house for the week, and she lives in Greenville. That's why I laughed. I'm in South Carolina now, too."

"You're in Greenville. South Carolina."

"Yes. What did you need to ask me?"

I usually didn't have much truck with coincidences, but I couldn't see how this could be anything but a very convenient one. "The photos you posted from your trip to Charleston. I noticed there weren't any from the gallery showing. I wondered if you had more photos from the trip that you didn't post."

"I do, actually. I like disposable cameras. I haven't finished using the last one from the trip, so I haven't had the photos developed yet."

That seemed an unusual preference for someone her age. "You don't use your phone?"

"I do, but when you take a hundred photos on a phone and pick the best one, it isn't as genuine as one quick snapshot," she said. "Photographs taken with phones look more posed. I like the rawness of disposables. And taking photos with disposables gives this worn in and grungy type of feel that's more authentic than photos with a phone."

Interesting. "Are there photos on your disposable from the gallery event?"

"Yeah, most of them are. I had like four cameras that trip. I grabbed a new one from my purse by accident when we went in."

"That was back in April..."

"Yeah, I kinda forgot about it. I brought it along to finish the roll at Grandma's."

"If I buy you a new disposable camera, would you be willing to have that one developed?"

"You don't have to do that."

"No, I want to get you a new camera. Can you meet me? Is Walgreens okay?"

"Sure."

"Which one are you closest to?"

"The one on Augusta Road."

"Can you meet me there at eleven-thirty?"

"My grandma and I have lunch plans. Would one-thirty be okay?"

"Sure. See you there."

"Nate?" Where had he wandered off to?

"Yeah," he answered from his office across the hall.

"Want to grab some lunch? We have a couple of hours."

He walked across the hall and leaned against the doorway, eyeing me speculatively. "What do you feel like?" His smoldering eyes told me exactly want he felt like.

"You are insatiable."

"Yes, I am. As a matter of fact, I think the condition is getting worse." He crossed the room, stepped around the desk, and reached down from behind me to fold me into his arms.

"You're going to be starving by the time we finish at Walgreens."

"I already am."

"Nate."

He went to kissing on my neck.

"Nate?"

"Yeah?"

"Focus. We have a case. New information. Missing girl."

He sighed and straightened. "You're right. But I refuse to apologize. You are a very pleasant distraction."

"About lunch? We have to eat."

"Feel like tacos? The Local Taco is on Conestee, just off Augusta."

"Sounds good."

He bent down and whispered in my ear. "That's not going to take two hours."

Samantha Blundell was every bit as perky in person as she looked online. She chatted with Nate and me while we waited for the photos to be developed. I paid for two sets, one for her and one for me. Over her protests, I bought her a replacement camera.

"Could you take a look at these with us, in case we have questions?" I asked when I finally had my copies in hand.

"Absolutely. Anything I can do to help find Kent."

I spread the pictures across the counter at Walgreens. The photo tech didn't object. There were twenty-three images, all from the inside of Evan's gallery. The first thing that struck me was that the artwork was completely different from what he was currently showing. "These are impressionist paintings." Was Kent drawn to him because his work was similar to hers?

"Yeah, that's what he said. I don't know much about art, but I thought they were pretty. Lots of bright colors."

"He's showing abstracts now. A completely different line. I wouldn't think he'd have a big opening in April with impressionist paintings and switch them all completely out by October. Do painters work that fast?"

"Beats me," said Nate.

I scanned the people in the photos. Hell's bells, my brother, Blake, had been there—with Calista McQueen. Were they an item? There was Kent chatting with two folks I didn't know, a guy and a woman. Kent with Evan, apparently discussing one of the paintings. I looked closer. I couldn't make out much but the colors and the sky over their heads. The painting must have been a landscape.

My eyes stopped short on a posed photo. Kent and Evan smiled on either side of a distinguished gentleman with white hair. He looked peacock-proud standing between his grandchildren in his light blue seersucker suit and red bow tie. C.C. Bounetheau. With him and Evan side-by-side you could see a resemblance. "Nate."

"Is that who I think it is?" he asked.

"Indeed, it is." I said. "Samantha, who asked you to take this photo?"

"Kent did. I promised to email it to her. I just haven't had it developed until now."

"Did she introduce you to either of the other people in the photo?"

"Well, the young guy was the artist, and I'd already been introduced. She said the older gentleman was her granddad. She mentioned that he was a painter, too. And so was she."

"Did you talk to them any further?"

"No. I mean, I did chat with Kent before then, like I told you. She saw me snapping pictures and asked me to take one of them. After that, I was browsing with my parents."

"Thank you so much. You've been very helpful," I said.

"I'm glad," she said. "I hope you find Kent. And I hope she's all right."

"Me, too," I said. But I was reasonably certain Kent was anything but all right.

Doctor Redrick Lawrence's home was as fine as anything on McDaniel Avenue. It was large by anyone's standard and built of red brick. A courtyard wall in the same brick surrounded the property. An iron gate in the brick wall prevented me from ringing the doorbell. I tried the call box by the numbered keypad. A camera was mounted discreetly above in a tree. I couldn't be sure if no one answered because no one was home, or because they didn't recognize me.

"What now?" I scanned what I could see of the yard through the gates. It had a look of vague neglect, like maybe someone was keeping it up, but not quite often enough. The front porch planters had the remnants of summer flowers, now dead. Weeds popped up through the mulch beds.

"It's tricky," Nate said. "We need to be real certain no one's inside before we let ourselves in, check it out."

"I know," I said. "Let me think."

While I was thinking, a jogger came by. We smiled and waved, and so did he. My gaze followed him. From the other direction, a walker approached. "Maybe I'll try chatting her up."

"You want me to do it?" He grinned.

I rolled my eyes. "You'll likely have better luck. Go ahead."

When the thirty-something blonde was close enough, Nate called out, "Good morning."

"Good morning," she said, her voice guarded.

"I wonder if you could help my sister and me out." Nate gave her his full wattage smile.

She returned his smile and crossed to our side of the street. "I'll try."

"We were looking up Doctor Lawrence. He treated our mother for many years, and we need her records. But since his office closed, we don't know where to call. Mom's not doing well." He looked at the ground for a moment, then back up at her.

"I think they have all of that stored in the house. I remember when they brought it all in. Boxes and boxes. Takes up a whole room, Lynda said. She's his daughter."

"I see," said Nate. "Do you know what the proper procedure is to request a file?"

"I'm afraid not. Doctor Lawrence isn't well himself. In fact, Lynda had him moved to a facility near her...six months ago, maybe?"

"Could you tell us where that is?" Nate asked. "Maybe we could call her."

"Sure. She lives on Sullivan's Island. She's a doctor, too. At Medical University of South Carolina? I think her father is in a care facility in Mount Pleasant. I have Lynda's number here somewhere." She pulled out a phone and tapped it a few times.

I grabbed a pad and pen from my tote.

"Here it is." She called out a number and I wrote it down.

"Thank you so much," said Nate.

"You're welcome. I hope your mom's all right." She smiled and returned to her side of the street.

When she was half a block away, I punched Nate in the arm.

"What was that for?"

"Flirting. And calling me your sister."

"Hey, I got you what you wanted. I like to think I used my body in your service. I can do some more of that later on if you like." A grin slid up his face.

I wrapped my arm around his neck and pulled him down for a kiss. "I would like, very much. But first we have to get back to the lowcountry. We have a doctor to find."

Nate pulled back. His expression turned grim. "I know. Let's go."

TWENTY-SEVEN

We'd taken what we needed from Nate's condo when we left for lunch, so we left McDaniel Avenue and headed for Charleston. As Nate pulled onto I-385, I dialed the number he'd scored from the walker. Because we were still using the prepaid phones, the Sync system in the car wasn't working. I put the phone on speaker so Nate could hear.

"Hello?"

"Hey, I'm trying to reach Lynda Lawrence?"

"This is Doctor Lawrence."

"Of course—my apologies. Doctor Lawrence, my name is Liz Talbot. I'm a private investigator, retained by the family of Kent Heyward in the matter of her disappearance. You may have heard about it in the news."

"Yes, of course. That poor girl. Have they found her? I saw where her car was found—just awful."

"No, she hasn't been found yet, but as you might imagine, time is of the essence."

"How can I help?" She sounded truly confused.

"Through a rather complicated series of events, our investigation has led us to a patient of your father's from the early eighties. I wondered if we might speak to him."

She was quiet for a long stretch. "Dad isn't well."

"I understand. I promise we won't stay long. Just a couple questions."

"I don't think he can help you. Dad has Alzheimer's disease. He has good days and bad days, but for the most part his memory is gone."

Alzheimer's. Such a cruel diagnosis. I felt bad for the doctor and his family, and ashamed that it also occurred to me this was the worst possible thing he could have in terms of being able to help us. "I'm so sorry to hear that. I know that must be terribly difficult for you both. I wouldn't ask, except a young girl's life may well be at stake. Could we please try? We're in Greenville right now, but we'll be back in Charleston in a few hours."

"Let me speak to his doctor. If he says it's okay, that'll be fine. I have your number on my cell."

"Thank you so much. I'll look forward to hearing from you."

"It could be a couple of days. Between my schedule and his, sometimes it's difficult to connect with Dad's doctor."

"I understand. Thank you for anything you can do."

"I'll be in touch." She ended the call.

"Something tells me the doctor at the facility isn't going to allow us to speak with her father," said Nate.

"I have that feeling, too, though I'd be surprised to learn she actually spoke to the facility doctor."

"We may have to arrange for flowers—maybe a potted plant—to be delivered to the good doctor. Florists with a delivery to make often call around looking for patients."

"Indeed," I said.

"I'd say what we've learned supports your working narrative pretty well."

"It also explains why someone invested in hired muscle to scare me off. I was questioning Evan. It's not that the Bounetheaus didn't want me looking for Kent. They wanted me to leave Evan alone. Or possibly they just wanted Virginia's past kept in the past."

Nate said, "But that would mean that whoever hired those guys honestly believes there's no connection between Evan and his background and Kent's disappearance."

"Just because they want to believe that doesn't make it true."

"I wonder if Evan knows who his family is."

"I doubt it," I said. "My guess is Talitha might've planned to tell him at some point, but she died unexpectedly. Part of her deal all these years had to be discretion, and the Bounetheaus paid her a lot of money for that."

"Yeah, you're probably right."

"It was either Abigail and/or C.C., or possibly Virginia, who hired the thugs, though I think Virginia's a long shot."

We bounced theories back and forth all the way back to Orangeburg, where we stopped for a break. When we got back in the car, Colleen was in the backseat. Her expression was grim.

"You know what?" I said to Nate. "I'd love a Cheerwine. I'm sorry. I should've gotten it while we were inside. Do you want anything?"

"I'll get it. Be right back." He got out of the car and headed back into the convenience store.

"What's wrong?" I asked Colleen.

"Ask Nate to let you drive."

"Why?"

"We don't have time for why. Just listen. You drive. Drive as slow as you can. Stay as far away from other cars as you possibly can. Don't take your sunglasses off."

"What in the world? Colleen—"

"Avoid the trees."

Nate climbed back in the car and handed me my Cheerwine.

"Thank you. Hey listen, you've been driving a while. Why don't you relax and let me drive a bit?"

"I'm fine, but thanks."

"Nate Andrews, do you not trust my driving?"

I reached for indignant, but I was anxious. What was going on?

"It's not that."

"Then let me drive."

I got out of the car and walked around to his side.

He shrugged, unbuckled his seatbelt, and got out of the car.

I got in and adjusted the seat and mirrors. When I looked into the rearview, Colleen was gone. I took a long swig of Cheerwine. The section of I-26 not too far in front of us, between I-95 and Summerville, was one of the most dangerous sections of highway in the country. Hundreds of people had been injured in accidents there over the past several years. Many had died. I put both hands on the steering wheel and squared my shoulders.

Traffic was heavy. I eased back onto the interstate, trying my best to stay away from other cars. The speed limit was seventy. I held it at sixty-eight and stayed in the right lane.

After a bit, I found a spot several car lengths from the Escalade in front of me and kept my speed steady.

A stream of cars passed me. I could feel Nate studying me, but I kept my eyes on the road.

After a few minutes, he said, "You turned awful quiet. Anything you want to talk about?"

"Just focused on driving is all."

"If you say so."

The median between the east and westbound lanes was wide, the topography varied from flat to ravine. Clumps of trees appeared in the passing landscape. Gradually, they became thicker until few gaps broke the tree line. The shoulder dropped off steeply. Twenty minutes after we left Orangeburg, we crossed under I-95. My hands at nine and three, I gripped the steering wheel.

For long stretches, dense swamp crowded the right shoulder. Just past mile marker 188, the Escalade slowed way down. I thought maybe the driver had car trouble and was looking for a spot to pull over. But the SUV just kept going slower and held the lane.

"What's up with this guy?" Nate said. "The speed limit is seventy."

I signaled to pass. A motorcycle whizzed by us.

I pulled into the left lane. As soon as I passed the Escalade, it pulled in behind me.

A blinding white light shot through the windshield.

"What the hell?" Nate yelled.

I fought the urge to cover my eyes. Behind my sunglasses, I squinted, tried to see around the light. It was too bright and too big.

Beneath us, the surface changed. The tires rolled over the shoulder. I was drifting left, towards a deadly stand of trees in the median. If I overcorrected, I could slam into someone in the right lane. I braked.

The light was unrelenting.

Nate spat out a string of curses.

I slowed as much as I could and tried to ease over into the median, praying for a break in the tree line.

I must've caught a section of the median where it fell off steeply. The Explorer pitched.

I pulled right on the steering wheel.

The car teetered.

We rolled.

Time seemed to stop.

Airbags popped open. Brightly colored shimmers of light filled the air. Colleen?

The car slammed into timber.

Blackness.

I heard voices. I tried to open my eyes but couldn't. The voices faded. I slipped away.

Later, hours or days, I couldn't tell, I heard Merry talking. "It's time for you to wake up now. What do you want to hear today? More *Pillars of the Earth* or People Magazine? I could sing."

I groaned, or tried. So thirsty.

"Liz?" Merry's voice was urgent. "Liz? Please wake up. Hey! Somebody? Get a doctor in here. She made a noise."

Where was I?

Nate.

Oh Sweet Lord. Where was Nate? The car had rolled.

I mustered everything within me and opened my eyes.

"She's awake!" Merry jumped up and down. "Can you hear me?"

I blinked. I couldn't talk. My throat was so dry, my lips parched. I worked to make one word come out of my mouth. *Nate.*

Merry disappeared. "*Hey*! My sister's awake. Get a doctor. *Now*," she roared.

She came back to the bed and took my hand. Tears streamed down her face. "You're awake."

I blinked back tears. I tried squeezing her hand. How could I communicate with her? I was desperate to know that Nate was all right.

"You've been out for two days," she said. "I've got to call Mamma and Daddy. They just went to get coffee."

By the time she'd summoned our parents and called Blake, a doctor appeared and ran them all out.

"Liz, I'm Doctor Young," she said. "Do you remember what happened?"

I blinked. Then tried a nod. I could nod. Progress.

She shined a light in my eyes, checked me over.

"You're at MUSC. Today is Friday."

Friday? We'd been driving home Wednesday evening.

She reached for a cup and put a straw to my lips. "I know you're thirsty, but just a few sips right now, okay?"

I nodded again. Oh dear heaven, that water tasted good. I took two sips. "Nate?" I forced his name out. My voiced sounded like a ninety-year-old smoker's.

"Mr. Andrews is down the hall. His injuries—both your injuries—are miraculously minor given the condition of the car you were driving. You're both bruised up badly. But aside from the fact we couldn't get you to wake up for two days, nothing to worry about. You have a nasty concussion. We were afraid it might've been a fracture, but your CT scan is clear. We've had you both under observation for internal injuries, because, frankly, none of us can believe you don't have any. Do you remember who pulled you out of the car? The highway patrol officers haven't been able to find your Good Samaritan."

"No," I said.

"The officers asked me to call when you woke up."

I nodded.

"I'll give you some time with your family."

"Thank you. Can I see Nate?"

She smiled. "I don't think a team of mules could keep him away once I let him know you're awake. He's been sitting in that chair by your bed ever since he regained consciousness. I believe your sister ran him back to his own bed an hour or so ago."

"Sounds like Merry."

"I'll check back in with you before I leave today. You can go home tomorrow provided you remain stable."

"Thank you." Thank God. Thank Colleen.

She walked out and left the door propped open. In a rush came Mamma, Daddy, Merry, Joe Eaddy, and Blake. And Nate. He walked towards me safe and whole and I started bawling.

Mamma said, "Liz, honey, are you all right? Frank, get the doctor."

Daddy said, "Well, she just left, Caroline. Tutie's just happy to see us." Daddy looked me over, reassuring himself.

Merry said, "What do you need? You want some more water? Are you in pain?"

Mamma said, "Merry, close those blinds, it's too bright in here."

Blake walked up to the side of the bed. He was rubbing the back of his neck, his stress tell. "About time you woke up. What the hell happened? Nate said someone blinded you."

I nodded. I was still tired, and I had a lot to process.

Then they were all talking at once, everyone telling the others to be quiet and let me rest. Over the roar, Daddy said, "Why don't we let Nate here have the chair? None of the rest of us is banged up."

"Thank you, Mr. Talbot."

"I told you before. Frank will be fine. Here, sit down."

Nate did as he was told and reached for my hand. "You had us worried, Slugger. I need to hear you tell me you're okay." His eyes glistened, too.

"I'm fine. Are you okay?"

"Unaccountably. Truck's totaled. Caught fire. Exploded. Apparently, we slept through a hell of a mess. I have no idea who pulled us out and away from there. One of the highway patrolmen said the first guy on the scene saw a red-haired teenage girl dragging me over by you—about twenty yards from the truck—but she disappeared."

Colleen. Colleen pulled us out. She'd been there. I remembered her shimmers.

Nate said, "I don't think I'm going to buy another grey Explorer. That combination hasn't been real lucky for us." He smiled weakly. The last one he'd had just like it had ended up in the water.

I smiled back at him and squeezed his hand.

"It's a good thing you were driving," he said. "I wasn't going to say anything because I didn't want to fight with you, but you were driving fifteen miles an hour slower than I would've been. Probably saved both our lives."

"I have a strong suspicion how so many Ingles have ended up dead in car accidents," I said.

"I was thinking the same thing."

Mamma approached the other side of the bed. "Here, sugar, this will make you feel better." She bathed my face with a cool cloth.

"Thank you, Mamma."

"Here now, put on a little lipstick." She handed me a tube of Estee Lauder.

TWENTY-EIGHT

As promised, we were both discharged Saturday morning with the usual warnings to rest. And we did. We went back to my house and let Mamma do what she does best—feed us. On her first stop of several, she brought homemade pimento cheese, which she knows I have a particular fondness for, a platter of fried chicken, deviled eggs, potato salad, green beans, and a chocolate cake. She insisted on fixing us plates of lunch before she left.

When she had us situated at the kitchen table and taken care of to her satisfaction she said, "I'll be back in just a bit. Don't worry about these dishes, now."

"This is incredible." Nate had a dazed look on his face. This was his first experience of being mothered by Caroline Talbot. "Thank you so much for all of this."

Mamma rested a hand on his shoulder and looked at him sideways. "You didn't think I'd let you go hungry, did you? Liz, call me if y'all need me to pick up anything on my way back." She hugged us and was gone.

Nate dug into his plate. "Mmm-mmm. Green beans never tasted like this when my mamma made them. She had one basic recipe she used for just about everything. Open the can, pour it in a bowl, microwave."

"Mamma doesn't countenance to food out of a can, with the exception of the creamy soups she puts in casseroles and all like that." I tasted the potato salad. "Yum."

"She's a sweet lady. Your whole family...they've taken real good care of us." Undercurrents churned in his eyes.

"Family does for family." This was the bedrock on which my world was built.

"My family doesn't operate this way. And I have to tell you, I'm not sure I'll ever get over the urge to apologize to your entire family, on behalf of mine and all our ancestors, for Scott."

I reached out for his hand. "Sweetheart, do not entertain such a notion. You are not responsible for his lack of character. Let it go. I have. So have they."

He raised his eyebrows, widened his eyes, and dropped his chin to the side. "Seems like a lot for them to overlook."

"I don't want to look back anymore. Let's focus on the future. I'm just so thankful we're going to have one. We're very fortunate to be sitting here right now."

"You don't have to tell me that. When I woke up in that hospital and didn't know where you were…" He twined his fingers through mine and held tight.

"I know. Me, too." It occurred to me then very likely no one had been there when he woke up. Merry had been by my side, and the rest of the family downstairs.

"Have you spoken to your parents?"

He shook his head. "No. The hospital didn't call them. You've been listed as my next of kin for years."

"Don't you want to call them? Surely they'd want to know—want to be here for you." I'd mentioned this in the hospital, but he'd avoided the topic.

"There's no need. I'm fine."

We'd barely finished lunch when Moon Unit brought over a casserole, followed by Nell and Ansley Johnson with a chicken pot pie. Nell had Ansley on a short leash. Her eyes had a medicated look to them. She didn't have much to say, only that Matt hadn't been released, and her daddy had retained her an attorney.

Calista came by next. She was annoyingly coy on the subject of my brother. Then came Grace, followed by virtually everyone else on the island. Nate and I did not go hungry, is what I'm saying. I ended up freezing way more than we ate. By Monday morning, we were itching to get back to work, if still sore.

We planned our day at the island in the kitchen, over our second cup of coffee.

I said, "As careful as we were, there's no way anyone tracked us to Greenville and laid in wait on the way home."

We'd been all through this, several times.

"Agreed." Nate set his mug on the counter. "I told you, I think Doctor Lynda Lawrence was our tripwire. Aside from Sonny and Blake, she's the only person who knew we were in Greenville. And you told her we were on our way back."

"But how'd she get herself caught up in this mess?"

"Someone kept tabs on Redrick Lawrence. When his daughter put him in an assisted living facility, they probably contacted her, or, more likely, hired someone else to do it. Made up some story about how someone might try to harass her father, and for his protection, if anyone ever called, she should call this number, and so forth."

"That begs the question. Is someone now on high alert at the assisted living center?"

"Maybe," Nate said. "Or they could be figuring on doing a more effective job of getting rid of us."

We both fell quiet. Clearly, at least one of the Bounetheaus had tried to have us killed. It had only served to make us more determined to solve our case.

As it turned out, there were only two Alzheimer's care facilities in Mount Pleasant, so it didn't take many florist inquires to ascertain which one housed Doctor Redrick Lawrence. It was a couple blocks off Johnnie Dodds Boulevard.

Nate and I walked through the front doors at nine a.m. and asked to see someone regarding Nate's mother, who would soon be needing full-time care. We both apologized profusely for not having made an appointment. This was a difficult time.

The lady at the front desk was very understanding. She got the director, who gave us a detailed tour, and all sorts of brochures. Fortunately, patients' names were posted outside their rooms. We went back to the director's office to discuss the financial aspects of care. Soon after, I excused myself and asked directions to the ladies room.

I made my way back to Doctor Lawrence's room. He sat in a chair by the window, watching birds fluttering around an empty bird feeder.

I knocked twice on the door, though it stood open. "Hey, Doctor Lawrence, how are you today?"

"I'm fine. How are you?"

He spoke clearly. His eyes were focused.

"I'm doing real good. Do you mind if I sit and talk with you for a few minutes?"

He was seated, but I made him for over six feet. His hair was white, his skin mottled and red in spots. He smiled wryly. "Not at all. Few people do. I'm happy for the company."

I smiled and sat in a chair next to him. "I'm Liz. Someone needs to fill the feeder for the birds, don't they?"

"I like the blue ones best."

"Those are my favorite, too. Blue birds of happiness."

"Sometimes," he said.

I didn't want to scare him, but I didn't have much time. "Doctor Lawrence, do you remember Kathy Ingle?"

He looked at me with shrewd eyes. "You mean Virginia Bounetheau?"

I almost stopped breathing. "Yes."

"Of course I remember her." He sighed. "I'm an old man. I can't tell you what I did yesterday, but I can tell you most anything you want to know about the eighties. Not that anyone ever asks. I've been parked here to die where I don't upset anyone with my illness."

"That's just horrible." I hurt for him. He had family close by. Who does that kind of thing?

"Since you took the trouble, young lady, I'll tell you whatever you want to know."

I smiled at him gently. "Thank you. This may help us find a young girl who's gone missing. Do you know what happened at the hospital in Greenville? What happened to the twins?"

He looked at his hands as he spoke. "It was Abigail. I knew C.C. in school. We were fraternity brothers. Abigail was mortified that Virginia had married beneath her social status and gotten herself pregnant. She offered me quite a lot of money to tell Virginia those babies died and put them up for adoption."

"Is that what you did?"

"I would have. I'm not proud of that. But the aunt—I can't remember her name—grabbed the babies and ran. Things were different in the eighties. It was easier to walk out of the hospital with children, especially if you worked there, knew people, and knew procedures."

I heard heels clicking in the hall. Someone was coming. Then I heard Colleen. "Help me find my mother. She's missing from her room." Footsteps hurried in the other direction. Colleen's new skill of materializing was getting a workout.

"Go on, please," I said.

"When the nurse discovered the babies were gone, I had to think fast. I told her they were with their mother, then asked her to check on another patient. The aunt had been with them moments before. She had to've taken them. I called Abigail. Told her the aunt had the babies and I was done with the whole mess. Abigail sent a limo. It was waiting out front within minutes. I put Virginia in it. The driver took her straight to Charleston. I let Abigail deal with her. I assume she told her the children had died.

"I simply told the staff my patient had checked out against medical advice and taken the babies with her. If you think I've done something illegal, I'm afraid you're out of luck. I have dementia, you see."

"Yes, I see." If he had committed a crime, surely the statute of limitations had expired. "How is it that a neighbor recommended you to Virginia? Are the Elmores involved in this?"

"Not at all. Abigail told me where Virginia was living. She has her sources. I'd seen Vicki Elmore for years. I let drop I was taking on new patients, said I was expanding the practice, and asked if she had friends or neighbors she might send my way. If Virginia had lived in another neighborhood, I'd have gotten a different patient to recommend me."

"Do you have any idea what happened to the babies' father?"

"I understand he was killed in a car accident. If you're asking me if I was told to expect some misfortune would befall him, no, but it didn't surprise me, either. But that was all Abigail. I had nothing to do with it."

"Is there anything else I should know?" He seemed eager to unburden himself.

"If you mess with Abigail, you'll likely end up dead."

"Yes, I know." Every cell in my body went cold. "Thank you."

"Take care of yourself, young lady."

I nodded and made my way quickly back to Nate.

"Sweetheart," he said, as I entered the administrator's office, "are you still feeling unwell?"

"I'm afraid so. Bad shellfish." I looked at the administrator.

"I'm so sorry," she said. "Perhaps you could take the information to look over and schedule an appointment to finalize a care plan."

"Thank you. That sounds perfect." Nate stood and escorted me out.

Once in the car, I brought him up to speed.

"Clever people," Nate said. "Ruthless and clever."

TWENTY-NINE

Nate and I mulled our next move while staring at the ocean from the Adirondack chairs on the deck snacking on pimento cheese and crackers. Brushes with death typically induced a few days of stress eating for me.

I washed a bite down with a swallow of Cheerwine. "Abigail may be capable of arranging for subpar grandchildren to be adopted. But it's hard for me to imagine she'd have one of the pedigreed ones killed, even to protect her secrets. And that's assuming Kent somehow found out. Except I don't see any other theory that fits what we know."

"Mrs. Bounetheau has an awfully lot at stake. Think about it. She contracted Turner Ingle's death—and possibly Talitha's, though I don't think we've established a motive for that. No statute of limitations on murder," Nate said.

"But you know her fingerprints are so far removed from that murder she'd never be convicted, or even arrested. All we have is the word of an eighty-some-odd-year-old doctor of questionable mental faculties."

"There's more evidence somewhere to be found, or she wouldn't be trying to get rid of us."

"I guess that makes sense. I'm not convinced Virginia Heyward knows to this day either of the twins survived," I said. "And how much does Colton Heyward know? I think that family has lots of secrets from one another."

"I find myself wondering just how clean C.C. Bounetheau's hands are. Is all of this Abigail? Or is he just as guilty?"

"I think it's time we talk to these folks, one-on-one, starting with the least threatening—Virginia. Let's get her version of what happened in nineteen eighty-one and see if she can think of how this might relate to

Kent. There was some weird vibe going on between her and Abigail from the first time I met them."

"All right," said Nate. "But we can't just call the Heyward home and ask to speak to Virginia. William Palmer would report that post haste to Abigail, and she'd release the flying monkeys."

"We need to get Virginia to leave the house by herself, then intercept her."

"What makes a woman like that, one with servants to run mundane errands, leave the house on a Monday afternoon?"

I mulled that. "We don't have enough information about her daily habits to make this elegant. How about we do a UPS delivery?"

"Signature required?"

"Naturally. It'll have to be the fake variety. We can't get a real one delivered today. I'll work on the letter and label. We need a medium-sized box. One that looks like it would be something she'd purchased online. I have several in the garage that would work."

"I'll grab one."

I hopped up and hauled my still aching bones to my office. First, I called UPS and asked for a package pickup that afternoon at my home on lower Legare. I gave them the address across the street from the Heyward residence. They told me they'd be by between three and three-thirty.

I typed a letter to Virginia, asking her to meet me alone at White Point Gardens, on a bench near the bandstand, at four that afternoon. Likely, she understood her family dynamics far better than I did, and would understand my need to employ such methods. I also told her to tear up the letter and flush it down the toilet after she read it. Then I created a UPS label using the small business application.

Nate carried in a box. "How about we put a couple books in here? I found some bubble wrap with the boxes. We could fill up the box with that."

"Perfect."

He assembled the package. I put the letter in an envelope on top, and he sealed the box.

Anxiety gnawed at my stomach. "Do you think Abigail is so paranoid at this point even a package delivery would trigger a call from Mr. Palmer?"

"That's a possibility. Especially since we have no way of knowing if Virginia's ever received a signature-only delivery. It may be he's reporting anything out of her normal routine."

"We need to give Abigail something more urgent to focus on."

After a minute, Nate said, "Or we prevent William Palmer from making any calls."

"The cellphone jammer is easy, but how are you going to disable the landline quick enough after doing the UPS delivery?"

"I'll get it done."

At two-forty-five, I pulled Gram's Caddy to the right side of Legare several houses before the Heyward home. Nate unfolded a map and spread it across the dash—just a couple lost tourists. Legare was a narrow, one-way street. A carriage tour driver cast us an aggravated glance in the midst of his animated tale, but pulled in front of us and went on with the show.

The UPS truck passed us at three fifteen. The driver stopped in front of the house across the street from the Heywards, got out of the truck, and headed to the front door. I slid in behind the truck. Nate hopped out of the car and jogged to the main entrance of the Heyward house. His uniform was exactly like the driver's, but his cap was pulled lower, and a black hairpiece stuck out from underneath. A fake mustache and wire-rimmed glasses completed his disguise.

This operation depended on perfect timing. I needed that UPS truck to sit in the road until Nate was outside the Heyward garden. Ideally, I needed the driver occupied on the porch long enough for Nate to hop inside the truck and slip out the other side just in case anyone was watching. I kept my eyes on the driver. It wouldn't take long for him to find out there'd been a mistake and no package awaited pickup.

He started down the steps. He could now see Nate when he emerged from the Heyward garden. I reached to open the car door. I needed to create a diversion. Directions. I'd ask for directions. The car door stood open two inches.

From Carolina sunlight, Colleen appeared on the sidewalk. She appeared to trip over the uneven stones and fell, landing hard, near the back corner of the truck.

"Oowww." Colleen rubbed her ankle.

The driver rushed to her aide.

I eased the car door closed.

He knelt by Colleen. She gestured and moaned, made a lot of racket.

Nate came out of the gate and glanced at me. I nodded towards the truck. He walked straight to it and climbed into the driver's side and stepped across, waiting at the passenger side. The driver helped Colleen to her feet.

"I can't thank you enough," she said loud enough for me to hear.

When the driver slipped behind the truck on his way around, Nate came out the passenger side. As the truck rolled forwards, he climbed in the car.

With practiced speed, he removed the hat, wig, and mustache. "Cellphones are jammed. Landlines are out."

"How did you do that so fast?"

"I made it to the box before I went to the door with the package. That's what took me so long. Virginia came to the door pretty quick after Palmer called her. Must've been in the living room. It was almost like she was waiting for me."

"We caught a couple breaks," I said, thinking the break's name was Colleen.

"What was going on with that driver?"

"He was helping a girl who tripped on the sidewalk. Those things are dangerous." I pulled away from the curb and headed to White Point Gardens.

At three-thirty, I parked on South Battery and made my way to the bench closest to the bandstand. Nate stayed in the car. We agreed Virginia would be more forthcoming with just one of us—not feel outnumbered, et cetera. Estrogen made me the better choice.

Virginia arrived early, only a few minutes later.

"I was too nervous to wait." Her eyes darted around the park. We weren't alone. A couple on a quilt picnicked nearby but out of earshot. The park was lightly dotted with tourists and locals. Lovers rambled hand in hand. Mothers strolled and chased children. Finally, she sat beside me.

"I apologize for the ruse," I said. "I wanted to speak with you privately. I don't think that's possible in your home." The canopy of live oak trees cloaked us.

She gave me an assessing look. "You were a good choice of investigator."

"I have some difficult questions for you. Please know I wouldn't ask them unless I needed to know the answers. I'm trying to find Kent."

"I understand." Trepidation settled on her face.

"Tell me about your first marriage, the children." I kept my tone neutral.

She brought a fist to her mouth, rocked back and forth. "Oh, no."

"Mrs. Heyward? I'm so sorry to put you though this, ma'am. But I think it might be important."

"No...I mean, I'll tell you." Her face paled. She took slow, deep breaths. "It's just, I've prayed so hard Kent's disappearance had nothing to do with all of that ugliness. I know what my mother is capable of. I told myself she wouldn't harm Kent. She's always doted on her. Kent's her only granddaughter." Her voice got higher and faster, like maybe she was working up to hysteria.

"Ma'am, I don't know for sure there's any connection. I just need more information to figure that out." I tried to sound calm, reassuring. I needed her coherent. "Start with when and why you left Charleston."

She drew a couple ragged breaths, seemed to steady herself. "Mother wanted me to go to college. Prepare myself for my position in Charleston society. Then she wanted to pick my husband. I was in love with Turner Ingle. He was a wonderful man. But he had no money, no social position."

"So you eloped?"

"Yes. Turner was a welder, and he'd heard GE was hiring. We thought Greenville would be far enough. Honestly, I thought Daddy would prevent Mother from interfering with us. I thought once I was damaged goods in her eyes she'd write me off and that would be that. All I wanted was to get away from her."

"Except she didn't let go that easy."

Virginia shook her head slowly, with precision. "No. I knew something was up with Doctor Lawrence after the twins were born. After we heard about Turner's accident. The doctor seemed very nervous. Then, Talitha, Turner's sister, overheard him talking to an attorney, arranging an adoption. I knew Mother was behind it. I begged Talitha to take the twins and leave. Eva was in an incubator. I knew it was a risk. I prayed Talitha could get to MUSC in time. I told her she could trust Daddy, but never Mother."

"Did she do that?" I knew the answer, of course, but I needed to know what Virginia knew.

Virginia rubbed her arms. "I didn't know for a very long time. Doctor Lawrence drugged me and Mother sent a limousine. The driver brought me straight back to the house. Mother had a doctor come to treat me at home. I was frantic about the children. I told Daddy everything. He was livid with Mother. I've never seen him like that."

Tears slid down her face. She dabbed at them with a handkerchief. "They told me the twins had both died at the hospital in Greenville. A part of me died then, too. I just didn't care anymore. Turner and my children were gone."

I waited for her to continue.

"My parents covered it all up. Told everyone I'd been traveling abroad. It was as if none of it had ever happened. A year or so later, they began orchestrating occasions where I spent time with Colton. He's a kind man, a good man." She looked up at me. "I needed a way out from under my mother's thumb. He gave me that. I tried to put everything behind me. And he's been good to me. Kent came along...we had a good life. But now...I can't understand how after all this time...."

"Did you ever hear from Talitha again?"

She shook her head. "No. I saw in the paper a while back where she'd been killed in a car accident, and was survived by a son. She'd never married. I knew...I just *knew* that child was mine. I went to her funeral. I thought Mother would have a seizure. William Palmer reports everything I do to her."

Why in the name of sweet reason would a grown woman tolerate this?

A jogger approached down the path to our left. Virginia stopped talking. Her eyes followed as the jogger retreated in the opposite direction. She seemed lost in thought for a moment. Then she looked at me directly, her eyes bright with anger. "I saw my daughter's tombstone. I saw Evan. He looks so much like my father.

"I went to Daddy. He admitted he'd made a deal with Mother, and with Talitha. He would take care of Evan, and Mother would leave them alone. If she didn't, Daddy said he'd promised her a divorce and a criminal investigation. Part of the deal was I was never to know Evan was alive. Mother wouldn't budge on that. His existence would've ruined everything."

"How is that?" I scrunched my face at her.

"Mother thought Colton would never marry me if he knew I'd been married before—had children."

"Really?"

She looked up at the sky through the tree limbs. "I don't know if he would or wouldn't have. But Mother was convinced he wouldn't. And she'd had him handpicked for years."

"And he still doesn't know any of this?" How could you build a life with someone and have secrets like this between you?

"If he does, he's never mentioned it."

"Seems like the kind of thing that would come up in a marriage."

She nodded. "It does. Then again, maybe not. Colton is capable of sweeping it all under the rug if he thought no good could come of bringing it up. And how could I ask him if he knew? That would be the same as telling him."

It was hard to wrap my brain around that kind of marriage.

"Have you approached Evan? Does he know Talitha wasn't his mother?"

"I haven't done anything—yet. I was wrestling with what to do. Talitha was a good mother to him. It was clear at the funeral how much he loved her. The last thing I wanted to do was hurt him. And then Kent disappeared, and I haven't thought of anything except her."

"Did you know Kent had become friends with Evan?"

Virginia looked stricken.

"No...how do you know that? I was stunned when Ansley mentioned his name. I assumed they were acquaintances. They had a common interest."

"She'd been to his gallery. He told me that she saw a painting of his in a friend's home and came in one day to look around. They struck up a friendship."

"Neither of them could have known they were half-brother and sister."

"I think perhaps she was drawn to his work because some of it is similar to hers."

Virginia nodded. "Kent didn't talk about her artist friends. She knew it upset her father."

"It's suggestive, I think, that she disappeared soon after Talitha's death."

"What do you think that suggests?"

"I think Talitha's death may have been a catalyst. You learned that one of your children had survived, the other brought home for burial. The past was stirred up again. It could be your mother felt threatened by that."

"But why harm Kent?"

"That's what I'm trying to figure out. I need a better way to reach you privately." I handed her a disposable phone. "My number is saved, as is my partner's. Call us if you think of anything, if you need us, or if anything happens you think we should know."

She took the phone. "All right."

"One more thing I think you should be aware of. Someone tried to kill Nate and me in an incident intended to look like an automobile accident."

Virginia jerked her head up and stared wide-eyed at me. "Turner."

"Yes, and perhaps Talitha. Maybe even their parents."

"Oh, God. I'll speak to Daddy."

"I'd appreciate that—but only if you're positive his hands are clean in all of this."

She held my gaze. "I'm sure."

"Let him know I'd like to speak with him. Can you do that without your mamma finding out?"

"Yes. We have lunch together once a week, sometimes drinks at the club before dinner at home. I'll ask him to meet me this evening. No one will be suspicious of that. I'll ask him to meet you here tomorrow. What time would be convenient?"

"Eleven a.m.?"

"Very well."

"Mrs. Heyward?"

"Yes?"

"This is a personal question, and beyond what you and your husband hired me to concern myself with. I apologize in advance for that. But I can't help but wonder why you don't tell your mother to mind her own business and fire that William Palmer."

She stared out across the park for a long moment. "The last time I stood up to my mother, two of the people I cared most about died, and I lost having my son in my life, probably forever. Would you cross her again?"

I didn't have an answer to that.

THIRTY

I called Evan and asked him to meet me at Bin 152 at eight that evening to discuss the case. He agreed, seemed happy to hear from me. He tried to change the venue to his apartment. I told him maybe we'd stop there for a nightcap. That seemed to placate him. He wouldn't be pleased to find Nate at Bin 152 in my place, but I won the coin toss. Even if Evan left mad straightway—which he likely wouldn't do—that still gave me two hours round-trip travel time.

Nate texted me as soon as Evan pulled onto the seven o'clock ferry to Isle of Palms. That was my go-ahead to commence breaking and entering.

Evan's gallery had a security system, which took me thirty minutes to disable. Then I entered through the back door. I'd already seen the gallery. I checked out the back room and found two file cabinets. It didn't take long to locate Talitha's bank statements. As expected, there were regular deposits going back to 1981 from a company named EDI, Incorporated. Evan Drew Ingle. I'd bet the company was owned by another company, and it would take hours of research to tie it to C.C. Bounetheau. I thought I'd just talk to him instead. I snapped photos of a sampling of the bank statements from over the years.

Then I climbed the stairs to Evan's second floor apartment. It was tastefully decorated and no doubt feng shui certified. I decided to come back to it if I had time. No news from Nate was good news. I climbed the stairs to Evan's third floor studio. It was light and airy, and looked like one would expect a painter's studio to look—easels, paint, brushes, drop cloths, et cetera.

The partially done painting on the easel was another abstract, similar to the ones currently in the showroom. I scanned the room, which took up most of the third floor. Three doors ran across the back wall. I checked them one by one.

The first door revealed a half bath. I checked the medicine cabinet. It was empty. The cabinet above the toilet held nothing but tissue. I moved on to the second door. A large closet held a dozen or so framed paintings. I turned on the light and flipped through them. These were more impressionist paintings, landscapes and seascapes. All were signed Evan D. Ingle. They were good. I'm no art critic, but I liked them much better than the abstracts he'd replaced them with.

I turned off the light and moved on to the third closet. More framed paintings. I turned on the light and studied them. More impressionism. Landscapes, seascapes—one of a Charleston streetscape similar to the one that had caught my eye in Kent's bedroom. None of this group of paintings was signed. Were these Kent's work? He'd said she'd brought a few paintings for him to look at, but he didn't mention she'd left them. And there were more than a dozen pieces here. Why would she move her paintings to Evan's studio? Was this part of him helping her? Were they going to photograph them to put on the website?

I checked the time. It was eight o'clock. Nate and Evan should be discussing how I was still recovering from my accident and was under the weather. Nate needed to befriend Evan, but not let on we were romantically involved. Evan would wonder why I hadn't called and cancelled. Nate was to tell him I'd taken the earlier ferry to do some shopping, but had tired myself out. I felt bad at the last minute, but knew Evan had already left. I was resting at a friend's house and hoped to join them shortly.

When I finished my work, I would call Evan, apologize, and reschedule. Meantime, Nate was just being a buddy. The one thing we hoped to glean if Nate could do it without sounding suspicious was why Evan had switched the paintings out—the abstracts for the impressionist exhibit. That detail continued to bug me, though I couldn't say why.

I glanced around the studio one last time, then went down to the apartment. The great thing about Evan being in Charleston was that I would have plenty of time to get out once he headed home. I took my time with his apartment, leaving everything exactly as I found it.

The whole apartment was very clean and orderly for a bachelor. The layout was simple, one bedroom, one bath, and a large combination living/dining room with a galley kitchen in one end. There wasn't much in the refrigerator. I checked the kitchen drawers and cabinets. Nothing there but the usual kitchen stuff. He must like to cook. He had a good selection of spices, vinegars, and oils.

The high-backed, leather barstools matched the dining furniture. Six dark wood chairs with leather seats and backs surrounded a round pedestal table with a compass inlay. Mamma made sure I knew a thing or two about furniture. Evan's was quality.

The dark woods and leather motif continued into the living area. A sofa, two armchairs, and an ottoman appeared to be from the same collection. Matching tables flanked the sofa, which faced a flat-screened TV I pegged at sixty inches. There was nothing in the living or dining area to search.

I wandered through the bedroom into the bath. A large tiled shower with a glass door took one wall, a vanity with a sink the other. I opened the door at the end. Nothing in the water closet except the toilet. I checked the tank. Just water.

The vanity drawers held a mix of the usual male condiments—razor, shaving cream, toothpaste, et cetera. Nothing remotely interesting. Disappointed, I went back into the bedroom.

His closet was neat. No shoeboxes of old love letters. Just jeans, shirts, shoes, two suits, and a few ties. I turned towards the dresser. Surely I was not going to spend an hour on this apartment and come up empty. I searched each drawer, running my hands through the clothes and along the inside frames. In the bottom of his sock drawer I found an envelope. I sucked in a breath. My heart went to cantering.

I slid it out carefully. The return address on the envelope was Hamilton Law Firm in Atlanta. It was addressed to Evan at the gallery. I slid the contents of the envelope out. A single sheet and another envelope. I unfolded the heavy stationery.

It was a letter from Mr. Hamilton to Evan, explaining that Talitha Ingle had retained him to hold the enclosed envelope and mail it in the event of her death. The second envelope had simply "Evan" scrawled on the front. I slipped the letter out. There were two typed pages.

My Dearest Son,
My fondest wish is that you will never read this letter. If you have

received it, I have gone to a better life before I summoned the courage to tell you all the things you should know. Because we live in an uncertain world, I've left you this so you can protect yourself. I have kept these secrets these many years to keep you safe....

My eyes raced through the letter. It was all there. Turner. Eva. Virginia. Abigail. Talitha had left this letter to Evan so he would know everything. She must have chosen an Atlanta lawyer because it was outside Bounetheau turf.

She'd signed it, "Your loving mother."

Evan knew he was a Bounetheau.

I looked at the postmark. It had been mailed a week after Talitha's death. My head spun with possibilities. He hadn't contacted Virginia. She would've told me in the park. So was he sitting on this information, deciding what to do with it, if anything?

I laid the letter on the dresser and took photos of each page, plus the cover letter and the outer envelope. Then, I carefully reassembled the contents and returned the envelope to Evan's sock drawer.

I made my way back downstairs, reset the alarm, circled the building, and walked back down the street to my car.

Once I was back inside my house, I poured a glass of wine. After a few sips, I called Evan and apologized profusely for missing dinner. He was very understanding. I could hear Nate laughing in the background, playing his part.

"So let me make you dinner tomorrow night," Evan said.

"I'd love that." I put a smile I didn't feel into the words. I would cancel that date as well. Hopefully by this time tomorrow this case would be wrapped up.

I had no idea whereby I came that hope.

Nate made the ten-thirty ferry and was back at the house by eleven-twenty. I filled him in on what I'd found over nightcaps.

"That's a lot to ponder." He swirled his bourbon slowly in the glass. "Revenge, greed...several possible motives there."

"Did you find out why he pulled the impressionist exhibit?"

"I found out the topic makes him nervous. Asked him if he still had any of the impressionist paintings he was showing back in the spring. Told him you had a special fondness for impressionism. He said they'd all been sold except a few he'd sent to other galleries."

"Well, that's a lie. I saw a dozen of them in a closet in his studio tonight. And even more of Kent's work."

"Seeing as how he's taken a shine to you, I find it very strange he wouldn't want to show off work he knows you like."

"He said to me once that his technique had a way to go. Maybe he feels like his impressionist paintings aren't ready for prime time."

"Maybe."

THIRTY-ONE

C.C. Bounetheau walked towards the bench where I'd met his daughter the afternoon before. He smiled and waved. As he approached, I could see the resemblance to Evan. Now that I knew to look for it, it was more obvious. C.C.'s hair was white, but the men were of a similar build. Odd how happy he seemed to see me, all things considered. How far could I trust his jovial demeanor?

I stood as he drew near. "Thank you for coming, Mr. Bounetheau."

"Happy to help any way I can." The man positively radiated Southern friendly. It was hard to conceive of such a man married to the monster Abigail had shown herself to be.

"Shall we sit?" I asked.

"By all means." We settled onto the bench.

"You're not wearing a wire, are you?" His blue eyes twinkled with amusement. He reminded me even more of Evan.

"No, sir, Mr. Bounetheau." That much was true. I wasn't wearing a wire.

"Call me C.C. All my friends do. I consider you a friend. Am I right in that estimation, Miss Talbot?"

"Yes, sir. I believe so. As far as I know, our objectives are the same. Find Kent. Bring whoever is responsible for her disappearance to justice. Mrs. Bounetheau, however, I believe, has different priorities."

He sighed wearily. "Virginia told me of your troubles. I'm deeply sorry about that. I give you my word you have nothing further to fear. I have taken care of the situation."

Could I trust that? Virginia had been adamant her father was not involved in her mother's schemes. She'd trusted him all those years ago—told Talitha to trust him. From where I sat, it looked like C.C. had held up his end of the bargain. "That's very good to hear. Thank you."

"I'm sure you'll understand, I can't let you have my wife arrested."

I tilted my head at him.

"My dear," he said. "Abigail insulates herself well. You'd never prove it. It would just be fodder for the gossips. No point in all that. Nothing good would come of it."

"You've cleaned up a few of her messes," I said, remembering Virginia saying he'd cleaned up after Peyton and Peter many a time.

"Family looks after family," he said. "Virginia tells me you've discovered our Evan."

"Yes. And I'm aware that you know Kent had as well."

"They are friends." He nodded. "I have to tell you, that gives me a great deal of joy. Neither of them knows about their relationship."

"You're certain of that?" I thought about the letter in Evan's sock drawer. Had C.C. not considered Talitha would do such a thing? And if Abigail had been behind Talitha's death, had she not considered this consequence?

He shrugged. "As certain as I can be of anything. Kent and I are quite close. I think she would tell me if she knew Evan was her half-brother. She would ask me straight up to explain it all."

"And Evan? I saw photos of you with him and Kent at his opening in April. The three of you looked quite happy together. You were just there as a patron of the arts? Not as his grandfather?"

He chuckled softly. "I might have bought a painting or two. Evan's talented." He shook his head. "Truth be told, Kent has far more natural talent. To the untrained eye, some of their work is similar. Any expert could tell the difference. Unfortunately, Kent's father and my wife disapprove of painting as an occupation." He stared at the ground for a moment. All traces of joy had vanished. "But to answer your question, no. Evan has no idea I'm his grandfather."

"Did your wife arrange Talitha's death?"

"No. In fact, I believe that's one of life's ironies. Talitha's death in a car accident is what stirred all this nastiness up again. Abigail would've had no reason to do such a thing."

I'd need to ponder that a great deal before I decided whether I believed Abigail's hands were clean in the matter of Talitha's death. Perhaps she had considered the consequences and hadn't arranged Talitha's accident. If so, C.C. was right. It was indeed ironic that her death had brought the secrets she'd kept so long to light. "Does she know Evan and Kent connected?"

He studied me for a long moment, looked away. "I don't believe so. It's possible Kent innocently mentioned him. She wouldn't have known the danger there."

"How do you think Abigail would've responded to that?"

"She would've tried to put a stop to it."

"Talitha was the only person alive who knew the whole truth. Everyone else knew only pieces."

"That's not true, my dear. I know the whole truth."

"If I were you, I'd be really careful."

He laughed. "Abigail will never harm me. She knows the terms of my will."

"I thought everything was owned by family trusts."

"To a point, that's true. But what happens to the management of those trusts upon my death, how much money she has access to...let's just say her life is easier now."

"Is Evan provided for?"

"As he always has been."

"Don't you think he's wondering where all the money comes from? Where it's come from all his life?"

"Talitha told him his father had a substantial insurance policy which she had invested well. She told him she established the trust. The attorneys have been instructed to back up that story."

"So you think everything is tied up with a bow—there's no way he can learn the truth?"

"I suppose there are ways he could. My hope is that he's happy and has no reason to question what he's been told."

"What do you think would happen if he found out?" I asked.

"Honestly, not much. He would come asking questions. I would tell him the truth, to a point. If he suspected the circumstances of his father's death, that could prove problematic for Abigail."

"And how do you suppose she'd respond to that?"

"She would never hurt Evan. She knows I would have her sent to jail."

"And Kent?"

He gazed across the park for a moment. Then he gave me a sad smile that didn't reach his eyes. "My dear, Abigail is brilliant. She has some unfortunate sociopathic tendencies, to be sure. But to her mind, everything she does is for one purpose: to protect those she loves most. Kent is at the top of that list. Her grandmother adores her. She is safer than any of us from Abigail."

"Would it be safe to assume that everyone in your family would know that Abigail harbors protective instincts towards Kent?"

He regarded me solemnly for a moment, assessing me. "If you're asking me if other family members—perhaps with secrets of their own—would know that harming Kent was not an option, no matter the reason, the answer is yes. I can tell you to a certainty that Abigail would deal harshly with anyone who harmed any of the grandchildren."

"Except Evan."

"Sadly, yes."

"And if it were one of her own children who harmed Kent?"

"She might not have them done away with. But there would be consequences they would find intolerable."

THIRTY-TWO

I climbed into the passenger seat of the Escape. "Did you get all of that?"

"Clear as crystal." Nate zipped the case where the listening dish was stored. "I sent the voice file to you and stored it in the cloud lock box."

"I'm not sure we'll be able to use it for anything. But it's always better to hold cards you don't play than not to have any."

"You think we should sit on evidence of at least one murder?" Nate looked troubled.

"I think if we hand that recording over to local law enforcement, someone will make sure it disappears, and us along with it. Let's focus on Kent for now."

"I'm listening."

"I want to talk to the neighbors." There were still missing pieces. I needed to go back to the beginning.

"The ones who complained to the police? I thought you already did that."

"Not the Walshes. I want to walk the route she took when she left home that Friday night and talk to anyone along the way who is willing to speak to us."

"Really?" Nate asked in a tone that signified surely I must be kidding. "You want to do a door-to-door canvas in this neighborhood?"

"I do. Someone saw something." I stared at patches of blue on the other side of the park, where sunlight reflected off the water. "People don't just disappear. Someone drove her car to Magnolia Cemetery. I don't think it was her. But whoever was in the driver's seat, the car left lower Legare at seven-forty-five the night she disappeared."

"Don't you think the police have already done this?"

"Probably. But since we never received a file, we're going to have to bother these nice folks again. Let's start with the neighbors across the street." I was energized, eager. This felt right.

Nate started the car. "As you wish." He still sounded skeptical.

We knocked on twelve doors on lower Legare. We spoke to whoever would talk to us. At two houses, no one answered the door. At the other ten, folks were just as nice as they could be. Everyone wanted to help, from wealthy matriarchs, to the couple who'd turned their ancestral family home into a bed and breakfast in an effort to afford to keep it, to the help. Yes, they'd spoken to the police. They wished they could offer anything by way of assistance, but no one had seen a thing.

When we came to the spot where Lamboll dead-ended into Legare, I said, "She either turned left here, or went on down to South Battery. There she could've gone left or right. If it were me, I'd've turned left here, gone over to Meeting, made a left, and gone up to Queen. Based on where she said she was headed, anyway."

Nate sighed a weary sigh, nodded down Lamboll. "Let's start with that."

We'd worked our way halfway down the first block of Lamboll when we pulled through an open gate and into a driveway to get out of the narrow street. The house appeared to be in the last stages of a renovation. It was a sunny yellow Charleston single house—the style that sat with the narrow end towards the street and had stacked porches running longways down the front, which faced the garden. We climbed the steps and rang the bell. The antique lion's head doorknocker seemed more for decoration. The gentleman who came to the door was roughly my age.

"Hi," he said.

Nate and I said hey, introduced ourselves and whatnot.

"We've been retained by the Heyward family over on Legare to help locate their daughter, Kent. We believe she came by here on the evening she disappeared, and we wondered if you might have seen her. She drives a red Mini Cooper."

"Oh, yeah. I saw on the news where they found her car over at Magnolia Cemetery. That poor girl. Please, come in." Over his shoulder he called, "Emily, hon, could you join us?"

He stepped back, and Nate and I walked into the small foyer.

"I'm Mike Lowell."

A trim woman with a dark brown bob joined us. "Hi, I'm Emily."

We explained ourselves again.

"When did she disappear?" Emily asked. "Of course I've heard about it, but the specifics are vague."

"September twelfth. It was a Friday night," I said.

"Oh gosh, no wonder it's vague. We were gone all of September," Emily said. "My dad had a stroke. We were in Atlanta. Mom couldn't cope with everything by herself. He was in rehab for four weeks. It was awful because the contractors were in the middle of the kitchen. Anyway, I wish we could help, but we weren't here."

"Thank you so much for your time." I smiled and turned to go. Halfway into the turn, my eyes crossed the living room to my left.

The painting over the fireplace was a near duplicate to the one of Boneyard Beach hanging in Kent's room. I stepped towards it. "That's a lovely painting. Do you mind if I take a closer look?"

"Go right ahead," said Mike.

I glanced at Nate, delivering the message that this was big. He followed me into the living room. It was beautiful. It reminded me of Van Gogh's Starry Nights, just like the other painting had. "Who did this?" My eyes fell to the signature.

"Artist over on Stella Maris," said Mike. "Evan Ingle. He's a buddy of mine from way back. We went to Porter Gaud together. I'm happy to see him doing so well. We would've bought one of his paintings, regardless. Emily and I both fell in love with this one."

"It is remarkable," I said. "Do you mind if I photograph it?"

"Not at all," said Mike.

I snapped several shots. "Is this part of his current collection?"

"I don't think so. Like Em said, we were gone most of September. Evan kept an eye on things for us. Checked in with the contractor, made sure things were on track. When we got back, he invited us to the gallery. We had dinner and he showed us around. Emily wanted to see his studio. This one was upstairs. Like I said, we fell in love with it."

"I can certainly see why," I said, thinking how I'd bet my left arm Kent had painted it—not Evan.

"Thank you so much," I said. "We'll get out of your hair."

When we walked out the front door, from the porch I could see more of the backyard than I'd seen coming in. The driveway extended deep into the lot, and a detached two-car garage was near the back of the property. In front of the garage sat a large white covered trailer. "Is that yours?" I asked.

Mike shrugged. "Yeah, I bought it when we started the construction project. Came in handy, hauling supplies, furniture, all kinds of things."

"What do you tow it with?" I asked.

"F-250 in the garage." He looked confused.

"Do you mind if I look inside the trailer?" I asked.

"Sure. Do you need a trailer?" He started walking towards it and we followed. "I'll be selling this one soon. Bought it secondhand, but still. It's not something I'm going to need going forward."

"You never know when one of these might come in handy," I said.

The look on Nate's face told me he was thinking exactly what I was thinking.

Mike opened the back of the trailer and Nate and I climbed inside. A Mini Cooper would easily fit. "Do you have ramps, like to roll things in? My brother has a band, and some of his equipment is on wheels."

"Yeah, I've got them in the garage. If he's interested, have him give me a call."

A long red scratch down the left side caught my eye. I caught Nate's glance and directed his gaze with mine. He looked, then nodded. Neither of us mentioned it. Nate walked in front of me, shielding me from view. I snapped a quick photo of the scratch.

"I'll do that. I'm certain he'll be interested. I'd appreciate it if you'd let him have first dibs." We stepped out of the trailer.

"Sure thing," Mike said. "Let me give you my number."

I typed the number into my phone as he called it out.

"Thanks a lot," Nate said.

"It was so nice meeting y'all," I said.

"You too. Y'all have a good evening. I hope you find someone who saw something."

THIRTY-THREE

Nate drove a little further down the block and pulled as far to the side as he could on the narrow street.

I said, "We need to stay here and make sure nothing happens to that trailer while Jenkins and Bissell get a warrant. Then we need to go over to John Rutledge House Inn and find out which room Evan stayed in, and if anyone would have seen him leave after he checked in."

"Okay, I see where the red paint could be a scratch from a Mini Cooper. And I'm guessing you made that for one of Kent's paintings with Evan's signature."

"Exactly."

"Let's make sure we're on the same page. Walk me through what you're thinking here."

"Okay...Evan gets a surprise at his mamma's funeral—he had a twin sister. And twins—I've read lots of research about the connection between twins. To find out as an adult you had one. That had to be weird."

"Agreed."

"Next Evan gets the letter from the attorney in Atlanta. Now he knows where the money came from his whole life. And there's another shock, maybe the biggest of all. The woman who raised him is not his mother. *His* mother didn't want him—or at least that's how it would feel to me—but she wanted this beautiful young girl who showed up in his art gallery a few months earlier, who he had a connection with he couldn't explain until now. Are you following me?"

"Yep."

"Now maybe he resents Kent. And it turns out she's more talented on top of everything else. She's gotten everything. And his twin sister, who should've had the life Kent is living, is in a grave. Talitha made it clear she believed Eva would have lived if she hadn't been taken out of the hospital. Remember, Vicki Elmore and Virginia both said Eva was in an incubator?"

Nate said, "And maybe Evan suspects the Bounetheaus of killing Talitha because Kent stumbled across him, and as you said earlier, aside from C.C. and Abigail, Talitha was the only one who knew the truth."

"Very possible. So Evan has a whole lot of motive. Not the least of which is now he has a closet full of unsigned paintings he can whip out, sign his name to, and sell for a lot more money than the ones he painted. There's proof of that hanging in the Lowells' living room."

"And that's why he switched out the exhibits. C.C. said an expert could tell the difference, remember? If he planned to start passing Kent's work off as his own, he'd have to get his impressionist work out of circulation as much as possible."

I nodded. "And when Emily Lowell wanted to see his studio, he only showed her Kent's work. Then he signed the piece she wanted."

"We have a whole lot of theory, and very little evidence."

"Which is why we need to get Jenkins and Bissell over here to get a sample of that red paint ASAP. If the paint's a match, that's hard evidence. And we can tie Evan to the trailer. He had access to the house the whole month of September. No doubt they left him the truck keys just in case. Except that's the kind of question that will raise suspicion. We don't want to ask that until after the paint's been sampled. Everything will fall into place after we have that. Then we can start talking about art experts to examine paintings."

"Do we call Jenkins and Bissell, or Sonny?" Nate asked.

I pondered that. "Jenkins and Bissell do not have a lot of love in their hearts for us. But they might after this. For now, maybe we'd best call Sonny. If he takes it to them, they're more likely to listen."

"Agreed."

I called Sonny. Ten minutes later, he parked behind us on Lamboll and got into the backseat. "What do you have?"

I walked him through it. He thought so hard I could see a vein throbbing in his temple. Finally he said, "I'll call them. But a warrant is going to take a while."

"I bet good money if I call Colton Heyward he can get one lickety-split."

"Fair point," said Nate.

"Call him," said Sonny. "I'll stay here and wait for Jenkins and Bissell. Make sure no one disturbs the trailer, though that doesn't seem likely. Better to be sure. You go on to John Rutledge House Inn and see what you can do with Ingle's alibi."

"Sounds good," I said.

Sonny nodded. "Good job, guys."

I took a long slow breath and let it out. "Thanks. Except we still haven't found Kent. I think we'll go talk to Colton Heyward in person. This is news he shouldn't hear over the phone."

THIRTY-FOUR

We had a brief meeting with Colton Heyward in his office. I had asked for it to be just him. I didn't want to talk to Virginia Heyward just then about the implications. And the odds of William Palmer eavesdropping on a conversation in Mr. Heyward's office were significantly less than those of one held in the living room. All I told him was that we'd found red paint in a trailer nearby, and we suspected the trailer had been used to transport Kent's car. I didn't even try to put a positive spin on that.

His face seemed to fold into lines as I talked. He leaned on his desk, his perfect posture slipping into hunched shoulders. Finally, he made a phone call, promised a warrant was on the way. We showed ourselves out.

Nate found a parking spot on Broad a couple blocks down from the John Rutledge House Inn. With my previous phone call to the innkeeper in mind, and how she'd made a point of telling me she wouldn't give me information I didn't have, Nate and I came up with a pretext.

We climbed the grand marble staircase with its ornate green iron railings and columns. Nate winked at me and opened the door. We slipped into character as we passed through the vestibule and into the foyer with me hanging on him like I was trying to climb him. The gentleman at the writing desk which apparently served as both check-in and concierge services raised an eyebrow.

"Good afternoon," Nate said.

"Good afternoon, welcome to John Rutledge House Inn. Do you have a reservation?"

Nate said, "I'm afraid we do not. Would you have a room available by chance?"

"We do. How many nights?"

I blew in Nate's ear.

"Just one," he said.

"Darlin', ask about the room Evan had."

"Sweetheart, we can't be persnickety. We don't have a reservation." I pouted.

He sighed and gazed at me indulgently. Then he looked back at the concierge. "Sir, a friend of ours stayed here recently. I think he may be a regular. Evan Ingle. He raves about this place. Anyway, there's one room he especially likes. Would you happen to know where he usually stays, and if so, is that room available?"

He smiled and said, "Let me check." He typed a bit and read the screen on his computer. "Mr. Ingle typically stays in one of our carriage house rooms. They're out back, not in the main building. I'm sorry we don't have one available for tonight. All we have is the mini-suite here in the main house. It's quite lovely."

He looked at Nate. Nate looked at me, then back at the concierge. "We have certain privacy needs. I'm not sure the main house is a good fit. Perhaps we'll just stroll through the courtyard, then try you another time."

"Very well. Y'all have a nice day." He was a true professional. If he thought they were better rid of us, his tone didn't betray him.

We walked out the back entrance and down the steps. Two narrow buildings occupied the far side of the walled courtyard, with a wide walkway between them and a gate at the back. They were secluded from the main house. Another walkway led from the courtyard around the inn and back out to Broad Street.

"Let's check out the door locks." Nate crossed the patio and tried the knob on the carriage house to the right. "It's locked, but it takes an old-fashioned key, not an electronic one. He peered through the window in the door. "Locks on the rooms are identical. No records of anyone's coming and going."

"He could come and go as he pleased. No one would ever know the difference," I said.

"He could've," Nate said. "We just have to prove that he did."

"Here's exactly what he did," I said. "He waited for Kent at the house on Lamboll. Probably asked her to stop there and pick him up on the way to dinner that night, made some excuse—they could share parking, something like that. She pulled in. He knocks her out, or maybe he kills her right then. He drives the car into the trailer and hides it. Then he gets in his car and drives to the parking garage and goes on to the restaurant. He spends the evening with his buddies, giving himself an alibi, then he walks back here and checks in."

Nate said, "Then he leaves, walks back to the house on Lamboll, pulls the trailer over to Magnolia Cemetery, and dumps the car. The only problem is, Kent wasn't in it."

"But what better place to hide a body than a cemetery? We need to get over there, see who was buried the next day. What time is it?"

Nate looked at his watch. "Four-thirty."

"They're open 'til five. Come on." We jogged down the walkway beside the inn and back to the car.

I hopped into the driver's seat. "We need to let Sonny know we've broken Evan's alibi—at least hypothetically. And we also need to get to the cemetery before they close."

"Let's divide and conquer," Nate said. "Drop me off at the Lowells', or I'll drop you off. One of us can brief Sonny while the other talks to whoever is in the cemetery office."

"Sounds good. Why don't I drop you off? Jenkins and Bissell are there by now. Y'all can bond. I think they like you better than me. I found the car."

"Suits me."

I made a left on Legare and drove down to Lamboll. There was no sign of Sonny's car, Sonny, or Jenkins or Bissell.

I called Sonny. "What the heck? Where are y'all?"

"Inside the Lowell residence. Long story. We moved our cars inside the gate."

"Okay, thanks."

I pulled to the side of the road and waited for Nate to get out. "I'll be right back. This shouldn't take but a minute."

He slammed the door and I made a beeline for Magnolia Cemetery.

THIRTY-FIVE

I studied the lock on the gate on the way in. It was a padlock, an old one, but substantial, hanging from a chain. After hours, the chain was no doubt looped through the iron gates and secured with the lock. For anyone who cared to watch a YouTube video, it would be easy to pick.

I pulled over in front of the white, two-story building and went inside. A short vestibule led to an office. A smiling middle-aged lady walked towards me and met me at the door to the room. "Good afternoon. Can I help you?" She was a sweet soul—that much shined from her eyes. The way she emphasized the word help reminded me of the librarian at the Stella Maris branch.

"Good afternoon. Thank you so much." I showed her my ID and license. "I'm wondering if you could tell me who was buried here on Saturday, September thirteenth of this year."

She gave me a look that signified that was an unusual request.

"Ma'am, this is in regards to a missing person's investigation."

"Oh," she said. Her eyes got bigger. "Oooh." She nodded.

She turned around and went to her desk. She tapped the keys of her computer, wrote something down, and came back to the door. She handed me the piece of paper. "There was only one. Mr. Roger Vanderhorst. He was buried in the Greenhill section." She pulled out a white eight-by-ten photocopy of a map and circled the area I'd already seen up close, then made an x where Mr. Vanderhorst was buried. "It's back here. This used to be the eighteenth hole of the Navy base's golf course."

"Could you tell me when his grave would've been dug?"

"Probably Wednesday, maybe Thursday of that week."

"Thank you so much. I'm going to check this out right quick. Y'all don't lock me in, okay?"

"Okay," she said. "Bye-bye now."

I slipped the name inside my purse and headed for the door. Inside the car, I pondered how I was going to get anyone to authorize an exhumation based on my hunch. I pulled ahead along the same road I'd been on the day I'd found Kent's car. A chill made its way from the base of my spine to my brain as I drove between the two marshes.

It was nearly five. It wouldn't take but a moment to check out Mr. Vanderhorst's final resting place. I drove faster than one normally does through a cemetery, but there was no one around to witness my act of disrespect. I sent mental apologies to the deceased. Following the clerk's directions, I took the third left in Greenhill, crossed another dirt road, and stopped three plots from the end. I stared at a pink granite tombstone that read Roger Vanderhorst.

I got out of the car. If I wanted to hide a body so that it was never found, I'd bury it underneath another. I was betting that was exactly what Evan had done. Put Kent in Mr. Vanderhorst's grave, covered her up with just enough dirt. Maybe he had to dig a little more out first, but still. It would work.

How was I going to persuade Jenkins and Bissell to ask the family to allow us to disturb this poor man's final resting place? I knew in my bones Kent was buried with Mr. Vanderhorst. But this was going to be a hard sell. Colton Heyward would have to be on board. If I convinced him, he could maybe speak with the family.

"You should've let me make you dinner tonight."

I jumped. My heart seized. Evan.

He was behind me, must've parked one row over, his car shielded by the stand of trees and circled around. How had I not heard his car? Of course. It was an electric car. Could I make him think I wasn't on to him?

"Dinner would've been so much more pleasant." His voice held what sounded like genuine regret. "I'm an excellent cook. And I bought a very nice Russian River Valley pinot noir. I think you would've liked it."

"How did you know where to find me?" My skin prickled, like someone was sticking me with millions of tiny needles charged with an electric current.

"Mike and Emily were so concerned about that poor girl you were looking for. After you left, they wondered if I'd seen anything while I was there. So they called me. By the time I arrived, you'd just finished knocking on doors, I guess. I saw your car at the end of the block. I followed to see what you were up to."

"Did you?" I turned to look at him. "See anything while you were staying at Mike and Emily's?"

His expression held reproach, said *nice try*. "Sadly, I think you've figured it all out, haven't you? Otherwise, you wouldn't be standing here. It's a shame. You and I could've been good friends, maybe more." He took one step towards me. He had a rag in his hand. Chloroform?

I wasn't waiting to find out. He was between me and my car. *Sonavabitch*. My gun was in my tote.

I took off at a run, cutting between gravesites.

He followed. His legs were longer. I couldn't outrun him long.

I ran behind a live oak, putting it between us.

He crept around the other side.

I dashed for cover behind a tall monument and peeked out. He was looking the other way. I sprinted for the car.

I jerked the door open, put my right leg in. Almost there.

He grabbed my left arm and pulled. Rather than fall towards him, I hit the dirt and tried to roll away from the car, going under the door.

Just as I cleared the door, he pounced, straddled me, pinned me down.

I punched him in the face.

He recoiled, and I slid out from under him. I crab-crawled back, turned over.

I was almost up when he tackled me, knocking the breath out of me. I gasped for air and inhaled grass. I bucked and grabbed at him, but he was far stronger. He wrestled me over. He grabbed my right hand and held it above my head and reached for my left hand.

I jabbed him in the eye with my left thumb and gouged for all I was worth.

He screamed and let go of my hand.

I arched my back, rolled, and wriggled out from under him.

I jumped up and ran. I darted between monuments, crossed graves, zigzagged. Then I crouched behind a tall monument.

He wasn't far behind me. I could hear him coming.

I glanced up at the grave marker that shielded me. On the top was a carved angel.

Use the angel to smite the enemy. Colleen's words echoed in my head. Where in hell was Colleen?

Evan appeared from the other side. He reached for me.

I grabbed the angel. She was heavy, but whatever had once secured her to the base of the monument had come loose.

I grasped her just as Evan's arms came around my waist in a move meant to tackle me.

I brought down the angel. Gravity did most of the work. I'd aimed for his head, but hit him in the shoulders. He slumped to the ground with a grunt.

I didn't kid myself he was down for long.

I dashed back to the car.

I heard him behind me, not quite as fast as before. He stumbled.

I reached for my tote.

He grabbed my left shoulder just as my right hand gripped Sig.

I spun on him, brought up my weapon in both hands. "I will shoot you where you stand and sleep just fine tonight."

He was so close the barrel of the gun was nearly touching him. He hesitated, let go, then took three steps backwards.

It wasn't nearly far enough. "Back off," I said. "Now."

His left eye bored into mine, his expression crazed. His right eye was closed tight. He bent over and charged me.

I got off one shot before he slammed into me and my back hit the car.

He staggered backwards. Pure rage contorted his face.

He charged me again.

I fired twice more.

He went down.

I kept my gun on him while I fumbled behind me in the car for my phone.

I voice-dialed Nate.

THIRTY-SIX

My mamma's long-standing rule was that we discuss nothing unpleasant at dinner. She was hard-pressed to enforce her code of conduct that Wednesday night. A week had passed. Nate and I had spent the better part of it being questioned, talking to our client, and producing reports. My family was all done with being patient. Nate and I were barely inside the door when the questions started. Everyone was there: Merry and Joe Eaddy, who to everyone's amazement we'd not run off, Blake, Mamma and Daddy, and Nate and me.

We gathered in the family room. Daddy was pouring Jack. Mamma had opened a bottle of pinot noir. Normally she preferred merlots. I knew my mamma. Tonight, I would have my favorite. She'd likely made my favorites for dinner, too. I'd bet anything she had country fried steak with gravy in the kitchen.

Blake cut through the barrage of questions. "Just tell us what the heck happened. We read the paper. We want the details."

Nate started, and I jumped in. We left out any mention of Peyton and Peter, and glossed over Abigail Bounetheau's involvement. We tag-teamed our way through the case hitting the high spots: Talitha and Turner Ingle, Virginia Bounetheau, Evan and his twin sister, right up to the part where I dropped Nate off to update Sonny on how Evan really didn't have an alibi, and our theory of how he'd pulled off Kent's disappearance.

Nate said, "But we didn't know the Lowells had called Evan right after we left, before the police detectives showed up with a warrant to search the trailer. They were trying to be helpful, but they alerted Evan that we were on to him. Sonny pulled inside the gate and hid his car behind the Lowells just in case Evan showed up. We called Jenkins and

Bissell. They parked in a driveway a few doors down. Unfortunately, none of us thought about him following Liz. We were focused on the paint evidence. Jenkins and Bissell took a sample for the crime lab, which, as you no doubt read, was a match for the make and model of Kent's car. We didn't find that out until the next day."

I said, "Meanwhile, now that we had a timeline to work with, I was convinced Evan had left Kent at the same place he'd left her car: Magnolia Cemetery. He could bury her in an open grave, but he had to roll the car out of the trailer and into the woods.

"His timing was perfect. He followed me to the cemetery, and when he saw me park at Mr. Vanderhorst's grave, he knew I had it figured out. He probably knew he'd have to deal with Nate later, because the Lowells told him we were both at their house. But he didn't know we had the police involved already. And here I'm surmising, because he isn't talking. His first word when he woke up after surgery was 'lawyer.'"

"*E-liz-a-beth Su-zanne Tal-bot.*" Mamma was not happy. "What in this world possessed you to go traipsing around a cemetery under the circumstances? Why didn't you go back to the house where Nate and Sonny were?"

"Well, Mamma," I said, "I had no idea Evan had been informed I was on to him. I thought he was busy getting ready to cook dinner for me. If I'd known, I would have headed back over to the house on Lamboll lickety-split."

She gave me a censoring look by way of an answer.

"I'm just glad I didn't kill him," I said.

Nate said, "I'm mostly relieved he didn't kill *you.*"

"I'm happy about that, too. But I want him to answer for what he did. Death would've been too easy. I think he really wanted me to kill him there at the last. Why else would he charge at me when I had a loaded gun?"

Blake said, "Guy's a psychopath. Who knows why he did anything?"

Joe Eaddy's grin took up his whole face. His eyes were bright, eager.

"Did they catch the guys who sent you the snake and threatened you? Are they the same ones who caused your car crash?"

"*They* didn't catch them." I looked at my brother. "Blake, you want to tell this part? Or how about you, Daddy?"

Daddy winced. He took a sip of his Jack and Coke, then stared at the glass. "Oh, I'll let Blake tell it."

Blake cleared his throat. A look passed between him and Daddy. I knew exactly what made the two of them so fidgety: Colleen. But I would never get tired of hearing my brother tell this story. Thanks to my new redundant security system and its motion-activated cameras, I could also watch it. I'd gotten an alert on my phone, but had been otherwise occupied at the time.

"Yeah, okay," Blake said. "While Liz was running around the graveyard, Mom was getting Wednesday dinner ready. Dad and I decided to ride by Liz's house, check on things. We've been doing that regular since she called on the way to Greenville and asked me to take care of Rhett. I figured until she and Nate closed this case, chances were those two guys would pay her another house call.

"So, we pulled into her driveway, and right off I knew something was up. Rhett didn't come running out to greet us. That dog always flies out of the house when he hears a car. I knew Liz wasn't home because she'd told Mom she was in Charleston, that's why she wasn't at dinner."

He shot Daddy a look of disapproval. "Dad had his shotgun. I told him to wait in the car, which of course was a waste of breath. I checked the front door, and it was unlocked. I heard Rhett barking. He was upstairs. I found him later, locked in one of the guest bedrooms. I went inside to check the house. When I got to the kitchen, I smelled gas.

"I went straight to the garage and got a vice grip. I knew where the gas shutoff valve was—the meter's right outside the garage walk-thru door. I turned off the gas supply, then went back upstairs and started opening windows. The two rent-a-goons were still there—they must've just turned on the gas when I got there. Maybe they tried to leave and saw Dad out front on the porch where he had no business with a shotgun."

Daddy interjected, "Seems to me that worked out just fine."

Blake rolled his eyes. "Yeah, Dad, I guess. Anyway, they'd run upstairs. After I opened the downstairs windows, I went upstairs to let Rhett out. These two guys came barreling out of the hall bath about the same time I opened the bedroom door to let Rhett out. One of 'em rammed me from behind—knocked me down. I guess they must've been afraid to fire a gun in the house, not knowing how much gas was in the air. They ran down the stairs. Rhett chased after them, raising unholy hell. I jumped up and was right behind him. Rhett skidded in the hall and I tripped over him." He shook his head, grabbed the back of his neck.

"They tried to run out the back onto the deck." Blake stopped. His face drew up like a prune. "For some reason, they couldn't get the back door open." He knew, and I knew from looking at the footage and talking to Colleen, that they had gotten the door open just fine. My brother was using selective memory.

"I had gone around back," Daddy said. "Come up onto the deck. Tell them what we saw, son."

Blake glared at Daddy. "I don't know what you saw."

Daddy laughed, shook his head. "It was real pretty, whatever it was. Bright colors, all shimmery. It was a wall in front of the door. These two guys had the door open, they just couldn't get out, is what it was. On account of this shimmery wall."

"Man," said Joe Eaddy. He was mesmerized.

Blake said, "I don't know what you're talking about. Maybe you were drinking before we went over there."

Daddy was indignant. "I had one Jack and Coke. Not enough to make me see things, I can assure you of that."

Colleen appeared, stretched along the back of the sofa like a cat. "I love to hear them argue over this."

I smothered a grin.

Blake made a swiping gesture with his arm. "For whatever reason, they turned around and ran towards the front. And I was ready. I had my weapon out. Theirs were under their shirts. Not to mention they didn't know I'd cut the gas. I hollered, and Dad..."

"I couldn't get in the back because of that wall," Daddy said.

Blake shook his head, a disgusted look on his face. He walked over to the wet bar and poured himself a drink.

I thanked Colleen again with my eyes and in my thoughts. I knew now why she had told me up front to use the angel statue, and why she wasn't in the cemetery when I needed her. She'd saved my daddy's life that same evening, by keeping those armed thugs from coming out on the deck. They wouldn't've fired in the house. But once outside, the two of them against Daddy...Of course he did have his shotgun. But if Colleen had been there, he needed her there. Maybe Blake did, too. Who knows what might've happened.

Daddy said, "I ran around and came in the front. Held my gun on 'em while Blake cuffed them. Then he called Clay Cooper for back up. But we had 'em by then."

Blake took a long pull on his drink. "They lawyered up fast. I'm hoping they'll eventually make a deal that gives us whoever hired them, but I'm not holding my breath. Whoever it is, they're more afraid of him than jail."

Nate and I exchanged a glance. C.C. Bounetheau was cooperating with the police up to a point. But he'd made it clear that Evan was the only family member going to jail. Mr. and Mrs. Heyward—the whole family—had closed ranks. They'd acknowledged that Evan was Virginia's son. Their story was that Evan had a mental breakdown shortly after Talitha's death, brought on by the surprise of finding out she wasn't his mother. They weren't standing by Evan. He'd killed Kent. But they would spin things to protect the rest of them.

"I can't believe the Bounetheaus kept that quiet all these years," Merry said. "Virginia being married before and having children."

"It's an awful mess," I said. "I feel really bad for Colton Heyward. He's a little gruff, but a nice man. He's having to deal with finding out his wife was married before, and not only did she have children, one of them killed his only child."

Nate said, "I feel bad for the Ingles. That whole family was victimized by the Bounetheaus."

I cut him a look. He and I had decided, after protracted discussion, not to raise our suspicions about Talitha's death or Turner's. It would be virtually impossible to prove their deaths were anything other than accidents. Our own story about being blinded had been quickly explained away by the investigating officers. Some unexplainable reflection, they thought. How much had that cost Abigail, and who had she paid off? My primary concern was keeping all of us safe.

I'd taken C.C. Bounetheau at his word when he said he'd put an end to Abigail coming after Nate and me. But either C.C. had lied to me, or he'd overestimated his control over his wife, because the thugs had tried to blow us up after that. We'd considered giving the recording of our conversation with C.C. to Jenkins and Bissell, but with C.C. in her corner, that would make us all targets for Abigail and her considerable resources. Since Evan's arrest, and with Virginia's first marriage in all the papers, Abigail had no reason to come after us now. We wanted to keep it that way. We'd agreed to let the task force handle bringing down the remaining Bounetheau criminals. Hopefully Abigail would be caught up in the indictments handed down. But we couldn't talk about any of that until the task force finished its work.

"I heard Charleston PD released the boyfriend," said Blake.

I nodded.

"Matt Thomas is free, but not doing well. He lost his girlfriend and his unborn child." When I'd spoken to Matt, he was crumbling under the guilt, blaming himself because he hadn't been excited about the baby. He was killing himself with "what ifs." I'd told him, and I believed, it wouldn't've changed a thing. Kent's death had nothing to do with him. Ansley was trying her best to provide comfort, but she was in pieces herself.

Daddy said, "That poor little girl." He shook his head slowly.

Everyone was quiet for a moment. Mr. Vanderhorst's family had agreed at Mr. Heyward's request to ask for an expedited exhumation. Kent's body had been recovered on Friday, along with her laptop and iPad. Clearly, Evan had thought there was evidence there that could lead back to him. I hoped he was right, and I prayed it could still be recovered. The more evidence, the better.

I was glad we'd been able to give the Heywards some sort of closure. But I felt a darkness pressing in on me. How could family heap such cruelty on family? Watching news accounts of such chilling inhumanity to those closest to you was one thing. Witnessing it firsthand was another thing entirely.

"Autopsy report back yet?" Blake asked.

"No," I said. "But there were no obvious wounds. The handkerchief he had at the cemetery when he came for me tested positive for chloroform. And they found two syringes of heroin in his car—fatal doses meant for Nate and me. I think it's a safe bet that's how he killed Kent. Though honestly, I'm surprised he knew where and how to buy heroin. There's no evidence he's a user."

"That just creeps me out," Merry said. "You came so close to being buried under someone else."

"It was dicey, I admit. But if anything, I think this proves I can take care of myself." I looked at Nate.

Mamma and Nate displayed similar looks of consternation.

Blake worked his jaw.

"With a little help from your friends," said Colleen.

I smiled and thought, *thank you.*

Merry squinted at me. "What are you smiling about?"

Colleen bray-snorted.

I had to come up with something on the fly. I glanced at Nate. He shrugged as if to say, *your call.*

"I have happy news. I didn't want to share it during this particular topic. Maybe after dinner?"

Mamma said, "I think we've already given far too much of our evening to discussing that poor girl and her family's misery. We could all use some happy news." Mamma smiled, like it was my choice, but her tone informed me otherwise.

I reached for Nate's hand.

He wrapped his around mine.

"Nate and I are engaged," I said.

The room erupted with happy sounds and congratulations. We all hugged. Mamma cried. Daddy slapped Nate on the back.

I overheard Blake say, "You take good care of my sister."

Nate responded, "Always."

Mamma said, "I need to reserve the church. Are you thinking May or June?"

"I like October better." Nate grinned at her.

"A fall wedding?" Mamma asked. "Those can be quite lovely. I won't have any trouble getting the church for next October. That will give us more time to plan." She beamed a sunny smile at Nate. She was so happy with him in that moment.

"I was thinking this October," Nate said.

Mamma's smile evaporated. That quick, Nate fell from grace. "That's just not possible."

Merry and I exchanged grins.

Blake, a pot stirrer from way back said, "Sure it is. They could go to Vegas."

Mamma looked horrified.

Nate looked grateful that Blake had drawn fire.

"How about a Christmas wedding?" I asked.

Mamma regarded me with displeasure. Her expression softened. "Not many folks are doing those. I could probably arrange for the church in December." Her tone was a bit grudging, but I could tell she was warming up to the idea. Likely it occurred to her she should marry me off as quick as she could.

Daddy had slipped out unnoticed. He came back from the kitchen with two bottles. "Merry, get the glasses."

"Champagne." I smiled. "Thank you, Daddy. How sweet." He hadn't been at all in a celebratory mood the last time I'd announced an engagement.

He set the bottles down on the wet bar. Grinning, he said, "I like this one. I hear he knows how to handle a shotgun. Nate, do you fish?"

"Every chance I get." Nate smiled back at Daddy.

"Oh yeah," Daddy said. "This one's gonna work out much better."

Susan M. Boyer

Susan loves three things best: her family, books, and beaches. She's grateful to have been blessed with a vivid imagination, allowing her to write her own books centered around family, beaches, and solving puzzles wherein someone is murdered. Susan lives in Greenville, SC, and runs away to the coast as often as she can.

Her debut novel, *Lowcountry Boil,* won the Agatha Award for Best First Novel, the Daphne du Maurier Award for Excellence in Mystery/Suspense, was an RWA Golden Heart® finalist, and hit the USA TODAY bestseller list. Susan's short fiction has appeared in *moonShine Review, Spinetingler* Magazine, and *Relief Journal* among others. Visit Susan at www.susanmboyerbooks.com.

In Case You Missed the 1st Book in the Series

LOWCOUNTRY BOIL

Susan M. Boyer

A Liz Talbot Mystery (#1)

Private Investigator Liz Talbot is a modern Southern belle: she blesses hearts and takes names. She carries her Sig 9 in her Kate Spade handbag, and her golden retriever, Rhett, rides shotgun in her hybrid Escape. When her grandmother is murdered, Liz high-tails it back to her South Carolina island home to find the killer.

She's fit to be tied when her police-chief brother shuts her out of the investigation, so she opens her own. Then her long-dead best friend pops in and things really get complicated. When more folks start turning up dead in this small seaside town, Liz must use more than just her wits and charm to keep her family safe, chase down clues from the hereafter, and catch a psychopath before he catches her.

Available at booksellers nationwide and online

Visit www.henerypress.com for details

In Case You Missed the 2nd Book in the Series

LOWCOUNTRY BOMBSHELL

Susan M. Boyer

A Liz Talbot Mystery (#2)

Liz Talbot thinks she's seen another ghost when she meets Calista McQueen. She's the spitting image of Marilyn Monroe. Born precisely fifty years after the ill-fated star, Calista's life has eerily mirrored the late starlet's—and she fears the looming anniversary of Marilyn's death will also be hers.

Before Liz can open a case file, Calista's life coach is executed. Suspicious characters swarm around Calista like mosquitoes on a sultry lowcountry evening: her certifiable mother, a fake aunt, her control-freak psychoanalyst, a private yoga instructor, her peculiar housekeeper, and an obsessed ex-husband. Liz digs in to find a motive for murder, but she's besieged with distractions. Her ex has marriage and babies on his mind. Her too-sexy partner engages in a campaign of repeat seduction. Mamma needs help with Daddy's devotion to bad habits. And a gang of wild hogs is running loose on Stella Maris.

With the heat index approaching triple digits, Liz races to uncover a diabolical murder plot in time to save not only Calista's life, but also her own.

Available at booksellers nationwide and online

Visit www.henerypress.com for details

Henery Press Mystery Books

And finally, before you go...
Here are a few other mysteries
you might enjoy:

BOARD STIFF

Kendel Lynn

An Elliott Lisbon Mystery (#1)

As director of the Ballantyne Foundation on Sea Pine Island, SC, Elliott Lisbon scratches her detective itch by performing discreet inquiries for Foundation donors. Usually nothing more serious than retrieving a pilfered Pomeranian. Until Jane Hatting, Ballantyne board chair, is accused of murder. The Ballantyne's reputation tanks, Jane's headed to a jail cell, and Elliott's sexy ex is the new lieutenant in town.

Armed with moxie and her Mini Coop, Elliott uncovers a trail of blackmail schemes, gambling debts, illicit affairs, and investment scams. But the deeper she digs to clear Jane's name, the guiltier Jane looks. The closer she gets to the truth, the more treacherous her investigation becomes. With victims piling up faster than shells at a clambake, Elliott realizes she's next on the killer's list.

Available at booksellers nationwide and online

Visit www.henerypress.com for details

PILLOW STALK

Diane Vallere

A Mad for Mod Mystery (#1)

Interior Decorator Madison Night has modeled her life after a character in a Doris Day movie, but when a killer targets women dressed like the bubbly actress, Madison's signature sixties style places her in the middle of a homicide investigation.

The local detective connects the new crimes to a twenty-year-old cold case, and Madison's long-trusted contractor emerges as the leading suspect. As the body count piles up like a stack of plush pillows, Madison uncovers a Soviet spy, a campaign to destroy all Doris Day movies, and six minutes of film that will change her life forever.

Available at booksellers nationwide and online

Visit www.henerypress.com for details

NUN TOO SOON

Alice Loweecey

A Giulia Driscoll Mystery (#1)

Giulia Falcone-Driscoll has just taken on her first impossible client: The Silk Tie Killer. He's hired Driscoll Investigations to prove his innocence and they have only thirteen days to accomplish it. Talk about being tried in the media. Everyone in town is sure Roger Fitch strangled his girlfriend with one of his silk neckties. And then there's the local TMZ wannabes—The Scoop—stalking Giulia and her client for sleazy sound bites.

On top of all that, her assistant's first baby is due any second, her scary smart admin still doesn't relate well to humans, and her police detective husband insists her client is guilty. About this marriage thing—it's unknown territory, but it sure beats ten years of living with 150 nuns.

Giulia's ownership of Driscoll Investigations hasn't changed her passion for justice from her convent years. But the more dirt she digs up, the more she's worried her efforts will help a murderer escape. As the client accuses DI of dragging its heels on purpose, Giulia thinks The Silk Tie Killer might be choosing one of his ties for her own neck.

Available at booksellers nationwide and online

Visit www.henerypress.com for details

BET YOUR BOTTOM DOLLAR

Karin Gillespie

The Bottom Dollar Series (#1)

(from the Henery Press Chick Lit Collection)

Welcome to the Bottom Dollar Emporium in Cayboo Creek, South Carolina, where everything from coconut mallow cookies to Clabber Girl Baking Powder costs a dollar but the coffee and gossip are free. For the Bottom Dollar gals, work time is sisterhood time.

When news gets out that a corporate dollar store is coming to town, the women are thrown into a tizzy, hoping to save their beloved store as well their friendships. Meanwhile the manager is canoodling with the town's wealthiest bachelor and their romance unearths some startling family secrets.

The first in a series, *Bet Your Bottom Dollar* serves up a heaping portion of small town Southern life and introduces readers to a cast of eccentric characters. Pull up a wicker chair, set out a tall glass of Cheer Wine, and immerse yourself in the adventures of a group of women whom the *Atlanta Journal Constitution* calls, "... the kind of steel magnolias who would make Scarlett O'Hara envious."

Available at booksellers nationwide and online

Visit www.henerypress.com for details

Made in the USA
Coppell, TX
02 October 2022

83932947R00164